Revolt
in
San Marcos

Revolt
in
San Marcos

Robert Carver North

HOUGHTON MIFFLIN COMPANY BOSTON

The Riverside Press
CAMBRIDGE · MASSACHUSETTS

Printed in the U.S.A.

To

the three women in my life

Irene, Woesha, and Kris

Foreword

The San Marcos where Carlos Chichayan became a man cannot be found on any map, nor is Ronca's state listed among the nations of the world. The reader will search in vain for dictionaries of the Nacheetl language, for none exists, and Xlalak is an unspoken tongue. And although a number of Spanish expressions appearing in the book were designed to suggest the colloquialisms used by many Central American peoples, an effort was made to avoid the speech pattern of any particular locality. The whole story, in short, is fiction, and yet there resides in all this fantasy a fundamental reality. For the book is a sublimation of actual experiences too real to be forgotten.

Contents

Revolt
in
San Marcos

I. The Village

A MIDWIFE WENT to the hut of a certain woman who was in labor and delivered her of a man child. She washed the infant, strapped him into a cradle of fibre netting and wood, and hung it from the roof by ropes. She also brewed lemon-leaf tea for the mother against her weakness and burned rosemary in an earthenware bowl as protection against the evil eye. And the mother took steam baths which purified her after her confinement. These she took in her bathhouse, which was of rough stone laid in clay mortar.

During the first night the infant twitched in his sleep, and the mother knew that his spirit had gone away. She called, "Come, thou must stay here." The child stopped his twitching, and the spirit returned to the body.

On the following day the woman washed her baby in a wooden basin, swaddled him into a bundle, and slung it from her shoulder; whereupon she and her husband set forth with friends and relatives upon a trail that climbed from their village to the temple of Dios at Xiltak. The husband carried a machete by a strap from his hip and also a calabash of water; but the woman carried only her child.

When they had gone up to Xiltak, they entered the temple of Dios, called the Church of Santo Domingo, which was sweet with the smoke of copal. There the woman undid the bundle and gave the child into the hands of a priest for christening. Now the priest, being a priest of Dios, was not a priest of Sun or Moon, but only of Dios. Likewise, the copal smoke was not a sacrifice, but incense upon the altar of Dios. For Dios was now God in the land.

Sometimes Sun was God. People would not say this; nevertheless, they knew in their hearts that Sun was sometimes God. Today, how-

1

ever, Dios was God, and the child was baptized in the name of Cristo.
After the baptism, the priest, taking quill and ink, wrote upon the
records:

> *On this eighteenth day of November, 1910, in the Parochial
> Church of Santo Domingo of Xiltak, I, Don Felipe Mendoza,
> vicar of the curacy, did solemnly baptize Carlos Juan, son of
> Pablo Morelos and Juana Flores, Indians of the village of Zalapec.
> The godmother was Maria Fuentes, and I instructed her in her
> spiritual duties to the child. (signed)* FELIPE MENDOZA.

When the priest had written his name, the woman took her child and
went down with her husband to their hut in Zalapec on the shores of
the lake called La Perla. Then the man picked up his hoe, which was
made of wood, and climbed to a hillside that he was clearing for corn.
With his hoe and his machete he hacked at the undergrowth, and he
burned the brush that had accumulated. As he worked, he girdled the
larger trees and built fires at the foot. Some burned and toppled over,
while the rest remained standing, charred about the roots.

This was one cornfield, and on the hillsides were many others.
Indeed, the slopes were like a quilt with many patches. These were
Nacheetl cornfields, and no one knew when the first had been planted.
The land was old and had grown many generations of corn. The land
was old, but there was still a yield. In each field the tiller raised a
cross that Dios might smile upon his corn, and about the cross was an
image of the sun that the blessings of Dios might be augmented.

As the man labored in his particular field, the woman worked,
grinding corn and attending to the duties of her hut. This hut was
adobe with a roof of tule thatch, and a red hibiscus grew at the
entrance. There were earthenware jars on either side, and they were
fat-bellied and filled with water.

Within the hut the woman worked, and she kept it clean. The air
was laden with dust, and there were chickens that got inside, but she
kept her living place clean. She swept the floor which was dirt with a
palm-leaf broom, and upon it she sprinkled water to lay the dust. In
these duties her daughter helped, and they cared for the hens and sows
and shoats, and they saw that the man child came to no harm.

Each morning before the lifting of the dew the woman and her daughter went to a stream near by, and with them they took shirts and pantaloons belonging to the man, and they took also their own soiled clothing. In the waters of the stream they soaked the clothes, and they scrubbed them against a rough rock. Any grey then left they beat from the clothing with paddles, and the sun bleached white cottons whiter.

While the man child lay strapped in his cradle near the foot of an oak, the woman and her daughter picked bougainvillea to brighten their hut. They plucked these blossoms and arranged them upon lily pads in designs according to their fancy. The daughter also picked two wild roses. One she placed in her own black hair, and the other she placed in the hair of her mother.

As moons waxed and waned, the man labored in his fields and saw that his corn grew. At night when he returned to the hut he was soaked with sweat which he washed from his body in the bathhouse. And the woman worked about her cooking and washing and saw that her child grew.

While his body grew, for lengths of time his life was outward-looking, and he spoke in smiles and gurgles, and next he would turn within himself. In his fifteenth month he stood upon his feet and looked about, and he seized his father's sandal and threw it, and this was part of being a man child.

During weeks that followed he learned about persons and about a few of the differences among them, and he became afraid of strangers. He was sure of his mother, and he was also sure of his father and sister, but he was not sure of others, and there was no way to know. He was afraid of strangers, but he had words. Not many words, of course, but words. Papa was a word, but it was something more, and mama was a word, and much more, but he had other words that were just words.

Months passed, and he developed I-ness, and he learned that along with I-ness there is also a you-ness, and between these two there can be much conflict. There is I-ness that is good, and there is I-ness that is bad, and it was not easy to learn the difference. The learning was difficult, and what he willed, he might not, and what he could, he would not.

There were many impulses within him. Some were clinging, and others were pushing away. There were times when toward what he wanted he felt a pushing away, and for that which he did not want he felt a clinging. Between his wants and his want-not's there was much confusion.

There was great awareness of himself. Part of this I-ness was in wanting, but there was also other I-ness. There was I-ness in hands and feet and face and in the organs of sex. The whole body was, in fact, an awareness, and about it he found much to explore. This was all-important.

There was also an inside I-ness that was more. This was the real I-ness, and it fought with you-ness. He did not think about this awareness, but it was there. "It's mine!" he said, and that was I-ness of a certain kind.

He came to know many things. He knew four walls and a thatched roof. He knew dirt floor and fire that pinched his fingers. He knew griddles and ladles and pestles and bowls and earthenware jars of cold water. He knew by sight and touch and by taste and smell. He knew flies and mosquitoes and fleas. He knew chickens and puppies and kid goats. He knew sunshine and rain and grass and chirping crickets. He knew round stones and flat ones and sticks for chasing baby pigs. He knew frogs and worms and snakes that slithered out of reach. He knew thistles and spiny cactus fences.

He came to know rocks that stubbed his toes and mules that kicked and children like himself. He came to know tunnels through tall grass and streams of water to dam with moss.

The family was four, and these four were also one. Each was one, and each was four, and all were a family, and they were We. The family was like a four-leafed clover. Each person, being a leaf, was a part of the clover which was four-in-one.

That was the family, and father was God-protector. He was strong and stern because he was father and God-protector, but in him there was also a measure of gentleness to make him We. So that was father, and mother was softness, love, and care. She had also a measure of sternness to make her We.

Such were father and mother. They were man and wife, which are different, but they were both parents; whereas son and daughter were child. All the parts were in balance, and all the balances made one, and the one was a symmetry.

The symmetry was not always perfect. For one thing, the girl was older than the boy, and because of this, she was often son as well as daughter. Usually she was more daughter than son, and often she was very much mother, but occasionally she was too much son and even father.

They were playing in the grass near the shores of La Perla, and she was six while he was not yet three. He reached for a bee that was sucking honey from bougainvillea, and her "no-no, Carlito" was mother-sister. At other times she said "do this, Carlito" but "not that, Carlito," and it seemed that her words were strong and stern and God-protective; thus she was sometimes father.

This time they were playing in a pasture. He lay in the grass while she was catching butterflies. He followed his thoughts and did not know when she was gone. And while he thought, lying in the grass, a ram grazed near.

This was a horned beast, patriarch of a mighty flock, and skin hung in grey wrinkles about its aged face. It came close to the boy and raised its head, uttering a hoarse blat.

Startled, the boy looked up; his eyes saw slit pupils and bloodshot globes, the folds of grey skin, and curled horns. He heard heavy breathing as the beast nosed near, and he smelled the musky odor that came from its nostrils. He sat terrified, his baby face distorted, and he tried to scream, but managed only a brief gasp that rattled in his throat. It was a beast that he saw, and it was fear. It was a fear in his baby mind, alive in demon shape; it was the fear he had known and what he had imagined and fears of the womb and of his parents and of their forebears. It was the fear of his tribe back through the ages, the fear of man and the fathers of man. It was fear of what he could not understand.

The fear arose from deep in his belly and spread about his anus and climbed his spine. He was stricken.

His sister came, and drove the beast away, and when the face was gone, he screamed. She gathered him in her arms. She was sister and mother, but she was also father and slayer of demons. She was God-protector.

She carried him home because she knew he had the fright. She carried him to the hut, and ran for an old woman who knew about fright, and the old woman came to the hut. She burned copal in an earthenware dish that was full of water, and while the copal was burning, she carried a small jug to each of the corners of the house.

Clapping the mouth of the jug with her hand, she called out loud. "Come to your house!"

Three times she went about the house, whereupon she sucked the man child's arms with her lips.

She burned more copal, and on the under side of the ashes, against the water, she found a ram's-head picture. She made the man child drink from the water. He gulped it down along with some spirit herbs.

These were a purge, the spirit herbs, and when they worked, they carried out the excrement, and with the excrement came the fright from the man child's body.

So the fright was taken away, and the sister who had gone for the old woman was more than ever God-protector.

2

No one knew for certain what brought sickness to the village. Some said that it flew down out of the sky on the wings of night, and others said it was a damp, dark vapor that oozed out of swamps and earth wet from rain, and still others insisted that it was an evil spirit, perhaps even the Devil himself, who got into the sick man's body and built a fire.

Whatever caused it, the sickness came and settled in the bodies of men and women and children. In the bodies of sturdy shepherds it burned hot, laying them low upon their sleeping mats, and they could not move away. It settled in the bodies of farmers, and the smoke from their belly fire spread through their arms and legs and made them heavy, and the victims dropped their wooden hoes and crept into the coolness of their huts where they lay and suffered. It settled in shepherds and farmers and it settled in their wives and children. There was nothing one could do.

In all the village, in all the mountain region there was not a soul who could stop the sickness. When it burned too hot in the belly of a victim, Dios took pity, laying his hand upon the man and calling the spirit from the body and taking it off. When the spirit was gone, there was nothing for the fire to burn upon. It went out, and the body was cold, and relatives took what was left and buried it in the campo santo.

It was in the third round of seasons after the boy's birth that the great sickness came among the mountains. It arrived overnight, and it spread rapidly about, seizing upon many people in the land. It seized upon the man and upon his daughter, and at last Dios laid his hand upon them both, and when he called upon the spirit to come forth from the body, the spirit came. Thus Dios gathered up the spirits of the man and of his daughter and left only the bodies behind, and stinking zopilote-buzzards came to sit upon the roof and croak.

On that very day the relatives began to wail, and even while the flesh was warm, they laid the bodies out. Two crosses were marked upon the adobe floor, and a body was placed upon each cross. On the chest of the man his saint's picture was placed, and the picture of his daughter's saint was laid upon her bosom. Candles were lit and placed in each dead hand, and the light glimmered through cracks in the adobe. Meanwhile relatives, going forth into fields above the lake, gathered flowers to cover the dead and to fill the adobe hut with fragrance.

Seeing death, the elder children among the relatives stood apart, wide-eyed and afraid; but the man child saw only candles, and he was delighted by their glimmer.

When both bodies had been carried off and buried with their heads toward the west, the woman went back to her hut, and swept the dirt floor with a palm broom and sprinkled water to lay the dust.

Now the family was two instead of four.

The man child learned from the woman, and from the woman's brother, who was Uncle Vicente. He learned shdish Dios li for thanking after eating and shdishe shina which was the proper reply.

From the woman and from the woman's brother he learned Nacheetl right and wrong. Calmness was good, and so were truth and obedience and respect for elders, but agitation and willfulness and lies were evil, and that was Nacheetl teaching. Thus he learned the tranquillity of inner virtue and the inner turmoil of guilt, the bowel pangs, the tail-between-the-legs grip that goes with evil.

From Uncle Vicente he learned to care for sheep. It was a small flock that Uncle Vicente tended, and the child in his fifth year became the shepherd.

As he watched sheep on warm slopes and listened to the tinkle of his bellwether, the child saw the valley and all that was in it, knowing each thing well. He knew the corn boy and the bean girl and the maguey cactus. He knew the pepper trees, both berry-giving "man" and the "woman" with her blossoms. He knew the willow, the nopal or prickly pear, the castor plant, and the organ cactus, which was used for hedges against his sheep. He knew the condor and the hawk and the black bird of death called zopilote.

He knew the mountains roundabout and the lake called La Perla.

He also knew Lightning, whose cave is in the sierra to the north. At night he put tortilla crumbs upon a rock for Lightning to eat, and he knew that Lightning is the Rain God and keeps jars of water in his cave for making storms. This he knew, for he had seen Lightning strike at night, blazing with fury and pouring rain upon the earth. He had seen Lightning terrify his sheep and make kindling wood of mighty oaks.

Yet he did not fear Lightning becaue he knew the words María Purísima, which were magic words and powerful when used against the Rain God. During storms at night the child hid his head in serape folds and whispered María Purísima, and Lightning did not strike. Trees also muttered María Purísima, and Lightning did not strike such trees. Many of them lived to be old as gods because they knew these words and could not be struck.

He was not afraid of the corn boy and bean girl. They were his friends. So were the willow and the nopal and the castor plant and the organ cactus. So were the mountains and the pastures and the lake. So was Lightning if one whispered María Purísima. He was not afraid of such things as these. But los aires were different.

He knew los aires and how they caused trouble and sickness and pain. He knew how they lurked over foul swamps and behind boulders in deserted pastures and in the poisonous air of night. He knew how they attacked their victims unaware and entered into the most secret recesses of the human body. He knew that a brain lost in thought was defenseless and easily captured by them. He knew all the pain that they could cause. He had heard them make helpless babies scream at night; he had felt them pounding in the veins of his own temples.

Fortunately there were cures and potions. He knew that a paste made from copal would draw the inflammation from boils caused by los aires. He knew that for muscle pains it was best to rub the skin with powder of the prickly cactus called "bad woman" or drink urine and rub it into the body pores.

He knew los aires, and so also he knew fright. He knew how this evil could steal appetite from husky cargadors and make a good woman lazy. Fright had tossed him about at night, sleepless on his pallet, and had brought the ram's head to him in the darkness.

The child was afraid of fright and of los aires, of dwarfs in the mountains and of the devil, too.

The world was full of all these demons. Once they got inside a man, they lived in all his thoughts and nighttime dreams and thrashed about and drove him mad or sent him off alone among the mountains to kill himself.

Dios could protect one from all such evils because Dios was more powerful than dwarfs and devil. Yet he did not rely altogether upon Dios. He propitiated María Madre and the Saints, and also the Departed Souls. From time to time he went to the campo santo where lie the bodies of Departed Souls, in order to leave a few flowers and a pot of beans on the graves of his father and sister.

Earth was also powerful. Everything that the man child had was given him by Earth, and in appreciation he must give something back to her. From time to time, therefore, he helped Uncle Vicente kill a turkey or a lamb, and they let the blood soak into the ground. This was always pleasing to Earth.

Some said that Earth was the same as María Madre.

A day came when the man child was in his sixth year, and Uncle Vicente took him out for a walk, and they sat upon a rock above La Perla.

"You are now a shepherd," said Uncle Vicente, "and before many seasons you will be a man. That is right, but in order to be a man, you must know the duties of Nacheetl men. Do you think you are ready?"

"Yes," he answered, "I think I am ready."

"The duties of Nacheetl men are of two orders," Uncle Vicente told him. "For it is known among us that Man has duties to Dios, and Man has also duties to Fellow Man. These duties are Nacheetl duties, and they are as old as the Nacheetl people. Man belongs to Dios, and that is in a large sense. Man also belongs to the Village, and the Village belongs to Man, and each is responsible to the other."

"What does Man do for the Village?" the man child asked.

"Man mends the roofs of public buildings such as the church and the Council House. Man repairs the streets and gutters and cleans the spring. Man sits upon the Council when he is asked. Man does all that the Village asks, and he seeks no recompense."

"What does the Village do for Man?"

"The Village is Man protecting Fellow Man," explained Uncle

Vicente, "guarding his hut when he goes to market, cultivating his corn when he is sick, caring for him when he is old, and feeding his aged widow after Dios lays his hand. Village is Man helping Fellow Man."

"The laws of the Village," Uncle Vicente continued, "are these laws. Man must work always for the good of Fellow Man by giving to the Village a portion of his labors. Man must care for Fellow Man when he is sick or in trouble or weak from age. Man must feed Fellow Man's widow when Fellow Man is dead. Man must tell no lies to Fellow Man nor speak slander behind his back. Man must not steal. Man must respect age, that he may be respected when he is aged. Man must not be boisterous lest he show his weakness. Man must not kill save only in defense of himself or Fellow Man. Man must do nothing to Fellow Man that he would not have Fellow Man do to him. These are the laws, and it is the duty of the Village to enforce them."

Thus Uncle Vicente spoke to the child, and he took him to the Council House in the Village.

Over the Council House was a bell, and the presidente sat inside with the Village seal. He had white hair, this presidente, and he spoke to the man child from behind his improvised desk, and he called the man child Carlos.

That was the Village, and it was Man and Fellow Man working together.

3

AFTER DAYBREAK Carlos drove his sheep along the trail that led through the village and beyond, and during the sun's journey across the sky he watched them graze in pastures above La Perla. Each day he did this, and at nightfall he drove them back down the trail, and now and again it happened that a man on horseback passed.

E-e-yah! he was a sight, this man on horseback. He wore a huge sombrero that was not of straw, but was stiff and black and had tassels sewn about the brim. He wore a jacket that was also black, and it was tight and smooth and shiny, and his shirt was sometimes yellow and sometimes red or blue. His jacket was tight, and his trousers were tight, and the legs of the trousers were embroidered with silver and gold.

He rode up the trail on a black horse, and his spurs were of silver, and they jingled, and the saddle was mounted with gold, and so was the bridle. As he rode up the trail, his horse struck sparks on the cobbles with its shoes, and the sheep scattered on this side and that, and his spurs jingled, and he cracked the air with his whip.

Carlos wondered about the man on horseback, and he asked Uncle Vicente.

"That is Señor," answered Uncle Vicente.

"What is Señor?"

Uncle Vicente shrugged. "Just Señor."

"Is he Fellow Man?" Carlos wanted to know.

"Never!" snapped Uncle Vicente. "That he is not."

"Is he then Dios?"

The old man was studying his nephew curiously. "Come, let us walk about the lake in the cool of evening and let us consider this thing."

They strolled slowly along the shores of La Perla, and Uncle Vicente sucked at his pipe and pondered, and Carlos saw that he was gathering thoughts like strayed sheep, and when he had gathered them together, he spoke.

12

"This village is Zalapec," he said at last, "and the lake is called La Perla, and Xiltak and the Church of Santo Domingo are above. These you know, and the valley you also know, and the trees and cactus and sheep. You know the mountains and winds and the skies at night. You know the seasons and the times for planting and harvest. There are other matters you do not know, and these are the matters about which I intend to speak."

Uncle Vicente found a rock that was near the edge of the water, and he sat upon it, and Carlos sat beside him. "These are strange matters," he continued, "and they require much thought."

The sun had sunk behind the mountains, but the sky still burned red in the west. Uncle Vicente turned his head that way, and in his eyes was a far look, and he said, "In the beginning, there was Chan, and he was God of the Universe. Chan was Sun, and he was God of the Universe, the only being who walked abroad."

Carlos heard these words, and he saw the direction in which Uncle Vicente was looking. He tried to see what Uncle Vicente could see, but there were only the mountains and the sky with the red in it.

"Now it happened that Chan went down one night from his palace of stone," continued Uncle Vicente. "He went down to bathe in one of the lakes of his garden, and a bright moon lighted him over the cobblestone path that led to the edge of the water. There he removed his cotton tunic and loincloth and braced his nakedness against a breeze of warmish air."

"Was it a lake like this?" asked Carlos.

"Ay-yah, like this," replied Uncle Vicente. "Exactly like this. On the surface of the water Chan saw the moon's image with blue sky all about; he saw white clouds and saw-toothed mountain ranges; he saw also his own body rippling on the lake. Even as breezes brushed the surface, he saw his muscles ripple in his water-image, and the sight stirred man-ness in his blood."

"What is man-ness?" asked Carlos.

The old man hesitated, tugged at an ear. "You'll know some day," he told his nephew. "It's a kind of belly cramp that makes slaves of men and men of slaves. It is life shut up in a small place wanting to get out. It is a seed that needs planting. It is all of these things, and Chan felt it, and to himself Chan said, 'I am Chan, God of the Universe, and this is my body that surrounds me, and there in the water is my body-image, and the moon floats beside it. In the moon there is beauty, and in my body, strength; and beauty and strength are love. I am Chan, God of the Universe, and tonight I shall wed the moon.' "

"I see it now," said Carlos, "I see the moon there in the water. Was it like that?"

Uncle Vicente's mouth widened in a toothless grin. "Yes, exactly so, and as Chan spoke, the moon's image smiled, and Chan's manness swelled in response. He gazed upon the moon's image, and his blood flowed hot. He said aloud, 'I am Chan, God of the Universe, and thou, O Moon, art Tana, and tonight thou shalt be my wife.' Thus Chan spoke, and from the silvery spot in the lake rose a maiden-figure. She was brown of body and beautiful to look upon. She came to him across the water, arms outstretched, and her lips spoke words of love. 'Behold, look upon me,' she said. 'For I am thine.' "

"What did Chan do then?" asked Carlos.

"He looked upon her hair and saw its blackness," explained Uncle Vicente. "He looked upon her shoulders and saw that they were smooth and full. He looked upon her breasts, and he saw that they were round and pointed. He touched her skin and found it soft. He held her close, and his chest felt the throbbing of her heart. 'Take me not to thy chamber,' she said, 'but make for me a bed beneath the skies. Let thy garden be our chamber.' Breezes blew warm upon their bodies, and the stars shone, and nighttime saw creation."

"I do not understand," objected Carlos. "What is this — creation?"

Uncle Vicente chose his words carefully. "You have helped sow maize in fertile soil," he reminded Carlos. "You have seen a seed planted and you know how it burst with life and sprouted and broke through the earth. So it is with gods and men. Woman is man's earth, and he plants his seed in her belly. It grows there until the moment it is ready to live, and then it comes out. You have seen how it is with corn and sheep, and now you know about men."

"About Chan and Tana, also."

"Yes, about Chan and Tana," Uncle Vicente agreed.

"When Chan had planted his seed, dawn was a step below the horizon. He took his morning bath, and the maiden helped him bathe. 'We must hasten,' she said, 'for my time is short. With the first rays of dawn I must go.' Chan seized her hand. 'No, Maiden Moon, thou goest not from me. I am Chan, God of the Universe, Light of the World, and I have wed thee for my wife.'

"Tana shook her head. 'I am thine, but I cannot linger. Yet from time to time I shalt seek thee out in thy heaven. Thou shalt find me there.' She drew away from Chan."

"Did she go?" asked Carlos.

"She went away. But she has kept her promise. From time to time she seeks him out in his heaven. And in her belly the seed grew. It grew and took shape, and she could feel it kicking inside, and in time she gave it birth."

"As a ewe has her lamb in the pasture?" asked Carlos.

"The same," replied Uncle Vicente. "It burst forth from Tana, and it was a man child, and she showed it to Chan. He looked upon it and saw that it was good, and he took it unto himself and called it Na-chee-tl."

"That is us," observed Carlos. "We are Nacheetl. You and I and my mother and the people of the village are Nacheetl."

"Yes, we are all Na-chee-tl," Uncle Vicente agreed. "Seed-of-my-Loin is the meaning therein."

The son of Chan and Tana was the first Na-chee-tl, the old man explained to Carlos, and his body grew in the image of his father. He was strong, and in the garden of Chan he grew and planted corn. There he lived and prospered, and in time he was given a sister. The child of Chan and Tana was this sister, and Chan looked upon her and saw that she was good, and to Na-chee-tl he gave her to take to wife.

"Did Na-chee-tl plant his seed in her belly?" Carlos wondered.

Uncle Vicente nodded. "He did that thing. 'Take this woman,' Chan told Na-chee-tl. 'Take her as thy wife. She shall tend thy house and draw thy water, and at night she shall share thy bed. In her thou shalt plant thy seed as in the earth thou plantest corn.' Na-chee-tl took her, and he planted his seed, and it prospered and grew. He planted his seed and had sons, and his sons planted seeds and had sons."

Year after year the corn was planted and tended and harvested, according to Uncle Vicente, and it spread over the face of the earth. So it was likewise with the sons of Na-chee-tl and with their wives, and there was much happiness. They took the name of their father, Na-chee-tl, and it is thus that they are known to this day. In those times the soil was fertile, and it gave forth bountiful harvests of maize. The land was rich to overflowing. Nacheetl men thrived and saw that life was good. Therefore they built temples of hard stone in honor of Chan and of Tana and of the lesser gods who likewise brought them good fortune, and the gods saw and were pleased.

Season after season men hoed their fields and harvested their crops, and smiths learned to beat out vessels of silver and copper and gold. "All the land was for all the people," Uncle Vicente explained.

Carlos was confused. "How was all the land for all the people?"

The old man tugged at an ear as he sought words to make the meaning clear. "It was an ancient way of living," he said. He explained about seasons long ago when only Man and Fellow Man lived within the Village. In these times, the corn that Man grew belonged also to Fellow Man, and the pottery that Fellow Man shaped with his fingers belonged to Man. There were storehouses for the harvests, and Man placed his grain therein. He filled his storehouses as he was able, and he drew from them according to his need, and there were neither rich nor poor.

So it was with the harvests, Uncle Vicente explained, and the land was not my land, nor was it thine, but it was Nacheetl land for the good of all. "You know about the Village today," the old man pointed out. "It is divided into barrios, and in each barrio Man and Fellow Man attend to the streets and gutters, to the training of children, and to the caring for widows and orphans and those who cannot work. Well, in old days, all Nacheetl land was common, and there was no mine-and-thine."

The small boy frowned. "What is mine-and-thine?"

Uncle Vicente tapped his chest. "It is each man taking for himself alone. It is I-ness grown too big."

"From what place came it?" Carlos asked.

The old man sighed. "The white man brought it to us." He told how long ago the Spaniards had come riding into Nacheetl towns upon their horses, and how the people knelt before them and trembled at sight of the snorting mounts and fell flat upon the earth when thundersticks roared and lightning found its mark. Thus Nacheetl men and women marvelled and rejoiced in the white strangers as mighty gods. But yet a little while, and Nacheetl eyes were opened, and people saw that the horsemen were only mortal like themselves. Even more remarkable, they lusted after gold as though it were something precious.

"Is it not then precious, this gold?" Carlos wanted to know.

Uncle Vicente shook his head. "It is the beginning of mine-and-thine. Now, even among our people, it has become more desired than food and joy and sun and rain and love and life itself. Yet I think it is only a stone out of the earth. But for it these strangers had a lust. They stripped our temples of it and seized our lands in hope of finding more. Anger then rose among the Nacheetls. 'These men are hungry for yellow metal. We must take our flint swords and drive them from among us.' For a number of years there was much killing between the two peoples. The white men spread like locusts over the country; one being killed, another took his place. Thus they plagued the Nacheetls and drove them out of fertile valleys into the mountains. They made our people dig holes deep into the earth and go down into the darkness after yellow metal. They built many towns and a city called San Marcos."

Carlos was angry. "Why didn't Chan drive them out?" he asked.

"They brought their own god called Dios," Uncle Vicente said, "and Dios is greater than Chan. They tore Nacheetl temples apart, and they used the stones to build temples of the cross."

"We say our prayers to Dios, don't we?" the small boy queried.

"Yes, we all pray to Dios, and to Jesucristo Salvador, and to María Madre."

"But why do we pray to Dios if he helped the white people take everything away from us?"

"Because if we pray to him, he will love us and save us, but if we do not, he will become very angry and we shall burn for many ages."

"We pray to Chan sometimes, too," said Carlos, "and we put Chan around the cross in the cornfield to keep the birds away."

"That is because Chan is more interested in our corn than Dios is, and he watches and makes it grow, whereas Dios has many other things to do and forgets sometimes about Vicente's little field. Thus we go on, even though the white man took our land, and everything now is mine-and-thine."

Carlos edged closer to Uncle Vicente. "We have some land, though, don't we?"

"Ay-e-e-ah, but the land is not Nacheetl. It belongs to Señor in the big house above Xiltak."

"But the cornfield is a Nacheetl cornfield."

"We work in it, but it belongs to Señor. And the sheep also."

"I do not understand."

"Listen, while I tell. The white man came upon his horse and killed Nacheetl warriors and tore down Nacheetl temples and made himself owner of many lands, a hacendado. The people fled to the mountains and were peasants, and their huts were adobe huts with ridgepoles of ocote pine. The roofs were tule thatch, and these roofs kept out the rain. The Nacheetl man lived inside, and so did his woman. The man labored in his fields, planting seeds and watching them break through the earth. The stalks grew high and bore ears of corn. Then the man gathered in his harvest, and as soon as it was gathered, Señor sent for the greater part and took it away."

"Did Señor eat it all himself?"

Amusement flickered about the old man's mouth. "No man could eat all that corn himself," he told Carlos. "Señor sent it away to the great city and sold it for silver and gold. That was what happened to the corn, and Nacheetl men kept only a small part which they took each to his woman. The woman watched over the hearth, and she ground the corn kernels with mortar and pestle. She ground flour, and from the flour she made tortillas on a clay griddle. She also carried water from the spring in earthen jugs and washed her babies and kept the floor clean. From time to time the man planted a seed in her belly, and she was great with child; yet she worked then, likewise, until she was in labor, when the man called the midwives to draw forth the child. The woman stood on her knees to deliver, as is Nacheetl custom, and after the child was drawn forth, the midwives cut the cord, and the child was washed. As soon as it was clean, the woman suckled it."

"Like ewes in the pasture," suggested Carlos.

The old man smiled. "A-e-yah, like ewes in the pasture. When the child had suckled, she laid it aside and went back to work. Once a week the man went to market, and the woman followed. The man carried his load with a tump across his forehead; the woman carried hers with a tump across her chest. On the trail they met white men who rode fine horses; but the Nacheetl man travelled on foot. So did the woman. The white men wore fine linen and jackets with shiny buttons. The man wore cotton drawers and a white shirt; and the woman wore a cotton skirt with stripes. The woman also wore a blouse and a rebozo."

"That is how it is today."

"Yes, that is how it is. The white man was always Señor, but the man was just man, and the woman was just woman. The man tipped his hat and said, 'adiós, Señor.' The woman kept her eyes on the ground, but she also murmured, 'adiós, Señor.' The man and the woman trudged home to their hut, while Señor rode to his hacienda with the high walls or to his house in the great city where Señora lives. Señora wears dresses of silk and satin and earrings of gold and a necklace of precious stones that sparkles in the sunlight."

"There is a hacienda with white walls above Xiltak," said Carlos. "Does Señor live there?"

Uncle Vicente stood up. A nighttime breeze blew across the lake, and the stars were out.

"A part of the time Señor lives there," he stated, "but most of the time he lives in the great city. When I was a young man we all belonged to Señor. We were like his horses, only they were fat and had sleek hides. Like beasts we belonged to Señor. Then there was a great battle fought on the plains near the big city. They called it a revolution. After that they said we did not belong to Señor. But it was all the same." Uncle Vicente knocked the ashes from his pipe. "It is dark, now," he told Carlos, "and soon los aires will be about."

Together they walked down from the rock above the lake. There were lights in the village where ocote torches had been lit. Carlos could see streaks of yellow streaming through cracks in the adobe houses. A dog barked somewhere in the distance. Carlos gripped Uncle Vicente's hand tighter. "I hate Señor. Why did he do these many evil things?"

The old man sighed. "Señor never did evil for the sake of evil, Carlos; Señor acted in the name of Dios."

4

SEASON FOLLOWED SEASON, and Carlos grew and tended Uncle Vicente's sheep. He was eight years old, and he had a flute upon which he played, and the notes were shrill and echoed among the crags above La Perla.

He was playing a tune to his flock when a shout was raised in the village, and he could see that women and old men were running this way and that. They took up the shout, and the heads of families came down from their cornfields, and in the village was much milling about. Then the log drum outside the council house boomed, and Carlos felt prickles along his spine.

After a time Uncle Vicente came up to the pasture. He was puffing, and his face was red, and the veins about his neck stood out like hempen cords.

"Drive the sheep down from the pasture," he said. "Bring them down into the corral."

Carlos close-herded his flock, and he drove them down into the village. The streets were full of men and women and children and dogs, and there was much laughing and shouting and waving of flails and sticks.

"What has happened?" Carlos asked Uncle Vicente.

"Never mind, just get the sheep into the corral!" ordered Uncle Vicente.

Carlos drove them through an opening in the cactus fence, and he shut them in. Then he followed Uncle Vicente to the village square. People had clustered about the council house. They were all excited, and everyone was talking at once. After a time the presidente appeared on the steps, and he was surrounded by men of the council. Uncle Vicente took his place among them. Carlos had tight hold of Uncle Vicente's hand, and he felt very important to be right there among the chief men of the village.

The presidente raised a hand for silence. Immediately the crowd quieted down. He paused a moment and ran his fingers through his white hair before he said:

"People of Zalapec! Stories are flying like bees among the cactus. But still your voices a moment while we hear from one who knows. A runner has come to me from the Barrio of the Frogs in the great city beyond the mountains. He has seen with his own eyes."

The presidente stepped aside.

On the threshold of the council house stood a short, square-set man dressed in shirt and pantalones that were brown from dust and spattered with mud. A machete was fastened about his waist, and a calabash of water hung by a leather thong from his right shoulder. He spoke Nacheetl with a strange, clipped accent.

"People of Zalapec! José Ronca has seized the government in the name of the Democratic-republican Party. The army of our oppressors is in flight. Last night our liberator, El Presidente José Ronca, issued by decree an Agrarian Law which restores all land to those who till it. Long live the new government!"

For a moment the crowd was silent; then Carlos heard a low rumble of voices that grew louder like thunder rolling over the mountains. "Viva Ronca! Death to the oppressor!"

A young man pushed his way through the crowd and sprang to the steps of the council house. "To the hacienda!" he roared. "To the Hacienda Santa Marta!"

"E-e-e-yah, to the hacienda!"

'Let's go, muchachos! Let's go!"

The crowd reached for the young man and would have lifted him high as their leader, but Uncle Vicente stepped forward. "Wait!" he ordered. Slowly the shouting subsided. "Are we a pack of stray dogs yelping in the streets? If we go to Santa Marta, let us go under our proper leader." He turned toward the presidente.

After running his fingers once more through the white hair that covered his head, the presidente spoke slowly and distinctly, "This is a moment in the ages. Do we go to the hacienda?"

"E-e-e-yah, e-e-e-yah, to the hacienda!"

"Then let us go as Nacheetl warriors with the blessings of the Great Dios and Jesucristo Salvador." He turned to Uncle Vicente. "Fetch the crucifix and bear it," he said.

Carlos followed Uncle Vicente into the council house, and Uncle Vicente took down from one wall a high crucifix which showed Jesucristo Salvador with a gaping wound in his side, and one could see the rib bones white as ivory. Uncle Vicente carried it out onto the steps, and the people raised a shout.

"Now let us go to Santa Marta!" the presidente announced.

Carlos felt important because he was directly behind Uncle Vicente and Jesucristo, and they were directly behind the presidente. Only the runner from the Barrio of the Frogs was ahead, and he ran so fast that he was soon out of sight in the direction of Xiltak.

The presidente was an old man, but Carlos saw that his legs were as sturdy as oak palings. He led the way at a steady pace, and Uncle Vicente moved close behind with Jesucristo held high above his head, and all the men and many of the women and children of Zalapec followed.

The trail was a steep trail and filled with cobblestones that many rains had laid bare. It was Señor's trail, and the cobbles were the very cobbles from which the hoofs of his horses had struck sparks these many years. Carlos was made to think of this, and he was made to think of Señor and his huge sombrero that was stiff and black and had tassels sewn about the brim, of the jacket that was tight and smooth and shiny, and the legs of his trousers embroidered with silver and gold. He was made to think of these things and of the presidente leading with Jesucristo Salvador looking over his shoulder and the crowd following with machetes and clubs and flails.

They climbed higher, and the trail zigzagged into the mountains, and already La Perla was far below. They took a short cut that by-passed Xiltak, and the hacienda loomed like a fortress directly above. For many generations it had stood there upon a bluff overlooking the valley, and its walls reminded Carlos of high cliffs among the mountains. They climbed higher, and one could see another trail leading up from Xiltak that was already below, and a line of men was moving on it.

"Let us hasten," the presidente called over his shoulder, "or those lazy Xiltaqueños will get there first!" He quickened his steps, and Carlos marvelled at the strength in his knotty legs.

The trail led up to a pair of oak gates that barred the only passage through the walls. Carlos saw that they were at least three times the height of a man, and he wondered how anyone could ever get in. As the men of Zalapec approached, however, the presidente ran ahead and pounded on the massive panels. A slot was opened from the inside, and Carlos saw a brown face and black eyes.

"Open the gates!" ordered the presidente.

"What do you want?"

"José Ronca has seized the government," the presidente explained. "The land belongs to those who till it. We have come for Señor El Dueño."

"Well, I don't know," hesitated the man inside the gate. "The patron — "

"Listen, Felipe, I knew you when you were a baby, and I knew your father before you. We want no trouble with you. If you open the gates, you'll be a free man. If you don't — " The presidente nodded toward the crowd of Zalapec men with machetes and clubs and flails.

"Pues, only one little moment then," answered Felipe.

Carlos heard the rattle of bars sliding in their grooves; the great gates swung inward with a screech of rusty hinges. There was a lone little man standing there in what appeared to be Señor's cast-off jacket and breeches. Beyond was a large cobbled court in which the whole village of Zalapec could have been placed with room to spare.

"Señor El Dueño is here?" demanded the presidente.

"Sí, pues."

"Where?"

"In the chapel at mass. The household is there."

"Good!" The presidente turned toward the crowd. "You, Pedro, and Miguel Flores and Enrique Santo, yes, and you, Lorenzo! Guard the chapel. Make certain that no one escapes."

Pedro and Miguel Flores and Enrique Santo and Lorenzo stepped forward; Carlos knew them well for they were young men of Zalapec. They went off with Felipe toward the chapel.

"Vicente," the presidente continued, "take good care of Jesucristo Salvador. Let him see everything and enjoy the looting. Now, you Zalapequeños, this is indeed a moment in the ages. After these many seasons of corn and after these many generations of men, Santa Marta is yours. Go to it, muchachos!"

There was no noise, this time. Not a single shout. The crowd merely dissolved. Within a moment the courtyard was empty. Men, women, children, all disappeared among the courts and halls and reception rooms of the vast hacienda.

"Come!" Uncle Vicente said to Carlos, "you and I will take Jesucristo around to see the sights. All my long years I have wanted to see the inside of Santa Marta, and I suppose he has been waiting much longer than that."

They crossed the court and pushed open a thick mahogany door. It was dark inside, but then their eyes became accustomed to it. Uncle Vicente gasped. "María Madre, I never thought it! No, I never dreamed it! E-e-e-ah, I've seen the church at Xiltak. I've seen the gold candlesticks and the gold plates and the colored windows. But this — why, this is where Señor lived! Look, those chairs, they are taller than the tallest man! And that table — all the men in Zalapec could sleep upon it!"

Carlos could only gape. He gaped at the table and the chairs, at the tapestries and paintings, at the mahogany sideboard with its cruets, its goblets, its ladles and trays of silver, its candlesticks of gold, at the chandelier with its prisms of glass. He gaped for a moment, and while he gaped, a man from Zalapec dashed through the door.

"Here, here it is!" he shouted. "Here is gold! Here is silver!"

Ten or twelve others squeezed through the threshold as sheep squeeze through a narrow gate. They squeezed through and spread over the room like locusts. They seized the candlesticks of gold and they tore down the chandelier and smashed the prisms into tiny splinters. They ripped off the paintings and bashed them in with their bare feet.

"Out with the chairs!" an old man yelled. He picked one up and ran for the door. But the chair was too large to pass through.

"Out the window!" screamed another. But the chairs were too big for the windows.

"Smash them up! Cut them to bits!"

They whaled into the furniture with machetes and clubs. They smashed the chairs and carved up the gleaming surface of the table and used the heavy mahogany legs to bash the sideboard.

"Let us go elsewhere," Uncle Vicente told Carlos. "Let us see all there is for our own sakes and for the sake of Jesucristo Salvador. This is indeed a sight to be remembered."

There were more buildings than Carlos could count. There were buildings for Señor and his family; there were buildings for the kitchen servants and the house servants and the grooms. There were countless buildings, and in certain of the buildings there were many rooms. Here was a room where Señor slept, and in it was a bed the like of which Carlos had never dreamed. It was soft and covered with silk, and above it was a frame from which curtains were hanging.

"Señor's bed is as big as our little house," Uncle Vicente remarked.

While they were examining the bed, a number of Xiltak men rushed into the room and tore it apart. They broke the frame and ripped the curtains and silks, and behind them came some Xiltak women who fought over the cloth that was left.

"Let us go to the stables," suggested Uncle Vicente. "In the stables is a milk-giving cow. I well remember when they brought it up the trail from the great city. It was a beautiful little cow, a precious one. Caramba, it had such magnificent teats. On no other beast did I ever see such magnificent teats. Long as my finger they were, and fat as my thumb. We must see that cow."

Leaving Señor's bedroom, they passed into a court where a fountain was playing, and all about the fountain were flowers of every hue. There were bougainvillea and gardenia and a garden of orchids. There were plants that Carlos had seen in the mountains and others which he had never seen and a number that even Uncle Vicente could not call by name.

From this court they moved through a scullery into a larger court that was bordered by sheds and stables, and men of Zalapec were fighting with men of Xiltak over horses and saddles. One man had a fine roan stallion by the halter; he had drawn his machete and was swearing to kill whosoever should dispute his claim. Several men came near and threatened, and he struck out with his machete. As he did so, the stallion snorted and reared and broke away. With nostrils distended, the beast charged about the court, stamping and kicking and biting at the air with bared teeth.

Carlos and Uncle Vicente ran for cover, and so did most of the men from Xiltak and Zalapec. They ran for cover, and the stallion

galloped twice around the court. Fiery-eyed and snorting, the beast
was starting around once more when a hoof caught in an iron grate
that covered a drainage gutter. With a scream of terror he pitched
forward into a heap, a leg hanging loose behind.

The danger gone, men of Xiltak and Zalapec came from their cover
and headed back to recover the prizes that they had so recently
dropped in terror.

"Come, let us hasten to find the milking cow," said Uncle Vicente,
"or it will be gone." He and Carlos and Jesucristo Salvador searched
about until they found a smaller, ill-smelling court that was covered
with dung; facing the court was a low-roofed shed just large enough
to hold a cow. Uncle Vicente opened a broken-down door and peered
at the blackness within.

"Look, Carlito, there it is!" exclaimed Uncle Vicente. "The milk-
giving cow!"

As his eyes became accustomed to the darkness, Carlos saw a beast
that was smaller than a horse, yet much larger than a sheep, and it
was tan in color like a puma, and it had curving horns. "The milk-
giving cow — she is precious!" he murmured.

Uncle Vicente entered the shed cautiously, holding Jesucristo well
in front of him, but the cow appeared to mean no harm. It sniffed
of Uncle Vicente and nuzzled his arm. Taking courage, Carlos slipped
in close behind Uncle Vicente. The two of them stood there quietly
stroking the smooth, brown hide.

"Look, Carlos, the teats! They are even larger than I said!" Uncle
Vicente stooped down and touched one gently. "See, she does not
care. She allows me to touch. Perhaps I can bring milk!" He squatted
and began stripping the teats as he had learned to do with ewes when
he was a small boy. A fine needle of milk shot out. He cupped a palm
and held it beneath until he had caught as much as it would hold. He
raised it to his mouth reverently as though he were taking com-
munion.

"The milk of a cow!" he exclaimed when he had sipped. "I have
drunk the milk of a cow!"

"May I be allowed to drink?" asked Carlos respectfully.

Uncle Vicente squeezed more milk into his palm and held it to the
little boy's lips. Carlos sipped. The milk had a strange taste that did

not suit his tongue, but it seemed to give strength. He thought that he could feel the strongness running in his blood. "I too have drunk the milk of a cow!" he said proudly.

"After these many, many years!" muttered Uncle Vicente. "After these many, many years!" He caressed the cow thoughtfully.

"To what man belongs this cow?" asked Carlos.

"According to the new law," said Uncle Vicente, "the land belongs to him who tills it."

"And about cows?"

"It is the same. You have seen other men taking ladles and candlesticks and plates of gold. You have seen them taking the silks from Señor's bed. You have seen them take horses and a roan stallion that broke its leg. If I were a young man, I too would want a stallion. But I am old and my hair is grey and the man-ness is gone from my belly. With the milk-giving cow I could spend my last days in peace. With the milk-giving cow I could die with whiteness on my lips. Why, it is God-given. There is not another man between here and the great city who can boast it!"

"Then we can take home the milk-giving cow?"

"Jesucristo Salvador willing, we shall take home the milk-giving cow!"

Carlos was helping Uncle Vicente to untie the halter rope when a crowd of Xiltak men came reeling into the court. They were waving tequila bottles and shouting curses that echoed back from the mountains.

"E-e-e-yah, what have we got in here?" screamed a one-eyed man as Carlos and Uncle Vicente led the cow out of the shed.

"A four-legged barbecue!" answered one of his companions. "A four-legged barbecue."

"Come, old man, let us help you along!" suggested the one-eyed man. "We'll slaughter your beast and build you a fire and even join with you in the eating."

"No, no," protested Uncle Vicente, "this is not a beast for meat. This is a milk-giving cow."

"Ho! So it's a milk-giving cow! Jesus, now, who ever heard of drinking milk? We've got tequila, old man. We've got bottles of it, barrels of it, gutters flooded with it. Have a drink of tequila, old man, while we slaughter your milk-giving cow."

"It is for milk only," pleaded Uncle Vicente. "Look, it is a beautiful cow, a precious cow, a magnificent cow! It is not a beast for killing. It is a beast for giving milk. All my life I have dreamed of milk, amigos, and I am not a young man. All these many years, and only today I drink of cow's milk. Take what you want, amigos, take silver and gold and fine silks. Take yourselves a stallion and tequila by the barrels. I have no need for such things. But the milk-giving cow, amigos, spare an old man his milk-giving cow."

"Out of the way, old buzzard," snarled the one-eyed man, drawing his machete. "Let's go, muchachos!"

They threw the cow onto its side and slit its throat with machetes. In a moment they had slung it from projecting eaves and the one-eyed man was opening its belly while the others tore the roof off the shed for firewood.

5

FOR MANY MONTHS the people of Zalapec talked about the looting of Santa Marta. They talked about the seizing of the ladles and trays and candlesticks of silver and gold, and they talked about the ripping of silks and satins, and they talked about the stallion that broke its leg. They talked also about the Xiltaqueños who tried to take everything as though Dios had chosen them to be the looters of Santa Marta.

All these matters were discussed and rediscussed according to their many aspects, but the story that was told with the greatest delight was the one that had to do with the burning of the chapel. It was told in story and it was told in song, and the word was passed from village to village throughout the great sierra. Those who had seen it passed the details along to those who had not, and thus it was known throughout the land of Nacheetls that the people of Zalapec (or of Xiltak, depending upon who was telling the story), had shut Señor and his household in the chapel of Santa Marta and had burned it to the ground.

Those who knew the story best were Miguel Flores and Enrique Santo and Pedro Fuentes and Lorenzo Valles, for they had guarded the doors. They had first smelled the smoke and heard the crackling of the flames, and some say that they had struck the first spark, but about this matter there was much dispute. That they had heard the prayers of Señor and his household, however, was a known fact, and it was also known that they had answered the screams with curses and had reminded the pleading Señor of his sins.

Señor and his household were reduced to ashes, and weeds were already growing in the ruins of the chapel and choking the flowers that surrounded the fountain. There were those in both Zalapec and Xiltak who were now rich because of what they had seized and carried or driven away, and there were others who had nothing left but stories of the looting and memories of the joy that had come from ripping and smashing and destroying.

In the village square and in the adobe houses of Zalapec there was also much talk about the revolution. Some men said that matters were no better than they had been before; the only difference was that men now paid their taxes to a government tax collector instead of sending everything to Señor. Others insisted that men were now free and that the tax collector was only a servant of the people; they maintained that all the taxes were being used for the good of everybody and that the government was going to do big things for the poor man as soon as the leaders could get around to it.

For the people of Zalapec life was very much the same. Men planted corn and hoed their fields with wooden hoes and left offerings of tobacco to appease los aires; women bore their children in pain and washed the clothing of their men and kept the houses clean; and boys like Carlos tended sheep or goats and kept them from going astray or breaking into fields of corn. In other villages, however, there were men who had become overfond of looting.

During the brief span of the revolution, these men were patriots; they smashed down the gates of haciendas like Santa Marta and killed Señor and his household and made off with anything they could move. After the Ronquistas had seized the government and the haciendas had been looted, these men found the old ways too hard. They formed bands and attacked any man who had more than his neighbor. Some called them bandits, and others called them patriots, and there was much talk about which were which. Sometimes soldiers came out from the great city to hunt these bandits, and if they caught one, they hanged him from the nearest tree.

Carlos spoke to Uncle Vicente about it, but the old man had no answer. "The world is upside down," he grumbled. "I know nothing about it. Man has turned against Fellow Man, and there is too much mine-and-thine. Even the laws of the Village are forgotten."

Poor old Uncle Vicente was no longer the same. He was a sick man and had been ever since the looting of Santa Marta and the slaughter of his milk-giving cow. Throughout the harvest he lay on his pallet in the house and wasted away. The presidente came to see him and pointed out that Jesucristo Salvador had been there, and if Dios had meant for Vicente to have the milk-giving cow, Jesucristo Salvador would have kept the Xiltaqueños from slitting its throat.

Harvest followed harvest, until Dios laid a hand upon Uncle Vicente and took his life-spirit away. He died with his lips dry of cow milk, and the relatives came to wail. Candles were lighted, and upon the dead man's chest his saint's picture was placed. The body was carried off to the campo santo, and it was buried in the earth.

Carlos now felt that he was a man; he remembered all the words that Uncle Vicente had spoken, and he was filled with importance. He remembered about duties to Dios and to the village. He remembered about Man and Fellow Man and about the laws of the Nacheetls. He remembered all these things, and he determined to take care of his mother and be the head of the family.

But in the summer of the same year his mother spoke to him. "Carlos," she said, "it has been many years since you have had a father."

"Uncle Vicente was a father," Carlos replied.

"Vicente was a good man," his mother agreed, "but he is dead, now, and you have no father. It is not right that you should have no father."

"I am a man now," Carlos replied. "I am head of the family."

"Yes, but you are very young," his mother insisted. "You are too young to be head of a family. Yet that is no matter, because you are soon to have a new father."

"A new father?"

"Yes! Lorenzo Reyes has asked me to marry him."

"I don't want a new father!" Carlos blurted.

His mother talked with him and explained about this Lorenzo Reyes. He was a Xiltaqueño, and since the revolution, an owner of many sheep, and he was a man respected in his village, and he had sat upon the council there. Dios had laid a hand upon his wife during the great sickness, and she had died, leaving him with a young son named Diego. Since then Lorenzo Reyes had been both father and mother, and he had raised Diego from a tiny boy. He longed for a woman in the house, and Diego wanted a mother.

So it was explained, and Carlos knew that there was nothing more to say. He knew that this Lorenzo Reyes had spoken and that his mother had answered. The marriage had been arranged, and that was all. Indeed, the nuptials took place after harvest; whereupon the family was four.

The family was four, but these four were not one. Carlos soon found that his new father was a harsh voice, and Diego was a grabbing hand, and his mother became merely a woman in a dream. These were three of the new family, and the fourth was himself.

Lorenzo was a harsh voice, and Carlos kept his distance, but the grabbing hand was always close about, and there was no getting away from him. It was soon after the marriage, and Carlos was lying on his belly in the grass that grew about La Perla, and he was playing on his flute. It had once been a wild reed, and just as Carlos was making it sing wild notes like doves mating, Diego came.

"Let me play," demanded Diego, and he seized the flute.

"Give it back," snapped Carlos. "It's mine."

"Try and get it," taunted Diego.

"I'll black your eye," threatened Carlos.

"You don't dare," replied Diego.

"I'll tell my mother!"

"What do I care!" said Diego. "My father can whip your mother."

"He can't do that thing."

"I saw him."

"You didn't either," grumbled Carlos. "When?"

"The other night, because I saw them. My father threw your mother on her bed mat and pinned her down."

"Well, I can black your eye."

"I'd like to see you."

Carlos tried, but Diego fought back; they grappled, and soon they were rolling on the grass, fighting as boys do, and Carlos tore his shirt. It ripped down the back, and it was in two pieces. They stopped fighting, then, and they went home by different trails, and when they reached the hut, Lorenzo Reyes was there.

Lorenzo was there, and when he saw the shirt, and when he saw how it was torn, he sent Diego down to the stream bed to cut a willow, and Diego cut a thick one.

That was the first beating, and there were many more, and so it came about that the new father was a harsh voice and also a willow stick. That was father, and there was also mother, but more and more she was only woman-in-a-dream.

Lorenzo Reyes had many sheep, and one flock he drove down from Xiltak.

"This Carlos is lazy," he said, "but there is nothing wrong with him that work won't cure."

And so Lorenzo gave Carlos a flock. He counted the sheep, and when they were counted, he gave them to Carlos to tend.

"Take them into the pastures above La Perla," Lorenzo said. "Graze them on the green grass there. But do not lose them. Guard against coyotes, and pumas, too, and boas, and do not lose a sheep. That will be some work to do, and we shall watch and see."

Carlos was a shepherd, and with break of day he set out for the hillside pastures with his father's flock. He drove them slowly along the slopes above La Perla, and throughout each day they ranged among the hills, grazing, and when the sun was high, they folded up their legs beneath them and rested in the shade of oaks. During the heat of midday they rested and chewed upon their cuds.

Sometimes Carlos slept, and sometimes he climbed high among the crags above La Perla and searched the rocks for caves or for a nest of eagle's eggs. As he climbed he watched closely lest he be surprised by the devil or by los aires or by the Xlalaks, the Fire Mountain men with pointed teeth who lived on slopes beyond the ridge and drank babies' blood in place of water.

He carried his sling in hand, and when he saw a pebble that was large and round, he would pick it up and fit it into the leather pocket of his weapon while searching for a target. When he had spotted a tree trunk or perhaps a hawk swooping low overhead, he would measure the distance with his eyes; then he would swing the leather thongs about his head. Twice the pebble in its pocket would circle his head, and halfway around again. Halfway around, and he would loose one thong.

When the large, round pebble left its pocket, it sang a song.

Often the pebble missed its mark. Perhaps it would fall short of the tree stump and send up a tiny cloud of dust where it struck the earth. Or perhaps the hawk zoomed low, and the pebble got lost before the sun. Often the pebble missed.

But sometimes it found its mark. Sometimes it struck the stump with a thud and knocked out a shower of brown splinters; once it nipped a hawk and brought a small handful of feathers floating down.

When he lay in the grass, he dreamed. Occasionally he fell asleep and had real dreams. In his father's little house at night he might dream of snakes, or the devil hiding behind a rock above La Perla, but in the pasture his dreams were good. Occasionally he fell completely asleep, but more often he just lay still and dreamed what he wanted to. He had a number of dreams, and when he was tired of one, he would try another.

In one he was standing near the trail that led far over the mountains to the great city when a pack train came out of the hills. He could hear the bell that the bell mule carried, and he could hear the strange talk of the driver.

"Hrrrr, mula, hrrrr," shouted the driver. "Arriba, hrrrr."

Down the trail the pack train came from the far-off mountain pass called La Cumbre, and when the driver was abreast, he stopped to chat with Carlos.

"I am looking for a man," he said in Nacheetl. "I need a man to learn my trade." He said that, but he also talked about the weather, about the season's corn, and about the Xlalak bandits. While he talked, he squinted at the clouds and hawked and spat, but he really was watching Carlos and looking him up and down.

"Well, now, I must be going," he said, and he spat once more. "Tell me, now," he continued, "you wouldn't perhaps consider driving mules?"

Carlos heard the question and pondered it a while. "Well, now, I might," he replied after a time. "I might if a man made it worth my while."

It always happened something like that. "I might," Carlos would say, and next he and the driver would be on their way toward the great city.

He would be gone for many years. He would be in the big city or driving his own pack train deep into the mountains and during this time he always became a famous driver. Sometimes he drove trains of charcoal, and other times he drove trains of silver and gold. Whatever he carried, he became famous along the trail and in the big city.

Finally, when he had fifty mules, or maybe a hundred, he would drive through the village. Small boys would hear his bell and run to the trail's edge to watch him go by.

"Hrrrr, mula, hrrrr," he would shout. "Arriba, hrrrr!"

His mules would climb the trail past his father's cornfield. His father would be working there, and Diego, too. They would lean on their hoes, and his father would say, "Ho, now, look at that pack train, did you ever see such a one!"

"He must be a very famous driver," Diego would agree. "What fine beasts they are!"

Carlos would not look to the right nor left, but he would hear what they said. A little way on he would rest his mules, and while they were resting, he would go to see his mother. She would be slapping tortillas with her hands, and he would notice how tired she was and how hard she worked.

At first she would not recognize this fine strange man from the city, but at last she would. He would help her to her feet, and she would throw her arms about his neck, and he would comfort her while she sobbed.

"Can that be Carlos Morelos?" the neighbors would whisper. "Jesus, what a man!"

He would take his mother with him to the great city, and after that she would live with him forever.

6

BUT THIS CARLOS was a shepherd boy, and by day he watched the sheep, and at night he returned them to their cactus corral where Lorenzo took a count.

It happened once that when Lorenzo counted, a ewe was gone, and he sent Carlos back to search. Already it was late afternoon, and the boy was afraid to go, but he was even more afraid of the willow stick, and so he started out. He climbed above La Perla to the pastures where his sheep had grazed, but there was no sign of the ewe. He climbed higher, and as he climbed, the sun disappeared altogether, and a greyness spread across the slope.

Higher and higher Carlos climbed until he was above the pastures, and he came upon a saddle in the hills. Ahead of him among the rocks there was a branching of the trail. One path climbed higher toward terrifying peaks and crags where lived the Xlalaks with pointed teeth while the other dropped away across a desert valley towards the famous mountain pass called La Cumbre.

Which way to go? There were pumas in the mountains, fierce beasts with bloody teeth, while in the valleys lived giant boas, snakes that were big around as trees. Carlos was too terrified to venture on either path.

Through deepening dusk he peered ahead, and he saw the splitting of the trail, a white fork against the blackness of the earth. Irresolute, he stood and stared, and as he stood, he saw a movement among the rocks. He gulped. It could not be, and yet it was.

The devil was squatting in the trail fork!

Carlos could see his trunk, rough like a knotty tree stump. He could see a massive head with curling horns, and it looked his way and snorted. Carlos turned and bolted like a rabbit. He sped down the slopes with terror at his back. Around La Perla he raced, and into the village, and he did not stop until he was safe within his father's house.

"Where is the ewe?" Lorenzo asked.

Carlos tried to answer, but his breath came short, and he could only gasp.

"Leave him alone," his mother pleaded. "The boy has had a fright."

Thus they asked no more until he was able to talk, and then he told them of all that he had seen. He spoke of the white trail fork in the mountain gloom, of the knotty-looking torso and the head with curling horns. Lorenzo Reyes listened with morbid interest to every word and crossed himself, and Diego sat wide-eyed and quiet in the corner farthest from the door. "The devil had big eyes, red and green," Carlos added, "and he snorted at me."

Diego shuddered in the safety of his corner, and even Lorenzo Reyes was strangely silent. Carlos ate his supper and drank a pot of lemon tea, and not another word was spoken about the ewe that he had lost.

So it was that Carlos escaped a beating, but thereafter the devil followed close behind. When the small boy lay upon his mat at night, the devil came, growing out of darkness, and stood and glared at Carlos. While Carlos was awake, the devil came, and while Carlos was asleep, as well. He moved about in Carlos' dreams and snorted, and the boy smelled his musky smell. Huddled on his woven mat, he felt the bestial presence, and in his mind the devil was a frightful fear, alive in demon shape. It was a fear of all the horrors that he had known, and it was a greater fear of what he did not know, and he shrank within himself and screamed screams that were stifled deep within his throat.

He was terrified at night, but he could safely dream by day. And so, when he had taken his father's sheep to pasture, he would lie hidden deep inside a clump of grass and ferns and build pleasant visions in his mind. Sometimes he was a mule driver taking gold to market, and sometimes he was presidente leading all the people for the looting of Santa Marta. He was this or that, here or there, but always he was brave and good and strong, and Diego was always mean, and in the end, it was Diego who was made to suffer.

One day when he was driving mules to market, Diego attacked him with a band of bandits, and there by the roadside they had a fight. It was a terrible battle, but Carlos went after Diego and his robbers with a big machete. This way he slashed, and that, and he killed off all the others, and then he attacked Diego. He was strong, this Diego, and very brutal, but manfully, Carlos fought, and finally with a mighty stroke he struck off his brother's head.

It was a great battle, but when it was over, Carlos had a sudden thought about his sheep, and deep into his belly came a jab of fear. He jumped to his feet and looked about, and he saw that they had strayed away. In fact, they had broken into a near-by field of corn.

He chased after them full speed, and he scrambled over the cactus picket that grew about the cornfield, and he drove them out through the hole by which they had entered.

He drove them out as fast as he could, but he had come too late. They had sliced the field with their hoofs and had bitten into ears of corn and had stripped leaves from the tallest stalks.

The damage had been done — but who would know? He looked hastily about. There was not a man in sight — so who would know?

There were other sheep in near-by pastures. There were sheep grazing close beside the cornfield. There were sheep on the slopes just below. Who would ever know?

For a few moments he felt safe, but not for long. He felt safe until he had driven his flock back to the pasture where he had left them when his dreams began. He felt safe until he saw Diego watching from a boulder in the field.

He pretended not to see Diego, but Diego slid off the boulder and sauntered toward him. He looked mighty righteous, this Diego.

"Where you been?" Diego demanded.

Carlos shrugged. "Off yonder only," he said, "where the grass is greener."

"Where?"

"Off in there."

"In the García cornfield, you mean."

"No, no, there in the pasture only."

"Liar! Your sheep were in the cornfield. I know because I was there. I saw them."

"Why didn't you drive them out if you were there?"

"Never mind me. We'll talk about you only. You were sleeping in the grass."

"What're you going to do about it?"

"Do about it? I'll tell Papa. That's what I'll do about it."

"I'll tell him you saw the sheep in the cornfield and didn't drive them out."

"See if I care. He'll beat your hide off, but he won't touch me."

"Go ahead and tell!"

Diego shrugged and started down the hill. "I will."

"Snake!"

Diego laughed, and while he laughed, he continued down the hill. "Pig!" he shouted over his shoulder.

"Baby-puke!"

"Whore-son!" Diego replied.

Carlos stopped, fist doubled. "Don't say that!" he screamed.

"Whore-son, whore-son," taunted Diego.

Carlos stamped his foot.

"Whore-mother, whore-son, whore-mother, whore-son."

Carlos ran a few steps down the hill, stopped abruptly. With one hand he unwound the sling from his belt, while he scooped up a large, round pebble with the other. It was the size of a hen's egg, and it was hard and smooth. He fitted it into the pocket of his sling. Then he grasped the thong ends with thumb and two fingers of his right hand.

"Whore-mother, whore-son," sang Diego. "Whore-mother, whore-son."

"Take that back," screamed Carlos. "Take it back or I'll heave a stone."

"You wouldn't dare," laughed Diego. "Whore-mother, whore-son, whore-mother, whore-son."

Carlos began swinging the sling about his head, slowly, menacingly.

"You don't dare," Diego repeated, "and you couldn't hit me if you did."

"Could too!"

"Couldn't either. WHORE-MOTHER, WHORE-MOTHER, WHORE — "

Once more Carlos swung his sling, and this time he loosed the pebble. It arced into the sky, sailing high into the blue, and he was certain that he had overshot and that the pebble would travel over

Diego's head and kick up dirt beyond. He was certain, and yet — and yet — it was falling fast, that pebble. It was coming down, down, straight down.

"Diego," he screeched, "DIEGO!"

But Diego didn't dodge, and he didn't look back. He walked right ahead. He walked directly into the falling pebble.

Carlos saw the round, white stone strike Diego's head. He saw Diego fold quietly into a small heap upon the slope.

Carlos ran down the hill to Diego's side where he knelt on the ground and seized Diego's hand.

"Diego! I didn't mean it, Diego. I wanted to scare you only. I didn't mean it, Diego, I didn't mean it."

He held Diego's hand in his trembling fingers, but it was limp, and when he dropped it, he saw how it flopped on the ground.

A big, black zopilote swooped low, circling the spot where Diego's body lay.

II. The Great City

CARLOS RAN DOWN from the pastures into a thicket of willows in the stream bed below La Perla, and he followed it to its junction with the big river. There was a ford near by, and the water was shallow enough for him to wade across. By the time he reached the other side of the big river, night had fallen.

He thought he heard footsteps behind him in the dark, he thought he heard his father shouting, he thought he heard village dogs yapping on his trail. He ran faster than he had known he could. The trail, zigzagging, climbed steeply from the riverbank, and it was a path of round pebbles that rattled underfoot. He stumbled upward in the dark, and great cacti loomed on either hand, tall with outstretched arms. In the darkness they looked like Jesucristo Salvador upon the cross.

His breath came in hoarse gasps. His legs were sticks of wood that refused to move so fast. Looking once over his shoulder, he saw lights in the darkness, and they were ocote torches burning in Zalapec. At first they were over his shoulder and above, but after he had climbed and climbed, they dropped below. He quickened his pace as he heard the wind moan as it does in high places.

In time he left cactus plants behind, and there was a pine forest in front. The wind, blowing through their needles, sighed, and it carried a chill that brought a surge of terror. He remembered los aires and how the devil might be close behind his back, and he had more fear of these than of his father or the village dogs or even of Diego's corpse. He forgot that his legs were short and that he had climbed high. He forgot that the air was thin and that his breath was sulphur in his throat. Fear seized him, and he ran again.

Gradually the wind died down, and stars appeared in the sky; after them came a moon bright enough to show the way. It also cast shadows among the pines, and he saw monsters across his path and corpses of Diego lying by the trail. He saw all these things, and each time he looked ahead, there were more to see.

Suddenly he could move no more. Overcome by exhaustion and fright, he sank by the way and curled himself like a babe in the womb, and lying thus, he wept and felt safe and finally forgot his terror and fell asleep.

When he awoke in the early morning, hunger gnawed his belly, and he was weak. He wanted to turn back, and he almost did. But his eyes saw Diego lying dead in the pasture, and his ears heard the voice of Lorenzo calling, and he felt the devil breathing on his neck. He continued on his way, therefore, step by step, dragging himself to the top of a ridge. There he looked back, and in the distance far off and below, he saw Zalapec and the church of Xiltak a little bit above.

The trail dropped over the other side of the ridge where it entered a deep canyon. The bottom of this canyon was far below, and there was a stream running through it, a green ribbon. The trail entered this deep canyon, and it was only a shelf cut into the side of a cliff.

Carlos was weak, and when he came to a spring, he dropped to his belly on the ground, and drank the cold water, and it refreshed him. While he was sitting by the spring, a man came down the trail, driving a burro. The animal stopped to drink at the spring, and the driver spoke to Carlos.

"A good day to you," he said. "A very good day, and whither are you bound?"

"I am going to the city," Carlos replied.

"To the city? Caramba! That's a long walk for a chico like you." He examined Carlos with his eyes. "A long walk indeed. Are you alone?"

"Yes," gulped Carlos. "I am alone."

"It isn't often one sees a chico travelling so far alone," the driver noted suspiciously.

"Oh, I am going to my sister's," Carlos explained hastily. "I am going to my sister's to live, and I am going to become a soldier."

"Ah-yeah, then we can walk along together," said the driver. "For a

part of the way, at least. I go to Cahuatl which is within church-bell
distance of the great city itself."

The driver had tortillas which he shared with Carlos, and they
travelled along together and chatted. The driver had been among the
pines to gather ocote, and he told about life on the ridges. He told
about the burners of charcoal and the makers of shakes, about the
cattle grazers and growers of potatoes.

As they travelled along they were overtaken by pack trains coming
down from the mines, and the mules bore burdens, and the burdens
were metal, both yellow and white. Carlos liked the sound of the lead
mule's bell, and the words of the arrieros. The tinkle of the bell and
the words of the arrieros were a song, and this song was a song of
the trail.

> Ah-rrrrrr-ayyyyyyyyy
> Mooooo-laa
> Ah-rrrrr-aayyyyyyyyy
> Choooo-laa
> Ah-rrrr-eeeeeeee-baa
> Ah-rrrrrr-aayyyyyyyyy

Down from the mountains came men and women and mules and
goats and sheep, and the trails were as stream beds, and the men and
women and goats and sheep were streams. They overflowed from
their channels into the Great Valley, and in the center of the Great
Valley stood the city. Like streams on a delta they overflowed from
their channels, and when they converged, they converged upon the
city.

From a high point in the trail, Carlos saw far below where men
and women and mules and goats and sheep spread themselves across
the Great Valley.

In all his life Carlos had seen nothing but the mountains back of
Zalapec and the slopes and the narrow canyons and rocky stream
beds, and he had always supposed that the whole world was the same.
But here before him stretched a valley flat as the floor in his mother's
house. It was flat and crisscrossed with roads, and each of these
roads was lined with eucalyptus trees, growing in straight lines on
either side.

The trail came out upon a promontory and there, a little to the west, rose a mountain shaped like a woman's breast, and the top of it was glistening white. "That mountain!" Carlos exclaimed to the driver. "It is white on top, as if sheep's milk were spilled."

"That is the Volcán, the Fire Mountain," explained the driver. "There is fire in its belly. From time to time it opens its mouth, which is on top, and spits out fire and smoke."

"But the whiteness!"

"That is a strange matter known as snow," the driver said. "The mountain is so high that clouds bump against it and leave a part of their whiteness there. I have heard of men who have climbed up and seen that snow. They say it is soft as a cloud would be, but it bites the hand at touch."

"I would like to climb there," Carlos said.

"That is dangerous," the driver warned. "On the slopes below the whiteness live fire-mountain men. They have teeth pointed like the teeth of dogs. They kill those who come, and they suck the blood of babies. We take now a trail that goes safe around."

Thus they travelled along, Carlos and the driver of the burro, and the trail dropped down from the mountains. In the afternoon they entered the Great Valley and came to Cahuatl where the driver lived.

"To the city it is only a matter of church-bell distance," the driver said. "But legs go more slowly. Stay with me tonight, if you wish, and continue your way in the morning."

Carlos had seen the city from afar, and he could not wait. He thanked the driver, and the driver gave him some cheese, and he continued along the road. It was late afternoon, and he saw his shadow lengthen fast. As he came near to another village, he decided to find some place to sleep.

The streets of this place were deserted.

He hurried across the village square. There was not a person in sight, and the loneliness of the empty houses frightened him. As he neared the outskirts, however, he heard the beating of a drum ahead of him, and in a moment he overtook a procession of men and women and children. He mingled with them, and they were shouting and praying, and in front of the procession moved a man with a heavy cross of wood upon his shoulder.

This man was wearing a scarlet robe and a crown of thorns had been placed upon his head. There was blood streaming down his face, and upon his arms and hands also there was blood.

Men and women marched on either hand with leather whips, and they beat him as he struggled forward with his cross. After a time they stripped the robe from him and scourged his shoulders and back with their whips, and the lashes raised heavy welts upon the brown smoothness of his flesh.

"Crucify him! Crucify him!" screamed the mob, and they laid upon him anew with their whips.

The man with the cross stumbled and fell in a heap upon the ground, and while certain men were reviving him, others, both men and women, lashed at one another with their whips and prayed and yelped with delight. The lashes slashed their clothes and brought spurts of blood, and Carlos grew sick at the sight. He longed to run, but he was now in the center of the crowd and dared not.

They had raised the bearer of the cross to his feet, and again he was struggling forward under his load. The procession continued upon its way until it approached a small knoll near the road, and there it turned aside into a field.

"Crucify him! Crucify him!" screamed the mob, and as the bearer of the cross stumbled toward the knoll, they laid upon him with new vigor, and upon one another, also.

A woman turned to Carlos and said, "Get thyself a stick, boy. During the Fiesta of the Crucifixion it is wicked to be without."

Carlos turned and fled in terror. He ran down the road at full speed for as long as he could hear the shouting and screaming and beating of drums, and he dared not look behind.

Darkness fell as he came to a church by the wayside. There was a fountain in front, and he dropped upon his knees before it and bathed his face and neck and quenched his thirst. He could feel a burning in his throat, and his heart was thumping and skipping an occasional beat.

When he had quenched his thirst and recovered his breath, Carlos entered the church and crept forward along the aisle, moving as close to the altar as he dared. There he knelt and prayed to Dios to watch over him and protect him from the horrors of the world. He explained how sorry he was to have killed Diego and begged Dios not to hand him over to the men and women with whips.

"Diego made me the way I was," he explained to Dios. "He made me angry, and I meant to frighten him only."

When he had explained everything to Dios very carefully, he asked him to care for his mother and try to make her understand, and not to tell Lorenzo where he was, nor the men and women with whips, either.

Then he lay down upon a bench and slept until daylight.

2

THE GREAT CITY was rows of houses stretching up and down and across, and it was hundreds and hundreds of people hurrying this way and that, and it was carriages drawn by fine horses with plumes upon their heads. The great city was much talk and noise of cart wheels and barking of dogs and singing of peddlers selling fruit. The great city was all the world gathered in one place.

Carlos found a great open space, a square in the center of the city. On one side was a church with stone towers and with steps that were jammed with people. They were standing and squatting, these people, and some were begging, and some were selling candles that were long and white and they were also selling tiny images of hands and feet and arms and legs and heads. An old woman without any teeth accosted Carlos. She held out a candle, and she spoke in Spanish that he could not understand. She poked the candle under his nose. He backed away, falling off the steps into the path of a loaded burro.

The beast halted, standing still in its tracks while the owner beat upon its rump with a stick. Since the beast would not move, its owner stopped beating after a while and went after Carlos.

Carlos scrambled to his feet and dived into a stream of people. These were men in white shirts and pantalones, and women in full dresses, their heads covered with rebozos. These were men and women who were on their way to market, and many of them had loads upon their backs. Carlos lost himself among them, moving as they moved, and in a few moments he found himself in the market place.

He saw rows of buildings which were no sides and all roof. Each building had a stone floor, and spread out upon the floor were things to buy. Here was a man with pineapples built in pyramids of four, and there were bananas beyond. There were also papayas, limes, oranges, avocados, and mangos. In the whole building there was nothing but fruit.

From all directions were coming those who would buy and those who would sell. From all directions came herdsmen and farmers and potters and tinsmiths and glass blowers and tinkers and blacksmiths and jewellers and servants and public scribes and fortune tellers and musicians and priests and miners and magicians and fire eaters. There were Indians and there were white men, and there were mestizos. From all directions came covered oxcarts with wooden axles and wheels, and the squeak of these carts was the squeak of wood turning on wood. From all directions rode charros on spirited horses, and the charros wore felt sombreros and striped ponchos, and breeches with flute-key braid on the legs. Their spurs were silver, and their saddles were trimmed with gold.

Carlos stood near the building of fruits and watched the people come. He saw men and women and children and mules and sheep. He saw dancers in plumes and paint. He saw soldiers in blue and gold.

He saw buildings of stone beyond the market place, and the roofs of tile, the windows grilled with iron. All this he could see from the building of fruits. He moved along, and there were potatoes and corn lying in piles and heaps on the naked pavements, and chilis and indigo and cochineal and cacao and rice and cotton and sugar and salt and squashes and beans. The vegetables lay in neat piles that made designs on the pavement.

He found himself among the sellers of pigs. Each man had his pigs in a bunch, tied together by their hind legs, and there was a din of squealing and squawking. Beyond was a booth where a jeweller worked, and he had rings and pins of silver and gold and little figures of onyx and marble, and behind his shop was a beater of gold.

All these things Carlos saw. He edged along, and in the next building there were bundles of pinewood kindling and heaps of charcoal, and the men and women who were selling charcoal had black faces and hands, and their clothes were covered with black dust.

Carlos found a third building that was full of meats. There were mutton and kid and two or three haunches of beef and blue and red and yellow fish the likes of which he had never seen.

The fourth building had hats with high crowns and brims that were two arms around. It had hats and fat-bellied baskets, snakeskin belts, sandals, bracelets and earrings of silver and gold, purple sashes, axes, machetes, and knives.

Never had he seen such knives. They had steel blades which caught the glitter of the sun, and the handles were of horn, and some were mounted with silver and gold. He stood at the edge of the building, eyes fixed upon the knives as they lay on the floor in rows. They were a sight to see, and for a moment he forgot that he was alone and afraid until the knife-man came up. "Go away!" growled the knife-man in Nacheetl. "Get away, or I'll cut your ears off."

The knife-man seized a knife with a long, curved blade, and sliced the air as though he were cutting off ears. "Get along!" he rasped.

Carlos hurried away, and he felt a twitching where his tail would have been if he had been born with one, and that twitch was a tail-between-the-legs twitch even though he had no tail. He scurried until he came to a cypress tree so large that it shaded a whole corner of the market place. Many people were gathered under this tree, and those behind were stretching their necks to see over those in front.

As he came closer, Carlos heard music, and this was the music of a marimba. He got down on his hands and knees and squeezed between people's legs. Once he poked his head under a fat woman's skirt, and she squealed like a pig. He scrambled away before she could see what had been under her skirt, and in a moment he was near the trunk of the tree. There he stood upon his feet, and the marimba was right in front.

At many fiestas in his village Carlos had seen marimbas. He had seen marimbas from Guatemala and faraway Chiapas, but this was the largest of all. The man who played the deep-note end was old and grey-haired and wrinkled across the face, and the music he made was the sound of raindrops in an earthenware jar. He played the deep-note end, and a younger man stood next, and another, and more beyond. There were six altogether, and playing the high-note end was the smallest of all. He was not half the size of Carlos, this high-note one, and he was standing on a box to reach.

This marimba was right in front, and beyond was a man with a monkey on a string, and beyond him was a clown.

The clown had a yellow face and a nose that was bright red. He danced to the music, and he made faces at the monkey, and sometimes he tried to peek under a woman's skirt. He would dance up close to the circle of watchers, and the girls and women would giggle. One-two-three, he would pass them by, and then he would turn and grab the hem of a skirt.

Carlos watched, and he liked the music, and he liked the monkey, and he liked the clown. He liked the lifting of the womens' skirts.

But his stomach was empty.

He had eaten nothing since the night before. Looking at the pine-apples he had not been hungry, nor in looking at the meat. He had been afraid, he had been alone, but he had not been hungry.

Now he was hungry.

He scrambled under people's legs again, and when he came up, he could smell broiled chicken.

Following the scent, he came to a white sunshade that was mounted on a mast. It bulged slightly under a gentle breeze and thus reminded Carlos of sails used on La Perla. Beneath this sunshade sat an old woman, broiling chicken over a charcoal spit. Carlos moved near and watched, trying to look as hungry as he felt. If he looked hungry, he thought, this old woman might feel sorry and give him a piece of chicken.

In the mountains one felt sorry for the hungry and gave them chicken. That was a law in the mountains. But although Carlos stood looking hungry for a great length of time, the woman gave him no chicken. The longer he stood there looking hungry, the hungrier he got, but the woman paid no attention. He moved closer.

"Get away, piglet," she snarled in Nacheetl. "Get away before I set you afire!"

Carlos backed away, but he was too hungry to go far. He stood in the shade of a pepper tree and watched while a man with a long bull whip went up to the woman and bought a leg of chicken. Carlos saw the man strip away the meat with his teeth, and when he was finished, the bone was bare. The man tossed it aside, and it fell in the dust where flies came to crawl upon it.

As Carlos watched the flies, an urchin sidled up and spoke in Spanish.

"No compren'o," Carlos said.

"Do you like chicken?" the city boy asked in Nacheetl. He seemed to be older than Carlos, though not much taller.

"The stomach grumbles," Carlos answered.

"Then listen, and we shall both eat chicken. The old woman, yonder, see how she raises on her knees to turn the chicken? I shall go behind the sunshade and poke her between the legs with a stick. She will get up very fast and scream. That will be the time when you grab the chicken. You will do that?"

"But that is to steal," Carlos protested.

"Cabrón, how else can one live?" the stranger demanded. "Do you want to eat chicken? Then do as I say." He sauntered away in search of a stick, and when he had found one floating down the gutter, he picked it up.

The ragged urchin circled like a sheep dog, and when he was beyond the sunshade, he sneaked forward. Soon he was directly behind the old woman, and there he paused. In a moment she rose on her knees to give the chicken a turn. Nodding to Carlos, the lad poked with his stick.

The old woman lurched to her feet with a howl, upsetting the charcoal grate, and danced this way and that, holding her backsides as she danced. Carlos darted forward, and as he ran, she caught sight of the boy with the stick who turned and sprinted across the square. She followed as fast as her aged limbs would allow.

Carlos seized the chicken out of the ashes and fled toward the nearest alley. He splashed through a gutter and dodged into an alley that was narrow and dark. There he stopped and looked back. The old woman was standing in the market place. About her was a crowd of men and women and boys, and a dog was barking at her heels. She was pointing at the grate that lay in the sand, overturned, and she was spewing a stream of Nacheetl and Spanish.

Carlos stuffed the chicken under his blouse and moved deeper into the alley. Soon he came to a small square with a well in the center, and there was a stone trough at which he knelt and drank. His mouth and throat were parched from running and sweating and fearing, and he drank until the water sloshed about in his belly as it does in a goatskin bag. When he could drink no more, he sat upon the edge of the trough and waited.

It was then that he realized what he had done.

All his short life he had lived in the mountains where men did not steal. There might be bandits who lived in the mountains and stole, but the people of the mountains never did. That was a law among them, and it was very old.

He had stolen, and he was both frightened and ashamed. He was frightened lest he be caught by soldiers and shot, and he was ashamed because men from the mountains do not steal. He was frightened and ashamed, but his fear was greater than his shame. He stared about him as though he had been pursued and brought to bay.

If he could hide the chicken, no one would know, and he could go his way unharmed. He looked about, and he thought of the well. He was on the point of dropping the chicken inside when he was stopped by a voice.

"Aye, there you are, cabronito. Dios, I thought you'd made off with the chicken." It was the stranger who spoke. "Come, let's get away before those pigs catch up with us." He seized Carlos by the arm, and off they went together.

"Will they send the soldiers?" Carlos asked.

"Soldiers? Jesus, what do soldiers care about an old woman's chicken? Unless they took it first. They're great thieves, those soldiers, only they're too lazy to go to much trouble. Ay-yah, we'll take Señor Chicken to a new roost, and there we'll answer the grumblings of our stomachs. It was nicely done, that chicken-taking. We work well together, you and I. There is much in this city to take. Today we took a chicken, but for us a chicken is nothing. Today a chicken, tomorrow a knife, one day a ring with many jewels."

"Don't they shoot men for stealing?"

"Shoot men for stealing? Suppose they do! Men are shot for many reasons, and hung, too. You know that tree in the market place? The cypress? Many a man I've seen hanged on that tree. Mostly políticos. Ah, now, those are the men who get hanged, those políticos."

"What are p'líticos?"

"Caray, what a mountain goat you are! What a precious mountain goat! Where did you come from, little goat? What are you called? E-e-yah, who cares where you came from? What matter? Your name, though, that is another thing. What are you called?"

"Carlos."

"Carlos? And why not? It's a good name, Carlos. As good as the next. Men call me Pepillo. Listen! Do you hear that? My stomach grumbles. Tear off a leg, Carlos. Tear a leg from Señor Chicken."

So he talked, this Pepillo, and the two of them crossed the city. They passed through the street of the glassblowers and on beyond the leather workers and potters and ironmongers and makers of coffins. They crossed the city by a devious path. They followed twisting alleys and crossed squares too small for sunlight to reach, and they came at last to a high-banked river. Pepillo showed Carlos a path that zig-zagged downward to the water's edge. "That is where we go," he said. He led the way down this path until they found themselves beneath a bridge.

"See, this is my roost." Pepillo pointed to a recess in the foundations.

Carlos saw that there was a sort of cave. It was much smaller than those in the cliffs above La Perla, but there were sheepskins on the floor, and there was a charcoal grate like the one from which he had taken the chicken, and there were faggots of pine splinters, a kettle, and a number of pots.

"Make us a fire, Carlos. Put red heat in the charcoal, little goat. Light a fire whilst I get water. Hot coals, that's what we want. God, how I hate cold chicken!"

3

"I COULD NOT LIVE in the mountains," Pepillo said. He was lying on a sheepskin in his cave, and the light of a candle shone upon his face, and there was chicken grease on his nose and about the edges of his mouth. "In the mountains all things come through work. Oh, I have heard all about that work. One digs away the sod with a wooden hoe and plants a seed, and one gets down on the knees to pull out weeds, and after many months the good Dios is pleased to present one with an ear of corn. Ah-yah, that is right for the one who likes to work only. But for Pepillo, no! In the morning he goes to the market, and there is precious corn, all spread out on a stone floor like yellow gold. Ha, I like that!"

"That is to steal," Carlos insisted. His stomach was full, and on a full stomach, stealing is stealing.

"From what man is it to steal? From the fat pimp who sits behind the corn? He planted no seed, that man, the corn is not his. Was not the good Dios pleased to touch the seed and make it grow? Was not the good Dios pleased to bring forth an ear of corn? Was he not pleased to present it to the poor fool who dug away the sod with a wooden hoe and pulled out weeds? Then what do I care if he gave his corn away for the pimp's greasy silver? What do I care for the pimp? I take the corn."

Carlos shook his head. "That is to steal only."

"I want no mountains," Pepillo persisted. "I want no wooden hoes or sweat or getting down on the knees in dirt. Look here in my roost. What more would I have? From the tinsmith I get a pot for coffee and for chocolate another. From the glassblower I get a jug, and a good jug, at that. See, there is the Holy Mother blown into the glass! I get my coal from the carbonero, the very best grade, and from the church, my candles."

"From the church?"

"There the candles are best. They burn well, and there is little waste of tallow. You see, there is nothing that I want."

"Have you always gotten things that way only?"

"Oh, no, once for a time I worked. I worked for my sister every day, and nights too. She lives on the Calle de las Mujeres. She has a place there, and I used to go about the streets pimping."

"What is that — to pimp?"

"Can it be? E-e-yah, you know nothing, little goat, nothing at all. Well, there are women who sell their bodies — "

"Yes, that I know," Carlos said. "There was one such in my village who would sell herself for sugar candy."

"Not here in the city, not for sugar candy! Here they go to bed for silver only. In my sister's house there are three girls — ah, three precious, fat ones. I used to go about the market place and the hotels and cantinas getting men. Not your barefoot ones, no, but a man with shoes, a guapo. To this man I go up just right, and I say to him, 'Señor, would you like zig-zig?' And if he says yes, I take him to my sister's house. Maybe he asks how much, and then I tell him a little too much. Of course, all the time my eyes, they have been seeing everything. His shoes, his clothes, his hat, all these things my eyes have been seeing, so I know what price to ask."

"Do you find many men?"

"Oh, many, always many men. It is a good business because zig-zig, that is something every man wants. If he does not want it, there is something wrong with him. He is old, perhaps, or maybe his health is bad. There are some men who do not like it. They are strange ones, but they buy other things. A few want an exhibición only. My sister, she does not give exhibición, but on the same street I know a house gives very fine exhibiciónes, really precious. You would be surprised the things they give at that house, things you would never think. One day we shall go and see what they do. You will not believe."

"To sell these things for your sister — that is to p-p — "

"That is to pimp. I do not do it longer. There is much money that way, but that is no business for a man. All the other chicos I meet, they point the finger at me and shout pimp. To my face they call me that. No more for me. I don't want that kind of silver, I like this way better. Do you like women?"

"I don't know," Carlos replied.

"You are too little, perhaps, but I am not so sure. There is a chiquito I know, he is more or less eight years old, he is very fond of women. I take him to my sister's house, and he likes it fine. He wants to go all the time after that. We'll go there, you and I, and we'll find out. If you don't like to stay, we'll wait a while. In ten or twelve months, who knows? Many things can happen in ten or twelve months. E-e-yah, it's time for a smoke."

From a small ledge in the wall of the cave Pepillo took down a wooden box from which he drew a cigar. "You like to smoke?"

Carlos shook his head. "I do not smoke."

"It's time for you to learn," Pepillo said, and he broke the cigar in half. "The rich man has fine horses, and he has women, and he has a cellar full of wine. For fine horses and beautiful women and wine it takes much silver. But for a cigar, pff! If a poor man cannot steal a cigar, he can pick up a few leaves. Silver is not needed for picking up a leaf or two. Tobacco is like corn. A seed is planted, and soon the good Dios presents us with leaves. 'Here you are, Pepillo,' says the good Dios, 'have a smoke on me.'"

"I do not smoke."

"It is very easy," Pepillo insisted. He stuck half of the cigar in his mouth, and drew a light from the candle. "There! I have a smoke as good as the great Judge Cervantes. Ay-yah, he is a true guapo, that Judge Cervantes. He has the best horses, and they say his wine comes straight from Spain, and when he was a young stallion he had many mistresses, too. All that he has to himself. And cigars? Verdad, he buys the best. He has commissioned Díaz to make them of the finest blends, and Díaz does that, cheating only a little. Old Díaz makes the best for Judge Cervantes. Pepillo knows this, and Pepillo knows the drawer where they are kept, and Pepillo says to himself, 'what is good for Judge Cervantes can do no harm to me.' It's a good smoke, Carlos, the very best, believe me."

Pepillo held out the lighted cigar to Carlos, and Carlos took it with shaking hand. He put the end into his mouth and drew in a small amount of smoke. It tasted good. He drew in more, but this time it crept down into his throat. It was biting and hot and it burned his lungs. He choked and fell into a fit of violent coughing.

"Oh, well, smoking is not a matter to hurry into," Pepillo explained, taking back the cigar. "A smoke is like a woman or a fine horse, it throws a timid rider. Tomorrow night we try again."

Pepillo smoked and chatted. He chatted about this and about that, but the this's and that's had always to do with the great city. It seemed that there was no part of San Marcos that Pepillo did not know. Just as Carlos knew the pastures above La Perla, just as he knew the crags and the caves and the springs of water and the moods of the winds and rains, just as Carlos knew all these things, so Pepillo knew about the city. He knew about the streets and the squares and the hideouts of thieves and the shops of fences. He knew about the pimps, about the men who wished men and the women who lay with women and about the men who lay with beasts.

He chatted about these things, puffing upon his cigar, and when the cigar had burned short, he pierced it with a splinter and held it thus until even the butt had crumbled in ashes. Then he stretched. "E-e-yah, the lids grow heavy," he said. "It is time for sleep."

They lay upon sheepskins, Carlos and Pepillo, and they drew skins about their shoulders, and they were ready for sleep.

Pepillo was soon asleep, but not Carlos.

With his face buried in the sheepskin, Carlos forgot Pepillo and the great city with its whores and pimps and he thought only of his mother and step-father and Diego, of La Perla and the pastures and crags and caves, of the sheep and how they bleated and how they smelled and how they cropped the grass close to its roots. He had seen all of the city that he wanted to see; in the morning he would go back to Zalapec. At break of day he would get up and sneak out of the cave without waking Pepillo. He would find the trail that led back into the mountains, and he would follow it until he came to the Village. He would go to his mother, and she would be overjoyed to have him back. She would take him into her arms and comfort him, and he would tell her about the big city. He would tell her, and his step-father and Diego would listen, and they would scarcely believe what he would have to say.

It brought tears into his eyes to think of his mother, and he buried his face deeper into the sheepskin, and his fingers clutched at long strands of wool. A great lump rose out of his belly into his throat, and lodged where he swallowed, choking him, and his breath broke into heavy sobs.

He was weeping, but this weeping was happy, because in the morning he was going back to Zalapec. He was going back to his mother and to the pastures and caves, and he would drink cool water from the springs, and he would feel mountain breezes blowing against his face.

He would take his father's flocks to pasture and would watch them carefully and never let them stray, and he would even love —

Diego was DEAD!

He remembered that Diego was dead. It was not a word, this dead. No, this dead was a hand that flopped to the ground when let go. Dead was a silence you heard when you spoke to Diego. Dead was zopilotes circling over.

This thought stopped his sobbing and made him afraid. Listening to Pepillo, he had not been afraid, but now his whole body felt a pang of fear that twisted in his belly. Fear was a sharp knife that turned in his belly and carved it to pieces, and that was the place where he was most afraid.

He did not think about his mother any more, or about his stepfather or Diego. He did not think at all. He merely lay on the sheepskins in the dark and felt his belly hurting.

There was no time any more, there were only fear and hurt. There was no time, and there was no line between awake and asleep. At first he was hurting awake, and later he was hurting asleep, and that was the only difference.

Yet hurting asleep was worse, because awake he did not think, while asleep, he dreamed.

There was a white cliff with a shelf of rock where he was lying, and his body was all alive except his right leg which was dead and brown and soft like rotten wood, and he could not move it. He touched his thigh, and his fingers felt, but his leg did not, and there was no life in it. While he lay there, the leg began to grow like putrid flesh swelling in the sun. It grew bigger than his body, and still it bloated larger, until it was like a tree trunk fastened to his hip.

He struggled to lift his leg, but it broke away just below the hip, and the end where the foot belonged rose high above him in the air, and thus it stood. He watched in horror, and two rigid arms grew out from the leg and formed a cross. The foot sagged down, and Carlos saw it become a head. A body appeared below it, hanging there in crucifixion.

The head flopped to one side, and he could not see it, but something told him that it was about to turn, and he was terrified. He tried to look away, but he could not move his eyes. They were fastened upon the head, waiting for its turning.

The body on the cross stirred, writhed, twisted in convulsions. Carlos waited for the head to turn. He expected to see Diego.

It was not Diego.

The head turned, and the face was a bestial face with grey skin hanging in folds and eyes that were slit pupils and bloodshot globes and two horns that curled about the temples.

Carlos screamed, waking himself, and he sprang to his feet in Pepillo's cave. "Chi-*cha*-yan! Chi-*cha*-yan! (Ram's head! Ram's head!)" he shrieked.

Pepillo sat up. "What passes? What passes, Carlos?"

"Chi-*cha*-yan!" repeated Carlos. "Hanging on the cross."

"Sh'liga! What a nightmare!" muttered Pepillo. "Lie down and go to sleep."

Carlos sank back upon the sheepskins. Pepillo put a hand upon the boy's shoulder and found it soaked with sweat. "It's only a matter of a dream," Pepillo chuckled. "Do not be afraid, Carlos — Carlos Chichayan!"

4

WHEN THEY HAD BATHED in the river, they ate tortillas and beans, and as soon as they had eaten, they went forth upon the streets of the city. The world was alive, and they watched burro trains coming off the bridge from the other side of the river. They watched burro trains and mule trains and men with heavy loads upon their shoulders. This one had faggots of wood, while that one had bags of charcoal, and a third had earthenware pots, each nested within another. Some of the men were alone; whereas others were followed by their women, and they moved quickly, both men and women, but the beasts moved slowly with heavy feet.

Carlos and Pepillo stood upon a cobbled curb to relieve themselves of water. They stood upon the curb, feet apart, hips forward thrust, and loosed two streams into the gutter.

"Ah-yah, what a delicious feeling," Pepillo muttered. "This outward flow of water! After a long night one has such power! Shall we try for distance?"

They squirted high and far, as boys do, each one straining to increase his span.

"Dios mío, Carlos, what a magnificent stream!" exclaimed Pepillo, enraptured. "Hombre, how you must be put together! Go it, chico! Splatter the middle of the road, Carlito! There! Blessed saints, you're over the middle! Oh, precious, precious! What a belly, Carlito, what a powerful belly!"

"That isn't so far," Carlos breathed modestly. "See, it's falling off. Already I am done."

"Oh no, chico, don't say it," answered Pepillo with admiration. "Believe me, it was magnificent. Over the middle, and no small street, either!"

"It was not so much," Carlos insisted. "In Zalapec they do better."

"I do not believe. Indeed, this is a great city, and I know many brave chicos with great power in their bellies. But over the middle? Never! Do all your men have such power in their bellies?"

"To herd sheep is belly-power," Carlos answered.

"I never knew," Pepillo admitted. "For me, I am a city goat, although I have often seen mountain men. They come to this market from many sides. They come in the early morning, just as you see, and on their backs are heavy loads. Like burros. Pft! Not for me. Now the Xlalaks — they are another thing. Caray, they are real stallions, those Xlalak boys."

"I have never seen a Xlalak."

"You have never seen? Oh, precious! The Xlalaks indeed! They sharpen their teeth like arrow points. Men say they drink the blood of babies, I don't know. Kill you just like that! Watch, now, along this street, and perhaps you will see."

"How do men know a Xlalak?"

"How does one know a stallion from a jackass? Do they come with backs bent under heavy loads? Not the Xlalaks. They come on horses like true Españoles. They come on horses with a lariat tied to the saddle. They come with leather boots in the stirrups and spurs on the heel."

"Are they Españoles, or are they only men?' '

"Oh, they are men — but not Nacheetl. Not white like Españoles, nor bent under a load like Nacheetl. No, they have skin like tanned leather and a straight back, too. But wild! They are bandits, those Xlalaks."

"Do they steal?"

"Magnificently! Oh, they are precious ones. Not a chicken from some miserable old bitch's spit. Not those chicos. For them it will be nothing but a mule train of gold fresh from the mines or the governor's coach at the very least."

"From the very city, they steal?"

"Oh, not from the city so much. No, but on the royal highway."

"What is the — the — ?"

"The royal highway? That is the road to Santa Cruz."

"And that?"

"What thing?"

"Santa Cruz of which you spoke."

"Madre mía, what a mountain goat! What a precious mountain goat! One cannot talk to you. What-is-this, what-is-that, I-do-not-know. Ah, well, I shall explain to you, I shall make all things clear." He showed Carlos around the city and told him about the things they saw.

They made their way southward along the Street of the Bridge of the Holy Saints of the Cross, splashing through gutters and examining the refuse that flowed through open sewers. As they came into the Central Plaza, Pepillo explained to Carlos about all the wondrous buildings that stood there before them. On the right was the Gran Hotel San Marcos with a two-wheeled cab waiting in front, while a brown sandstone building occupied the opposing corner.

Pepillo turned left. "This is the Banco San Marcos, this building here," he told Carlos. "Inside they keep all the gold. It is piled up like heaps of potatoes on the floor, and a man shovels it around with a great big spade. Madre mía, chico, how would you like to get your hand onto that much gold?"

Carlos had no ideas about that. He was not accustomed to think of piles of gold.

Next to the Banco San Marcos was the highest building Carlos had ever seen. It had three stories, Pepillo said. "That is Preetee-mans," he explained to Carlos.

"What is Preeteemans?" Carlos asked.

"They are Yanquis," Pepillo replied. "You know about Yanquis, Carlos?"

"N-no," Carlos replied doubtfully. There were so many of these things he had never heard of before that he began to doubt if he could remember even if Pepillo did explain.

"Cabrón, you will learn a thing about these Yanquis," Pepillo warned. "Oh, they are precious bad." Set in the sandstone front near the doorway of the building was a shiny brass plaque which bore two words: *Prettyman Enterprises*. Pepillo backed off, aimed with puckered lips and spat. His saliva hit the brass and dribbled down between the two t's of Prettyman.

Carlos cast a wary eye about, but there was no sign of anything that could possibly be a Preetheeman or that other thing of which Pepillo had spoken. The door was a precious sight, however, since it had glass all up and down its middle, but you couldn't see inside because of how the light was shining on it.

"Let's go!" said Pepillo, splashing into the gutter again. Together they moved eastward past the great cathedral and along the Calle Florida that entered the University quarter.

"See those chicos there?" Pepillo asked. There was a low stone building with an iron gate, and lounging in front were five or six young men in black suits, with tight-fitting caps upon their heads. "Those are students. In the University they learn all there is to know, and by night they come to my sister's house. What guapos! Pues, of all her customers, these students are among the best."

They made their way eastward as far as the Avenue of the Bees, and thence Pepillo headed southward to the Calle Bolívar and westward until they reached the Alameda. There before them was a mighty palace bigger than all of Zalapec and Xiltak, too. It was made of stone, with enormous walls about, and the oaken gates, studded with iron, were higher than the banana trees that grew near by.

There were gorgeous gardens on either hand, and there were fountains playing, and walking guard around the walls were soldiers in uniforms of blue and gold. Their shakos were high and plumed, their swords all gold about the hilt. "That is the Palace of the Lions," Pepillo said. "In the front the Governor has a precious place to live, but behind there is another court which is prison and dungeons deep within the earth. When the soldiers catch a man, they throw him in a pit, and lions eat him up."

They took a long bypass around the Palace of the Lions, and Carlos watched it closely. He was afraid that the soldiers would see them and come and take them to the beasts. But nothing happened. They passed another mighty building where the presidente, General Ronca, lived. They entered the Street of the National Army which skirted the southeastern edges of the city. They passed the brown-stone parapets of El Castillo barracks where the garrison stayed, and Carlos saw soldiers drilling by the hundreds, and he heard the sergeants shout commands. Thence they retraced their steps westward and crossed the Avenida de Todos los Santos where, Pepillo said, the rich men lived.

At length they reached the Calle de las Pumas and, turning north-ward, they followed it to the Armory of the National Militia. There they headed eastward again, in the direction of the Calle de las Mujeres and the market place beyond. "Ho! I see come chicos down the street," Pepillo said. "They are brave boys, those chicos, you will see. Oh, very brave. Come!"

Carlos and Pepillo ran down the street and dodged in front of burros and splashed through gutters, and thus they overtook the chicos.

"Ah-yah, c'm'stás, Pepillo?" asked one.

"Qu' dic'?" demanded another.

"Buen' día'," said a third.

All three were gutter boys with ragged clothes and dirty faces.

"Qu' ta'?" answered Pepillo. He continued running, and the others followed close behind. He led them into an alley where they sloshed through mud. The alley led into a small and dingy square on which an ancient church was standing. Pepillo stopped abruptly and sat down upon a step. Carlos did the same, and the others, too.

A man in tattered shirt and pantalones lay drunk in a doorway opposite, but otherwise the square was empty. Pepillo leaned forward, elbows on his knees, and tried to spit upon a spider that crossed the step below. He missed, and the spider disappeared within a crack.

"Who has a cigar?" one of the boys asked. He had no shirt, and his ragged pantalones ended just above his knees. In place of a belt, he had a length of rope tied tight about his waist. There were no buttons upon his fly, and so, when he sat down his pantalones opened wide.

"Cigars? I find all I want," Pepillo said. "And I do not beg from others. But there is another matter, chicos, which I have to speak about. Listen you little goats, this is Carlos who has come with us. Carlos Chichayan."

"C'm'stás, Carlos!" This one had pantalones patched so much that Carlos could not decide which color was the original.

"Qu' dic'?"

"Buen' día'. Please, Pepillo, a cigar!" begged the chico with the open fly.

"No, hombre, no cigar! Listen, chicos, you know the Street of the Twenty-Eighth of June?"

"Sí, pu's."

"Very well, and you know where this Street of the Twenty-Eighth of June crosses the Street of the Bridge of the Holy Saints of the Cross?"

"Sí, pu's."

"You know how wide is the Street of the Twenty-Eighth of June where it crosses the Street of the Bridge of the Holy Saints of the Cross?"

"Sí, pu's, that we know."

"Very well, now I tell you one little thing. This chico here, this most precious hombre stood on the cobbled curb at the south side of the Street of the Twenty-Eighth of June and squirted a magnificent yellow stream well beyond the middle of the road."

"No!"

"Indeed, no, Pepillo, that we do not believe," said patched pantalones.

"It cannot be!"

"This hombre —" Pepillo tapped Carlos on the shoulder with a forefinger, "this little hombre did that thing."

"But the Street of the Twenty-Eighth of June is far across," exclaimed open fly.

"He did that thing, Chu-chu."

"But the street is thirty steps across at that place. Thirty steps, eh, Paco?"

"Not thirty steps, Chu-chu," corrected patched pantalones.

"Thirty steps!"

"Twe-e-enty, Chu-chu!"

"Cabrón, it is thirty!"

"Twenty, thirty, who cares, chicos! Pepillo says this little hombrecito here can splatter beyond the middle. That I do not believe."

"Right, Tito," agreed Chu-Chu, "that we cannot believe."

"He did that thing," Pepillo insisted.

"No man could splatter beyond the middle," Tito said.

"That is true," agreed Paco. "No man could."

"Carlos can do that," Pepillo said. "Carlos Chichayan can do that thing."

"I'll believe it if I see it, chicos," Chu-chu announced.

"Sí, pu's, let us see that," Paco suggested. "Let us go to the place and see."

"Oh, that is far," Tito said. "Let him stand on these steps only. Let him stand on the top step and splatter the road."

"But that is less far," Chu-chu protested. "That is much less far."

"Let him reach the middle of the street, then," Pepillo said confidently. "Caray, it is a miserable little street. Let him stand on the top step and sprinkle the middle."

"That is good," Chu-chu agreed.

"All right, Carlos Chicayan," said Pepillo, "go to it, man. Show these young capons what power you have in your belly."

"But I cannot do," wailed Carlos.

"Hmph!" snorted Chu-chu. "He cannot do."

"That I know," said Paco.

"Why cannot you do?" demanded Pepillo.

"I have no water. It was left in the middle of the Street of the Twenty-Eighth of June."

"Ah, well, that is nothing," sighed Pepillo. "Now he cannot do, but later — it is a small matter."

"I do not believe," Chu-chu stated. "This chico has no power in his belly. He cannot sprinkle beyond the toes of his feet."

"By all the Holy Saints, he can reach the middle of this street," Pepillo swore solemnly.

Chu-chu shrugged. "Then let him do it."

"But it is only a little tiny matter of lack of water," moaned the exasperated Pepillo.

"Let him do it," repeated Chu-chu stubbornly.

Pepillo's eye measured once more the distance from the top of the steps to the center of the road. It was indeed a great span for the spraying of water, but he knew that Carlos could do it. He seized the boy's shoulders with his hands. "Listen to me, hombrecito, listen, little mountain goat, Carlos Chicayan, you must do this. You must take your place at the top of the steps and try!" He guided Carlos to the proper spot.

Carlos stood at the top of the steps. There he poised himself, feet apart, hips forward thrust. It was the position for greatest power. But it was no use; he had no water.

"Ah-ya, ay-yah," wailed Pepillo, "hombrecito, what shall we do, shall we — Dios Padre, I have it! Oh, you little goat, how stupid is Pepillo! You must drink, cabrón, you must refill your belly with water! Oh, water, where is water?"

"There is none here," said Paco. "I think no well is close."

"Over there under the eaves of the church!" Tito exclaimed. "That big old earthenware jar has water in its belly, I have no doubt."

This earthenware jar was under the eaves, and indeed, it had much water. Pepillo tipped it until the contents began to spill. "Drink, Carlos Chichayan! Drink, you precious stallion."

Carlos drank and filling his stomach was like filling a goatskin bag. He drank and drank, and when he paused for breath, they urged him on.

"More, Carlos, drink more! Fill your belly!"

He drank more, and he could hear the water splashing into his stomach. He could hear it, and he could feel it sloshing around. His belly felt stretched, and he wanted no more.

"Drink, drink, man!" shouted Pepillo. "Empty the jar, little Carlos."

"I cannot," Carlos gasped.

"You can!" growled Pepillo, and he pushed as if to cram him into the jar.

Carlos drank until his sides began to ache, and then he drew away, but Pepillo pushed him back.

"More! More!" shouted Pepillo.

"More!" shouted the other chicos.

Carlos drank.

"Empty the jar!" ordered Pepillo.

"Yes, empty the jar!" shouted the others.

"No! María Purísima! I cannot! I cannot!"

"Perhaps that is enough," Pepillo conceded. "He might drown inside."

Carlos drew his head out of the jar, but he could not stand straight. Pepillo steadied him.

"Ay-yah, what a water bag!" exclaimed Pepillo. "What a magnificent water bag. Up the steps, now, cabronito. Up the steps."

"I cannot! Oooh, I cannot. Let me lie down, oooh, let me die!"

"Ay, you chicos, help me get him up the steps," snapped Pepillo.

They pushed him to the top step and stood him at the edge.

"Now, little goat, let it go!" directed Pepillo. "Sprinkle the middle of the street!"

"I cannot!"

"No, no, that is right," Pepillo agreed. "He cannot. These matters take time. Let him rest and gather power."

They stretched him out upon the top step.

"How long will this take?" asked Chu-chu.

"Not long," Pepillo replied with confidence.

They sat about and waited, and while they waited, Paco slipped away to the nearest tobacco shop from which he stole a package of brown cigarettes. These he took back to the church steps, and when he rejoined the chicos, Chu-chu was already restless.

"Now!" Chu-chu was saying. "I think now."

"No!" snapped Pepillo. "Not now."

They smoked the cigarettes down to short stubs.

"Now!" Chu-chu repeated.

"No!" snapped Pepillo.

"Yes, yes!" Carlos suddenly screamed. "Now — hurry — help me up!"

The chicos sprang to their feet and yanked him up, and they balanced him on the edge of the top step, feet apart, hips forward thrust. They balanced him there and helped him to loose a stream.

"Hmph!" grunted Chu-chu. "It has no color."

"No color, perhaps," Pepillo admitted. "But power! A little more high, Carlos, a little more high. Oh, magnifico!"

"It's only on the bottom step," sneered Chu-chu.

"No-no, it's in the road!" Paco corrected.

"A little more high, Carlos, just a tiny bit more high!"

"It's — it's — no — yes, it is!" shouted Paco. "It's splattering the middle."

"That is no splash," gasped Tito in admiration. "It is a magnificent gush. Oh, perfecto!"

"Oh, it is that, it is that!" agreed Paco. "Look, chicos, he's beyond the middle!"

"He is! He is!" Pepillo was jumping up and down on one foot. "He's crossing the street! Oh, go to it, hombrecito, go to it, mountain goat. What a fountain! Oh, what a precious, precious fountain!"

"I do not believe it!" muttered Chu-chu. "No, that I cannot believe."

5

"YOU ARE A GOOD CHICO," Pepillo conceded. "You have power in your belly and you can sprinkle the center of the road. But for this life that is not enough."

It was early morning, and he and Carlos were bathing in the river beneath the bridge.

"I stole a chicken from the old woman's spit," Carlos reminded him.

"That was no great thing," sneered Pepillo. "What would become of me if I stole nothing but chickens from helpless old hags? No, Carlos Cichayan, you must do better than that if we are to work together. One day we shall steal like Xlalaks — a mule train of gold fresh from the mines or the governor's coach or maybe even the National Bank."

"To steal in Zalapec was against the Village Law."

"That was different. The people there were friends. Here the whole matter is another color. There are rich, and there are poor, and the poor must work or steal or starve. Some men choose to work, and then there is a drought, or a war is fought, and pfoof! Of what use is all the work? No, Carlos Chichayan, the político can draw his pay, but honest men like you and me must steal or starve."

"But the revolution!" Carlos protested. "In Zalapec it was said that the Ronquistas set men free."

"Madre! I know a thing about the Ronquistas," said Pepillo. "For two weeks I marched with Ronca. I hear his words. 'Come along with us!' he shouted. 'Fight for us and we will make you free.' He was just a poor Indio like us in those days. Never had his feet in shoes. So I stole a machete and joined his army. We marched and fought and raped and I picked up a bullet in the anca. Dios, we won the war, and then you should see this Ronca! He got himself a pair of boots and a blue coat off some dead Nacionalista, and he was General Ronca. Rode around on a black horse and carried a sword that dragged on the ground and chopped a poor chico's head off because he didn't salute. Next he got himself a black coat and a tall hat, and then it was Presidente Ronca. Rode around in a gold trimmed coach with sixteen horses pulling. That's all right for Ronca, I said, but what about Pepillo?"

"Didn't he set you free?"

"Free for what? Free to starve, sabe, free to starve! There was no more corn than before. There was less. Did you ever stuff your belly with freedom, Carlos? It's the same as gas on the stomach."

"Maybe matters will be better soon," suggested Carlos. "There were men in Zalapec who said that."

"With Ronca buying diamonds for his corbata and chasing whores around the government palace? No, chico, steal or starve, but don't wait for better times. Oh, you'll do all right. Practice is lacking only. Come, let us leave this water and dry ourselves. I have an idea for you."

"What is this idea for me?" Carlos asked as they were drying in the sun.

"Oh, it is a small matter," explained Pepillo. "More than an old woman's chicken, perhaps, but nothing great."

"What is it, Pepillo?" Carlos was impatient.

"You have been to church, chico. You know how the money is dropped in the almsbox."

"That I know."

"It is blessed."

"That I also know."

"Holy money is lucky money," said Pepillo. "We could use some, Carlos."

"You mean to steal," gasped Carlos. "You mean to steal from the church?"

"It is a small matter," answered Pepillo. "It is really too small to talk about."

"That is holy money," Carlos said firmly. "People have left that money to Jesucristo for giving to the poor and for keeping the household of Dios. He would not like me to take that money, Pepillo."

Pepillo shrugged. "I have no time to talk about so small a matter," he said quickly. "It was an idea for practice only. I like you, Carlos, and I have precious admiration for the power in your belly. But if you cannot do this little thing you will be no good for big. There are many brave chicos who are begging to work with Pepillo. Think about that, Carlos Chichayan!"

"Jesucristo Salvador is my good friend," Carlos protested. "He went with Uncle Vicente and me to the burning of Santa Marta. He would not like me to do this."

"In my cave there is room for two," Pepillo said. "If I get another chico — "

Carlos saw himself alone in the great city. He saw himself wandering through the streets with nothing to eat and no place to sleep. He saw himself fleeing down dark alleys to escape soldiers and police.

"I will do it, Pepillo," blurted Carlos. "Only tell me how, Pepillo, and when."

"That is for you to decide," Pepillo replied. "For me there is no how or when. For me it would be very easy, but that is not the matter about which we are talking. The how and the when are your deciding. You will be the one."

"I will do it today," Carlos promised. "Now!"

"As you wish," answered Pepillo.

They dried their bodies in early morning sunlight, and when they had finished, they put on their shirts and pantalones and scrambled up the river bank to the city above.

"I shall go right now to the church," Carlos said firmly. "I shall do it now."

"Very well," said Pepillo. "As for me, I shall go with you to the square. I shall be waiting there when you come out with the money."

Together they walked along the Street of the Bridge of the Holy Saints of the Cross to the place where it entered the Plaza of the Nine Martyred Heroes. On the eastern side of the square stood the cathedral, and there were crowds of people filing out.

"There has been a mass," explained Pepillo. "In the box there will be many coins. After this we shall live well, Carlos."

"I am afraid," Carlos admitted.

"So! It has turned out as I thought in the first place. You have only water in your belly, Carlos. You will be of no use to me."

"No, no, Pepillo, I did not mean it," Carlos urged.

"Good. You will find the box inside the door on the left. It is fastened to a pillar, but the wood is old and soft, and the box hangs loosely on its nails."

"I cannot take the whole box," protested Carlos. "The day is bright. I will be seen."

"Can it be that only now you begin to think?" scolded Pepillo. "To me the matter is small, yet I would have planned each precious movement."

"This box is large?" asked Carlos.

"The size of a man's head, no more."

"Then I will take off my shirt and carry it in my hands. I will tear off the box and wrap it in my shirt."

"That is better, Carlos. It will be a small matter, I tell you. The church is dark, and in a few moments there will be no one about. Do not run when you leave the church. Many people carry bundles from church. It is expected. Run only if someone chases."

"I am ready, Pepillo."

"Go, then, cabrón. Go!"

Carlos walked away from Pepillo. As he made his way across the plaza, he felt that the whole city was watching. He dared look to neither side, but with his eyes straight ahead, he went toward the steps of the cathedral. The crowd had already left, and now only a few aged women and cripples were straggling out. On the bottom step a vendor of candles and holy images was gathering his wares into a sack. A bit higher a blind woman was squatting, and as he climbed toward the church door, Carlos heard her whining voice. "Have pity," she begged in Nacheetl. "Have pity upon a poor old woman who cannot see. For the love of Dios, have pity on a sightless one."

Carlos walked quickly by and entered the cathedral. It was dark inside, as Pepillo had said, and there was no one about. At first his eyes saw nothing but the vastness of the building. It seemed that the rafters arched upward into the sky itself, while the supporting columns might have had the weight of heaven upon them. Sunlight, filtering through the stained windows, tinged the walls of the chancel with a red glow as if a fire had been kindled behind the altar. Carlos

felt that this was indeed a holy place, holier by far than the church
in Xiltak.

As his eyes became accustomed to the dimness, he saw the almsbox
hanging loosely from a column on his left. He moved nearer and
touched it with his hands. As Pepillo had said, the wood was old and
soft, and the weight of the coins had enlarged the holes made by the
nails. A sudden twist would tear the box away.

The whole matter was much simpler than Carlos had feared. There
was not even a reason for haste since the cathedral appeared to be
deserted, and a person entering from outside would be half blind
in the reddish gloom. It was so easy that Carlos felt uncomfortable
about what he was going to do. He looked toward the chancel again,
and he saw Jesucristo Salvador hanging on the cross. He decided suddenly that he ought to explain.

He would go up the aisle to the foot of the cross, and he would
kneel before Jesucristo and explain. "I really do not want to do this,"
he would say. "But Pepillo says that I must. He says that I must take
the almsbox for practice only. Of course the money in the box is for
you to give to the poor people, but you see, we are poor, too. When
you and I and Uncle Vicente went up to Santa Marta, it was different.
We were not poor then. There was plenty of corn in the field, and
Uncle Vicente used to hoe it every day, and he kept out the weeds."

Carlos was walking up the aisle toward the chancel, scarcely aware
of what he did. He was thinking of how he could explain his troubles
to Jesucristo. "Yes, there was plenty of corn, and I took good care of
the sheep, too. Of course, Uncle Vicente did want his milk-giving
cow. That was the only little thing he wanted. Some men wanted ladles
and trays and candlesticks of gold and silver, and some wanted silk
from Señor's bed, but Uncle Vicente wanted the milk-giving cow
only. Why didn't you give it to him, Jesucristo? Why?"

He was near the foot of the cross, now, and he knelt instinctively
and bowed his head. "Yes, that's when we began to have all the
trouble. Uncle Vicente was very sad when the men from Xiltak killed
the milk-giving cow because that was the only thing he wanted.
Maybe you thought that Uncle Vicente did not know much about
milk-giving cows. Maybe you thought he would not take care of it.
Yet Uncle Vicente knew all about animals, and he was a good man,

and he gave life to things. He could even make corn grow tall in stony soil. The milk-giving cow would be very happy living with Uncle Vicente."

"So you see," Carlos pleaded, "when you did not let Uncle Vicente have it, he felt sad, and after a while he got so sick that Dios had to take his spirit away, and we buried his body in the campo santo. I was head of the family, then, and I was going to take good care. But then my mother married this Lorenzo Reyes who is a harsh voice, and there was Diego who is a grabbing hand. So you see, Jesucristo, you really started all this trouble, and that is why you must not mind if I take your box this single time."

"That is a very tearful story," Carlos heard a voice say. "But there is a thing you have not said. You have not told me why you left home."

"It was that I could not live with them," Carlos sobbed. "Diego took my flute and Lorenzo Reyes beat me, and I could not live with them."

"Why did you leave home?"

"I was going to be head of the household, and I would have taken very great care, but my mother married Lorenzo Reyes, and he made me work for him, and if I lost a sheep he beat me."

"Why did you leave home?"

This time when Carlos heard the voice, he heeded. For a moment he was in the pasture above La Perla, and he was swinging his sling. He swung it around his head and loosed a pebble that arced into the sky. It went high into the blue, and he was certain that he had over-shot, but the pebble was falling — falling — falling fast. It was coming straight down. "Diego," he screamed. "DIEGO!" Diego didn't dodge. He walked directly into the falling pebble.

Jesucristo Salvador had seen that!

"Are you Carlos?" asked Jesucristo.

"Yes," replied Carlos, who was no longer in the pasture but kneeling in the cathedral. "I am he."

"Why did you leave home?"

Carlos was afraid to look; yet even as he shrank from looking, he felt Jesucristo making him look. He raised his eyes a little, but terror of what he might see drove him to cover his eyes with his hands and sob. The impulse to look continued. He could not hold his eyes away much longer. Then, as he knelt there in the dim light with his hands hiding his eyes, it happened that the organist took his place in the loft and touched a bass chord with his fingers.

The pipes uttered a deep snort that vibrated among the rafters and made the stained windows tremble. To Carlos, kneeling in the dark, this was the snort of a beast, and hearing it, he knew well what was hanging on the cross. He knew how the skin hung in grey wrinkles about the face and how the eyes had slit pupils and bloodshot globes. He felt the monster's hot breath upon his neck. With his tongue cleaving to the top of his mouth, Carlos rolled over backward and scrambled to his feet and ran.

He fled down the aisle, knocking over a wooden bench, and he bolted through the door of the cathedral, and in his terror, he upset the blind woman on the steps and sent her rolling to the ground.

6

"WHAT YOU SAW in the church is a small matter," Pepillo said. He was hot and ill-tempered after following Carlos in blind flight halfway across the city. He sat down on a curb and thought a while, chin resting in cupped palms. "You are of no use to me," he added abruptly.

Carlos was silent. He was overcome with shame, and at the same time he had not recovered from his terror.

"To me you are of no use whatever. You would only get us into trouble with your horned beasts and crucifixions."

Once more Carlos pictured himself wandering alone about the streets of the great city. Each moment he expected to see Pepillo get up and leave him there on the curb.

"As a thief you are worthless," continued Pepillo with a snap of his fingers. "There is nothing but water in your belly."

Pepillo would leave him there on the curb, and there would be nothing to eat, and he would have to steal a chicken from some blind old woman in the market place.

"I have known chicos who were afraid of the police," Pepillo pointed out. "I have known chicos who were afraid of soldiers and even priests. But never have I known one who was afraid of — of — of that thing of which you are afraid. No, you are worthless as a thief, and I do not know what to do with you."

Pepillo would leave, and Carlos would have nothing to eat and no place to sleep, and there was no Uncle Vicente and no presidente and no Jesucris — he shuddered.

"You cannot live in the cave with me," Pepillo said, "and the other chicos will pass you by. There is no place for you at all. I know of one thing only. Yes," he added with conviction, "that is the thing. Come along, Carlos Chichayan, come along with me."

Pepillo ran ahead, splashing in gutters and swinging his arms, and he chattered like a monkey as he ran. "A-e-yah, this is the only thing. We shall go to the house of my sister in La Calle de las Mujeres. She will know a place for you, I think. Magdalena has many good connections. Oh, yes, very good connections."

When they had nearly recrossed the city, they entered a street that was narrow and sticky with mud. A scrawny sheep bolted from a doorway where it had been lying and ran ahead of them, bleating piteously.

"This street is not much to the eye," admitted Pepillo. "But my sister's house is another matter, you will see."

The door of one house was open, and Carlos saw two women on the threshold, and he stared when he saw them. Never in his life had he seen such women. One was slender and had a water jar balanced upon her head. The other was plump, and she was standing with her hands upon her hips, a broad smile across her face. One was slender and one was plump, but the eyes and cheeks and mouths were what Carlos saw. There was blackness painted about the eyes and on the lids, especially, while the cheeks were pink and the lips scarlet.

In Zalapec the women had no such eyes or cheeks or lips, nor in Xiltak, either. María Madre in the Parochial Church of Santo Domingo had such, but she was made only of wood. These were real women, and they smiled at Pepillo, and the plump one winked. "Qu' dic', Pepillo?" she asked.

Pepillo winked back and jerked his buttocks in a way that made the women laugh.

Carlos and Pepillo continued along the street until they came to a house that had two iron-grated windows in front. "A precious house this once was," Pepillo explained as he pounded upon the door. "A precious house. My sister has done well to be in such a house."

A wooden shutter was thrown open. "A-ló!" a soft voice called down. "Oh, Pepillo!"

"Business, business!" Pepillo taunted. "A-ló! Even your brother you greet like that."

"I did not know, Pepillo, I did not know! Only one little moment, and I'll let you in."

The shutter banged shut.

"It is a magnificent house," Pepillo boasted. "You will see."

Carlos heard light steps inside and the rattle of a bolt. The door opened, and standing on the threshold was Pepillo's sister. She was slender, like the girl they had seen further up the street, and her eyes and cheeks and mouth were brightly painted, but Carlos liked her better than either of the other two women he had seen. She was much more beautiful; she was almost as beautiful as María Madre.

"Pepillo, it is so long!" she said. "Time moves with funeral feet when you are gone. How goes it, chico?"

"So-so," replied Pepillo. "This muchacho is my friend, Carlos Chichayan."

She held out her hand, and Carlos felt how warm and soft it was. He knew that he was going to like Magdalena.

"Come in, come in," she urged.

When Carlos walked across the threshold, he saw that this was indeed a magnificent house. He was standing in a stone passageway, and beyond was a court almost as big as his mother's adobe house in Zalapec. There were flowers growing in it — gardenias and bougain-villea and orchids hanging from a trellis. Around the court was a small portico where chairs were placed, and from the roof of the portico hung cages of canaries and parrakeets.

Magdalena sat down on one of the chairs, and Pepillo sat down on another, and Carlos watched because he was not certain how it was done.

"Sit down, sit down," urged Magdalena.

Carlos backed into a chair, flushing over his awkwardness, but Pepillo and Magdalena were too busy talking to notice what he had done. They talked rapidly, now in Spanish, now in Nacheetl, and it was not easy for Carlos to follow what was said. He sat very straight in the chair, his bare feet dangling a palm's thickness from the ground. With wide-open eyes he gazed about him.

Behind Magdalena was an open doorway partially obscured by a lavender curtain, and beyond the curtain was a bedstead which was not as large as the one he had seen at Santa Marta, but it was even more georgeous to him because it had shiny knobs on the posts and grillwork, and it was covered by a pink spread. While he was looking, a small white poodle jumped down off the bed and trotted through the doorway. He stopped close to Carlos and sniffed at the boy's bare feet and licked at the toes with his tiny red tongue. Pepillo laughed coarsely and made a remark which Carlos could not understand. Magdalena stamped her foot, and the little dog trotted back and jumped onto the bed.

Carlos saw two more rooms opening onto the court. There was also a wooden stairway leading upward to another story. In a far corner of the court stood a board shack with a crooked roof beneath the eaves of which stood two large ollas to catch rain water. Inside the shack was a charcoal grate made of bricks and red tile, while wooden ladles and clay utensils hung here and there on the walls.

From time to time one could hear the padding of bare feet on tile floors or a muffled giggle, but Carlos caught no sight of those who were moving about. He listened to what Magdalena was saying.

"Oh, yes, Pepillo, he spoke well of you!" She leaned forward as she said it, and Carlos was embarrassed because of the way her low-necked blouse fell away from her breasts. "He said he was an old compañero."

Pepillo shrugged. "I do not know. Under Ronca I knew many chicos."

"It was Salvador Díaz."

"Oh, that boy!" exclaimed Pepillo with contempt. "He was a loud-mouth and a bully."

"In those days, perhaps," Magdalena said. "Now — qué guapo! He is in the Federal Police, and he rides a magnificent horse. Rode it to our door, sabes, and swung from his saddle like a true caballero in shiny boots and spurs that tinkled. He — "

"I do not understand," Pepillo interrupted. "What are these Federal Police? I have never heard of such."

"Oh, that is a new matter, I tell you. It is Ronca who has done it. Only the best are chosen, you understand — the horsemen, the intrépidos."

"Yet Salvador Díaz was only a loudmouth."

"You are wrong, Pepillo, about that you are wrong," protested Magdalena. "You are wrong about Ronca in the same way. He is a great man, this Ronca, muy fuerte, a real stallion. You will soon see about these Federal Police, also. Salvador had shiny black boots and a pistolera of polished leather. His uniform was grey, almost blue, and his shirt the same, and his sombrero, Pepillo, it was high and had a precious brim, and the material was truly felt!"

"Tell me just this," growled Pepillo, levelling a finger, "tell me where this Ronca gets these sombreros of truly felt!"

"Bien, I will tell you," Magdalena retorted. "Ronca gets those hats from the North Americans."

"From the North Americans?"

"Verdad! Salvador Díaz sat in that very chair and showed me. It was written in his sombrero."

"How do you know that? You do not know letters, nor does Salvador Díaz."

"These letters he knew, and they were there in the sombrero to see. Oo-aissay-ah!"

Pepillo snorted. "Because this Ronca gets felt sombreros from the Yanquis you think he is a great man. You forget one little thing. I served under Ronca. I marched for him, I fought for him." He patted his buttocks. "For Ronca it even now carries lead."

Magdalena laughed. "In which direction were you going, Pepillo, when you picked up lead in a place like that?"

Pepillo slapped the muscle of his right arm, crooked at the elbow.

"You will see," Magdalena insisted. "You will wish you had stayed with Ronca. Salvador Díaz thinks you might even now get in. The Federal Police, that is. The age is seventeen, but Salvador Díaz says the exact years are a small matter, especially if one marched with Ronca."

"I got my bellyful of that one."

"Carbrón!" Magdalena ejaculated. "Bien, will you eat, Pepillo?" Without waiting for an answer she called up the stairs, "Josefa, come!"

Carlos heard bare feet padding on the floor above, and a moment later a girl appeared on the wooden stairway. She was not altogether a woman as Magdalena was, but had narrow hips and breasts which had only begun to bulge. Carlos felt her looking at him and flushed.

"Coffee, Josefa, and pan dulce," Magdalena ordered.

"Sí, señorita."

"And fix yourself, Josefa, you look like a pullet in the rain."

"Sí, señorita." She disappeared into the farther bedroom.

"She is new," Magdalena said. "Do you need a girl, Pepillo?"

Her brother shrugged.

"When we have eaten, perhaps," she suggested. "How about your little friend?"

"He is very young," Pepillo said.

Carlos hung his head.

"One never knows," Magdalena said. "It comes at different times with different chicos. We'll let Josefa find out. After coffee."

"In regard to this muchacho there is a small matter," Pepillo mentioned.

"What thing?"

Pepillo replied in a torrent of Spanish that meant nothing to Carlos, but his gestures were unmistakable. He was telling Magdalena about the almsbox in the cathedral. Carlos turned sidewise in his chair and began to draw designs in the dirt with a toe. Poco-á-poco into the church, Pepillo was saying, quiet, so quiet . . . . . chitón . . . . . chitón . . . . . and then . . . . . zape! . . . . . z-z-z-z-z-z-z-z pfouf!

"Qué precioso!" murmured Magdalena, and Carlos knew that she was watching him with her soft, big eyes.

They switched back to Nacheetl. "He is a good boy, just the same," said Pepillo. "Do you know what he did? This boy stood on the cobbled curb at the south side of the Street of the Twenty-Eighth of June where it crosses the Street of the Bridge of the Holy Saints of the Cross. He stood there in that place and squirted a precious yellow stream well beyond the middle of the road!"

"No! That I do not believe, Pepillo."

"It is so!"

"Magnífico!" exclaimed Magdalena. "What a monstrous little man! Josefa must hear that thing."

"Now you see," Pepillo continued, "he is no mean cabrón, this Carlos! That is why we must find a place."

"Of what sort?" asked Magdalena. "What can he do? What *else* can he do?"

"That is no small matter," Pepillo explained. "He is only a little mountain goat. He has herded sheep only."

"Oh, but there are other matters. Many important men come to this house, many rich men."

"This is no matter for a too important man," said Pepillo. "We speak only of one mountain goat not so big."

"There is Salomón Rodríguez," Magdalena suggested. "Since many years he comes here. Since I was like Josefa under the old proprietress."

"Who is this Salomón Rodríguez?"

"He is head cook for Judge Cervantes. A real guapo! Why, he wears underpants of silk only. Qué fino!" Magdalena rubbed thumb and forefinger in appreciation.

"Is he a man of — of authority?"

"Complete! Judge Cervantes has great faith in him. If Salomón Rodríguez likes this chico, I promise you there is no other matter. Josefa!"

"Sí. señorita! I am coming, señorita!"

Carlos kept his eyes fixed upon the ground, but he could hear the pad of Josefa's bare feet and the clatter of crockery in the kitchen shack.

"Come, Josefa," Magdalena called.

"Sí, señorita!" She appeared with cups and coffeepot and pan dulce on a woven tray. Her lips and cheeks were rouged, and she had done her hair in a knot at the back of the head. She served Magdalena and Pepillo. Then she moved toward Carlos.

He could smell her scent of violets and feel her warmth as she sidled close. He drew back against the chair and looked only at his feet.

"Take coffee," Magdalena said gently, "and pan dulce, too."

Without looking up, Carlos grabbed awkwardly for the cup and upset it on the tray.

"Pig!" teased Josefa under her breath.

"Get him another cupful," Magdalena snapped at Josefa.

When the young girl returned, Magdalena took the tray. "You do not yet know how to take care of men," she said to Josefa. She gave Carlos the cup with her own hand, and a pan dulce. Carlos took them from her and smiled shyly.

"I do not think the sap runs yet in this bush," Magdalena told Pepillo. Turning to Carlos, she said, "One day you will remember my house, and you will have a great desire to return. Do not be afraid to come. I think Josefa will be more glad to serve you then."

III. The Gate

"AVENUE OF ALL THE SAINTS number ten," muttered Pepillo. "This is the place, Carlos Chichayan."

The house in front of which they stood, the street itself, were impressive to behold. The Avenue of All Saints was wide enough to hold four carriages abreast, while down the center was a narrow parkway with tall cypress trees and swards of grass and a bridle path where the most debonair charros of the city paraded their mounts and their trappings of silver and gold. That was the street, and the front of the house abutted it, with only a gutter between.

It was a mansion of brown sandstone, with Moorish windows and a single entrance, like the gateway of a medieval castle, by means of which horsemen and carriages could pass through the outer walls into central courts. This giant portal was closed by gates of three-inch oak, studded with spikes and swinging on hinges of hand-wrought iron. Through one of the gates, however, a narrow foot entrance had been cut; this, too, was shut and locked, but a bell rope hung through for the convenience of any person who might wish to enter.

"Ring the bell, Carlos," Pepillo said. "Here is the gate of your future!"

"This house — it is greater than Santa Marta," gasped Carlos. "Pepillo, I am afraid."

"Ring the bell only," repeated Pepillo.

Carlos pulled the rope. Somewhere within the stone belly of the mansion a bell tinkled. He heard the scuff of sandals on paving flags. A bolt rattled on the other side, and the door of the foot entrance creaked on its hinges. An old, white-haired Indian stood on the threshold.

"We want nothing today," he announced irritably. He was dressed in a threadbare sackcoat with pockets that sagged from overstuffing.

"We have come to see Salomón Rodríguez," Pepillo announced stoutly.

"Madre mía, and who are you to be seeing Salomón Rodríguez?" snarled the old one. "Don't you know that Salomón Rodríguez is a busy man? Indeed he is an important personage with no time to waste on guttersnipes."

"It is about this chico here," Pepillo explained as he indicated Carlos. "Salomón Rodríguez has made a promise to Magdalena López that this small chico is to work for him."

"Why did you not say so in the first place?" grumbled the gatekeeper. "Salomón Rodríguez has indeed spoken to me about this chico. Come in, but — " he wagged a gnarled finger at Carlos — "do not think that you will see Salomón Rodríguez only like that."

"This chico does not speak Spanish," Pepillo said. "You will have to speak in Nacheetl, old man."

"Does not speak Spanish! Caramba, now of what use is a wild pig that speaks no Spanish? One does not speak Nacheetl here."

"He will learn," Pepillo promised.

The passageway in which they now stood was actually a tunnel through the front wing of the mansion. There were grooves in the flags on either side where the grinding of carriage wheels had worn into the pavement, and there were calkmarks on the stones between. Beyond the passageway was a court with flower beds, a circular drive, and in the very center a fountain gushing water that was green.

"What is your name?" the gatekeeper asked Carlos in Nacheetl.

"His name is Carlos," Pepillo cut in quickly. "Carlos Chichayan."

"Chichayan, Chichayan, that is a strange name, Chichayan," the old man muttered. "Bien, bien, there is no need for you to see Salomón Rodríguez, Carlos Chichayan. He is a very important personage. It is I who will instruct you as regards your duties. I am an old man, you know, and sleeping on the flags at night is hard on my bones. Do you know how long I have slept on these flags here at Señor's gate? Every night for seventy years I have slept on those flags. A-e-e-yah, on the night that Don Ricardo was born it was I who let the doctor in. Already it was twenty years I had slept on those flags; on the night of old Don Alberto's wedding it was I who opened the gates for his coach. In those days I was a chico like you only. My bones were young and soft and fitted gently against the pavement."

The old one stood gazing at a spot on the flags. "Tonight you will be the one," he said with sentiment. "There is much for me to teach, much for you to learn. First, one speaks Spanish. One says sí, señor, and no, señor, and muy bien, señor. One does not keep Señor waiting, nor Señora, nor young Don Juliano, nor Señorita Dolores, but opens the gates rapidly with great dispatch. One does not keep Salomón Rodríguez waiting, either. One learns also those to let in and those to keep out. One learns the footsteps of each member of the house, yes, and the voice and the ringing of the bell."

"Does one sleep at the gate only?" asked Carlos.

"One sleeps at the gate, but during the day there are other things one does. One greases Señor's boots, his riding boots, that is, and the boots of young Don Juliano, too. One carries luggage to the coach when a member of the house is about to leave, and one receives luggage out of the coach when he returns. In the passageway and on the drive one cleans where the horses have dirtied. One cleans also the gutter in front, and one kills rats in the sheds and snakes in the flower beds. All these things one does."

"How does one speak when one knows no Spanish?"

"That I must teach," the old man replied. "It will take time, but I shall teach. During the period of learning, one will say sí, señor, and no, señor, and muy bien, señor. Another little thing," he added in a low voice. "After one knows Spanish, one hears many matters. These one does not remember or repeat. In truth, what one hears is not heard, and what one sees is not seen. That is how things stand."

Carlos liked the old man, and he understood the old man's gruff speaking. He felt grateful to him and grateful to Señor and grateful to Salomón Rodríguez, and most of all he felt grateful to Pepillo and his sister Magdalena. He turned to thank Pepillo, but the passageway was empty. While he and the old man had been talking, Pepillo had slipped away.

"There is yet the matter of the parts of the house where one goes and the parts where one does not go," the old man explained. He took Carlos across the court and through a second passageway that pierced the south wing of the house. Beyond was another court flanked on one side by kitchen and storerooms, and on the other three sides by sheds, stables, a smithy and the saddler's quarters. There was a sweep well in the center of this court, while under the many eaves were ollas to catch rain. Unlike the front court, which was neat and cultivated with many flowers, this one was muddy and strewn with manure in which chickens and turkeys were scratching and pecking.

"This is greater than Santa Marta," Carlos said thoughtlessly "only they looted Santa Marta and burned Señ — " He checked himself.

"Of what place did you speak?" asked the old man quickly.

"A place I heard of," said Carlos. "The name I cannot remember."

"This place they will never loot," said the gatekeeper. "There is no man who would dare. Never, not even José Ronca and his bandit Republicans. They marched through these streets, the Ronquistas did, right by the gate out yonder. A-e-e-yah, and Don Ricardo opened them wide. They were raping and looting, those cutthroats were, and hanging the richest señores from oak trees, too. Half drunk on tequila and liberty, they were, and lusting to kill, and Don Ricardo opens the gates. There was no guard, either, none but me, Pablo Larra. Pues, my fear was a rat chewing at the belly! I, Pablo Larra, stand alone in the passage. I hear drums along the Avenue. R-r-r-r-tat, r-r-r-r-tat, r-r-tat-tat-tat. I look down the way and there they are. Caramba, what cutthroats, with machetes and clubs and guns, yes, and axes. There is Ronca riding a nag out front. A serape Indio, no more, with bare feet stuck in the stirrups!

"Right down the bridle path he rode that nag. A youngish man, but hunched, and his face — Dios! It was mahogany carved. Behind him came a chico with the Republican banner — a scorpion ready to attack and then the soldiers screeching out words from the 'Virgin Whore' — that's their marching song. Down the street they came until Ronca was here, in front of this very house. He stopped his horse, and the soldiers halted behind him. The singing stopped, and the shouting also. His nag began cropping grass that grows along the bridle path. 'To what señor belongs this mighty house?' Ronca shouts. To me he shouts that, you understand, to toothless old Pablo Larra. In my throat is a cricket. 'To Señor Don Ricardo Cervantes y Gómez,' I answer back, my words squeaking. 'To Señor Don Ricardo Cervantes y Gómez, Chief Judge of the Superior Court of the Nation.'

"Madre mía, how the sweat oozed," Pablo exclaimed in recollection. "You have seen water bags sweat on a summer's day? Bien, I have spoken, and I am waiting to be shot, to be hacked to pieces, to be devoured by those coyotes. But no, there is no shooting, there is no hacking. No-no! This Ronca does nothing at all. He does nothing but bow a little, ever so little, you understand, and touch the brim of his straw sombrero. 'To Señor Don Ricardo Cervantes y Gómez,' he calls back, 'to the Chief Judge of the Superior Court of the Nation, greetings from José Ronca, the Democratic-republican!'

"That was all, you know. There was nothing else. Ronca jerked on the reins of that old nag. He rode up the street, and the soldiers came after. R-r-r-r-tat, r-r-r-r-tat, r-r-r-tat-tat-tat. He passed on with his soldiers, and he left the city and swept over the countryside. Ronca is general, Ronca is presidente. Ronca has all the power of the land. He loots many haciendas and burns them to the ground, he hangs many fine señores from many trees, but to Don Ricardo he bows, like this, and tips his hat!"

Pablo led Carlos to the door of the kitchen. "It is here that you will eat," he explained. "And you will eat well. But one does not ask Salomón Rodríguez for food. No-no. He is a very busy man. He is an important personage. One asks Tomás Méndez for food. He is second cook. Now I will show you where one washes the shirt and the pantalones. In this house one keeps both the shirt and the pantalones always clean. I will show you the house, the parts one enters, and I will show you the doors leading to the parts one does not enter."

Thus Pablo showed Carlos all the places that he should see and told him the matters that he should know. And when the bell rang at the gates, Pablo went with Carlos to open the small door. He explained the workings of the oaken panels and showed how they swung inward on their hinges. The whole of the day passed in this manner, and after supper Pablo brought out a fibre mat and spread it on the flags near the small door.

"One lies on this," he explained to Carlos. "One sleeps, but an ear is always open. It happens that tonight Don Ricardo is out. One will hear his step and unbolt the small door for him to enter."

When Pablo had left him, Carlos lay still on his mat and thought about all that had happened. Indeed, he marvelled at how he had found a new home, and he was sad because he had let Pepillo slip away without being thanked. With this thought and with thoughts about Magdalena and about Pablo and about José Ronca on a nag of a horse, Carlos drowsed and finally fell asleep.

He was awakened by a loud ringing of the bell. He sprang to his feet in terror before remembering where he was and what he was supposed to do. His fingers still trembled as he drew back the bolt and opened the door. Immediately his eyes were blinded by the light of a lantern. He stepped back, blinking. A giant of a black bearded man stooped to enter, stopped in the passageway, and held the lantern in front of Carlos.

"Aló, aló! I don't believe I know you," he said. "You must be the new gate boy."

"Sí, señor!" Carlos answered without having understood a word the great man had said.

"I am Don Ricardo," he continued. "This is my gate you are watching. Pablo has watched this gate for seventy years. He watched it when my father was a very young man. Do you think you can watch it that long?"

"Sí, señor!"

"Seventy years is a long time. How old are you now, my boy?"

"Sí, señor!"

"I say how old are you?"

"Sí — no, señor!"

"Oh, so that's it! I don't believe you have understood a single word I have said, now, have you?"

"Sí, señor!" answered Carlos, confused and frightened.

Don Ricardo laid a huge hand upon the boy's head. "We shall have to see first of all that you learn some Spanish," he said. "What is your name — Pepe, Juanito, Pancho?"

"Carlos! Sí, señor!"

"Very well, Carlos, first of all you will learn some Spanish." He smiled, and Carlos smiled shyly back. "Watch my gate with care," he added with a chuckle. He walked into the court, swinging the lantern and whistling softly to himself.

Carlos spread his mat back upon the flags and curled up like a kitten. He could still hear the steps of Don Ricardo and the notes that the great man was whistling. Carlos pursed his own lips and caught the air. He closed his eyes, completely happy.

2

THE HOUSE of Don Ricardo was like a village surrounded by walls of stone, and day by day Carlos came to know its many parts and the people who lived and worked there. First of all he knew the gate and the outer court with its gravelled drive lined with palms and heavy-scented magnolias. He became accustomed to the crunch of wheels and the chomp of horses hoofs, and he learned to run and hold the bridles while Señora and the young Señorita Dolores came out of the house to take their places in the closed carriage that would whisk them off to mass or to the house of a friend. Half terrified of the spirited team, he would stand at arm's length from their tossing heads, and at the same time he would steal quick glimpses at the two mysterious women.

The Señora was a quiet little figure in black. Her skin was white and drawn tight over the delicate framework of her bones, her eyes yellow from malaria. Pablo Larra explained that she had a snake in her belly that ate up all her food, and that was why she was so small and thin and pale. There was something sorrowful about her, Carlos thought, but Señorita Dolores was another matter. Her skin was white, too, but there was a lustre like polished ivory, and she had large brown eyes, soft and friendly and even a little frightened, like the eyes of the fawn that Uncle Vicente had once found among his sheep. She was not much older than Carlos, and he thought that he might like her very much but he never had a chance to find out about that.

For in this teeming village that was Don Ricardo's house there were two kinds of people. One kind included Carlos and Pablo Larra and all the people of the inner court. These were the blacksmith and the saddler, the hostlers and the cooks, the laundresses and maids, and all

91

the other servants. Greatest of these, of course, was Salomón Rodríguez who presided over the kitchen and matters that pertained to it
and who had charge of food and was therefore respected and even
feared by all who cared to eat. These were one kind of people, and
they were Indians of one sort or another, or else they were mestizos
like Salomón Rodríguez.

Inside the house, in the front part, lived another kind. There were
Don Ricardo and his Señora, the young Señorita Dolores and her
brother, Don Juliano, Father Timoteo who came to hear their confessions, and all those who rode up in magnificent carriages or astride
prancing horses and entered through the door in front. These people
were people of a different kind, and Carlos was half afraid of them.

On the day after his arrival at Don Ricardo's gates, Carlos saw
young Don Juliano ride forth through the gate on a dancing palomino.
He was a wondrous sight, this young caballero. He was older than
Carlos by two or three years, and he had a slender, delicate face with
lips that were thin and with brown eyes hidden behind long black
lashes. He rode out through the gate and was gone during the morning. When he returned, the horse was sleek with sweat, the rider's
boots dust-powdered.

Pablo Larra rose out of a flower bed where he was pulling weeds
and seized the reins which Don Juliano tossed over the horse's head
as he slid to the ground. "The Señor's boots!" Pablo called in Nacheetl
to Carlos. "Hurry after and clean the Señor's boots!"

Carlos darted out of the gateway and started to follow Don Juliano
through the front door of the house.

"No! No!" Pablo Larra shouted, horror-stricken. "Not through that
door, boy, no, never!"

Carlos stopped on the edge of the driveway. "Where?" he asked.
"Where does one go?"

Pablo Larra had not yet recovered from his pious shock. "The back
door, boy, through the kitchen. Always through the kitchen."

"And from the kitchen?" Carlos demanded. "Where does one go
from the kitchen?" He followed as Pablo Larra led the palomino into
the inner court where the stables and saddlery and blacksmith shop
were located.

The old man paused near the kitchen. "In through there one goes only," he said. "Through the scullery and the kitchen, and through the pantry, and there one sees a door on the left, but one does not enter. One goes farther through the darkness of a hall, where there is a door on the right, but one does not enter. Beyond is a third door, also on the right, and one enters, and there one finds a stair and climbs straight-straight to a hall above, and there one goes straight, also, and in front of the nose is the room of Don Juliano. The boots are outside, and one picks them up and takes them to the court and cleans them and takes them back." Leaving Carlos by the scullery door, Pablo Larra led Don Juliano's horse across the inner court past the well toward the open doors of the stable.

Timidly Carlos entered the scullery, a dirt-floored wooden shed where a Nacheetl woman was grinding corn with a mortar and pestle. Beyond lay the kitchen. Cautiously he ventured in. Here the floor was of flagstones, and along one side were enormous charcoal stoves of red tile. Each firebox glowed pink below steaming terra cotta pots. The air was warm and heavy with the scents of garlic and bay leaves. Squatting on the flagstones Tomás Méndez was busy shelling beans. Carlos started toward the door leading out of the far side of the kitchen, but stopped short when he caught sight of Salomón Rodríguez.

Don Ricardo's chief cook was seated on a chair, a dapper middle-aged figure in a black serge suit surmounted by a celluloid collar. His skin was light brown, his dark hair neatly trimmed, and on his lip was a thin, bow-shaped mustache. On his nose were cracked spectacles with plated rims and a black ribbon fastening them to the winged lapel of his coat. Carlos circled cautiously as a dog circles a cat. Tomás Méndez chuckled softly. "Easy, boy, the Great One sleeps."

Carlos slid through the door into the pantry which was long and narrow, a mere passageway hung with trays and cluttered with Nacheetl baskets that carried an aroma of fresh-baked bread. Here was the beginning of a hall, and Carlos found the door on the left, which he was not to take. He felt his way further along, touching oak panelling on either hand. There were more doors. There were doors on the left, and on the right. Carlos stopped. He could not remember which was the one to take. He tried the first on the right. It creaked open, and Carlos saw a long table surrounded by chairs with carved backs much higher than his head. Along one wall was a mahogany sideboard with teapots and platters and ladles of heavy silver. Far beyond the table were windows opening onto the patio and the entrance gate.

He tiptoed down the hall and tried another door. It disclosed a chapel almost as big as the church at Xiltak and far richer to behold. The altar was carved like white lace, and there was a chalice of gold upon it, and up above hung Jesucristo Salvador. On the walls around were saints with candles burning beneath them.

Carlos stood gaping, and as his eyes became accustomed to the yellow glow of the candles, he saw a figure kneeling at a rail just before the altar. It was a small figure draped in black, with its face raised toward Jesucristo. There was the sound of prayers mumbled. Carlos could not see beneath the black mantilla, but he was sure that it was the Señora kneeling there. He backed out into the hall and tried another door.

This one opened into a narrow stairway of stone. Carlos climbed it on tiptoe, fearful lest the very padding of his bare feet should bring some terrible fate upon him. He found the upper hall, and he followed it along until he discovered the boots side by side near a closed door. Inside was the sound of whistling, a cheerful sound quite strange to the sombre gloom which Carlos had so far penetrated.

He seized the boots and retreated as quickly as he dared.

So it was that Carlos saw for the first time what the inside of Don Ricardo's house was like. During months that followed, he climbed often to the upper hall in order to get young Don Juliano's boots, and he ran other errands about the house, but he was always half afraid. He was somewhat afraid of the Señora because she was frail and draped in black, because somehow she seemed almost dead. But mostly he was afraid of the stillness of the house where he knew he did not belong.

Young Don Juliano made him more afraid. Oh, he was always gay, this Don Juliano. He whistled and sang and shouted to his friends whenever he rode forth to meet them on the bridle path of the Avenida. Among people of his own world this Don Juliano was a sport indeed. But to people of Carlos' world it was very different.

When he clattered through the gate on his lively palomino, Don

Juliano was full of energy and youthful spirit, and so also when he tossed his reins and slid to the ground from his saddle. But the way his eyes looked through — that was a different matter. Did he see Pablo Larra at all? Carlos didn't think so. Pablo Larra was a gatepost for receiving the reins. Pablo Larra was nothing more, and Carlos was an opening of the gate and a shutting of the gate. He was not even a polishing of the boots, Carlos thought, because Don Juliano just put the boots out and brought them in, and how they got polished was not a matter for thought.

Thus Carlos saw that there were two villages within the walls of Don Ricardo's house. He saw, indeed, that Don Ricardo was Señor, and his house was Santa Marta. Yet all his life Carlos had hated Señor, while Don Ricardo did not look like a man to hate. Carlos did not feel like smashing Don Ricardo's table or looting his house or burning the chapel with poor Señora inside.

He did want to be seen. He did want to be a person for young Don Juliano to whistle and sing and shout at.

He decided to keep his eyes open and see for himself why Pablo Larra was Pablo Larra and Don Juliano was Don Juliano.

He wanted to find that out.

During his first year at the house of Don Ricardo, the Nacheetl boy came to learn all about the duties of gatekeeping, and he learned from Pablo Larra to speak Spanish. He soon discovered that learning Spanish was more than the learning of words; it was a new way of thinking. For Nacheetl thinking had to do with mountains and valleys and sun and wind and rain; it had to do with crops and seasons and plantings and harvests. It had to do with sheep and goats and pigs. Even more than these, Nacheetl thinking had to do with Man and Fellow Man, the Village Council and the Village Law.

Nacheetl thinking had to do with much that was mystical and difficult to understand; yet its mysteries were more simple than those having to do with Spanish thinking. From Pablo he learned words and their meanings, and he learned how to string them together and how to greet Don Ricardo when he came to the gate and how to answer the questions that Don Ricardo asked. These things, he found, were not difficult to learn. But there were other matters that also went with Spanish thinking.

It happened one day that Don Ricardo sent word down to the kitchen to bring two cups of chocolate to his study. It was Salomón Rodríguez who prepared the chocolate, for only he knew the secret of mixing the cinnamon and making the drink just right for the taste of Don Ricardo, but, because the serving man was out, it was Carlos who carried the tray.

As he approached the study, Carlos heard the voice of Don Ricardo, and he heard also the voice of Father Timoteo, who came often to the house. They were speaking in Spanish, but the words were not those of Pablo Larra, nor were they the words of vendors who came to the gates, nor even of Salomón Rodríguez. Carlos paused outside the door, and for a moment he listened, trying to remember the words. Don Ricardo was speaking now, and he was using words like free will and determinism in the Stoic form and natural right. Father Timoteo replied with words about one Marcus Aurelius and harmony with the universe and obedience to the will of God.

When Carlos had served the chocolate, he hurried out to the back court and hunted up Pablo Larra. "I heard new words," he said breathlessly. "I heard determinism and sto-stoic. What means determinism? What means stoic?"

Pablo straightened up from the flower bed he was weeding and crossed himself. "Those words I do not know," he said. "Perhaps they are words of evil. One does not repeat all words that one hears."

"They were the words of Don Ricardo," explained Carlos. "And of Father Timoteo, too."

"Bien, that is no affair of yours," Pablo advised. "No doubt those are words that go with being a judge. Or perhaps they are the words of priests. It is true that priests use many great words among themselves. They are men of precious learning. Father Timoteo is a man of learning. So also is Don Ricardo."

"How does one become a man of learning?" Carlos asked.

"Only white men like Don Ricardo become men of learning," Pablo answered. "They are born that way. Why, when Don Ricardo was born, it was I who was at the gate and let in — "

"Father Timoteo is not a white man," Carlos persisted. "He is an Indian. He has skin like ours, and he speaks Nacheetl."

"With priests it is another matter," Pablo explained. "I have known many who were poor Indians like you and me before they became priests."

"How does one become a priest?" asked Carlos.

Pablo shrugged. "One learns to read books. In books there is every kind of knowledge."

"I want to read books."

Pablo chuckled. "For an Indian it takes much study," he said. "It is not for people like us."

"Why is it not?"

"We are not priests," Pablo reasoned. "We are gatekeepers. It is enough to sleep on the flags near the door and to listen always for the bell."

"But why does one become only a gatekeeper?" demanded Carlos. "Why does one not become a priest?"

"Because one is not meant to be a priest," replied Pablo testily. "It is God's wish that certain men be gatekeepers. Who would tend the gates," he added with indignation, "if all men became priests?"

Month succeeded month, and Carlos tended the gate and greased Don Ricardo's riding boots and the boots of young Don Juliano; he carried luggage to the carriage when a member of the house was about to leave, and he received luggage out of the carriage when a member of the house returned. In the passageway and on the drive he cleaned where the horses had dirtied, and he cleaned the gutter in front, and he killed rats in the sheds and snakes in the flower beds. During these many months the matter of becoming a priest was in his thoughts constantly.

Often it happened that Father Timoteo rang the bell at the gate, and when Carlos let him in, the priest always smiled and had a good word to say. Within Carlos was a desire to speak to the priest about that which troubled him, but Father Timoteo had come to tutor young Don Juliano and to catechize Señorita Dolores, not to answer questions at the gate. It was left only to ask Don Ricardo, and day after day while he was busy about his duties, Carlos worked out questions in the best of his Spanish. But when Don Ricardo passed through the gate, whether on foot or on horseback, the words would not come, and Carlos could say only "Good morning, señor!" or "Good afternoon, señor!" and there was nothing more to it.

When Carlos was nearly fifteen, it came about that Don Ricardo rang the bell at the gate just as a thunderstorm broke over the city. Rain came down in heavy torrents, and so it was that he waited in the passageway until the storm should lift. He shook the water from his hat and from his black beard and from his sackcoat, and with a dry rag Carlos wiped the mud and moisture from his boots.

"A tostón for your trouble," said Don Ricardo, handing him a half-peso. "You are a good boy, Carlos. Let me see, now, how long are you tending my gates?"

"Almost two years I am in your house, sir," Carlos replied.

"Two years? Can it be that, indeed? Two years is a long time when one is young. If you are here as many years as Pablo Larra, you will discover that time runs faster."

"Sir, I do not wish always to tend your gate only," Carlos said quickly.

"So? Well, now, I am sorry to hear that, Carlos. Has everything not been right? Perhaps we need some new arrangement."

"Oh, no, sir, it is not that!" Carlos summoned all his courage. "It is that I do not want to be a gatekeeper only." He gulped. "It is that I wish to be a priest."

Don Ricardo looked at him with astonishment. "I should have known," he said at last. "Let me look at you, Carlos! Let me see your eyes! Yes, they are clear and bright! Too sensitive, perhaps, but clear and bright! Do you have the courage, Carlos? To be a priest takes many, many years."

"I want to be a priest only!"

"We'll see about it," Don Ricardo promised. "I shall speak to Father Timoteo tomorrow. Can you read, Carlos? Can you write?"

"No, señor."

"Of course — who would have taught you? We'll see about this matter, Carlos, we'll see!"

Soon the rain ceased, and Carlos was left alone in the passageway. Although the boy scarcely dared believe in what had happened, Don Ricardo did not forget. Within a week Carlos had entered a parochial school that belonged to the very cathedral from which he had once intended to steal the almsbox.

The various classes were held by monks who taught many things in

addition to reading and writing. They spoke of strange lands beyond
the sierras, more distant even than Zalapec, and of oceans that were
water as far as man could see. They spoke of places called Egypt
and Babylonia and Assyria and Phoenicia, of Israel and Judah. They
spoke of the earth that was round, and they told how God had
made it.

There was much else that Carlos learned. In the school was a picture of Ronca's nation, and it was called a map, and on it Carlos saw
what the shape of the country was. Through a tremendous neck of
land was the Sierra Madre extending east and west, and the San Marcos
Valley was like a navel in the mountains.

The Sierra Madre was only a narrow belt extending east and west,
and to the north lay foothills and a strip of savanna land, and all the
rest was jungle, low and hot and mostly unexplored.

Rising among the western mountains were the Río Mosca and the
Río Pongo and the Río Colorado, and they came together and became
the Río Negro which flowed northward into the Bay of Pearls where
Santa Cruz was situated. More to the east was the Río Papagayo,
emptying into the Caribbean Sea, while flowing southward from the
sierras were two short rivers, the Macha and the Río Puma that passed
through San Marcos and emptied into the Pacific where the port town
of Cocamba lay.

In the country were two large cities, San Marcos, and far off Santa
Cruz, and the Royal Highway stretched between. There were other
towns like Tolca and La Trinidad, Tumaco on the Río Mosca, and El
Palmar and Sabara, and a dozen others, but they were small, yet
larger, Carlos learned, than Zalapec.

In the school were many other maps of far-off places called Europe
and Africa and Asia, and each of these places was made up of countries that one knew by their colors. England was pink, and Spain was
brown, and Russia was green, and China was yellow. Some of these
countries were good, and some were bad, and others were neither
good nor bad, but very strange. France was a good country, and Spain
was a good country now, although she used to be bad, and China was
not especially good and not especially bad, but the people ate birds'
nests and did everything backwards. Of all the countries, there was
only one that was particularly bad.

This country was called the United States of North America, and none of the monks had a good word to say for it. To begin with, this terrible country was inhabited by heretics called Yanquis who were always trying to do harm to the True Faith. In addition to that, they had a law called the Monroe Doctrine which said that they could walk into any little country in Central America or South America and tell them how to run things. A long time ago they had sent terrible armies into Mexico and had captured the capital and had taken away more than half of the country. They took Texas and California and New Mexico and a lot of other places away and made them into their own states.

Even after taking all of that land, the Yanquis were not satisfied. Some time ago they had started a war against Spain, and they took away Cuba and Puerto Rico and the Philippine Islands, and next they stirred up a revolution against Colombia and seized part of Panama. All of this was bad enough, but to make themselves even more hateful, they kept insisting that all of these conquests were really for the good of the people.

As he learned these truths about the world, Carlos was happy that he had decided to become a priest. There was much that he did not understand, and he asked many questions. Certain of the questions were answered, and others were not, and when the monks did not answer, they spoke of faith.

A large part of each school day the monks devoted to God and the Church, and as soon as Carlos could read a little, they gave him stories from the Old Testament. It happened once that he was reading aloud about the sons of Adam. "And Abel — was a — keeper — of the sheep," he read. The words came slowly and painfully. "And in — time it came — to pass — that Cain — brought — of — of — the — ground — an of-of — "

" — offering," the monk supplied.

"offering — un-to — the — Lord." Thus Carlos read, word by word, and he read how Abel brought the firstlings of his flock and of the fat thereof. The Lord had respect unto Abel and to his offering, but unto Cain and his offering he had no respect, and Cain therefore was very wroth. Unto Cain the Lord said, if thou doest well, shalt thou not be accepted, and if thou doest not well, sin lieth at the door.

"And — Cain — talked — with Abel — his — brother; and it — came
— to — pass, when — they — were — in — the — the — the — "
" — field," the monk supplied.
"field — that — C-C-Cain — rose — up — a-a-a — "
" — against," said the monk.
" — against — Abel — his brother — and — sl-sl-sl — "
" — slew him."

Carlos burst into tears burying his face in his arms upon the desk
at which he was sitting. When the monk tried to comfort him, he
jerked away and scrambled to his feet. In grief and terror he stumbled
from the schoolroom out into the open air, and once he was in the
cathedral yard, he began to run.

Blindly he fled through the streets, and he had not the least notion
of where he was headed. He knew only that he had killed Diego in
the pasture above La Perla. He had seen Diego fold quietly into a
small heap. He had held Diego's hand, and when he had dropped it,
the whole arm had flopped lifeless on the ground.

3

CARLOS WAS RESTLESS, and he had difficulty falling asleep at night. After his reading of the Cain and Abel story, he had stayed away from school for two whole days through nervousness and fear, but then some word of his truancy had reached Don Ricardo who gave him the choice of going back to the monks, or giving up school forever. A part of his uneasiness might well have sprung from this, but he had also become gradually aware of changes in his body and mind.

Most of his trouble had begun after the marriage of Señorita Dolores to a member of the Medina Del Campo family, a handsome lad not much older than Don Juliano. Pablo Larra had been saying for months that it would happen soon because all during that time there had been much going and coming between the two families, and Don Ricardo had received the young fiancé and talked with him in the judge's study.

It was a tremendous wedding with music and feasting, but to Carlos the whole affair was mostly a matter of taking down luggage from this carriage and that and greasing boots by the dozen.

There was feasting for the servants, of course, and there was dancing for them in an empty stable, and everyone joined in except Salomón Rodríguez, who was too important a personage to mingle socially with the lesser servants. But Carlos, stationed at the gate, could hear only the music and laughter and chatter from the front of the house and he felt left outside. When no one was about, he crept close and climbed into a pepper tree from which he could see through an open window. The massive table in the dining room was loaded with more food than Carlos had ever seen outside the market place. There were roasts and sauces and pastries, cheeses and ices, oysters and clams and fishes, sweets and fruits and mysterious dishes which Carlos had never imagined.

Carlos could see all these foods, and he could see a hall festooned for dancing. He could hear tangos and waltzes playing inside, and as he watched couples dancing, he felt more outside than ever before. After a time he slid down the tree and went back to the gates where he squatted upon the flags and tried not to listen.

Thus Señorita Dolores was married, and after the reception her husband helped her into a waiting carriage, and they clattered away together and began their journey toward his home somewhere beyond the mountains.

Pablo Larra grinned at Carlos. "Tonight he will plant a seed in her belly," he said gleefully.

This startled Carlos. Señorita Dolores had seemed young, and for some reason it had not occurred to Carlos that anything like that would happen so soon. "The seed will take root then," he remarked half to himself, half to Pablo, "and there will be a baby."

The old man nodded. "If Dios is willing."

Carlos pictured the planting of the seed in all its remarkable detail, and from these thoughts he derived a most peculiar sensation. He considered the matter with some pleasure, and he was not astonished when Señorita Dolores slipped from his mind and he found himself remembering Magdalena. After that he thought more and more about the house on La Calle de las Mujeres.

Asleep on his mat, he dreamed one night that he met Pepillo on the street and went with him to the house of Magdalena. She greeted them both as before and took them into the court which was really not her court at all, but the front court of Don Ricardo. Suddenly Pepillo wasn't there any more, but Magdalena was, and she came over and gave Carlos a kiss. Carlos picked her up and carried her into a bedroom and laid her gently down upon a bed that was like the one at Santa Marta, and the sheets were pink and made of soft silk. He got into bed with Magdalena, and she leaned over him, and as she did so, her blouse fell away from her breasts, and Carlos touched them with his hands.

Carlos held her very close to him and he felt that he wanted to do a very strange thing, but Magdalena did not want him to. He tried to force her, but she struggled with all her strength, and she got her fingers about his throat and squeezed until he was ready to choke, and then he woke up.

In the morning he felt ashamed of what had happened. He was sure that he had sinned and that now he could never be a priest. His conscience told him that he should confess to Father Timoteo, who had been catechizing him for his confirmation, but he lacked the courage to broach the subject even in the vaguest way.

He promised himself that he would stamp from his mind all recollections of the occurrence and think only of God and Jesus Christ and the prayers that he had learned. Yet he could not rid himself of the dream, and, what was worse, the bliss which he had felt during his nocturnal vision persisted during the day and dilated beyond his control. He found himself thinking only of Magdalena, or of matters related to Magdalena. The swish of a skirt about a servant girl's ankle, an aroma of violets, a cup of coffee, a white dog examining a tree near the bridle path, all reminded him of Magdalena and swelled his excitement.

After school he went around by the Bridge of the Holy Saints of the Cross to see if he could find Pepillo. On the way he told himself that for many months he had intended to visit Pepillo, although his conscience insisted that he was not really searching for his friend Pepillo, but for Magdalena's brother. The trail leading down from the street to the river's edge, however, was overgrown with weeds, and flood waters had filled the deserted cave with silt. He scrambled back up to the street, and for a moment he was on the point of looking for Magdalena. Then he remembered with shame that he was studying to be a priest. He felt that God and Jesus Christ and Mary the Virgin were looking over his shoulder and reading his thoughts and making note of his every sin.

He hastened home in panic and hid himself in a dark corner of Don Ricardo's stable to pray. "I confess to almighty God, to blessed Mary ever virgin, to blessed John the Baptist," he prayed, "and to the holy apostles Peter and Paul, to all the saints, and to thee, Father, that I have sinned in thought, word, and deed." Thus he spoke, and his words were those that Father Timoteo had taught him. "Through my fault," he sobbed, "through my fault, through my most grievous fault!"

When he had gone through his prayers, he felt momentarily better, but night came at length, and when he lay down upon his mat, his mind turned again to Magdalena. He saw her as he had seen her in his dream, and he felt himself touching her bare breasts, and it was as if she were really there. A great ecstasy overwhelmed his body when he allowed his thoughts to feast upon her, and he soon discovered that he could direct them to even greater frenzies than he had yet imagined. No longer was he lying on his mat with only hard flags beneath; with a twist of a thought he was wallowing in a silk-covered bed, and Magdalena was with him, and their bodies were merging in a rapture that could drive him mad. They writhed together in joyous anguish until his whole being found release and spilled its passion.

It was over in a moment and he was cold and exhausted and overcome with guilt. His mind now recoiled from the very thoughts which he had found most delicious, and he swore that he would never indulge himself again.

The next morning he arose early and worked especially hard at his chores, and at school he fastened his mind upon everything that the monks were trying to teach, and he was exceptionally devout at prayers. Occasionally he found his thoughts touching upon his guilt, but they recoiled in such abhorrence that he was convinced that he was forever safe from temptation. And so he was for nearly a week; then one night he dreamed again.

He had almost summoned courage to speak to Father Timoteo when the holiday was announced.

"Out of respect for our great liberator and president, General José Ronca," read the notice on the schoolroom door, "there will be no classes held during the Anniversary Day of the Great Revolution. Viva Ronca!"

All the schools were closed, and so was the University of San Ramón where Don Juliano was now a student.

The schools were closed, and a fiesta was proclaimed, and Don Ricardo told Carlos to guard the gates. "Open them wide," he said, "as Pablo Larra did before."

Carlos had never seen the city as it was this day. Flags hung from every balcony, and there was bunting on the lamp posts and an arch of triumph stood in the square. Militiamen guarded the streets, and the band got out its instruments, and even the symphony orchestra was in a special rehearsal against a command performance.

According to Don Ricardo's orders, Carlos swept the gateway and the gutters no cleaner than on other days. But he swung the gates wide open.

It was midmorning and Carlos had just taken his post when a bugle sounded. He peered up the avenue, and there he saw the reason. It was a squadron of cavalry, he thought at first, and then he saw the powder-blue uniforms and high sombreros of the federal police.

The troop approached on prancing mounts, and sunlight glittered on their buttons and polished metal. Every horse was black and wore a purple plume, and the bridles were trimmed with silver and the saddles with gold. The troopers carried yellow braid upon their shoulders, and their gloves were white and their pistol grips butted with ivory.

They were abreast of Carlos when the bugler sounded a second call. The troop halted, and the men swung from their saddles and swaggered stiffly about, leading their horses. Carlos watched them with bulging eyes, and he was fascinated by all that he saw. He liked the jaunty tilt of hat brims, the slap of gloves against thighs, the click of leather boots upon the cobbles. He liked the sight of sleek horses cropping grass on either side of the bridle path.

Most of the troopers lighted long cigarettes and sauntered about in search of diversion. In a moment servant girls had lined the walks in front of neighboring houses, and many of them giggled and flaunted their skirts, and the troopers laughed and strutted. One broke away from the group and strode toward the house of Don Ricardo.

Carlos, terrified, took his place between the gates. He felt his knees shaking, and his stomach turned over, and his heart pounded in his throat. Perhaps the trooper would turn aside! But he didn't. He came on toward Carlos, and the cartridges in his belt glittered in the sunlight.

"Guard the gates," Don Ricardo had said, "as Pablo Larra did before."

Carlos held his ground. The trooper stepped neatly over the gutter and entered the drive.

"Madre mía! Carlos!" he exclaimed. "Carlos Chichayan!"

The trooper in the powder-blue uniform and the white gloves and great sombrero was Pepillo!

"Oh, you precious chico, how you have grown!" He threw his arms around Carlos and kissed his cheek. "I should have known it! I should have known that you'd be standing at the gate. You're big, Carlos, a tremendous little man!"

Embarrassed, Carlos could only grin.

"So you're not in jail, chico! I thought maybe you'd gone back to stealing chickens or even almsboxes from the church!" Pepillo roared good-naturedly and slapped his thighs with his white gloves. "But no, I see you have done so-so for yourself in another way." He felt of the jacket Carlos was wearing. "Don Ricardo was ever dashing, a real guapo. What are you doing for yourself, chico?"

"I work here only," Carlos replied. He was somehow ashamed to tell Pepillo that he was going to school and hoping to be a priest.

"That's good enough," agreed Pepillo with a wink. "I wager Don Ricardo has some sly wenches in his house. A man needn't want for loving, eh? Bien, I suppose you wonder how I got into this kind of harness."

"I went to find you under the bridge," Carlos said.

"Oh, you precious! Well, Magdalena — you remember Magdalena?"

Carlos felt his heart plop over in his chest.

"Well, my sister Magdalena was right about this Ronca. Pues, that I must admit! Soon after that day we were there — at her house — I saw these federal police. Madre, you have seen them. You know how they strut about. What stallions, eh? They were looking for chicos like me. Oh, Ronca's a sly one. I thought not, but I did not know. Money? Dios, he can squeeze gold out of a rock. And he pays well. I tell you, one take-this is worth two I-will-gives. Ronca knows that, so pues! he pays."

"Do you go after bandits?" Carlos asked timidly.

"Bandits, yes, and other matters as well," Pepillo explained. "This Ronca is a man of force, a true stallion. He knows what it takes to rule. It is better than living under a bridge, working for Ronca. In the old days what did we earn? A louse-eaten chicken from some old bitch, a box of cigars, maybe a candlestick to sell to an old pimp in the thieves market. In the old days we worked for that. With Ronca it is

another matter. There is a rich man, say, who makes trouble, and
Ronca sends two or three chicos to explain how matters are. In that,
one earns more than a chicken, Carlos, e-e-e-yah, much more than a
chicken. But for old friends that is not an affair for talk. Tell me,
chico, have you been to see Magdalena?"

Carlos flushed and shook his head.

"Oh, now, precious one, let me look," Pepillo explained. "Let me
study your eyes. Yes, the sap has long since been running. Is there
then a muchacha in the house of Don Ricardo? That is no reason for
forgetting Magdalena. Or Josefa, either. Let me tell you, she is delicious, that Josefa. In those days she was only a yearling, perhaps,
but the last time I tried her she was a ripe little apple."

"It is lack of time to go there only," Carlos explained lamely.

"What a tender lie! Caramba, there is a wench in this house. That
is no matter. Perhaps tonight there will be a little hour or two when
we can go together. Yes, you and I together shall go this night indeed.
It is many months since I have been to the house of my sister. Pues,
and the sap runs high. Oh, there are plenty of women near the constabulary, believe me, and delicious ones, too, but we are men of
great responsibility and have much to do. Tonight we shall go to
Magdalena's and have a try."

"I do not think — "

A bugle blast drowned out what Carlos said.

"There it is!" Pepillo announced. "We must mount. Do not forget
tonight!" He darted into the street, caught his horse by the bridle,
and swung astride his saddle.

Carlos could hear a ruffle of drums and a shrill of fifes coming
nearer. The troop swung into formation and waited motionless. Men,
women, children, dogs, and burros crowded back of the gutters on
either side of the street. Carlos peered down in the direction from
which the troopers had appeared. No question about it, Ronca was
coming!

The colors came first, the national banner and the scorpion of the
Ronquistas borne side by side. Next came a regiment of the National
Army in dress uniforms of dark blue and shakos topped with waving
plumes of scarlet. As the procession came near, the troopers moved
forward, their horses in pace with the music, and the fifes broke out
with the shrill notes of the "Virgin Whore."

Carlos stood in the passageway and watched them pass, and directly behind the regiment came a man on a prancing palomino. He was dressed in blue with scarlet cape turned back to show its silver lining, and the buckle of his belt was gold, and his epaulets were of yellow braid. He looked straight ahead, and his face was hard and sharp and the color of baked clay.

"Viva! viva! viva!" screamed the crowd. "Viva Ronca! Viva El Libertador!"

He was coming abreast, and Carlos felt a pang of terror. Suppose Ronca should stop before the gate of Don Ricardo as he had done before! Suppose he should demand the name of the owner! Old Pablo Larra had answered, but Carlos would not have the courage. There had been a cricket in Pablo's throat that other time, but the old man had answered. "To Señor Don Ricardo Cervantes y Gómez belongs this house," Pablo had shouted, and José Ronca, the liberator, the great Democratic-republican, had bowed, ever so little and had tipped his hat.

There he was, the terrible Ronca! This time he was riding no nag, and his sombrero was not of tattered straw. General Ronca, the powerful presidente, was astride a prancing palomino, and the hat upon his head was a plumed shako with a strap of polished leather crossing his chin. A sabre hung from his side, and the hilt was gold that flashed in the sunlight. He looked straight ahead, and his face was hard and sharp and the color of baked clay. He rode by without a glance at the house of Don Ricardo. He rode by without a bow or a tip of his magnificent hat. Without seeming to see on either side and without seeming to hear the cheers and the shouts, General Ronca passed on by.

Carlos had been standing there with legs of wood, his own breath burning in his throat. Now the danger was over, and he felt limp.

A moment later Don Ricardo and a blondish gentleman came out of the house and dallied about the gateway, looking up and down the Avenida. At first they spoke only in English, but after a while Don Ricardo switched to Spanish. "There will be no trouble from official sources this time," he said, "but the rabble will soon be drunk."

The blondish gentleman peered in the direction of the plaza. He was about Don Ricardo's age, Carlos thought, although he seemed younger because of his light skin and yellow hair. He had a small mustache that was carefully trimmed. He turned toward his friend triumphantly. "See how they flock behind him, Ricardo? No matter what you or I may think about it, you can't blame old Prettyman for backing a man like that. In this kind of country it's a sound investment."

"For Prettyman!" Don Ricardo snorted. He, too, was staring down toward the Plaza in the direction of Ronca's procession. "The King of Spain himself never bled them drier than Ronca does today, and yet they scream and shout and wave their hats. A slogan, a shiny sword, and a fine horse. *Sic itur ad astra!*"

For a few moments more the two men stood in the gateway, chatting. Carlos loitered near. He was trying to summon courage to speak to Don Ricardo about the matter that troubled his mind. For weeks he had dreamed only of Magdalena, but now that Pepillo had suggested a visit, he was afraid to go.

He was afraid to go because he was ashamed of what he had been dreaming and because she might look at him and somehow know what he had been thinking. That she had slept with hundreds of men did not occur to Carlos. To him she was still a beautiful woman with lips and cheeks as red as the lips and cheeks of María Madre in the Church of Xiltak. She was a beautiful woman about whom he had been thinking wicked thoughts, and he did not want her to know. That was one fear, and his other fear was guilt.

He was guilty because he had determined to become a priest and, having made up his mind, he had wallowed about in silken beds and touched the bulging breasts of a woman and wrapped himself about her naked body. He told himself that he had tried not to think these thoughts, but the thoughts had come, and he had lacked strength to drive them out. Thus he had sinned, and now, if he went to the house of Magdalena, he would sin again. He must not see Pepillo.

Carlos knew that Pablo Larra was the proper one to ask, but the old Indian was crabby, while the judge — "Sir!" he said timidly as Don Ricardo and the blondish gentleman turned back toward the house.

"Yes?"

"Sir, I would like please not to guard the gate for a few hours tonight!" He was embarrassed, and his voice faltered, and his words did not come in proper order.

Don Ricardo looked at Carlos quizzically. "Ah — so?" He turned to the blondish gentleman. "This is the boy I was telling you about — the one who wants to become a priest. Carlos, this is Mr. Nash. You know he is manager for Prettyman here in San Marcos."

Carlos bowed slightly as he had learned to do.

Mr. Nash extended a hand genially. "So you want to be a priest, eh?"

Don Ricardo turned toward the niche in the wall where Carlos kept his books. "What are you reading now?" He drew out a volume, spread it open on one palm, and held it up for Mr. Nash to examine.

Mr. Nash squinted at the page before him. "Well, now, my Latin's rather rusty. What's this — Saint Jerome, eh?" He faced Carlos. "Are you certain that you wish to become a priest?"

"Yes sir."

Mr. Nash laid a hand on Carlos' head. "Well, stick to it, son, and you'll come out on top!"

Don Ricardo replaced the book, clapped his friend across the shoulder. "Bueno, Frank, time for a little copacita, eh?" The two men moved out of the gateway.

Carlos followed a step behind. "Sir!"

Don Ricardo turned. "What is it?"

"Sir, about tonight, I would like please not to guard the — "

Don Ricardo winked at Mr. Nash. "Well, of course, there will be much to see," he chuckled. "Yes, for a boy there will be much indeed to see. Go ahead, chico! Some old one will watch the gate!"

4

CARLOS RAN into the streets and headed for the cathedral. The city was jammed with soldiers and militiamen and police and crowds of people. There were all kinds. There were rich men in high-wheeled coaches and barefooted Indians from mountain villages and lanky, fearsome Xlalaks on prancing horses and craftsmen from the smithies and pottery shops of the city. There were muleteers with coiled whips and black mustachios. There were priests. There were brown-faced women in full skirts of red or blue or yellow. There were young men and old and boys like himself and babies slung from their mother's backs. It seemed that all the world had come to jostle and gape and shout for Ronca.

There was fear of meeting Pepillo, and because of it, Carlos chose dark alleys and avoided squares. He bent low and darted like a tramp dog, and no one noticed.

Carlos came to the cathedral and slipped inside, making his way to Father Timoteo's study.

The priest looked up from the book that he was reading by candle light, and he greeted Carlos and motioned toward a chair. "You look troubled," he said.

"Yes, Father."

"You wish to tell me?"

"Yes, Father."

"It is perhaps a matter of some small sin that has been committed?"

"Yes, Father."

"A lie, perhaps?"

"No, Father."

"A blasphemy?"

"No, Father."

"Hm!"

Carlos gulped. "It is a matter of a nighttime dream."

"So?"

"Yes, Father."

"What is the nature of this nighttime dream?"

Carlos studied his toes.

"This is perhaps a matter of a woman dream?" suggested Father Timoteo.

Carlos nodded.

Father Timoteo closed his book and faced Carlos squarely. "It is a part of man-ness to have such dreams," he said. "Since the days of Adam they have come at night to plague us."

"It is not then wicked?"

"You know the story," Father Timoteo admonished. "You remember how in the beginning both the man and the woman were naked, and they were not ashamed. But the serpent tempted Eve, and she ate of the apple, and Adam also ate. Thereafter, they knew that they were naked, and they were ashamed, and thus has man condemned himself to sin. You have heard the story. You have read the words."

"I thought it was a matter of an apple only," Carlos said.

"Now you have come to understand?"

"Yes, Father, I have come to understand."

"The dream is a thing that comes in men's sleep. It is a whispering of the devil in one's ear. It is a memory of sin long forgotten."

Carlos was relieved. "It is then only a memory!"

"Ah, but wait!" Father Timoteo raised a forefinger. "A memory, indeed, but not to be enjoyed!"

Carlos flushed.

"You see! A memory, yes, but a memory to be thrust aside! A memory to be pushed back into the night. A memory to be flogged into oblivion. Do you understand?"

"Yes, Father."

"If only you did! I tell you, boy, it is beyond your comprehension. You have smelt the devil, Carlos, but you have not yet seen his face. For you who intend to become a priest, this is only the beginning.

What has happened cannot be concealed. It is written in your face. The dream came, and you embraced it. You gloried in it. You wallowed in it. You awoke and longed to be asleep. You went over it in your mind. You thrust it aside — and hauled it back."

"Yes, Father."

"This is the beginning only. The devil has found you, and henceforth he will track you down. Wherever you go, there he will be. There is no escape. By day he will peer over your shoulder and breathe down your neck; by night he will stretch out his body upon your mat. He will stand behind you and before you and about you, and you must test your strength with him. It will be a long fight. Are you strong, Carlos?"

"I do not know, Father, I do not."

Father Timoteo reached for a narrow shelf that was pegged to the adobe wall behind him, and he took down a book.

"You are now a man, Carlos," he said. "In body you are a man and, to a limited extent, in mind also. There is quickness in your thinking, and there is also a power to grasp. The hour for great decisions is not far off. It is your duty to be prepared. Are you going to be ready, Carlos?"

"I do not know, Father."

"You must be ready," Father Timoteo warned. "Now observe this book. It is one that you will come to know. You will rely upon it. You will look upon it as a weapon, yes, each word will be a rock for your sling. Draw near, now, and look at these pages. See, we have here the story of two cities. There is a City-of-the-World, and there is also a City-of-God. Two cities, and between them there is no sharp division. The people of one jostle with the people of the other. Indeed, there is no certain proof as to which men live in the one or the other. Ah, but there is a difference, for those of the World City are doomed, whereas the people of the City-of-God are chosen among all men. There will be a great separation, and the Godly shall be saved, but lo! those of the World shall be damned unto eternal hell fire."

Carlos shuddered.

"Now mark this!" Father Timoteo paged through the book until he had come to a certain place. Here the margins were noted, and several words had been underscored with black lead. "Let us remember that the City-of-the-World is a city of raw flesh, whereas the City-of-God is a place of strength and mansions of the spirit. We come now to a private matter." The priest spoke in lowered voice. "We have spoken of the serpent and of the woman and the apple. So man was doomed to sin, and he cannot shake off the desire that plagues him. In his punishment he lusts after woman, and he is begotten through lust. It is allowed to man through the sacrament of marriage that he indulge his lust for the purpose of begetting only. Yet even then he is ashamed. Only in the darkest regions of his private chamber does he indulge himself lest his neighbor perceive, and the virtuous man would do without."

"It is a matter not easy to understand," Carlos suggested.

"In what respect?"

Carlos hesitated. He was thinking of Uncle Vicente and his story of Chan and Tana. He remembered how Chan went down by night from his palace of stone and looked upon the image of the moon. She rose out of the water, brown of form, and she went to Chan with arms outstretched. Breezes blew, Uncle Vicente had said, and the stars shone, and nighttime saw creation. "I do not understand," Carlos said at last, "because in our village we plant maize in the soil, and after a time the seed bursts with life, and it sprouts and breaks through the earth. I have seen that, and Uncle Vicente used to say that woman is man's earth, and he plants his seed in her belly."

"That is true," Father Timoteo conceded. "But think of this. Is there lust in the planting of corn?"

"No, Father, there is no lust."

"Ah, you see? That is how it is. Man cannot plant his own seed as he plants the seed of maize. The first is a matter of lust, whereas the second is of the mind only."

Carlos remained perplexed. "If man planted no seed in the earth, there would be no corn, and if he planted no seed of his own — "

"Those are different matters," Father Timoteo answered sharply. "When one speaks of corn, it is a matter only of corn, but when one speaks of man, one speaks of flesh and spirit. It is true that man dwells in the City-of-the-World, but through God's Holy Grace it is permitted to certain men that they may aspire to the City-of-God.

Propagation through lust belongs in the City-of-the-World and has
there its proper place, and in that manner men multiply. To those
who aspire to the City-of-God, the propagation of men is a lesser
matter than the cultivation of the spirit. So it should be, for the spirit
is eternal and of a higher order, while the flesh is of this world only."

"Is it then wicked for man to plant his seed in woman?"

"It is no sin within the matrimonial sacrament," Father Timoteo repeated, "so long as the act is for begetting only. We speak now of
men as such. For the Man of God there is no place for indulgence.
The Man of God must live within a spiritual kingdom, and he must
keep the borders of that kingdom inviolate. He must protect them
through the will-force of his spirit and through God's grace. The devil
will pound at his gates and seek to breach his walls. The devil will
open the sluiceways of lust in order to flood him out, whereupon the
Man of God will be alert and fearless, and he will call upon God
and the Host of Heaven to help him resist."

"That is to become a priest?"

"That is to become a priest," agreed Father Timoteo. "It is not
every man that is called, but he who is chosen bears before God a
sacred duty. I am counting on you, Carlos, to fight well."

Carlos squared his shoulders. He liked the priest's confidence in
him, and he felt already like a Man of God; he pictured himself
grappling with the devil hand to hand and throwing him to the earth.
"I think I'm ready to fight hard," he said.

Father Timoteo smiled briefly. "Be careful with words," he warned.
"You have not yet met the battle. You have heard only the shouts
from afar off. Remember this. The first battles are but small
skirmishes, but through them one takes on strength. Each small victory brings courage and power for the winning of a greater. At first
you will meet only a little temptation here and another there. It will
be a matter of scorning a nighttime dream and thrusting the memory
aside. Make certain only that you win every one."

"Yes, Father."

Father Timoteo put the book back upon its shelf, and Carlos got up
to leave. He padded across the room to the door where he paused
to thank the priest. He still felt strong and brave and ready to meet
the devil on any street corner. Father Timoteo waved off any thanks,

however, and Carlos stepped into a dark passageway beyond the door.

"Don't forget the two cities," Father Timoteo called after him. "Don't forget that the City-of-God is Abel's city, while the City-of-the-World is the city of Cain!"

At that moment a draft slammed shut the door, and Carlos was left alone to face the devil in the blackness, and he knew in his heart that he was Cain.

5

YEAR BY YEAR Carlos studied under the monks at the cathedral and under Father Timoteo as well, and as he studied, the world grew. He could not travel abroad and study in Paris as Don Juliano was preparing to do, but he could read books. Through them he saw beyond the valley of San Marcos and beyond the seas. He saw beyond the seas and into the past and into the thoughts of men and into their dreams and hopes and failures. He learned fast.

He learned Latin and read of battles in Gaul and the building of a bridge and the musings of a gentleman farmer in Rome. He learned Greek and marched across the deserts of Asia Minor parasang by parasang and sailed with Ulysses and watched rosy-fingered dawns as they grasped at horizons of the sea.

Thus he travelled afar off from the land of the Nacheetls and from the city of San Marcos and the parades of Ronca. He walked with Socrates and saw Augustine's City of God. He travelled afar off, and he saw two worlds, and they were not the same.

He saw that each had many phases of which he had never dreamed. These were not the phases of Uncle Vicente nor of Pepillo and Magdalena. These were the phases of Israel and Judah, of Egypt and Babylon and Nineveh and the land of Medes and Persians. These were the phases of Galilee and Corinth and Rome. There were all these phases, and many more, and there were galley slaves in chains and the fall of empires and Christians thrown to hungry beasts and a meeting of holy men in Nicea.

These were the phases of two worlds as Carlos saw them. He sat with open book in Father Timoteo's study and saw the slaughter of thousands in Thessalonica. He lay with open book in Don Ricardo's garden and visited Saint Anthony in an Egyptian desert. He squatted with open book in candlelight upon stone flags and saw the Lombards sack Cassino.

There were two worlds, and these were the phases, and in each phase he sought the World of the Spirit rather than the World of the Flesh, but both were there, and the Flesh was not easy to avoid. In his own phase there were Carlos the shepherd and Carlos stealing a chicken and Carlos opening the gate for Don Ricardo late at night. There was Carlos thinking of Magdalena, and there was Carlos dripping sweat and praying. There was Carlos killing his brother with a sling and there was Carlos studying to become a priest.

These were all Carlos-in-the-Flesh, and Carlos-in-the-Spirit was mostly a vision seen during moments of prayer.

There were two in everything, and of each two there was Jesucristo Salvador in one, and the devil himself in the other.

For the seeking of Jesucristo there was a way of grace which Saint Augustine explained. The beginning of the way of grace was baptism, which Carlos already knew, and there were other sacraments, and there were meditation and prayer. There was a way of grace, but it was not easy to find, and it was even more difficult to follow, and Carlos discovered that his thoughts wandered when they were supposed to be seeking the way.

He knew moments when he hated his flesh and mortified it with thorns and by holding his arm to flame. During the mortification he might perhaps control his thoughts, but when he was not mortifying, they wandered again and became one with his flesh, and he knew that the devil was to blame.

The devil came to squat in Don Ricardo's gateway and talk with Carlos. He was no longer the devil of the pastures back of La Perla, but the devil of Abraham and Isaac and Jacob, the devil that would sift Simon as wheat, the devil of Father Timoteo's teachings; and yet his face was one that Carlos had always known. It was loose skin hanging in folds; it was a pair of slit eyes red and green; it was curling horns.

He came always at night when Carlos had stretched himself upon a sleeping mat within Don Ricardo's gate. He came at night and squatted on the cold flags and talked.

"You are a chico very much to my liking," he said to Carlos.

"Leave me alone!"

The devil gave a friendly laugh. "Oh, now, I came for a little chat only."

"One of these nights I shall throw you out in the streets," Carlos boasted.

The devil chuckled. "When?"

"As soon as I am strong."

The devil slapped his thigh good-humouredly. "In that case we have plenty of time. You know, I like this place. I like you, too." He looked about him, and his shrewd eyes caught sight of a crevice where a block was missing from the arch of the gateway. There were five or six books standing there in a row. "What are those?" the devil demanded.

"Those are books," Carlos replied. "Each word is a stone for my sling."

The devil guffawed.

"What are you laughing at."

"You know as well as I," the devil chuckled.

"You wait," Carlos warned. "One day I shall confess to Father Timoteo, and then I shall drive you off."

The devil snorted. "You remind me of Cain."

Carlos twisted on his sleeping mat.

The slit eyes gloated. "He was the same, that Cain."

Carlos felt a surge of remorse. "I did not mean to do it; I wanted to frighten only. Anyhow, he was a grabbing hand."

The devil was sympathetic. "There is a secret to tell," he confided. He leaned toward Carlos, his ram's nostrils dilating. "That Abel was also a miserable fellow. People said he did everything right, always, and Cain did everything wrong. Actually, he was a grabbing hand. Oh, it was easy to talk to Cain."

Carlos buried his face in the crook of an elbow. "I wanted to frighten only," he repeated.

The devil patted Carlos with a hairy hand. "It was just so with Cain," he comforted. "No, it was not that way exactly. Cain *dared* to frighten only. He *wanted* to kill, but he dared only to frighten. Thus it was that I came to help."

Carlos looked up at the red and green eyes floating in blackness. "You?"

"Verdad!" The devil snickered wickedly. "I gave his hand a precious leetle push!"

Carlos writhed with anger and fear. He writhed with anger because the devil sat there within reach taunting him to his face, and he writhed with fear because he had killed like Cain and was weak and had not the strength to confess. He writhed, and the devil sat on the flags and chuckled. He writhed until sweat stood out on his face and shoulders and neck; he writhed until he fell asleep from exhaustion.

In his sleep were dreams.

Some of his dreams were simple dreams that he could forget, but others were woman dreams. They were soothing and tingling to the flesh, and he enjoyed them to the fullest. He enjoyed them in his sleep, and when he awoke, he remembered them and enjoyed them again and wallowed in recollection. He wallowed until he was satiated, whereupon he was seized with remorse. Then it was that he rememberd Father Timoteo, and he remembered the battles he was expected to win.

These were the small battles he was expected to win in preparation for the great, and he determined again to win them, and even as he determined, the devil slipped through Don Ricardo's gates and squatted upon the flags and chuckled.

"There is no importance in the small battles," he told Carlos. "They are little matters only. The big battle has been fought and decided and is already a matter of long ago. We are good friends, Carlos, so enjoy your dreams. There is no need to fight."

That was how the devil talked. He came often, and over the course of years Carlos, entering manhood, grew to know him well.

One night a month or so after Don Juliano's departure for France it happened the devil was sitting on the flagstones when Don Ricardo came home from a late excursion into the city.

More and more frequently Don Ricardo had been going forth at night, and it was often nearly daybreak before Carlos was awakened by his ringing at the gate.

On this particular occasion, Carlos had not been asleep. For a number of hours he had lain upon his mat and writhed under the devil's taunts. For a number of black hours he had writhed until he could bear it no longer; then he had jumped to his feet and had lighted a candle that was stuck in the niche with his books.

With the lighting of the candle, the devil disappeared from sight, but Carlos knew he was there and could feel the gaze of his slit eyes.

Carlos took down from among his books a certain one and began to read. It was the story of one who went up into the wilderness and was tempted of the devil. For forty days and forty nights he was there, and he fasted, and when he had fasted, he was hungered. The devil came to him and said, "If you are the Son of God, command these stones to be made bread."

This one answered, "It is written, Man shall not live by bread alone, but by every word that proceedeth out of the mouth of God."

Again it happened that this one was tempted, and again and again, but he struck out against the devil and said, "Get thee hence, Satan."

"Ho!" shouted Carlos aloud. "There was one who grappled and threw you." He was squatting on the mat with the book upon a knee, and the devil was somewhere opposite.

"That is of no significance to you," the devil stated. "You have been on my side from the beginning."

Carlos felt brave tonight. "Please God, I'm a man, now, and I'll throw you any day. Please God, I'll — "

Don Ricardo was tugging at the bell rope.

Slowly Carlos got to his feet and slid back the bar.

Don Ricardo paused on the threshold, eyes dazzled by the candle-light. "Caray! this is no time for a candle," he grumbled. He stepped in, and Carlos rebolted the door.

"I was talking with — I was reading a book only," Carlos apologized.

Don Ricardo noticed the books in the niche where the candle was burning. "So? What have we here?" He took down a volume and flipped through the pages. "Do you understand this?" he demanded.

"Yes, sir."

The judge put the book away and took down another. "One knows so little of matters in one's own house! How long now are you guarding my gates?"

"It is nine years, sir."

Don Ricardo pursed his lips. Carlos waited awkwardly, shifting his weight from one foot to the other.

"Nine years, eh?" Don Ricardo fingered his beard. "You know **my** study, Carlos?"

"Yes, sir."

"Come there tomorrow," he said, "and we shall have a talk."

6

"YOU HAVE TENDED my gates too long," Don Ricardo said when Carlos came to his study. The judge was sitting behind a mahogany desk almost buried under a pyramid of papers. "Do you think you would like another kind of job?"

"There is no tiredness in guarding your gates," Carlos replied.

Don Ricardo saw that his gatekeeper was fully grown, a Nacheetl man of medium height with small bones and long, flexible muscles. It was with genuine, almost paternal interest that the judge's eyes studied the impassive brownness of the young Indian's face. To the casual glance there was no expression, but Don Ricardo had long since learned to watch the thinness of the lips for a tiny quiver, the black eye-pupils for a kindling spark. "I know, I know!" He waved a long-fingered hand. "But there is waste in your guarding my gates. Look around you, Carlos, look at this study. What do you see?"

"Papers," replied Carlos.

Don Ricardo grunted. "Yes! There is no chair without a sheaf of papers," he agreed. "This room is a scholarly pigsty."

"There are also books," Carlos pointed out.

Don Ricardo was still watching Carlos shrewdly. Unless he had long since missed his guess, there was a battle raging somewhere far behind that calm indifference. "There are also books. There are all kinds of books." The judge glanced at the shelf-lined walls. "Take one down, Carlos."

"Which one do I take?"

Don Ricardo shrugged. "Any one at all."

Carlos selected one and took it down.

"Have you read it?"

"No, sir."

"Take down another."

Carlos selected a second book.

"Have you read it?"

"No, sir."

"It is a pity that time is short," Don Ricardo told him. "If we did nothing but read, there would still be so little time for all that we ought to read. Remember, Carlos, our lives are too short for that which is trivial. Would you like to read my books?"

Carlos nodded, and his eyes were glistening. "Yes, sir, I would read every one."

"They are not all of the same importance," Don Ricardo warned. "But the greater part are worth the reading." He toyed with a pencil. "How would you like to be my secretary?"

"Sir?"

Idly Don Ricardo tapped his desk with the pencil. "I need one in whom confidence can be placed," he explained to Carlos. "I need a secretary who will clean up these papers and keep them in order. I need a secretary who can copy my writing intelligently and who can read Latin and French. I need one who can be trusted."

Carlos hesitated. "I am studying a few years only."

Don Ricardo frowned. "You are the one I am asking."

Carlos gulped. "Yes, sir, I would like to be your secretary, but I study with —"

"Good. You will move into my house, and you will buy shoes this day, and your salary will be increased from that of gatekeeping to one of secretary. You will work in the mornings only, and in the afternoons you will go to school as before, and you will read my books. That is agreeable?"

"Yes sir, that is agreeable."

Carlos began a new life. For the first time he put shoes upon his feet, and he walked about with his feet the most important part, and he did not feel the shoes pinching. For the first time he slept upon a bed, and there was whiteness, and he sank deep in softness and could not sleep. The bed brought warmth and sweat, and in the morning his back ached from lying in the softness, and the second night he slept upon the floor.

This was a new life, however, and his feet came to accept their shoes, and his body the bed.

Each morning he arranged papers for Don Ricardo and copied letters and took dictation, and each afternoon he went to school under Father Timoteo and the cathedral monks, while at night he read.

Much of the reading was that which Father Timoteo had prescribed, and thus he learned theology and the history of the Church and the philosophy of Saint Thomas Aquinas.

Carlos saw that the path of reason led to God, and this path was a dialectic. It began with known authority and proceeded from there, and in the end it reached God. There was also faith, and it proceeded and reached God in the end, likewise, and there was no conflict.

There was also the reading in Don Ricardo's study.

Carlos took down a book from the judge's shelves and read about a life of reason warmed by love. He read it and put it away in exchange for another. The second volume was Voltaire who said that Jesus had been too noble a man to be insulted with the name of Christian. He read that and put it away and read an "Essay on Miracles" which said there were none. Thus he travelled from book to book, and as he read, he became confused, and at first he took his confusions to Father Timoteo.

He told Father Timoteo about a book called *Candide,* and Father Timoteo was not pleased when he found that Carlos had read it.

"It was inspired by the devil himself," Father Timoteo explained. "It was inspired by the devil and written to confuse Christians — especially young Christians." He asked Carlos what he was doing now that Don Ricardo had taken him away from the gates.

Carlos explained.

The old priest thought a moment, and the muscles in his face strained as he groped for the words he wanted. "Don Ricardo is my friend of many years," he told Carlos. "He is a courageous man and has a fine intellect, but he allows his thoughts to wander unchecked. I am afraid he entertains a number of very dangerous ideas. I would advise that you do your work without any regard for the books upon his shelves."

These were the words of Father Timoteo, and Carlos had such faith in them that for a time he went about his work without taking books from Don Ricardo's shelves. He did not read, but he thought about Father Timoteo's warning and about the book called *Candide,* and after a time he questioned Don Ricardo about dangerous ideas.

"What man has spoken of dangerous ideas?" Don Ricardo wanted to know.

"No man," lied Carlos. "I was wondering only."

Don Ricardo peered at Carlos searchingly. "That is a matter about which Father Timoteo might have spoken," he remarked. "If he ever speaks to you of such things, you must listen respectfully, of course, but do not heed. He is a noble man, this Father Timoteo, and his mind is good, but he dwells only in the past. He is afraid of nothing on this earth except that which is new."

"It was I who was thinking about dangerous ideas," Carlos insisted.

Don Ricardo struck his desk with a doubled fist. "There is but one idea that is dangerous," he snorted, "and that is the idea that ideas are dangerous. On the contrary, all ideas must be considered. There are those for acceptance, and there are those for rejection, but all must be considered. Indeed, it is the duty of an intelligent man to reflect upon them all."

These were the words of Don Ricardo, and Carlos had faith in them even as he had faith in Father Timoteo. Thus he was confused, and his thoughts did not know what course to follow. In his confusion he turned again to the shelves in Don Ricardo's study and took more books.

He read from an Italian named Beccaria. This man condemned in human society a tendency to confer on one part an extreme of power and happiness while the other part was reduced to weakness and misery. He read Beccaria, and when he had finished, he turned to a book by a Venezuelan named Roscio.

This Roscio was upon his knees, begging forgiveness of God, and his sin was submission to despotism. He had submitted to despotism and had used God's Holy Word to bind men in chains. Following the dictates of a false education, Roscio had overlooked "nature's holy book" and had remained ignorant of the "language of reason." He had hated as heresy the writings of learned philosophers and had observed no laws but those of despotism, no philosophy but the philosophy of ignorance, no truth but his own prejudices.

Those were the sins of Roscio, the Venezuelan, and for them he asked forgiveness of God.

Carlos read these books, and others, and after a time he spoke to Father Timoteo about Roscio, and the priest was angered.

"Have I not warned you against the words of heretics and sinners!" he exploded.

"I do not understand," Carlos protested. "What is the sin of this man Roscio? Did he not get down upon his knees and beg forgiveness of God?"

"I do not know about that," admitted Father Timoteo. "I have never seen his book except upon the shelf of Don Ricardo. But this Roscio was an infamous man. He forsook the teachings of our Holy Church and followed the path of heretical reason. Yes, and he raised the banner of revolt against established authority."

Carlos was confounded. "Did not Saint Thomas himself prove that reason is but another road to grace?"

"Reason stemming from true premises established by our holy philosophers does indeed lead to grace," Father Timoteo replied. "That you know, Carlos, that you know well. But this heretical reason is a pagan thing."

"I do not understand what is so holy about established authority," Carlos persisted.

Father Timoteo was aghast. He seized Carlos by the arm as he spoke. "Carlos, Carlos, have you delved so deep that your mouth speaks the very words of the damned? Have you forgotten how Jesus spoke to the Pharisees and Herodians, saying Render unto Caesar the things that are Caesar's, and to God the things that are God's?"

Carlos was trembling with doubt and contrition. "I have not forgotten."

The priest seemed to tower. "Then cast away your misbegotten heresies and harken to me," he said with anger. "Do you not remember how Saint Augustine taught of the City of God which only the elect may enter? There you have the concern of Jesus and the concern of holy men through the ages. It is to prepare sinners for entrance into the City of God that you have chosen to seek the garb of a priest. Your concern is with the spirit and not with the laws of man. Carlos, Carlos, can you not yet distinguish Caesar's world and the world of God?"

Carlos covered his face with both hands. "I am confused," he said passionately, "I am very confused."

Father Timoteo touched the boy's shoulder gently. "Of course," he said, "and you are tired as well. Go to a cell this night and fast and pray, and when you have ordered your soul, we shall talk more."

7

When Carlos returned to Don Ricardo's house from the cathedral, he felt himself sufficiently strengthened by Father Timoteo to resist whatever heresies he might encounter; carefully ignoring the books upon the shelves, therefore, he went straight to work among the papers which the judge had asked him to sort, classify, and file away.

The great house, Carlos found, was even more silent and apparently deserted than it had seemed on that first morning nine years before when he had ventured through the kitchen and scullery in search of Don Juliano's boots. The Señora had grown feebler with each passing season, and now, since the departure of her son, she had asked to have trays sent to her quarters at mealtime, and Don Ricardo usually ate there with her.

As the family had grown smaller, Don Ricardo had not seen fit to replace any servants who died or left his service. Indeed, he had disposed of all but a few of his horses, so that only two hostlers were necessary in the stables, while in the house Salomón Rodríguez and Tomás Méndez and three Nacheetl women were the only ones remaining out of the teeming populace of the inner court that had impressed Carlos upon his arrival within Don Ricardo's gates. In certain respects he was relieved that so few of the old ones remained. To the ancient Pablo Larra this transition from Carlos the gatekeeper to Carlos the secretary was merely an act of Dios which required no explanation. In the others, however, Carlos felt a resentment which all but Salomón Rodríguez sought to conceal.

Had the household been as large as in previous years, it would have been difficult for him to have faced all the big, brown accusing Nacheetl eyes. As it was, the women who served him came always with lowered lids, while Carlos carefully avoided the kitchen and overlooked the almost aggressive indifference with which Salomón Rodríguez chose to scorn the former keeper of Don Ricardo's gates.

In the meantime, Carlos was kept busy with the papers which were to be put in order. It was an enormous job under any circumstances, but Carlos hindered his own progress by yielding to curiosity and examining the remarkable documents which Don Ricardo had collected. There was, for example, a report compiled by a Yanqui investigator for the Prettyman Human Welfare Foundation in New York. Scribbled across the top of the first page were a few pencilled phrases. "Financed by the Old Man's conscience," the handwriting said. "Ironic, eh? — Frank."

Carlos read the pages that followed. There were rows of statistics about the Ronca state, figures which suggested that the country was perhaps the most backward in the Western Hemisphere. San Marcos was one of the few inland capitals of the world which were not yet connected with a seacoast by so much as a single railroad. It appeared that the whole Ronca state had escaped the track-laying fever which had spread across Latin America in earlier years, and only recently had plans been made for the building of a line between San Marcos and Santa Cruz.

Two per cent of Ronca's people, according to this report, owned eighty per cent of the country's land. One of the leading families held an estate larger than Holland and Belgium combined. The largest single holder was the Church with twenty per cent of the nation's territory in its grasp, but there were two thousand haciendas consisting of more than twenty-five thousand acres each.

Carlos learned that the average income for tenant farmers was two cents a day in United States money, while the average wage for skilled labor was seven cents an hour. Carlos was not sure how much these figures represented in centavos, but it was obvious that the Yanqui investigator didn't think that they amounted to much.

Upon reading farther, Carlos learned that eighty per cent of the population could neither read nor write, that three quarters of the people were believed to be living on a slow-starvation diet, that sixty per cent of all babies born were doomed to die before they were six years old, and that the average life span of those who reached maturity

was thirty-seven years. The country was plagued with malaria, ty-
phoid, intestinal parasites, yaws, syphilis, pinto, and a number of other
diseases of which Carlos had never heard. There was an average of
one doctor for every fifty thousand people.

Such figures meant almost nothing to Carlos. What astonished him
was the fact that the Yanqui was so much upset about these conditions. The report had noted, for example, that three out of four of
the population had never slept in a bed. Carlos wondered what was
so unusual about that. He himself had not laid eyes upon a bed,
except for the one in the hacienda of Santa Marta, until Pepillo had
taken him to his sister's house on La Calle de las Mujeres.

Carlos filed the report away in a wooden filing case which Don
Ricardo had bought and attacked another pile of papers. Here was a
series of lectures which Don Ricardo had delivered to the University
law school, and there, tied with red ribbon, was a packet of legal
documents which turned out to be deeds and mortgages. With an
uneasy twinge of guilt, Carlos examined each one with far more care
than was necessary for their proper filing, and, as he went through
the bundle, his curiosity grew. It was clear that Don Ricardo owned
a large section of San Marcos itself. Here was a single deed covering
five city blocks between the river and the market place. There was
also a mortgage on the Gran Hotel San Marcos, while a third document indicated that the judge was sole owner of *Las Noticias,* the
city's oldest newspaper. Carlos saw that his patron was indeed an
influential man.

The next sheaf of papers included detailed records of a dispute
between Prettyman Enterprises and the National Government of pre-
Ronca days. The case, which seemed to have something to do with
mineral rights, extended over a number of years and ended only
with the extinction of the old government. Carlos could make slight
sense of the legal language, but from the documents he did learn
something about Prettyman power. He found out, for example, that
Prettyman Enterprises not only held several million dollars worth of
government bonds, but also controlled a dozen or more of the country's
richest mines, several rubber concessions, an enormous banana planta-
tion on the Rio Mosca, a steam-navigation franchise on the Río Negro
and a voting majority among stockholders of the Banco San Marcos.

Carlos sorted out the documents, arranged them in some sort of order, and filed them in Don Ricardo's cabinet, in a dossier marked PRETTYMAN.

Another pile of papers included a series of pencilled notes which Don Ricardo had pinned together. The first page had a quotation scrawled upon it. "Any people anywhere being inclined and having the power have the right to rise up and shake off the existing government and form a new one that suits them better. This is a most valuable, a most sacred right — a right which we hope and believe is to liberate the world." After the quotation was a dash followed by the words "A. Lincoln, Mex. War Speech."

Underneath was a similar sheet with a second quotation. "When a long train of abuses and usurpations, pursuing invariably the same object, evinces a design to reduce them under absolute despotism, it is their right, it is their duty, to throw off such government, and to provide new guards for their future security — U.S. Dec. of Indep."

Thus, stack by stack, Carlos went through the papers that cluttered Don Ricardo's study. Sometimes the judge himself came in to read or to scribble voluminous notes upon any one of four or five pads which he kept upon his desk for that very purpose. Usually when first he entered, Don Ricardo was too preoccupied even to notice Carlos, but after a time a passage from a book he was reading might strike his fancy, or perhaps some new thought would flash across his mind. "Listen to this!" he would exclaim, and Carlos, squatting on the floor, would settle back, ears wide open.

There was a certain fascination in putting together all that he had come to know about Don Ricardo and trying to guess the rest. The judge liked Father Timoteo, but hated the Church. He was tolerated, even respected, by General Ronca, and yet he talked increasingly about overthrowing the government. He believed in a people's right to revolt, but he sincerely hated violence. He opposed Prettyman and ranted about what he called the "Yanqui colossus," and at the same time he liked Frank Nash and quoted Jefferson and Tom Paine and Abraham Lincoln and carried on a voluminous correspondence with a large number of lawyers and professors and scientists in places like New York and Philadelphia and Washington. This much Carlos knew.

Speculating further, Carlos suspected that the judge had more to do with General Ronca than had so far come to light. This suspicion was strengthened when he came across a bundle of records from Don Ricardo's court. Most of the documents, aside from clearly criminal cases, dealt with Prettyman mining claims, property suits rooted as far back as the days of earliest royal grants, disputes with various Yanqui, English, and German concessionaires, contested water rights and similar controversies which had taken place over nearly three decades. The dispute which caught his attention, however, concerned one Pepe Ronca, accused by the National Government of smuggling arms from an alien ship into national territory by way of beaches adjacent to Cocamba.

It appeared that the defendant, having been apprehended, had made good his escape only to deliver himself back into the custody of the Government after an interval of nearly two years. In the course of his eventual trial, this Pepe Ronca was duly acquitted and set free. Since the defendant was obviously, even admittedly, guilty, the trial, Carlos thought, was more than a little peculiar. What caught Carlos' particular attention was a quotation in the finding. "I hold it that a little rebellion, now and then, is a good thing. . . . It is necessary for the sound health of government." The author of the statement, Carlos discovered, was Thomas Jefferson, the Yanqui democrat.

After comparing the various dates in the case, Carlos concluded that while the smuggling had been carried on before the Democratic-republican revolution, the tongue-in-cheek court decision had been handed down several months after the Ronquistas had come into power.

Carlos was puzzled. How many governments did Don Ricardo intend to overthrow?

His fingers trembled slightly from excitement as he examined the evidence, and he was so absorbed that he did not hear footsteps on the threshold. In fact, he was not aware of Don Ricardo's presence until he glanced up, uneasily, and saw the judge standing near his desk. A bit too hastily Carlos dropped the papers.

Don Ricardo raised his bushy eyebrows, tugged his beard. "So! You have found something," he chuckled. "A matter truly scandalous, I have no doubt."

On Carlos' face was the abashed expression of one caught prying. "It was n-nothing," he stammered.

Don Ricardo puckered his brows inquisitively. Curiosity aroused, he stepped over and picked up one of the documents. Gradually an expression of recognition spread across his face. "Hmph! How times change!" he snorted. For a few moments he stared down at Carlos as though weighing something in his mind. At length he said, "I suppose you are wondering exactly where I stand?"

Carlos nodded. "It isn't clear."

Don Ricardo took out a long cigar, lighted it, drew heavy drafts until the tobacco was burning well. Then he went over and sat down behind his desk. There was a silence while he leaned back in his chair and gazed at the ceiling reflectively. "The first matter to understand is this," he said finally. "In our country there are two forces. First, there are the landholders who look always backward into our feudalistic past and sigh for the King of Spain. They are afraid to lose their haciendas and the labor of their peons. They hate any forward change. That is one force, and attacking it are those of us who wish to modernize our country and give the people things to buy and money to buy things with. We look at our great Yanqui neighbor to the north and see what he has done, and we wish to do the same."

The judge puffed furiously on his cigar, and a red ring of fire ate into the tobacco, leaving gray ash behind. "Fifteen years ago," he continued, "my friends and I gave a lot of money to José Ronca. He was to rouse the peasants, organize them, overthrow the government. Eventually we were to step in and build a state like the Yanqui democracy. Well, we got our revolution started, and Ronca swept the country, and it looked as though we might succeed. Then the Yanquis landed Marines in Santa Cruz in order, they said, to protect foreign interests and to 'insulate the fighting.'"

Carlos thought of the Prettyman dossier. "Who was responsible?" he asked. "Did Prettyman have anything to do with it?"

Don Ricardo answered cautiously. "Such matters are difficult to prove, Carlos. Let me tell you the rest. The Marines were with us only six or seven months, but during that time Ronca sold out. He owed everything to us, of course, but he had ambitions of his own that were large out of all proportion to his conscience. He made a pact with landholders and the Church and most important of all, with Mr. Prettyman.

Carlos stirred among his pile of papers. "Through Mr. Nash?"

"No, no, that was before Frank came down," Don Ricardo said. "The story goes that Ronca spent two nights aboard Prettyman's yacht out in the Bay of Pearls, but that may be only rumor. In any case, Ronca secured a substantial loan."

"And now you seek to overthrow again?"

Don Ricardo flicked the ashes of his cigar onto the rug. "There is no other way," he told Carlos. "Church and landholders will go along with Ronca until the country is squeezed as dry as a cast-off lemon. What do they care about the deals he makes with Prettyman and other foreigners so long as they have land and peons to work upon it? Some of your hacendados would rather go back to a king altogether and even reunite with Spain, but lacking that, the Ronquista government serves. So you see, Carlos, rebellion is our only choice. After that we can make a government, a constitutional, democratic government, and then we'll modernize. With Yanqui help we'll build railroads and factories, we'll give people jobs and wages and things to buy, we'll establish schools and hospitals and — "

Carlos rose on one knee. "With Yanqui help? You spoke only now of Marines in Santa Cruz!"

Don Ricardo was amused. "Do not judge a people," he warned, "by an individual or by a faction or even by the government in power. It is true that Prettyman channels a monstrous part of our national wealth into his own private reservoir. It is also true that Yanqui Marines landed in Santa Cruz. The Yanquis have intervened in Latin America on fifty or sixty different occasions, and at the very time when they had troops in our country, they had similar forces in five or six others. But that sort of policy is done for, and most Yanquis know it. They are beginning to realize that we Latin Americans must prosper, if only for purposes of trade with them. There are many Yanquis who are not imperialists; there are many Yanquis who are willing to be good neighbors. We must win their confidence, Carlos, for our destiny is bound irrevocably to theirs. That is why it is important for us to found a democracy in the Locke tradition."

Carlos did not fully understand. "What is the Locke tradition?" he inquired.

Don Ricardo explained about Locke's theory of contract government depending upon the consent of the governed. It was a civil compact with checks and balances to restrain the power of the governing, and these checks and balances implied a doctrine of letting be. "Freedom of speech and press," Don Ricardo said, "freedom from unwarranted search and arrest, guarantees of a speedy trial, protection of private property — these are the benefits of contract government." He leaned over to a bookshelf and took down a volume. "Essentially, that is the kind of government the Yanquis have, and I have a deep admiration for it. But you must not think that it grew overnight. On the contrary, the Yanqui government is the result of a thousand years of development. It is the result of centuries of Common Law; it is the result of centuries of trial and error, of struggle against oppression. So you see, if it took them the better part of a thousand years to develop their still imperfect freedoms, we cannot expect to achieve those same blessings in three or four."

The judge flipped through a few pages of the book which he held in his hand. "In this you can read something about their kind of government," he told Carlos. "Come, I will make you a present!" He took a pen from his desk, and on the flyleaf of Locke's *Treatises* he wrote: *to Carlos, from Ricardo Cervantes y Gómez, magna est veritas, et prevalebit.* "Study this carefully," he added, "for in it lie our only hopes for a decent future."

Carlos took the book and thanked Don Ricardo. That night he read by the light of a kerosene lamp, and the more he read, the more certain it seemed that Father Timoteo must be wrong about Judge Cervantes and the things he stood for, and yet —

8

As LONG AS Carlos knelt in a cathedral cell, as long as he fasted there and prayed, as long as he was close to Father Timoteo, he was alone with himself and perhaps with God. Even while he worked in Don Ricardo's study there was only curiosity to disturb his thoughts. But when he went to his room, when he lay upon the softness of his bed, when he ceased to work or pray, his soul was torn two ways, and he was not alone.

He lay upon his bed one night, and while he slept, the devil watched over and waited for a chance to talk.

When Carlos awoke, it was black, for there were no candles burning, but he could see the devil sitting upon his bed, waiting to talk. Carlos sat up and said to the devil, "Get thee hence, I have made my peace."

The devil only chuckled. "With whom have you made your peace?" he asked.

"With Don Ricardo," Carlos replied, "and with his books."

The slit eyes glittered slyly. "So? And with Father Timoteo? Have you also made peace with Father Timoteo and with the Church?"

"The Church closes men's eyes," Carlos charged, "and leads them backwards, sleep walking."

The devil raised a horny forefinger. "Ah! Then Father Timoteo is a scoundrel," he suggested, "or a misguided fool."

"Get out!" hissed Carlos. "Get out and let me be!"

The devil sidled closer. "Have faith, Carlos! Have faith in Father Timoteo!"

"I have put an end to faith," Carlos interrupted.

138

The devil grinned. "You are through with Father Timoteo?"

"I am through with Father Timoteo."

"He is a friend," the devil reminded.

"He died a thousand years ago," Carlos muttered. "He lives no more."

The devil clapped his bestial hand. "Ho! You have found him out?"

Carlos nodded. "I have found him out."

The wicked eyes narrowed. "You renounce him altogether?"

"Already I have cast him aside."

"Good!" shouted the devil. "I am glad to hear."

This disconcerted Carlos. "Oh? Why are you glad to hear?"

The devil laid a hand on the young man's shoulder. "Because you have no faith in Don Ricardo, either," the devil explained. "You do not believe in him."

Carlos pulled away. "On the contrary, Don Ricardo is a noble man."

"He is indeed," the devil agreed, "but so is Father Timoteo."

"Don Ricardo has a keen mind."

The devil nodded. "He has indeed."

"Then why do I not believe?" Carlos demanded fiercely.

The devil shrugged. "Why indeed? Because Father Timoteo has a mind and soul as well."

Carlos sprang from his bed. "Get out!" he screamed. "Get out!"

The devil only laughed. "You have made your peace, Carlos."

"Peace? There is no peace!" Carlos threw himself upon his bed and moaned, and thin streams of sweat trickled off his neck and body and soaked the sheets.

Again the devil touched Carlos. "Is it peace that you seek?" he asked gently. "Is it peace that you really seek?"

"It is peace," Carlos gasped. "It is peace only that I seek."

"Why?" asked the devil. "Why peace, Carlos?"

"Because they tear me apart," Carlos groaned. "Father Timoteo — Don Ricardo — they tear me apart."

"Peace is a simple matter," the devil ventured. "Of all matters, peace is the simplest."

"In what manner is peace so simple?" asked Carlos doubtfully.

"You must put an end to both," the devil replied.

"To both?"

The devil was pleased with the boy's interest. "To both. You have put an end to Father Timoteo. You must also put an end to Don Ricardo."

"That is no answer," Carlos scorned. "It is far too simple to be an answer."

The devil chortled. "Indeed? Oh, come, Carlito, consider only a moment. Reflect upon those one meets in the market. Reflect upon the tamale vendor, perhaps, or the seller of pots. Look into their eyes and tell me: are they tearing themselves in twain?"

Carlos thought a moment. "I think not," he admitted. "I think not."

The devil leaned close. "Why is not the tamale vendor tearing himself in twain?"

"I do not know."

"It is a small matter," the devil advised. "The tamale vendor makes no choice. Between Don Ricardo and Father Timoteo he makes no choice."

An expression of eagerness spread across the boy's face. "There is peace?"

"Consider his eyes," the devil directed. "Look into them yourself and see!"

"There is a matter of thinking," protested Carlos. "There are times when one cannot stop."

"You just now put an end to thinking," the devil reminded. "When you pushed aside Don Ricardo, you put an end to thinking."

"That is true," Carlos conceded. "Yet at times the brain won't cease."

The devil raised a forefinger. "If the body is served, Carlos, the brain will cease."

"What is one to do?"

"Ho, Carlos! What is one to do indeed!" the devil leered. "We know, don't we, Carlos? We have waited all these years."

Carlos thought of Magdalena. As in his dreams he saw her naked in the softness of her bed. With a burst of self control he jerked his mind to heel. "It is wicked," he cried.

"It is a planting of seeds only," the devil corrected. "All things plant their seed."

The words of Father Timoteo came to strengthen Carlos. "Through the planting of his seed Adam brought sin to all the world."

"You do not believe that, Carlos," the devil reproved. "You do not."

The boy cowered against his pillow. "I am ashamed."

"There is no need for shame," the devil coaxed. "Put on your breeches, Carlos, and we'll start along."

"Another night, perhaps. Tomorrow, even."

"Remember your dreams, Carlos," the devil reminded him. "Remember how you lay upon your mat and dreamed of Magdalena? Remember how you lay in her bed, and it was pink and soft? Remember how you took her in your arms? Remember her blouse, how low the neck was, and how you touched her breasts, and they were warm?"

"That was a dream only."

"Yes, but after you had wakened, you sought sleep again and tried to dream," the devil recalled. "You tried to sleep and dream and could not, and, falling asleep, you dreamed awake. You remember that?"

Carlos was entranced. "I remember," he admitted. A gate opened in his mind, and a carnival of luscious memories came trooping through.

"This is the night," the devil tempted. "Let us go, and you shall sleep in Magdalena's arms. Put on your breeches, Carlos."

Carlos began to dress, slowly, at first, but faster as he thought of Magdalena. "It is very late," he said. "The door will be barred, and she will be asleep."

"Magdalena's door is never barred," the devil answered. "And Magdalena wakens quickly." He moved toward the threshold.

"Wait!" Carlos begged. "A moment only." He buttoned up his trousers.

They slipped out of Don Ricardo's house together, the devil and Carlos, and they went forth upon the streets of San Marcos. The hour was late, and only here and there a light showed through a battered gate, but the devil knew the way. He took Carlos through deserted streets and alleys and across squares he had never seen, and soon they came to La Calle de las Mujeres.

It was the same as many years before. The mud was deep, and

there were pigs asleep in corners. Candles burned in certain houses, and Carlos heard voices and excited laughter, and he heard a woman squealing.

"Magdalena will not know me," Carlos muttered. "She has forgotten."

"That is no matter for consideration," the devil said. "You are a man, Carlos. Nothing more is needed."

They proceeded through the darkness, and the devil showed him Magdalena's door. Carlos pounded upon it with his fist, and when there was no reply, he pounded harder. Soon he heard footsteps, and a window opened above.

A voice hissed. "Quien es?"

"It is I only," Carlos replied. "I seek Magdalena." He turned to the devil for reassurance, but the devil was gone.

"A little moment only!"

Carlos waited, and after a time the door before him opened a crack. "I seek Magdalena," he repeated softly.

The door opened wider, and Carlos stepped inside. A woman stood in the stone passageway, a candle in her hand. It was Magdalena! She was not young, this woman, but she was Magdalena. Tonight there was no paint upon her face, and her hair hung down in braids.

"It is late," she said. "What is it that you want?"

Without the devil at his side, Carlos was afraid, and his tongue was stiff in his mouth. He forced himself to speak. "You do not remember, but I am Carlos — Carlos Chichayan. I came once with Pepillo when I was very small. I — I —"

She held the candle high and studied his face. "Carlos Chichayan! Yes, I remember. He was a so small boy with great power in his belly. He came with Pepillo, and now — " she looked him up and down " — now he is a true man. Come, Carlos Chichayan! Come with me."

Magdalena led the way with the candle in her hand. She moved into the court that Carlos remembered, and by the light of the open flame he saw that gardenias and bougainvillea were still growing, and there were orchids hanging from a trellis. The small portico was the same, and the chairs, too, and from the roof of the portico hung cages of canaries and parrakeets, but tonight the birds were asleep.

She stuck the candle upright on a rough table, and she and Carlos pulled up chairs about it. She sat with her elbows on the table, chin cupped in hands, and she stared at Carlos. His face was brown and smooth and calm, and only the redness in the eyes betrayed a certain ferment.

"You are the one," she said at last. "You are Carlos Chichayan! The eyes I would know, and the mouth, also."

Her own eyes were soft, but not as clear and bright as Carlos had remembered. There was a malarial yellowness in the white, and about the corners were lines like the ribs of tiny fans, opened wide. She was not quite so beautiful, but she was Magdalena.

Her warmness comforted Carlos and gave him reassurance. "It is a matter of many years, " he said.

"Yes, many years," Magdalena agreed. "They are gone — like that!" She snapped her fingers.

Carlos had remembered the smallness of her hands, the slimness of her wrists. Both were somewhat grosser, now. "I would know you," he said. "Anywhere I would know you."

"No, no, the youngness has gone from me," she said. "About you — tell me, Carlos, are you going to be a priest?"

Carlos started.

"It is only that I heard," Magdalena added. "From Salomón Rodríguez I heard that you had become an important personage in the house of Don Ricardo and that you were studying to be a priest."

"I do not know," Carlos said, "I do not know."

Magdalena shrugged. "It is a matter of the spirit," she suggested. "There are those born to be priests, and there are others for the keeping of gates and the fighting of battles. Among women there are those who marry, and there are whores to make men happy. When have you seen Pepillo?"

Carlos told her of the day when Ronca had marched past Don Ricardo's gate.

"I remember, I remember!" Magdalena exclaimed. "He went back that night and you were gone. Why did you run away? He wanted to bring you here only."

Carlos flushed.

She laid a hand upon his. "You were not ready, I know. About

Pepillo — he is teniente, Carlos! Already he is third lieutenant! Madre! I do not like the things he does. Oh, I tell you, that Ronca has become a pig. 'Fight for us and we will make you free!' Those were his words, Carlos. Long ago those were his words. I believed them, too, and I sent Pepillo off to join the federal police. Believe me, he is guapo, my Pepillo, in that uniform he is guapo. But the things he does. 'All the land to those who till it!' Those were Ronca's words, and we believed them. All the Indios believed, and they took the land and called it theirs. Taxes, Carlos — you know of taxes?"

Carlos shook his head.

"Why, only last night there was one here from Xiltak," Magdalena continued. "It is far back in the sierra, this Xiltak, a village, only. There was one here from Xiltak, and he told the story. In the old days one gave corn or wool. To Señor el Dueño one gave corn or wool. Not under Ronca, El Libertador! No, no. Now one pays the tax. Not corn or wool, but money to jingle in the pockets of El Presidente. Pues, he was furious, this one from Xiltak. 'Where does one get the money?' he asks. 'There is no price for wool, nor for corn, neither. Where does one get the money?'"

Magdalena laid a forefinger close beside her nose. "I'll tell you this," she whispered. "One gets no money. One pays no tax. Then what? Then come the federal police. Then comes Pepillo, guapo in his boots and sombrero. Pft! Like that."

"Why does he not leave?" Carlos asked.

Magdalena lowered her eyes. "You would not want to see Pepillo," she said, studying her nails. "He has been around this Ronca too long." She looked up, and there was sadness in her face. "You know when it began, Carlos? It began when last you saw Pepillo. You know this Ronca, he is mad for women. Oh, truly mad! He plucks them like ripe fruit. Pues, you remember Josefa? Little Josefa? Believe me, she had become a sweet apple. Pepillo took her to Ronca. Pepillo took her to Ronca's house and this Ronca, he liked her! Indeed, he took her for his bed only! She wore satins and silks, and the jewels he had looted. She was a queen. For months she was a queen."

"And now?"

Magdalena shrugged. "He is after all a man, this Ronca," she said. "He tires."

"I would like to see Pepillo," Carlos ventured.

Magdalena shook her head. "It is better not," she warned. "His life is not for you, Carlos. It is better that you become a priest."

"To be a priest is not easy," Carlos told her, and he tried to explain about his studies and about the teachings of Father Timoteo and about Don Ricardo and the books upon his shelves.

"Those are matters I do not understand," Magdalena said. "This I know, that Father Timoteo is a good man and gives to the poor. He prays for all men and makes matters right with God, and I would listen to what he said, but as for Don Ricardo — he is another matter."

Magdalena's implication roused Carlos to defense of his benefactor. "He is wise," he stated, "and he — "

"Wise he may be," Magdalena admitted. "But he cares nothing about the poor. Look at that fat house and the gardens and the horses in his stables. Why Salomón Rodríguez says — "

Carlos flushed. "Don Ricardo is my friend," he said angrily. "Don Ricardo — "

"I am sorry, Carlos. I wanted only that you become a priest."

"I wished to explain," Carlos told her. "There is also another little matter. I — sometimes I — " He paused, afraid to speak.

"So!" Magdalena laughed gaily. "My little Carlito has become a man?"

Carlos nodded.

"That is already a matter of some years," Magdalena pointed out.

"I prayed," Carlos explained. "All night I prayed on my knees. But the devil whispered always in my ear, and tonight — "

Magdalena winked impishly. "Chst! That was not the devil," she said. "That was man-ness only."

"It is wicked for a priest, Magdalena."

Lightly she touched his wrist. "Jesus, and who is yet a priest? Not you, Carlito. I understand this. Books, no, nor manners of thinking. But I understand this."

"One cannot become a priest."

"In time, perhaps," suggested Magdalena. "It seeps away, this man-ness. It seeps away with time."

Once more Carlos felt an inside tearing. "But what am I to do?" he cried. "During the seeping, what am I to do?"

Magdalena grasped his hand in hers. "Go away, Carlito! You must go away for a year or so."

"But where to go?"

Magdalena sensed a tightness in the young man's fingers. "Beyond the mountains," she suggested. "The world is big. There is much to see. Pues, there is also much to do. Only today we had here a patron from far away. A gringo he was, and believe me, Carlito, he had seen the world. A gringo with yellow hair! He was telling us about a railroad, Carlos. They are going to build one, he said. Right here to San Marcos, he said. Can you see a railroad, Carlos? I can see a steamboat, but not a railroad."

"I have seen pictures," Carlos said.

"A railroad! Pues, you could make it, Carlos! The gringo was looking for men. Think, Carlos, you could make a railroad!"

The candle was burning low. "I would like to make a railroad," Carlos said. "Do you think I could, Magdalena?"

"You are strong, Carlos!" Their knees touched beneath the table. "You are very strong."

Fiercely Carlos felt his man-ness. This was his dream. This was Carlos in the courtyard of Magdalena. She would come to him and kiss his lips, and he would carry her to her bed and lay her gently upon the sheets that were pink and made of soft silk. This was his dream, and he wanted to tell her of it. He wanted to tell her of his passion, of his night time struggles, of her blouse falling away, of his hand touching her breast. These were the things he longed to tell, but his throat choked, and he could not.

"I think I could make a railroad," he said huskily. "Tonight I think I could."

IV. Steel

THEY CAME FROM HOME TOWNS like Binghamton and Muleshoe and Woodland. They came from Wichita and Evanston. They came from these places, and many more, and their names were Smith and Sherman, Gannon and O'Leary and Rafferty, Rossi and Milano, Hofstatter and Cohen and Sinciewicz. A few were from Cornell and M.I.T. and Carnegie Tech. A few more were from State College and University of Texas and R.P.I. Others were from night school and correspondence school and summer short course.

The rest were from hard knocks.

The rest were from Baltimore and Ohio and Central Vermont, New York Central, Katy, and Southern Pacific, Soo, Great Northern, Burlington, Chicago, Milwaukee, and Saint Paul, New Haven, Pennsylvania, Rock Island, and many more. They were all these, and they knew their stuff.

They had come to lay steel.

They had come to drive steel fangs into the country's heart.

They sailed through the Straits of Tiburón, past the island where the dungeons were. They sailed into the Bay of Pearls to the wharves of Santa Cruz.

They piled out of steamers with their transits and blueprints and specifications. They stood upon the docks with their feet apart and looked at Ronca's principal port.

A hundred and one in the shade, and they stood upon the docks and looked at Ronca's port. A hundred and one in the shade, and they saw cobbled streets and mud holes and heat waves shimmering over pavements of the Plaza Central. They saw adobe walls stained yellow by the urine of men and dogs. They saw pigs rooting in open sewers and Indians asleep against jambs of cantina doors. They saw sleek little men in Panama suits drinking at a sidewalk café. They saw vendors squatting on street corners. They saw goat meat for sale at twenty centavos a kilo, and it was lying on the curb, covered with flies.

They saw urchins wading in the gutters. They saw pus running from syphilitic sores. They saw the sombreros and black boots and powder-blue uniforms of the federal police.

The Smiths saw these things, and the Shermans, and so did the Gannons and O'Learys and Raffertys, the Rossis and Milanos, the Hofstatters and Cohens and Sinciewiczi, and all the other men who had come to build a railroad.

Azhol-of-tha-yooniverse, they said.

They stood upon the dock with feet apart, and they saw Santa Cruz, and beyond the city they saw palm trees and swamps and jungles. They saw palm trees and swamps and jungles, they saw greenness. It was lush, this greenness, it was greener than it should be, it was lewd.

They took up their transits and blueprints and specifications, their whistles and time books and dinner pails, and they found rooms or put up shacks and gathered crews and went to work.

They went to work on the docks, laying track, and they dumped fill in swamps beyond the city.

Their purpose was to drive fangs of hard steel into the heart of the greenness.

They blew whistles and went to work, and it was get them carts movin', goddammit. It was get them carts movin', goddammit, and it was more fill, goddammit.

Those were the words of the engineers and the technicians and the foremen. Those were the words of men who had come to build a railroad.

Carts movin', more fill, carts movin', more fill. Whazzamattereth 'ese goddam people, don't they ever get a move on? Carts movin', goddammit, more fill, goddammit. Chrisake, cancha find any one of these guys can read a blueprint? Carts movin', goddam it, more fill, goddammit. Ten pesos, eh? Well, how muches 'at in *real* money? Carts movin', more fill, build a form, grab me a whaler, Dear Honey, wish't I was home, more fill, a good screw, raise ya ten, a quart of likker.

Whazzamatter, can't nobody in this goddam country speak American?

The carts moved, and a dike of rock and earth was pushed across the swamplands. The carts moved and built their own roadway, and they dumped rock and earth into bottomless marsh. The carts moved and dumped rock and earth in the ooze where alligators had lately lain to sun themselves. The carts moved, and the screech of their wooden wheels scared flocks of green-feathered parrakeets and put them to flight.

Out across the marshlands moved the dike, and there was an army sweating. There was an army of Smiths and Shermans, Gannons and O'Learys and Raffertys, Rossis and Milanos, Hofstatters and Cohens and Sinciewiczi. There were engineers and technicians and foremen, and under them were bone and muscle. López and Morelos, Hernández and Núñez, Juárez and Díaz, Suárez and Rodríguez and Fernández, Flores and Rivas — these were the muscle and bone.

This was an army sweating. They loaded the carts and drove the mules and oxen. They dumped the fill and levelled it off. They filled in the swamplands.

It was an army, and it lived upon the dike. They built wattle shacks along the edges, and there they lived, and they brought women from the city, and the women lived there, too.

The men labored by day, driving mules and oxen, dumping fill and smoothing it off, filling in the swamplands. The men labored by day, and the women cooked and carried water.

There was an army, and it lived upon the dike, and at night there was eating and drinking and singing and carousing. There was fighting, too, and there was loving.

There was birth, and there was dying.

There was an army, and by day it labored, and engineers and foremen shouted . . . More fill, they shouted . . . get movin' . . . build a form . . . grab me a whaler . . . start pourin' . . . more gravel . . . more *ce*-ment . . . hey, guy witha straw hat, yousted, whazzer name, comb say yammer? Ya, you! Whadya say . . . Carlos? Okay, Carlos, we gotta pour, saby, pour, like this, you comprendy, concrete, *ce*-ment! Hey, Joe, whaddya know, I gotta guy here acks like he sabies. Letter roll, boys, letter roll, Carlos. . . . There she goes, there she goes, by

God we're pourin' . . . push 'em, Carlos, drive 'em, Carlos, that guy
over there, hey you, Rain-in-the-Face, Sittin' Bull, ya, you, get be-
hinjer baby carriage, start wheelin'. . . . Push 'em, Carlos, drive 'em
Carlos, time is money, Carlos. . . . Time is money, Carlos. . . . Time's
money, Carlos, time's money, time's money timesmoney-timesmoney-
timesmoneytimesmoney.

More fill . . . more fill . . . migawd, ain't this country got no bottom
. . . more fill . . . more fill . . . a good screw . . . more fill . . . drive 'em,
Carlos . . . timeismoney . . . a quart of likker . . . dear honey . . . more
fill . . . azholeofthayooniverse . . . more fill. . . . Dear Honey . . . no
bottom . . . more fill . . . what Ronca can do with thissere whole goddam country, he can . . . more fill . . . a good screw . . . a quart of
likker. . . . Him? Malaria.

I ain't a——n'ya, she was swallered up! Yesser, a whole goddam
Baldwin. What? Yeah, the fill jest mashed out like mush and down
she went. Nuttin' left but bubbles and green slime. What? Yeah,
downa Kilometer 10.

More fill . . . more fill . . . Yeah, in them mountains it's bounta be
better . . . more fill . . . gonna pour . . . drive 'em, Carlos. . . . Hey, you,
easy on that *ce*-ment. . . . Whazzat? Gravel, use gravel, hell, gravel
don't cost nothin'. . . . Yeah, but Chrisake, easy on the *ce*-ment. . . .
Drive 'em Carlos, timesmoney . . . Use gravel. . . . Goddam mosquitoes.

Yes, suh! This Ronca ain't so dumb. Don't suppose you all evah
heard tell of Porfirio Diaz? Well, anyhow, this Ronca, he reminds me
of Diaz. What? Yes, suh, that's him. Run Mexico, forty, fifty year.
Tough ol' hombre, he was, but by God, he knew how to put the feah
of God in them greasers. Made 'em work, too. Built railroads like ol'
Ronca's a-doin' down heah, and cleaned out the bandits, and by God,
you know, that country up theah was damn near safe for a white man.
Had a bunch of rahght smart Rurale boys like these heah federal
po-lice. Chris', any ol' greaser touch a white man, boy, howdy, they
strang him from the first ol' oak tree come handy. Howzat? Yeah,
hell, he got overthrowed. Yeah. Chris', you know how hit is in these-
hear greazer countries, a revolution's bound to come round sure's
Christmas. Yeah, I s'pose one of these heah days ol' Ronca'll git hisn.

You, Carlos, we gonna pour . . . more gravel . . . more fill . . . grab
me a whaler . . . yeah, but accordin' to the specifications . . . to hell wid

that, just go easy on the *ce*-ment . . . more fill . . . a quart of likker. . . .
Dear Honey . . . why, sure, in them mountains it's bound to be better
. . . yeah, like ah say, that goddam snake was twenty foot or ah ain't
from Texas . . . more gravel . . . we gonna pour . . . drive 'em, Carlos,
sweat their bloody heart out, drive 'em, boot 'em ina ass . . . more fill.

Well, fer Chrisake, I seen it wid my own eyes. Yeah, back at
Kilometer 342. Like I say, they was drivin' a well, and it just come
belchin' out. All black, it was. Splattered to hell and gone. You
heard me, goddam it, you heard what I said. Hell, yes, I know erl
when I see it. So, this track crew was pumpin' a hand car, and by
God, what they did when they seen it, they took off down that fill
to stake theirselves a claim. Belong to? Now fer Chrisake, how do
I know who that country belongs to. Belongs to Ronca, don't it?

There was an army sweating, and they pushed a dike across the
swamplands and laid a track of steel upon it. They laid a track of
steel across the middle of marshes and monsters moved upon it.

They pushed a dike across the swamplands and reached solid
earth where jungles grew, and there were tall trees, and the tops were
laced with vines.

High noon, and the sun was out of sight.

High noon, and it was gloomy in the jungle.

There were tall trees and hard trees. There were ebony and
mahogany, rosewood, and Spanish cedar. There were zapotes chicos
dripping gum, and there were rubber trees and bananas set in groves.

There were engineers and foremen shouting. There was an army
sweating . . . more axes . . . more oxen . . . logs movin' . . . top them
trees . . . damndest hardest wood . . . sure could make a bar . . . more
axes . . . more oxen . . . a good screw . . . a quart of likker . . . drive
'em, Carlos . . . deadly poison. . . . fer de lance. . . . Him? Malaria. . . .

Fill? What'n hell we gonna do with fill? Just take a look through
this-here transit. . . . Tell the super we gotta have picks. . . . What? Oh,
lessay a coupla hunnert . . . seen that labor they recruited? Right outa
the jungle, no kiddin'. Damn near bare-assed, 'ceptin' maybe diapers
. . . drive 'em, Carlos, swing them picks . . . quart of rotgut . . . raise
ya ten. . . . Oh, him? Malaria. . . .

Well I was talkin' to the district engineer and he seen the contrack.
Yeah, it says that, subsoil rights 'n all. It says they gotta lease for

thirty years. Yeah, oil, too, and every other goddam thing. Naw, not *our* outfit, we only gotta sub-contrack. Just lay the track, and we're washed up. Top guy? I dunno who the hell it is. Some big outfit that put up the dough. Yeah, must be Prettyman, I guess. Well, why not? What the devil would these-here greasers do with oil, anyhow?

Who, Ronca? I dunno, but he must of got an angle somewheres.

There was an army sweating, and they bored through a jungle where tall trees grew, and the tops were laced with vines. They bored through jungles where the sun was out of sight at noon.

They reached savannas that were wide and open, and they pushed steel across.

They reached foothills and began to climb.

There were gorges cut by swollen rivers, and there were cliffs and crags and condors soaring overhead. There were rattlesnakes sunning on a ledge. There were landslides.

There were cliffs and crags and the cordillera just behind.

There was the Fire Mountain, and its foot was in the tropics, while its peak lay buried in snow.

See that important looking guy over there talking to the super? Well, that's our boss man, the number one big shot in this job. Prettyman? Oh, hell no, that ain't Prettyman. That's Frank Nash. Prettyman, he don't fool around with no inspection details, he just sits in the Fifth Avenue office on his fat butt and pulls the strings. Well, let's getter rollin'.

There were engineers and foremen shouting. There was an army sweating. Dynamite? Hell, it'll take more'n that . . . never seen such goddam mountains in all my life. . . . Where'd you say? Texas? Why, you lyin' sonofabitch, they don't have no mountains in Texas. Not like these here, they don't. . . . It'll take three years to lay a track up them cliffs if it takes a day. . . . Me? Hell, I'm an old hand with powder . . . quart of likker? Hunnert pesos at the very leas'. . . . Goddam you-all, lay off'n that leetle squaw, or I'll bus' yo' ass. . . .

Hell, you ain't seen no gooks 'tall 'till you seen one of them Xlalak braves. . . . Why, sure, they file their teeth and every goddam thing. . . . Rahde the sweetes' leetle ponies this-heah sahde of Laredo . . . won't work, though, won't do a stroke of work . . . slit a guy's t'roat when he ain't lookin'. . . . Mountains? I never seen such mountains. . . .

Betcha they're two-three mile high. . . . Me? Ten whole goddam months to go. . . . Yeah, if I ever get my fat butt outa here, you ain't never gonna see me again, not down here, you ain't . . . picturesque, hell, if you was to ask me, I'd tell you it was the azhol of the god damn universe. . . .

Him? Malaria. . . .

Yeah, s'fact, they brang a hunnert wheelbarrers for them new laborers and the pore dumb sonofabitches loaded 'em up and carried 'em on their head!

I was talkin' to one of them survey parties, and the engineer, he said he'd rather lay out a railroad through the Grand Canyon some place. Yeah, them gorges 're that steep!

Hey, Carlos, c'mere. Over here t' the shack a minnit. Take a look at this, now. Know what it is? Well, it's dynamite, that's what it is. Enough to blow this whole goddam country to hell 'n gone, pretty near. Well, what I wanted to know, I thought maybe you'd like to handle it. Huh? No, no, I mean set it off. Look, now, take a look up ahead. See what we're comin' to? See them rocks? Well, we gotta tear 'em apart. We gotta make number two gravel outa them rocks. We gotta blast a leetle old grade right across the side of them mountains.

Naw, ya gotta drill deeper'n that. Yeah, 'nother half a foot. . . . Carlos, I guess you told all these-here braves of yourn what's gonna happen. I guess you told 'em they gotta go hide their ass behind a tree. . . . Tighter 'n that, Carlos, pack 'er in tighter 'n that. . . . Yeah, now cut her back this-a-way. . . . There, that's about right. . . . Yeah, Carlos, that's right. Now run like hell.

Sure gotta big laugh today. They're blasting Kilo 520, ya know. Yeah, they was showin' one of these-here Injuns how to handle powder. Well, anyhow, they slapped a couple dozen sticks into the side of a cliff and touched her off, and say, by Jesus, you oughta seen them Injuns clear out. Reckon they figgered the world had come to a end. Naw, not the guy that was settin' it off, I mean them headhunters they drug outa the jungle a while back. Bet more'n one of them braves hadda change his diapers.

Okay, now, look here, see that saddle way up in them mountains? Well, that's a little more'n nine thousand feet up, and that's where we're a-goin'. How far? Lemme see, well, I'd say not more'n thirty mile the way the crow flies. By the grade? Jesus, I dunno, maybe coupla hunnert.

Ya gotta git after them monkeys of yourn, Carlos, you gotta drive 'em, you gotta get all that busted rock outa here. . . . Track crew's been layin' on their ass coupla months. . . . We gotta get ready to blast, Carlos, yeah, say about a hour.

Who? Oh, that important-looking guy talking to the super? That's Frank Nash. Yeah, I'd give ten years of my life to have his dough. Why, next to old man Prettyman, he's. . . .

Jeez, that was a helluva landslide they had back at Kilo 500.

Hey, Spike, how many more years you reckon this job's gonna take?

Hell, yes, he's a gonner, but let's get him out, anyhow. . . . Yeah, I'd say he was just about in the middle of this-here rubble. . . . Chris', it was better when these Injuns was scared to death, what I mean, a man had less to worry about. . . . Watch it, there's his foot. . . . Pore bastard, where's that gas can? Lookit, now, let's sprinkle him good before ya toss that match. Last guy didn't burn so good.

O'Leary? Which one you mean, the section chief or that engineer bastard? Oh, him, hell, he went back to the states a year ago, maybe more.

By God, they'd better get in another batch of quinine quick.

Yeah, ya gotta hand it to him, that guy Carlos is pretty smart for a Injun.

Last name? I dunno, Cheat-your-aunt or some goddam thing.

That landslide on Kilo 510 sure was a pisseroo!

Thirteen more months, and my contract says I'm goin' home.

D'ja hear about that refinery they're putting up at Kilo 10? Prettyman? Naw, he sublet to some California outfit.

A thousand pesos says my track crew'll have steel laid across that goddam pass by Christmas.

2

FROM JUNGLE-COVERED FOOTHILLS the railroad climbed toward La Cumbre which was nine thousand feet above the sea. The grade was a narrow shelf cut in the face of cliffs, and it was a series of curves and bends and tunnels and switchbacks. Engineers claimed that in the whole world there was not another like it, and experts came from Europe and the United States to inspect.

Boss of the grade crew was Carlos Chichayan. He was a straw boss, and by day he drove his crew. They blasted and cleared away the rock and levelled for the ballast, and they were a part of an army sweating.

There were also ballast crews and sleeper crews, and there were the layers of steel. There was section maintenance. All together they were an army sweating. They lived upon the grade, this army. Men, women, children lived, died, were born upon the grade. Up and down the right of way they built their shacks, and on the edge of the grade, overhanging space.

The men sweated and pushed the grade ahead, and the women cooked over charcoal grates and carried water, and the children, as soon as they were big enough, also carried water.

The men sweated and pushed the grade ahead, and after a time the shacks were torn down and moved forward to another place.

Boss of the grade crew was Carlos. He had broad shoulders, now, and his chest was deep, and long muscles lay smooth beneath his shirt and breeches. His eyes were brown and quick to move, and his voice was sure from driving crews.

This was Carlos, the grade-crew boss, and the devil had not been to see him now for many months.

He had a shack for his private use, and he had a rough table and a gasoline lantern that shed a brilliant light. He had books in a box by his canvas cot, and after work he would remove his Yanqui boots and sit at the table to read, or perhaps members of his crew would drop in to chat, or a Yanqui foreman or even an engineer.

Whenever the grade had pushed forward and upward a mile or so, he would rip down his shack and have it carted ahead, along with the others.

Just now it was perched on the edge of the grade, and it jutted out over the edge of a cliff where it was propped with two-by-sixes, and Carlos could spit out a back window into the Rio Colorado a thousand feet below. For the canyon here was narrow, and the sides were hard, sheer cliffs, and from below the zigzagging grade looked like knife slashes across the face of a smooth stone wall.

On this evening Carlos was squatting at the grade's edge near his shack. He was gazing down into the chasm below, and his ears heard only the roar of river water pounding against boulders that obstructed its passage through the canyon bottom. The sun had already set behind western crags and ridges, but a purple light, touching the canyon rim and upper reaches of the reddish sandstone walls, merged gradually with black shadows in the chasm's depths. The open box of stone below Carlos had no measurable size, no ratio to anything he had known. The canyon could be small, gouged by a mason's chisel, or big enough to hold the rising moon should it come crashing down before his eyes.

The moon moved higher as he meditated, and the cool, silver light of its rays chased away the purple and probed into canyon depths to the river where it glistened on froth and foam kicked up by rapids. The box of the chasm now was neutral, had lost its color, was as cold and hard and severely chiselled as a gorge upon the moon itself.

The crunch of Yanqui boot on gravel smashed the peace of his meditation. "Hi, there, Carlos! Com'stá?" It was Cohen, a junior engineer. He sat down near Carlos, dangled his lanky legs over the side of the grade. "By God, now, there's a really dazzling sight!" For a silent moment he gazed at the diamond-sparkling river far below. "Why, the best damn artist in all the world couldn't paint that picture, even if he tried. Know what I mean?"

Carlos nodded. He did not feel disposed to talk.

"On a job like this, well —" the junior engineer groped for words " — you know how it is, a guy just gets so he don't even give a good God damn, blasting and pouring concrete and bawling at the goo — men." He stared with eyes half shut at the river which thundered through its constricted channel, and as he stared, he saw a vision growing. "Know what I'd like to do?" he asked Carlos.

"What?"

"Well, if I was running this country," he said, "what I mean, if I was General Ronca, know what I'd do? I'd throw a dam across that river right about down in there." He pointed at a spot where the walls pressed in against the tumbling waters. "You could squeeze enough power out of that river to push Ronca's railroad trains and light half the jungle besides. Yessir, I'd really make something out of this little country. Why, lookit, Carlos, you've got all it takes. You've got oil and steel and power and God only knows what else like tin and tungsten and mercury and zinc, a little coal, even, though I guess it isn't so good at that. But you've got the stuff to make it go, to turn the wheels, to start producing."

Carlos was interested. "Could we do that thing?"

"Hell, why not?" demanded Cohen. "You've got what it takes."

"We do not know how," protested Carlos. "We are a nation of Indians, peasants only."

"Teach 'em!" Cohen retorted. "Hire a bunch of us terrible Yanquis to teach 'em. Hell, there's not a God damn thing on this earth a white man does that a red man can't learn, or a yellow man, either, or a black. May take him a while. Even us Yanquis didn't come right down out of the woods and start making Fords. But damn it, what I mean, there's no reason you guys can't learn."

"We have no money," Carlos complained. "We have to sell concessions. As with the oil, we have to sell concessions."

"Who says so?" Cohen snapped. "It gripes my guts how bastards like Ronca sell you guys out. Hell, you got all it takes, like I said. You got oil and power and iron and tungsten and all the other goddam stuff us Yanquis 're aching to get our fingers at. So why don't you sit on it awhile, drive a real bargain? Get hold of some experts to come down and teach you guys how to run things. Only make sure you guys are boss, so Prettyman and his gang don't get you over a barrel. Hell, it isn't money that runs this world. It's production. It's being able to produce this or that better and faster than some other place. That means guys like you are right up a well-known creek, until you get to learn how to produce."

"It is no easy matter," Carlos insisted. "To learn is no simple thing."

"Hell, no, of course not," admitted Cohen. "But God damn it, Carlos, you guys have gotta begin sometime. Why, three quarters of this sonofabitching world is five — six hundred years behind. India, China, all places like that. Well, they gotta learn fast, and one of these days us Yanquis, we're going to learn that we'd better God damn well teach. What I mean, Carlos, this old world is just one big barrel of apples, and you know what happens when three or four start spoiling. Only it's worse than that. Half or maybe three fourths of the world is spoiling already, like you guys under Ronca."

So they talked there by the side of the Rio Colorado gorge, and after Cohen had left him, Carlos hurried into his shack and lit the lantern and spread a map of the country across his jerry-built table. There it all was in brown and green and black. There was the high cordillera, the Sierra Madre, running east and west across the southern quarter of the nation, and there were the foothills and the savanna belt, and north of the savannas stretched mile after mile of jungle, flat and hot and wet. It was all there, but the rivers were what Carlos saw tonight.

West of the Volcán rose the Río Pongo and beyond it the Río Mosca. They rose at nine or ten thousand feet and gushed down through precipitous ravines and into canyons a thousand meters deep. So it was with the Río Pongo to the west and with the Río Mosca, too, and east of the railroad rose the Río Malo and the Río Cocodrilo, and the Río Papagayo near the border. They pounded toward the lowlands in fierce torrents, and not one had yet been harnessed.

All these rivers flowed northward and emptied into the Caribbean. And flowing southward were the Puma and the Macha, both rising high among the mountains.

Cohen had mentioned power. Well, here was more than even Cohen knew. Carlos sank back in his hand-made chair, and saw power harnessed. He saw the building of dams, the halting of the rivers, the backing up of heavy waters. He heard the turbines whirring, heard the humming of wires under tension, the crackle of lightning harnessed.

Carlos saw all this, and he saw the land transformed. He saw factories built, he heard the grind of great machines, he saw roads and bridges and concrete buildings ribbed with steel. He saw clean white villages with paved streets and closed-in sewers, he saw schools and teachers and children learning. He saw all the things that he had seen pictured in Yanqui magazines and all the things that Yanqui engineers and foremen had talked about.

He, Carlos, would bring these things to be. He would go to school and study, and with knowledge he would build these things. He would go to New York, perhaps, and become an engineer. Or he would study law and enter politics, and in one way or another, he would replace Ronca, break Prettyman, run the government as it should be run, doing as Cohen said.

Sitting in his shack, he forgot about details. How matters came about was indeed a small concern. It was the vision that counted, the picture in his mind of power and gushing oil, of Nacheetl engineers and mechanics tuning motors, of a new nation learning to produce.

3

THROUGHOUT HIS YEARS OF WORK upon the railroad, Carlos had seldom seen the devil, for at night he was tired and ready to sink upon his cot and loosen his muscles and let them rest. When he was tired, his thoughts were plain. "Peace is a simple matter," the devil had told him once. "If one makes no choice, then peace is a very simple matter." So it was. When his body was tired, when his thoughts were small and calm, when body and soul were both at rest, then peace indeed was simple, and the devil seldom came.

After he had talked with Cohen, after he had seen his vision, came nights of tossing, nights of restless thinking. There were nights of engineering, nights of building dams and turbines. In Yanqui boots and leather jacket Carlos was an engineer, and he dammed rivers and erected turbines. He dammed the Pongo and the Mosca, the Colorado and the Cocodrilo, and he backed up heavy waters. He set the turbines humming, strung wires under tension, harnessed lightning, erected factories, saw the land transformed.

There were nights of engineering, and there were also nights of law. There were nights of reading books and trying cases, nights of study and nights of making speeches. There were nights of plotting. He stirred the nation, rallied men around him, and the people rose, tearing Ronca down, putting Carlos in his place. Then Carlos ran the government as it should be run, doing as Cohen said.

Here were two futures as Carlos saw them, and the paths to them were different. He saw them in his nights of tossing, in his nights of restless thinking. Having talked with Cohen, having seen his vision, Carlos sat upon the crossroads, and there the devil came to see him. "Peace is a simple thing," the devil said, "if one does not make a choice. Go back to work and stop the thinking."

Carlos dreamed. The people rose against Ronca, and they tore him down, putting Carlos in his place. That was the way it was when he lay upon his bed at night, and he did not stop to think how far he had drifted from those very people whom, in his dreams, he stirred

160

and rallied. For he had been shut away too long. Behind Don Ricardo's gates he had been a prisoner from the Nacheetl world, and Don Ricardo's study had been a confinement even closer, while on the railroad he had come to live with Yanquis and had bossed a crew of jungle Indians whom he scarcely understood.

Blas spoke to Carlos of these matters when the railway unions were being formed. He was a tough little Indian, this Blas, a hard-muscled track layer in blue shirt and tight-fitting jeans, a greasy shop cap askew upon his head. One Sunday he came to the shack where Carlos was and talked about the workers. "Pues, you know how it is," he said as he stuffed canvas gloves into a hip pocket of the jeans he wore. "A peso a day is not so much. Take your grade-crew chicos, Carlos, see how hard they work. In the morning out they go to the end of the shining tracks, and there they sweat until grey dusk falls, and back they come, tired-tired, with dragging funeral feet, and for all that work, how much does your Yanqui give? A peso only!"

Carlos admitted this. "Yet they could not do so well in the jungle," he pointed out. "A year ago they were half starving in their wattle shacks."

Blas shook his head. "In one's own little hut," he said, "the soul is light like a fountain bubbling. In one's own thirsty field of corn the hardest labor goes fast-fast, like fiesta dancing. Here you have another matter. Here are only rocks hot beneath the sun and sweat about the arms and neck, and in the pantalones one lonely peso does not even jingle. There is also this, Carlos. There is no food except that which is bought within the commissary car. Pues, look about you, chico! We are on a long stone shelf where even mosses do not grow. Well, then, one takes the peso to the commissary car and lays it on the counter. For what, Carlos? For a teeny can of fish!"

"The Yanquis say that prices cannot be helped," Carlos said to Blas, "because food costs so much to move. You know where it comes from, that little can of fish?"

Blas spat. "Sí, pues, I know," he replied. "From far-off Se-ah-tlay comes the tiny can of fish. But in regard to corn, Carlos, that comes from near at hand, and yet the prices – " he waved his arms above his head to show how high they were.

"What you say is so," admitted Carlos. "But what to do?"

Blas touched his nose with a forefinger. "There comes your union," he said. "We organize, Carlos, even as the oilfield workers do. Then we have a weapon, sharp-sharp like a blow-gun dart. When prices get too high, we call a strike."

Carlos was doubtful. "Unions are against the law," he pointed out, "and if we strike, there will be much trouble."

The track layer grunted. "Trouble will be good," he said. "We pay Preeteeman back in his own kind of trade, and that Franknass bastard, too."

This angered Carlos. "I don't know Prettyman," he said, "but Frank Nash is no bastard. He was kind to me when I was a boy."

Blas seized Carlos' shirt front with a grimy hand. "Hombre! Hombre! You are boss too long," he cried bitterly. "You are drunk with Yanqui pay."

Carlos backed against the wattle of his hut. "Bueno, see my grade-crew chicos, then," he said to Blas. "I do not care. They are jungle Indians, Blas. You will find they have ways of their own of fixing things."

Blas released his grip on Carlos' shirt. "That is true," he admitted, "and that is what we do not like. A wasp alone has one stinger only. Well, all right, Carlos, then I go to see your chicos." He left the hut and walked up the grade along the curve of tracks gleaming in the sunlight.

There were many days of work after this talk with Blas. The grade crew blasted and bit into piles of loosened rock with picks and shovels. Tall, long-muscled Indians, the grade crew was, and they moved debris in wheelbarrows or dragged it on fibre mats and dumped it into space beyond the shelf. Thus they worked each day, and while they worked, they sang.

These grade-crew chants were strange songs that no one understood.

> Ye-pe-la-ki-ya-me-kah!
> Ni-mah-ki-mo-ki-la-sah!

So they went, jungle songs, verse after verse, and if one asked the meaning, a grade-crew worker with tattooed skin and loincloth would laugh. "It is wind among the rushes," he would say, perhaps, or "the crocodile king makes love."

Thus they blasted and dug and moved loose rock and sang their songs, and the railroad climbed. From palms to pines, nine thousand feet, the railroad climbed, and it reached El Prado just before La Cumbre.

At El Prado the right of way cut across a mountain meadow, a patch of green among the cliffs. There was a cool stream of water here, and pine trees grew in thickets all around. Already the grade crew was blasting rocks beyond, but the tracks reached just half way across the meadow. There was a siding for the commissary and bunk cars and the caboose where blueprints were, while up and down the stream were workers' shacks, not clinging to the grade, this time, but firm on solid ground.

It was Sunday again, and Carlos sat on the bench before his shack, feet, clad in Yanqui boots, stretched out before him. The stream bed swarmed with women and children washing, while their men folk lay about in pine groves snoozing or talking in voices that were soft and low. As he sat there, Carlos waved to old Nika, a member of his grade crew. The jungle Indian, dressed up for Sunday in cotton blouse and pantalones, waved back. Carlos watched as the old man strode with springy steps toward the commissary car.

The sun was warm against the meadow, and Carlos closed his eyes and dozed. He was soon aroused by the shouting of his name.

"Hey, you Carlos!" It was Smith calling from the open door of the commissary car. "C'mere a minute, Carlos."

When he swung up the iron ladder of the freight car that served as commissary, Carlos saw that Smith was back behind the counter that separated old Nika from the shelves of food. The Yanqui was a short, thick-set man with a nature that was normally friendly. But today his breath was heavy with tequila fumes, and he was clearly annoyed at being disturbed by Nika.

Smith scowled at Carlos. "Ain't this here one of your boys?" he demanded. "Well, goddamit, gimme a general idear of what he's beefing about."

Carlos spoke in Spanish, and old Nika answered in a broken jargon that mixed Spanish with his native tongue. In his hand he clutched a five-kilo sack of beans.

"He says he's paid you already," Carlos translated.

Smith's red face was sweaty, his eyelids swollen as though he had been asleep. "The hell he has."

The old Indian broke into another tirade.

"He says he gives you the same money he gave last time for a sack of beans," Carlos explained.

Smith wiped his forehead with a blue bandana handkerchief. "Don't he know I can't help it if the price goes up?"

Carlos tried to make Nika understand how prices changed, but the old Indian was angry, now, and would not listen. A strange guttural of words came tumbling out, each syllable crowding the next.

"He says he doesn't understand about price," Carlos interpreted. "But his belly wants the same amount of beans for power."

"Tell him I don't have nothing to do with the price," Smith said.

As Carlos tried to explain, Nika tucked the sack under his arm and moved toward the door of the freight car. "Hey, he's gotta pay!" Smith shot out. He vaulted his chunky body over the barrier. Startled, Nika drew back, stumbled, and pitched backward onto the gravel ballast of the road bed. The sack broke open, scattering beans over stone and cinders. For a moment the Indian lay there stunned. Then he climbed slowly to his feet and limped away with all the dignity he could muster.

Carlos returned to his shack and tried to dismiss the whole unpleasant matter from his mind, but whether he read or went to a near-by shack where an all-day poker game was on, he felt uncomfortable, vaguely ill at ease. He was not uplifted when Tomás, a Nacheetl member of the grade crew, slipped into his shack and squatted solemnly upon the floor.

It was a Nacheetl trick to come and sit for an hour or two without uttering a word, but something about Tomás today warned Carlos that this was not an ordinary social visit. Eventually, as dusk was falling, Tomás coughed awkwardly. "Nighttime comes down out of the sky," he muttered, "like a zopilote with its black wings spread wide."

Carlos recognized this as an Indian preface to something more important. He pumped and lighted a gasoline lantern, set it on the table, and watched moths gather about the globe.

Tomás coughed again. "Nika is mad like a bull."

This snatched Carlos' eyes away from the lantern. "So!"

The old Nacheetl grunted.

"There is no cause for anger," Carlos said. "The whole affair this afternoon was a misunderstanding." He was not astonished when Tomás was silent, but he was worried. "What does Nika do now?"

Tomás grinned. "I think tonight he burns a spirit."

After a moment's thought Carlos took a serape from the head of his bed and folded it over one shoulder. "Let's go see Nika," he suggested, picking up the lantern.

Up the tracks a few hundred yards were the green clearings of El Prado. Tomás took Carlos to the shack where Nika stayed. A pine-faggot fire blazed on a dirt hearth, and the lowland Indian was squatting before it, molding a pudgy figure from a lump of clay. Carlos and Tomás sank down on their haunches to watch. The object in Nika's fingers was too crude to bear any resemblance, but Carlos was sure that it was intended to be an effigy of Smith.

The fire crackled and sent sparks flying upward through a hole in the roof. With the nighttime air cold upon his back Carlos moved closer to the flames and spread his palms to catch the heat.

When the figure had been molded properly, Nika laid it aside. Without a word to either of his visitors, he then tore a splinter from a pine slab and began whittling it down to needle sharpness.

"There is no need for anger," Carlos said abruptly. "The Yanqui Smith meant no harm. As he explained, he does not make the price."

Nika kept his eyes upon the whittling.

Absently, Carlos drew designs on the dirt floor with a stick of kindling. "The price depends upon what distance the beans are carried," he said. "Men far away from here decide what the carrying costs, and they are the ones who make the price."

Nika tested the point of his sliver against a calloused thumb. Satisfied with its sharpness, he picked up the clay figure. Like an angry child, he was elaborate in his attempt at ignoring Carlos.

"The beans must be carried far up here upon this shelf of rock," Carlos elaborated. He was growing a trifle annoyed with Nika. "That means the price is greater. We all pay more."

The old Indian held the figurine with his left hand, while with his right he began pressing the sliver point into the brown clay neck. It was as though Nika were slowly inserting a needle into rotten flesh.

Carlos experienced a disagreeable sense of fascination as though he had stumbled unannounced upon a morbid act. Nika's splinter passed into the fat clay neck and pierced the other side in skewer fashion.

A disturbing premonition seized Carlos. He had heard lurid stories about this jungle sorcery. "The Yanqui Smith was drunk," he added hastily. "Men do harsh things when there is tequila in the belly, Nika. You know that."

The old Indian turned slowly to face Carlos. "Tequila is madness from a gourd," he conceded. "That is true." He placed the figurine in a dark corner and added a faggot to the fire. As flames shot upward, lighting the shack, Carlos found himself amused at his own uneasiness. These lowland Indians had strange ways, but there could be nothing dangerous in a squat little figure of clay. "Tomorrow it will all be forgotten," he told Nika, "between you and this Yanqui Smith." He stood up to take his leave.

A fog was dropping low over El Prado as he made his way down the tracks alone, and in the dark and nighttime chill he felt once more a bit of the vague anxiety which he had experienced in Nika's hut. He was relieved to reach his own shack where four walls contained the light and gave it a certain friendly substance.

He had just begun reading when Smith rapped at his door. "Mind if I butt in?" the Yanqui asked. He was cold sober, now, and the biting air had brought an alertness to his eyes that contrasted with the dullness which Carlos had seen that afternoon.

Carlos made room for him to sit on the edge of the cot.

The Yanqui hesitated, obviously embarrassed. "Look here, Carlos, I just want to put myself straight," he said. "I didn't mean no harm. You know how it is when a guy's had a snifter. Hell, I wouldn't hurt that old goo — Injun."

Smith's simple honesty warmed Carlos. Most Yanquis were like that, he thought — so forthright that one felt forced to forgive their brashness and their swagger and their contempt for everything outside their own borders. "I have been to see Nika about this thing," he said. "In a day or two it may be forgotten."

The Yanqui looked relieved. "You really think so?"

Carlos could not be sure. "You Yanquis think we are strange people, and I think we must be because, you see, we think you are very strange people, too."

Smith clapped a knee with open palm. "By golly, I never thought of it just that way."

"Price means nothing to a man like Nika," Carlos explained carefully. "He probably came down to the commissary car for a friendly dicker. That's why he felt insulted. I think you should stay away from him until his anger cools." In the light of his shack, the sense of foreboding had disappeared, but he thought that Smith deserved a word of warning.

"Well, anyhow, like I say, I didn't mean no harm," the Yanqui repeated. "Why hell, Carlos, you know I don't have nothing to do with them prices. I don't even know who does. Probably some old skinflint bastard like Frank Nash."

Carlos laughed. "Mr. Nash gets it from all sides — Nacheetls, Yanquis, everybody. As a matter of fact, I think he is a very good man." He told Smith something about Don Ricardo and his friendship for Mr. Prettyman's agent in San Marcos.

"I don't know nothing about Frank Nash except only what I see," Smith admitted. "I always figured he wasn't in any misery, being he's Prettyman's number one man down here."

Thus Carlos and the Yanqui chatted for an hour or more, and the young Nacheetl was even a trifle disappointed when Smith decided that it was time for bed.

"Drop down to my shack some night for a copacita," Smith suggested. He was standing in the doorway, snapping his flashlight on and off.

Carlos promised. He went to bed in a cheerful mood, and he even lay awake for a time planning in his mind a trip that would take him to New York and Chicago and all the other fabulous cities where Yanquis lived.

It was a shock when he learned the next morning that Smith was dead.

A guard had found the Yanqui stretched out between the tracks, the gleaming flashlight lying among cinders near at hand. There was no apparent mark upon the body, and it was generally assumed that his heart had given out. Carlos felt his eyes drawn irresistibly toward the short, thick neck, and he thought — but he wasn't sure — that there was a dart prick about an inch below one ear.

4

Two DAYS before Christmas the grade crew reached La Cumbre, and the track crew followed. They laid a tie upon the exact summit, and Mr. Nash arrived to drive a last spike before the whole army of workmen began to celebrate. There was a solemn little moment during which Mr. Nash said a few words to the effect that they had pushed up to La Cumbre, carving a railroad out of solid rock, that now it was all down grade to San Marcos, and that he hoped Christmas would be a happy day for every man and woman and child who lived along the tracks.

Carlos stood aside a respectful distance during the driving of the spike and during Mr. Nash's speech, and all the time he was wondering whether or not he should go up and introduce himself to the famous Yanqui. Somehow it didn't seem right for a sweaty grade foreman to press himself upon this altogether guapo gentleman with the blond mustache so carefully trimmed, with the important-looking business suit, with the white shirt and dark blue tie.

Yet Carlos knew that Mr. Nash was a friendly man. There was not only the memory of long ago when the distinguished Prettyman agent had extended a genial hand to Don Ricardo's gate boy; there was also the friendly, soft-spoken Mr. Nash chatting with the district superintendent here by the trackside. Surely there could be no harm in approaching a man like that. Carlos stepped forward to introduce himself.

Mr. Nash listened attentively while Carlos explained who he was, and the blue eyes began to twinkle. "Why, yes, I do remember!" he exclaimed heartily. "You watched Don Ricardo's gate for many years." He asked Carlos a number of questions about his job. "Come around

168

to my office," he said, "as soon as the railroad is finished. There is always something for a young man like you."

The Yanqui was such a simple, friendly man that Carlos forgot his usual shyness. "I have saved some money," he said. "Perhaps I shall prepare for the university."

Mr. Nash exchanged a sly wink with the superintendent. "So much the better! Come around after you've been to school, and we shall have to pay you more."

Carlos left in a delighted daze. What magnificent men these Yanquis were! He whistled a tango as he headed for the cluster of shacks that lined the tracks just below La Cumbre. It was almost Christmas, and the sun was setting, and lights started to gleam in wattle huts and in the bunk cars that had been shunted onto a siding. There were lanterns that the engineers and foremen had lit, but most of the lights were candles and torches of ocote pine.

There were open fires, too, for at nine thousand feet the nights were cold, and about each fire were men and women and children with fingers extended over the flames. Older men sat hunched under their serapes, while their women boiled coffee, and children, many of whom had been born somewhere along the right of way, stood close to the crackling flames.

Older men sat hunched under their serapes, but the younger ones were up and down the tracks, singing, laughing, tipping bottles of colorless tequila, quarrelling among themselves. They were up and down the tracks or crowded into gambling shacks or searching for whores.

For two days and nights there was no work, but there was laughing, and there was singing, and there was fighting along the tracks. Now and then a knife flashed in the firelight; now and then blood spilled across a tie. And all this had come about because the tracks had reached La Cumbre and it was Christmas Eve and men were tipping bottles in celebration.

Scattered up and down the grade for two miles was a platoon of Ronca's soldiers. Barefooted, they padded back and forth in pairs, Mauser rifles slung, but along the tracks there was knife fighting just the same.

There was knife fighting, and there was praying.

Jesucristo hung in many of the shacks, a burning candle at his feet, and it was Christmas Eve, and there was praying.

Carlos had a shack for himself alone, and a rough table, and a gasoline lantern that shed brilliant light.

He was sitting at his table, and one of the Gannons was opposite.

"Carlos, I'd give six months' pay to be in my home town tonight!" This Gannon was young, and he was engineer for the grading crew. "Six months' pay! You can't even imagine what it's like with the streets covered with snow and the holly out and kids singing Christmas carols under the window." He poured a thimble glass of tequila from a bottle that was on the table and downed it quickly.

"I heard," Carlos said. "Last Christmas I heard, and the Christmas before, and the one before that I heard, too. At Christmas every Yanqui gets drunk and talks of how he wishes he was home. Three Christmases I have heard."

"Do you know where I was then? Three Christmases ago, I mean. I was home — outside of *De*-troit. Just a college kid home for the holidays, Carlos. Golly, though, I guess that doesn't mean much to you, at that."

"This year *De*-troit," Carlos said. "Last year it was Greenville where the grading engineer came from, the year before, Kokomo, and the year before that Brattleboro."

"I guess you get kind of tired listening to us guys weep," Gannon admitted. "Gee, Carlos, you ought to see that country up there. It's like — it's like — hell, it isn't like anything else in this whole damn world. Guess you don't exactly know what I'm talking about, but damn it, if you could ever get out of this stink hole and see for yourself, Carlos, you'd know what we've been talking about."

"I think I know a little," Carlos said.

"Yes, I guess maybe so," Gannon sighed. "Bet you've seen a hell of a lot of Yanquis come and go. Well, anyhow, we're getting you your railroad built. You know, we might make something out of this country, Carlos. Did you ever think of it that way? You have a railroad, now, and two or three pretty good refineries, and those swamps down there, I'll bet they're lousy with oil. You've got to hand it to this guy Ronca, he's a pretty smart Indian."

"A Yanqui would think that," Carlos said.

"Ronca's a pretty smart cooky," Gannon insisted. "As far as that goes, you're a smart sort of character yourself."

Carlos shrugged.

"Honest, I've been watching you, Carlos, and you're not like the rest of these boys. You must have had quite a bit of schooling."

"A little," admitted Carlos.

"You see?" Gannon bragged. "I spotted you right off. I saw you reading books, too." He glanced about the shack. "I see you got some right here." He reached over to a box at the head of Carlos' cot and selected one of the four or five books that were there. He opened it on the table and paged through it listlessly. "What's this, Carlos, what's it about."

"Locke," Carlos told him. "Locke's *Treatises.*"

"Wasn't he some kind of philosopher?"

"Something like that."

"That's what I thought. Academ majors in college used to study about those guys, but I never had time for anything that wasn't practical." Gannon flipped back through the pages and paused at the flyleaf. "Geez, what's this handwriting, I can read that. Look, it says 'to Carlos from something Ricardo something, *magna est veritas, et prev — prevalebit.*' What do you know, I can almost read Spik! You know, if I was to — "

"Listen!" Carlos interrupted. "There is a train on the grade."

Gannon cocked his head. "Hell, it can't be a train. The section engineer said he wouldn't let any trains up here only over his dead body. I heard him say that."

"It is a train!" Carlos stepped out of his shack, and Gannon followed.

A thousand feet below them a headlight stabbed through the night and lit a long strip of rock wall.

A train!

The word spread.

A train on the grade!

Carlos and Gannon swung into the section engineer's caboose on the siding.

"Over my dead body!" the section engineer was yelling into a phone. "Yeah? Well, the district superintendent can kiss my anca before I'll let a freight over this section on *my* responsibility. You know how these landslides are. Whole —— mountain's liable to give way any minute. There ain't no reason for running a freight up here, anyhow. What? Say that again, will ya? No kiddin', well, I guess that's a different story. Naw, I won't say nothin'. Not a word. Okay — okay! Yep, do the best I can."

The engineer slammed the receiver down on the hook. "Son-of-a-bitch! Hey, you, Carlos, you're the man I want. Yeah, listna me, now, you get your crew together or any bunch of men you can lay your hands onto and knock together three, four stock chutes — you know, to unload horses outa freight cars with." He grabbed his hat and jumped down out of the caboose.

Gannon gaped. "Now just what in hell would anybody want to unload horses in this goddam place for!"

Men, women, and children were milling about in the pass and up and down the grade. They all heard the puffing and wheezing of the locomotive, and they were talking and shouting and peering over the cliff at the headlight that stabbed through the night.

Carlos nabbed a couple of men here and a couple of men there. Some of his crew were drunk, and some were whoring, and some had gone to mass, but he nabbed a few and went to work. He sank piles into loose ballast and nailed down platforms and ramps, and when he had finished one chute, he dispatched his crew to build another.

Meanwhile, the freight was laboring up the grade. Men, women, and children peered over the cliffs and watched its progress. They watched the headlight stabbing through the night, and they waited while it passed through a tunnel, and they saw the red glow of hardwood coals dropping out of the firebox. They heard the puffing and the wheezing of the locomotive, and they listened for the shrill of the engine driver's whistle.

Carlos finished the fourth of his chutes, and a half-hour later the freight rounded its last curve before the pass. Women and children squealed as the headlight beam blinded their eyes, and dogs backed away, whining, and barefooted soldiers padded up and down, clearing the tracks.

A shout was raised. "Viene! Viene el tren!"

It was terrifying.

Up the last stretch of track wheezed the monster, and the sight was terrifying to see.

The driver eased his locomotive into the pass and nosed it up to the barricade where the tracks ended. Carlos stood back and watched.

The last car was a passenger car, and a man swung down the steps. He carried a lantern, and the rays glistened upon the buttons of his tunic and upon insignia about his shoulders and throat.

Carlos saw that he was an officer of the federal police.

He stood there, lantern in hand, and he had black boots that gleamed, and he had a uniform of powder-blue, and the butt of his pistol was ivory white. He spoke to the section engineer, and the section engineer nodded. A sergeant swung out of the passenger car and blew a whistle.

The word travelled. Man whispered to man, and woman to woman. They backed away a little, and whispered among themselves. "Federal police! Sí, sí, in San Marcos, a revolution! A whole squadron from Santa Cruz! To San Marcos to quell a revolution!"

The squadron detrained by the light of lanterns, and the men set about unloading their horses.

"A revolution!" The word was passed in whispers. "A revolution in San Marcos!"

V. Stone Pyramid

CARLOS TIED HIS BOOKS and a few other small possessions into a bundle, filled a calabash with water, and slipped away from La Cumbre. Merging into darkness beyond the locomotive's beams, he followed a short-cut trail which wound downward toward deep canyons and arid desert country in the direction of Zalapec and Xiltak and the city of San Marcos on beyond. It was a short-cut path along the fringe of Xlalak country, and by taking it, Carlos was certain that he could reach San Marcos before the federal police.

There was a trail cut deep into volcanic soil by the pack trains of three centuries and by Nacheetl runners. It dropped down from the oaks and pines of La Cumbre into the mesquite country below. Carlos travelled rapidly, and his eyes, growing large with the dark, saw junipers give way to pitahaya and organ cacti, and he saw massive buttes looming on either hand.

The sky was clear, and after a time the moon appeared in quarter phase. He travelled rapidly, and he heard no sound but the crunch of his Yanqui boots upon the cobbled floor of the trail and now and then a coyote yipping in the distance. He travelled rapidly, and the moon travelled, too, and by the time the moon had reached the west, Carlos found himself on a ridge above a narrow valley where a tiny lake glistened silver in the night.

There was a village directly below him, and as he loped down the trail through green pastures and fields of corn, Carlos realized with a pang that he was approaching Zalapec. Among all the adobe houses there was not a single burning torch, but each building shone clear white in the moonlight. Passing near the council house, he saw the hut where his mother lived with Lorenzo Reyes. Momentarily he felt an impulse to go close, to stop, even, and see her, but a dog barked

174

near by and threatened to arouse the whole village, and he was reminded that one who had killed his brother would not be safe in Zalapec.

He went down the trail to the river, and when he had crossed, he climbed up cactus slopes beyond. When dawn broke, he had reached oaks and pines, and soon he came out upon the ridge whence, as a small boy, he had first seen the smooth, white slopes of the Fire Mountain. This morning they were painted pink and red by the first faint rays of a rising sun.

The trail wound through a series of precipitous canyons. From far below came the booming echoes of a river tumbling through rocks and narrow gorges. Rapidly Carlos made his way downward, and the distances, he found, were not as great as he had remembered from his boyhood journey so many years before.

He skirted the edge of a butte and was coming out upon the plateau when two horsemen appeared from the shadows.

Horses and riders moved like dark ghosts, and they pulled up, one on either side of Carlos.

"A 'onde va?" asked one. He spoke softly, with a sprightly lilt.

"A San Marcos, no más," Carlos replied.

As they talked together in another language, Carlos recognized the liquid singsong of a Xlalak dialect. After some discussion, the taller speaker turned back to Carlos. "Come with us," he said in Spanish.

Carlos studied his captors. They were lank, straight men in white shirts and pantalones, with leather belts and spurred boots, with sombreros a-tilt at jaunty angles. Their faces were long and narrow and brown, their noses thin. "I go to San Marcos," Carlos told them.

The horsemen talked together in their native language. The taller one took out a tobacco pouch and yellow cigarette paper and rolled himself a smoke. The horses tossed their heads until the silver on their bridles jingled. They were high-strung mountain ponies sensitive to their riders' movements. It was clear enough that they did not like this waiting.

Both Xlalaks had fixed their eyes on Carlos, and he felt uneasy beneath their hostile stares. The shorter one jerked his head in the direction of the Fire Mountain. "Come!" he said.

"I go to San Marcos," Carlos repeated.

"There is revolution in San Marcos," the taller Xlalak said. He drew a finger across his throat and grinned, and in the moonlight, Carlos saw that the man's teeth were filed to a point.

"Come with us," the shorter one said again. He stirred slightly, and his horse responded by edging sidewise and nudging Carlos with a shoulder.

Carlos moved along, following the taller Xlalak, and the other came close behind. There was a faint trail through the mesquite, and they followed it to the westward, and Carlos saw the white slopes of the Fire Mountain looming before him.

For an hour or more he moved along with the riders who led him into a small box canyon where there was a water hole in the middle of a grove of stunted oaks. A horse, securely hobbled, grazed near by, and a camp fire smoldered in an open spot among the trees. A third Xlalak sat up on the spot where he had been lying, rubbed his eyes, and yawned.

"Sh'lau mala?" asked the sleepy one.

The taller rider answered in a long singsong of Xlalak syllables. He and the other rider dismounted and squatted near the fire.

There was a long silence. The sleepy one poked the fire, added a bone-dry stick, and moved a pot of frijoles nearer the coals. The other two lighted yellow cigarettes.

After a time the sleepy one spoke. "You are Yanqui," he stated in Spanish.

Carlos shook his head. "Nacheetl, only!"

After another silence, one of the riders reached down and felt of the boots that Carlos was wearing. There was more discussion in Xlalak, after which the sleepy one said, "Only Yanquis wear such boots."

"I am Nacheetl," Carlos insisted.

The sleepy one was now quite awake. He looked at Carlos out of the corners of his eyes, slyly. "You work for the Yanquis," he said. "You work on the railroad."

Carlos nodded. "For three years I am working on the railroad."

The one who had been sleeping shrugged. "It is the same," he told Carlos. "Your skin may be Nacheetl, but your heart is Yanqui."

"In what manner?" asked Carlos.

"You drive steel bars into our country."

"The railroad goes to San Marcos," Carlos told them.

"Into Xlalak country steel bars are driven."

Carlos shrugged. "I go now to San Marcos only."

"Why do you go to San Marcos?"

"San Marcos is my place of living."

The taller of the riders grinned. "In San Marcos is revolution!" Again he ran a forefinger across his throat.

"I know," Carlos said.

"Then why do you go to San Marcos?" asked the other rider.

"I am Nacheetl," Carlos insisted.

"José Ronca is Nacheetl!" The fire tender spat.

"José Ronca *was* Nacheetl," Carlos corrected.

"Has he changed his skin?" asked the tender of the fire.

"He has changed his heart!"

The three Xlalaks chuckled.

Carlos felt better. He looked closely at the fire tender; this time his own eyes were those that had the slyness. "At La Cumbre are federal police," he said.

The fire tender stirred the frijoles and moved the pot away from the fire a bit. No one spoke.

"At La Cumbre, *sí!*" Carlos added.

"Federal police," the fire tender said slowly, "They are everywhere, federal police."

"At La Cumbre are many horses," Carlos expanded. "At La Cumbre is a full squadron."

"La Cumbre is a strange place for horses."

"They do not stay," Carlos said. He waited for one of the Xlalaks to question him further, but none of the three spoke. After a time, Carlos added, "They go to San Marcos."

At this, the fire tender spoke rapidly to the riders, and they answered, pointing toward the trail from La Cumbre and the spot where they had found Carlos.

"They go to San Marcos to stop the revolution," Carlos charged. He watched the three Xlalak faces closely. "It is a great pity that no one is hiding beside the trail among the buttes."

The fire tender spoke quickly to the riders, and the taller one got up from his haunches and went to unhobble the horse that was grazing near. Then the fire tender asked, "At what moment do the federal police come?"

"In my warm footprints," Carlos replied.

Within a few minutes the third horse was saddled. The fire tender mounted and motioned Carlos onto the croup behind him. All three animals set off at a canter. They picked up the trail through the mesquite, slowing up as the growth became denser. The way back seemed long to Carlos, and indeed, the sun was several fingers above the horizon before they reached again the butte where the Xlalaks had first appeared from the shadows.

"E-e-e-yah!" shouted the fire tender. "Li mee-na-a-a-e sna-lu-u-u-u-ma-li-sha-a-a-yu poli-ci-i-i-í-as fe-de-ra-a-a-a-a-a-les!"

All three swung from their ponies and examined the hoof marks that had chopped up the trail. They talked rapidly among themselves in Xlalak, pointing toward San Marcos, and Carlos thought they were going to follow, but after much discussion and some hesitation, they remounted their ponies and turned aside. Carlos was undecided whether or not they had set him free. He dismounted and took a few experimental steps. "I go to San Marcos," he said.

The fire tender raised a hand. " 'di-ó-o-o-s!"

The other two grinned, and the taller ran a forefinger across his throat. The fire tender motioned toward San Marcos. "Go, amigo!"

Carlos glided away in a smooth, Nacheetl lope until, having left the Xlalaks well behind, he sat down on the edge of the trail and removed his boots. Then he tried walking upon the cobbles with his bare feet, but the soles had grown tender from years of wearing shoes. He sat down again, and taking a knife from his bundle, he cut away the soft tops of his boots and shaped them into sandals, using the rawhide laces for thongs. He tested them upon the trail, and they protected his feet.

Now he looked like a Nacheetl.

He proceeded along a trail, which led toward San Marcos through fields of agave. There were adobe houses here and there, and goats in cactus corrals. The people were Nacheetl, and they called out to him as he passed, and he tipped his sombrero and shouted back. Once he paused at a well to fill his calabash, and occasionally he picked tuna or an aguacate to stay his hunger. But most of the time he loped along, pushing distance behind him, and by late afternoon he saw San Marcos on the horizon.

When he had come within a mile or two, he left the trail and entered a field where he stretched out among the agave to wait. It was nearly dusk, and he wanted to enter the city by night and to make his way through alleys towards the house of Don Ricardo.

He watched the setting of the sun, and when night had come, he continued upon his way and entered the city. There was not much change, he thought, but the streets were empty, and only patrols were moving about. He slipped into an alley which as a boy he had come to know, crossed the Bridge of the Holy Saints of the Cross as the guard changed, and made his way to the Central Plaza.

After skirting the Plaza, he came upon the Avenue of All Saints within a block of Don Ricardo's gate.

A burro grazed in the parkway of the Avenue's center, but there was no other sign of life. Keeping within the shadows of buildings and garden walls, he came upon the gate, unperceived, and tugged the bell rope. There was no response. He pushed gently, and it opened with a rusty creak. He stepped inside. The gateway appeared to be unguarded. He moved across the flags where he had slept so many nights, and then his feet touched the gravel roadway in the garden beyond.

A voice barked. "Alto!"

Carlos stopped.

A man stepped out of the bushes. In the dim light of a moon beyond white clouds, Carlos saw the outline of a broad sombrero with tipped up brim, and he saw the gleam of polished belt and the ivory white butt of a pistol. Strong arms pinned his arms from behind, and he was pushed across the court and through to an empty stable behind.

The shed was lit by a lantern. A saddler's bench had been pulled in, and behind it sat a corporal of the federal police.

"He came in at the gate," said the voice of the one who held Carlos in pinion.

"Take off his clothes," ordered the corporal, "and we'll see what he carries."

"In his hand was this," said the voice behind. The bundle was tossed upon the bench.

The corporal untied the corners. There were books inside, a knife, and some sheets of paper, hand written. He examined one of the books, upside down, and as he leafed through the pages, he nodded wisely and grunted with deep satisfaction.

2

THE CELL in which Carlos was locked had stone walls on three sides and stone ceiling and floor, while the fourth wall was an iron grating. It was narrow — two paces wide, and its length was six paces, as Carlos learned through the night from many countings. There was no bed, but in one corner lay a fibre mat for sleeping. A slop bucket served for urine and for movements of the bowels and for vomit if the prisoner were sick. There was nothing else in the cell. Outside in the corridor hung an oil lamp that spread a feeble yellow light.

This was the provincial prison of San Marcos, a part of the old Palace of the Lions built by viceroys in the early days after the Spanish conquest.

Squatting on the fibre mat, Carlos considered the iron and stone that walled him in, and it seemed that the whole Ronquista state was a pyramid of cells. The bottom tier was the peasant tier, and above the peasants were vaults for small freeholders and market vendors, learned men and parish priests. Higher still was a tier for hacendados, officers of the army, politicians, and the greater clergy, and on the apex — General Ronca.

Each man was born into his proper vault of stone and iron, and there, with few exceptions, he was made to stay. That was the Ronca state, and it was a medieval structure, a feudalistic tomb, with a Nacheetl dictator astride the top.

For the first time Carlos understood properly the books on Don Ricardo's shelves, yes, and the volumes he himself had carried with him, and he understood why General Ronca feared them. How long could the Ronquista state tolerate John Locke and his state of nature? "Men living together according to reason, without a common superior on earth!" For a proper state, according to Locke, was a civil compact depending upon the consent of the governed.

There was freedom, Carlos thought. Locke had called for checks and balances to restrain the power of the governing, and the checks and balances implied a doctrine of letting be that Carlos liked.

That was Don Ricardo's creed, and with it he had attacked Ronca's pyramid of cells.

Thus Carlos pondered through the early hours of morning, and at daybreak a guard appeared with water for drinking and a tortilla covered with mashed frijoles, and that was breakfast. While the prisoner ate there were steps along the corridor, and they stopped outside the grating. Carlos looked up. In the yellow prison light stood Father Timoteo!

"Carlos!" It was a greeting of father finding son.

The priest grasped the grating with shrivelled hands that trembled. He was an old man, Carlos saw. The shoulders were bent, the hair, once grey sprinkled, was now long and white. Carlos sprang to meet him. "Father!"

"I heard that you were here," Father Timoteo said. He turned to the guard. "Unlock the door that I may enter."

The attendant put his key in the lock of the grating, swung back an iron door that hung from rusty hinges. Father Timoteo entered, and the grating was closed and locked behind him. He placed a hand on Carlos' shoulder, gazed paternally into the young man's eyes. "Where have you been, Carlos?"

Father Timoteo listened as Carlos explained about his work upon the railroad, and when the story was finished, he felt the long, smooth muscles in the young man's arms. "A man!" he exclaimed. "A real man, Carlos! Tell me, did you find what you were seeking?"

Carlos hesitated. "Sir?"

Father Timoteo searched his eyes with an anxious look. "When you left, you were seeking peace," he recalled. "You came to me on the eve of your departure and told me that you were seeking peace. Did you find it, Carlos?"

Carlos lowered his eyes, scuffed the stone floor with the toe of a sandal. This was a question he was not prepared to answer. "I do not know," he told the priest. "The work was hard labor, and at night the body was tired. At times it is not easy to distinguish between peace and tiredness."

Father Timoteo inclined his head a bit to one side, wet his parchment colored lips. "Before you left," he said, "I was tempted to warn that peace is not to be found in this place or that, nor by crossing mountains nor building a railroad. Peace is in the soul, Carlos, and that is the place to seek it. I was tempted to warn, but I knew also that for you San Marcos was an evil influence so long as you were confronted daily by the tempter. Therefore I bade you go. I trust you have found more peace than you knew."

Carlos looked up. "I trust so also."

"In truth I am not a little disturbed," Father Timoteo continued. "For it has come to my attention that when you were — were apprehended, you had upon your person a number of volumes that are — well, frankly — heretical."

"I had also the testament that you gave."

Father Timoteo folded his hands behind him, gazed abstractedly at the stone ceiling. "I was indeed pleased to learn that," he admitted. "But its presence alone does not nullify your possession of the others, Carlos."

"I had a battle to fight," Carlos said.

The priest gave a quick look into the young man's face. "I trust that you triumphed."

Carlos rubbed his face with an open palm. "I think that I triumphed, Father." He searched the priest's face anxiously. "Where is Don Ricardo?"

Father Timoteo cast his eyes upward with a gesture of despair. "I fear for him, Carlos, I fear for his soul."

"He is dead?"

"I do not know that."

"He is a brave man," Carlos said. "And a good one."

"I do not doubt his courage."

"Why do the federal police occupy his house?"

Father Timoteo sighed. "He was conspiring, I am told. He organized a plot against the government."

"That surely can be no sin," Carlos exclaimed. "To organize a plot against José Ronca can be no sin."

"Hist!" Father Timoteo flicked his eyes toward the attendant in the corridor. "For your own welfare, Carlos."

Carlos shrugged. "It can be no sin," he repeated in a lower voice.

"You do not know the whole story," Father Timoteo told him. "His plot was also directed against the Holy Church."

"It is not always easy to distinguish," Carlos said shrewdly, "between the affairs of José Ronca and the affairs of the Holy Church. How can that come about in the City of God?"

With disturbed eyes Father Timoteo examined the young man closely. "Carlos, Carlos, you have not changed."

"It is a matter I cannot understand."

Father Timoteo paced the length of the cell. "The policy of the Holy Church is not your concern," he chided. "The affairs of the Holy Church are directed from above by greater minds than ours. They are directed for the greater glory of God and the welfare of men's souls over the whole expanse of the earth and through ages of time. How can you and I here in the little city of San Marcos far back in the mountains — how can you and I judge what is best?"

"I certainly cannot believe that the way of Ronca is best. Why, everywhere — "

The priest took a step toward the younger man. "Carlos!" He straightened, throwing back his rounded shoulders, and he seemed to look down from above. "You must mend your ways, Carlos, ere it is too late."

Carlos avoided the old man's accusing stare. "I seek truth."

"And lose faith. I fear that your battle has merely begun."

Carlos felt his shoulders sag. "I am tired of the battle," he said. "All my life it is only battle. On the railroad with pick and shovel the body was often too tired, and yet sometimes at night — again the battle."

Father Timoteo sighed. "I came to administer," he told Carlos, "but I doubt you are ready."

"No, Father."

With both hands the old priest seized Carlos by the shoulders. "You must brace yourself, Carlos, and prepare," he admonished. "While you are here, prepare yourself, I adjure you!"

Carlos did not move. Slowly, reluctantly, Father Timoteo released his grip and called the guard who came and unlocked the grating. As he left the cell, the old man paused. "I shall be back," he promised Carlos. "I trust you to meditate and pray, and when the time is right, I shall come to help."

The gate clanged shut, and Carlos heard the shuffle of Father Timoteo's sandals along the prison corridor. In his own chest he felt the pounding of his heart, and it seemed that whatever he might have found during his years of labor had disappeared during these few brief moments. "Don Ricardo also plotted against the Holy Church!" Carlos sank down upon his fibre mat. Was there a pyramid for the spirit, too?

He was trying to straighten out his thoughts when the guard returned, unlocked the iron door again. "You are coming out," he said to Carlos. He pointed down the corridor.

Carlos hastened toward a solid iron door, while the guard came padding close behind. The door was unbolted and opened from the other side by a federal policeman. "Come with me," the trooper ordered. "You are going to Captain López."

The name meant nothing. "Who is he?" Carlos asked.

The trooper made no answer.

After passing through a series of dim, stone corridors, they came to an open court. They crossed this. The trooper paused before a heavy oak door on the far side. "Captain López is inside," he told Carlos. "When you go before him, you will stand at attention and salute."

Carlos objected. "I am no soldier!"

The trooper gave the door a sharp rap. "You will stand at attention and salute," he repeated.

After a short pause, a voice inside snapped "pasa!"

Carlos entered. The room was large and bare, the only furniture being an enormous desk behind which an officer sat in a carved-back chair. He appeared to be writing and did not look up. Carlos walked toward the desk, stopped a few paces off and waited, chin up, feet apart, arms hanging loosely at his side.

"Why do you not salute?" the officer asked in a voice that was oddly familiar.

"I am not a soldier," Carlos said, "nor a trooper, either."

The officer looked up from his writing. "Ho! Carlos!" he roared. "The same old Carlos! Oh, what a precious billy goat! What a precious mountain billy goat! You won't salute, eh, Carlos? You will not salute your old friend Pepillo! Ho, then, give me your hand as a comrade should!" He stood up and walked around his desk.

Carlos extended his hand, bewildered. "You knew — "

"Ho! You precious chico, of course, what else! When we seize the house of Don Ricardo you are not there. Why? Because for three years you are working on the railroad. Oh, yes, our records know. Cabrón! There is not one little thing our records do not know. Pepillo says to himself, he says, Carlos will be back. One, two, three nights Carlos will be back."

"And then I came?"

"Oh, precious, of course you came! Last night they tell me," Pepillo explained. "I do not disturb. But today, I send for you. Right off I send, as soon as Father Timoteo is gone. Now you do not salute. The same Carlos, the same precious billy goat, he does not salute!"

"You instructed the guard, didn't you, Pepillo?"

"A joke only, I tell you, it was a small joke only."

"Pepillo, tell me this, where is Don Ricardo?"

Pepillo put an arm about his old friend's shoulder. "You have nothing to worry about Don Ricardo."

Carlos drew back slightly. "You have not answered my question."

Pepillo removed his arm and shrugged. "I do not know the exact place, Carlos. Cabrón! I do not. But he will not be hurt."

"Are you certain?"

"Certain! Listen Carlos, you precious one, listen! In this country are many men, but Don Ricardo is Don Ricardo. We all know that. General Ronca knows that. Come, let me show you a thing." Pepillo stepped across the floor and removed the bar from an enormous shutter. There was a squeal of hinges. "Look through this window. Out there in the Plaza — what do you see?"

Carlos caught his breath. "I see — I see an oak tree — "

"Yes?"

" — from which men are hanging!"

Pepillo placed a hand upon Carlos' shoulder. "Those men conspired against the government and the Holy Church," he said. "They sought to overthrow Ronca and to divide church property among the rabble. Now I tell you this, Carlos. Don Ricardo also conspired. Don Ricardo also sought to overthrow Ronca and divide the property of the church."

"He is not there?"

"He is not there. A doctor hangs from that tree, and the writer of a newspaper, and a priest. Think of it, Carlos, a poor, precious little priest. Don Ricardo?" Pepillo shook his head. "Don Ricardo has gone away with his good señora. I do not think he will ever come back." He closed the shutter and reset the bar.

Carlos sighed. "There was so much about Don Ricardo that I did not know."

"A precious stallion," Pepillo agreed. "A precious stallion!" He returned to his desk and sat down. Taking two fat cigars from a drawer, he offered one to Carlos. "No? Then permit me!" He returned the extra cigar to the drawer. Biting the end from the other, he prepared to smoke. "Well, Carlos, you see how it is," he said as he struck a match.

"Yes," agreed Carlos, "I see how it is. I see exactly how it is."

"Bravo, little goat, I knew you would," Pepillo exclaimed. "So, now we have cinched the girth and are ready to mount. Listen, cabron! I have a most precious proposition for you."

"Really?"

"Oh, a precious one." He lounged back in the chair and waved a cigar. "Look, Carlos, with what man do you talk? With Pepillo? With the scrawny little billy goat of under the bridge? No, no, Carlos, not at all. Oh, no. The fact is, you, Carlos Chichayan, are talking with Captain López. Who is Captain López? Well, you might think that Captain López is only Pepillo in a powder-blue uniform. You might think that, but you would be wrong. The truth is that Captain López is a very good friend of — " He winked.

"I think I understand," Carlos said.

"I think you do," Pepillo agreed. "Good, and now for the proposition. How would you like a commission in the federal police?"

"A commission?"

"Yes! A third or second lieutenant, say, or perhaps even a first."

Carlos gaped. "I — I — "

"Cabrón! It is an opportunity, Carlos. Think only that I started out as a trooper. Twelve, fourteen years ago I began as a trooper, and now you will start a grade or two below where I am after all this time."

Carlos shook his head. "I cannot."

"A-a-h, you are going to be a priest, perhaps? I remember now how you ran away the night we were going to Magdalena's. What a bastard of a friend, I say to myself, and then I am told you stay away from women because you are going to be a priest."

"I am not going to be a priest," Carlos said.

"Then why do you wait?" demanded Pepillo. "You do not like Ronca, perhaps. He has sent Don Ricardo away, and you do not like him. I cannot blame you, Carlos. But consider that it is a small matter. Against what Ronca does for this country, it is a small matter only. Ho! I need not tell you what a precious man is this Ronca. You have worked upon the railroad. You have seen oil spouting from the earth. You have also seen the refineries. Jesus, but that is a small beginning! One day you will see roads across the mountains and auto trucks hauling out silver and gold. In the port of Santa Cruz you will see ships from many nations. You will see factories right here in San Marcos. On every corner you will see a shop, in every block a building touching the sky!"

"And in every oak tree a citizen hanging?"

"Oh, Carlos, you are precious! You have never changed. From the days when you would not steal an almsbox you have never changed. You really should be a priest!"

"To give you and Ronca my blessing?"

"You must not be harsh upon the Church," Pepillo said. "In every matter there are two sides. There is the moral, and there is the practical. We keep them separate. The practical is a matter for Ronca to arrange, while the moral — "

"I know!" Carlos interrupted. "But I am not going to be a priest, and I still do not like your proposition."

Pepillo stared hard at Carlos through half-closed eyes. "There is a further matter that you should understand," he said with deliberation. He opened a drawer of his desk and took out a sheaf of papers. After thumbing through them, he looked up sharply. "Do you know about the Falange?" he asked.

Carlos did not.

Pepillo leaned forward across his desk. "You have been to school," he said to Carlos. "You have studied history and know many things that poor Pepillo will never know. Bien, I do not have to explain matters about the glories of long ago, about days when the Spanish Empire ruled the sea. All right, Carlito, then tell me this. Why today are we stupid mountain goats, a banana country for Yanquis to laugh at?"

There was a silence while Carlos considered. "It is a long story," he said eventually. "First of all — "

Pepillo waved his hand with a scornful flourish. "Never mind," he interrupted, "the history is a small matter, Carlos. Let me tell you this. Our precious Motherland — " he tapped the desk with his knuckles — "our precious Motherland is once more a supreme realidad!"

"I do not understand," admitted Carlos.

The officer raised a forefinger. "A-a-ah, Carlos!" he exclaimed just above a whisper, "the old glories will soon return. Believe me, we now become a unit of destiny in the universe, and the Yanquis will never laugh again. Faith is with us."

Carlos examined Pepillo's face critically. Unit of destiny — those were not the words of Magdalena's guttersnipe brother. He paused a moment, forming a sentence. "The Yanquis do not only laugh," Carlos pointed out. "They also build railroads."

Pepillo smiled wisely. "Today, perhaps, but soon now we do not beg from them. No, cabrón! From those Yanqui atheists and their democratic mob we shall no longer beg. They shall beg from us!"

Carlos looked skeptical. "The Yanquis are a powerful nation," he protested. "There is nothing we can do against them."

Pepillo paused to relight his cigar. When it was drawing well, he picked up the sheaf of papers in his right hand and tapped them with the fingertips of his left. "Here we have a weapon, Carlos. Absolute Hispanidad — there is the shaft, and the sharp-sharp point is the Corporate State. That is our weapon, and with it we fight the badness of the world." He selected a sheet from among his papers and handed it to Carlos. "Read this, and you will understand our Acción."

Numbered on the page were twenty-seven points, and as he

skimmed through them, Carlos saw where Pepillo had found his pompous words. The points were a plan, and they were also a promise, and it seemed to Carlos that no man had been forgotten. Liberty was guaranteed along with human dignity and the integrity of man, and work was both a duty and a right for all people. But no political parties, no suffrage, no parliament! Down with the politicians, up with the State! Guard private property, divide the estates! Education for all, every man a soldier. Fight capitalism, slaughter the Bolsheviks. PATRIA! IGLESIA! FAMILIA!

Carlos hesitated. How was one to criticize? Where to begin? "I do not understand," he ventured, "in what manner one does these many things?"

Pepillo smiled warmly. "Pues, I will explain. We gather all men within the State, and there are many grupos. The hacendado and his workers — that is a grupo. The factory man with his laborers — that is also a grupo. They work together, and there is no need to strike." He told how representatives from each grupo would be incorporated into the State and would sit in place of the old-time Assembly. "It is very modern," he added, "and already in Europe it takes the place of worn-out, democratic ways. For Hispanidad, all men together! Faith against Jewish reason and Yanqui materialidad. Magnífico, eh?"

This diatribe against the Yanquis perplexed Carlos. It did not make sense, and yet he had never seen Pepillo more sincere. "I doubt whether Mr. Prettyman will like your program much," he said. He was watching his old friend closely.

The young officer smiled suavely. "Let me show you one little thing," Pepillo replied as he opened a drawer of his desk. He drew out a large, glossy photograph and handed it to Carlos. "Eh, now, tell me what you think of that!"

There were two men in the photograph. One was tall and silver-haired and distinguished, a benevolent-looking gentleman in formal dress. The other man, square-jawed and squat in a military blouse that gleamed with medals, was draping a decoration about his companion's neck. Carlos knew both faces well, having seen them in newspapers and in Yanqui magazines. "When did this happen?" he asked Pepillo.

"Only a month ago, more or less," Pepillo replied. "While Mr. Prettyman was in Rome, he was entertained and decorated, as you see."

Carlos was puzzled and vaguely shocked. "Yet surely Mr. Prettyman would not like that sort of thing — not over here, anyway."

Pepillo spread his palms. "One does not speak for Mr. Prettyman, of course, but why should he object? For a man like him there are worse things than what Il Duce offers. Too much democracy in a country like this is not so good for Yanqui business, and Bolshevism would be the end of everything."

"I do not believe you," Carlos charged. He tossed the photograph onto Pepillo's desk. "After all, what is a picture? It means nothing."

"Perhaps not," Pepillo admitted. "Yet Mr. Prettyman visits Rome, and he visits Madrid, also. Meanwhile, our new order grows, and Mr. Prettyman does not object. He does not apply pressures for the landing of Marines. He does not fly down to San Marcos to stop us. He does not even send Mr. Nash to us with hard words. So what is one to think? On the other hand, let us suppose that Mr. Prettyman does not like, then what? Very well, amigo, let me tell you this!" He levelled a finger at Carlos. "Let me tell you that no one can stop this new order. No, not even Mr. Prettyman with all his mines and railroads and ships. Not all the Yanquis put together, either. You will see."

Carlos found himself both annoyed and pleased with Pepillo's simple honesty. "I do not believe these things," he stated stubbornly.

Pepillo chuckled with expansive good nature. "You will learn, Carlos! Oh, I tell you, it is sweeping the world, this new order, and in ten years our country will be altogether another thing. What plans, Carlos! Believe me, cabronito, you have no idea. One little railway is a small matter, sí pues! There will be roads and factories with wheels turning fast-fast and airplanes and auto cars. There will be battleships that will make those Yanqui fighting boats look like tubs of wood. Oh, we shall have a mighty army, great with proudness."

"We cannot do these things," Carlos protested. "Alone we cannot do them."

With a forefinger Pepillo touched his nose. "We shall have great help!" he promised in an impressive whisper. "So now, Carlos, what about my precious little proposition?"

Carlos shook his head. "Thank you," he replied. "But really, Pepillo, I do not like it."

Pepillo's disappointment seemed real. "Is that a certain matter, Carlos?"

"That *is* certain."

As Pepillo considered this, a new thought struck him. "Perhaps you do not understand," he confided. "In the Corporate State we troopers will have many things to do." He winked slyly. "One could not do better, Carlos."

"Yet I do not like," Carlos insisted.

"Oh?" Pepillo's manner changed somewhat. His eyes lost the sharpness of their focus, and momentarily he seemed preoccupied. "I hope you will not regret," he added absently. He replaced the sheaf of papers and fumbled with another drawer of his desk. "There is yet a matter to be discussed, however." He opened the drawer and took out a number of small volumes. "You have seen these before?"

Carlos blanched slightly. "They are my books," he admitted.

Pepillo opened one and began reading the title. "*The Spirit — of — Conquest — and U-sur — u-sur-pa-tion —* you will pardon, I do not read well, Carlos — by — by — "

"Benjamin Constant," Carlos supplied.

"Yes, and this other is — " he examined a second volume carefully. "This is — "

"The *Treatises* of John Locke."

"Precisamente! and it is forbidden. It is on the Black List. This one, also, and that."

"How about that one there?" Carlos asked. "Is not that also forbidden?"

"That? Why, that is the Holy Bible, Carlos."

"I wondered."

"You joke with me, Carlos, but do not forget!" He raised a forefinger. "One little book can hang even a priest."

Carlos started.

"Bien!" concluded Pepillo. "Now you see how matters are. What do you think of my proposition?"

Carlos hesitated. When he spoke, his tongue and lips were dry. "I-I want no part in your federal police."

"Things might go very bad with you, Carlos," warned Pepillo. "There is still time to change the mind. For friendship's sake, there is still time."

"I-I do not want!" Carlos insisted.

There was a long silence. Carlos felt the heaviness of his own breathing.

Abruptly Pepillo stood up. "Bien, bien, you old mountain goat!" he said good-humoredly. "We shall have to get together again, eh? It is a so short chat. What a shame we have no more time." He took Carlos by the arm familiarly and moved toward the door. It opened as they came near.

Carlos hesitated. "Do I go now?"

"Guard!" called Pepillo. "Show my friend to the gate!" He held out a jovial hand to Carlos. "Cabrón! It is a sorrow to see you go."

"Adiós!" muttered Carlos.

"Hasta la vista!" Pepillo waved gaily. "Hasta la vista!"

3

CARLOS SAT under the sagging colonnade in Magdalena's court, and as he talked with her and drank from a tumbler of red wine, he decided that matters were no longer going well in this house on the Street of Women. The table before him was the same table that he had first seen with Pepillo many years before, but the legs were loose, now, and the top was warped. An afternoon rain was drumming on the tile roof above his head, and a thin drizzle came down through a hole, just missed the table, and bloated a puddle on the dirt floor near his feet.

Magdalena laughed harshly. "In two days it was over," she said. "They had no chance for a revolution." She gulped a small glass of tequila, shook her head clear of fumes, and poured another drink.

Carlos stared dully at the rain-soaked patio. The shower was slackening, and already a mother hen and her chicks were scratching for worms in the loose, dank earth beneath a banana tree. He took a deep breath and held it a moment. The moist air with its sweetish, vegetal aroma refreshed him after his night in the provincial prison. "In what way did Ronca find out?" he asked Magdalena.

Her shoulders shrugged beneath the coarseness of her peasant blouse. "How should I know?" she demanded irritably. "What about my bastard brother, Carlos?"

Carlos described his seizure in the house of Don Ricardo and his night spent in prison, and he told about Pepillo with his impressive desk. He left out nothing, and as he spoke, he watched Magdalena. In her face were lines that in the gloom of a rainstorm looked deeper, perhaps, than they really were. Her teeth were yellow, and one in front was missing. She coughed incessantly, and Carlos smelled the odor of her breath.

"My brother would eat up Ronca's puke," she snarled, "if he thought it would help him any."

Carlos tried to explain to her his feelings for Pepillo. "Pepillo does not forget a friendship," he told her. "He could have put me back in prison. He could have had me hanged."

Something flashed deep in Magdalena's eyes. "He would not dare!"

"You know better," Carlos contradicted. "What Pepillo wishes, Pepillo dares. He has no fear."

Magdalena smiled grimly. "All right, all right! What about Don Ricardo? What did Pepillo say of him?"

Carlos told her what he knew.

Magdalena wrinkled her nose, "I don't weep for him," she said.

"Why?"

Indignation crossed Magdalena's face. "He does evil things against the Holy Church. Salomón Rodríguez told me young Don Juliano is fighting now for the Faith in Spain, but his father does bad things. Pues, about Father Timoteo — did he do nothing for you?"

"He inquired about my soul."

Magdalena tossed her head. "That Father Timoteo is a good man, just the same."

Carlos sipped slowly from his glass of wine, and the liquid warmth was soothing to his fingers. He said nothing about Father Timoteo.

"But he *is* good," Magdalena insisted.

"Yes, I know he is," Carlos admitted. "But I do not like his thinking."

Magdalena shrugged petulantly. "All his life he is working among the poor," she said. "All his life!"

Carlos agreed. "Father Timoteo is a good man. Yet he will do nothing against Ronca."

Magdalena said fiercely, "he is not afraid, Carlos. You know he is not afraid."

"No, Magdalena, Father Timoteo is not afraid," Carlos answered. A network of lightning flashed across the clouds. Magdalena crossed herself. "Father Timoteo is not interested in the welfare of man's earthly body," he continued. "The soul and the life of the soul hereafter — "

"He gives to the poor," Magdalena protested sentimentally. "Always he gives to the poor."

"He gives alms," Carlos agreed. "He gives charity."

"And Don Ricardo! He never gave a peso to the poor."

The patio grew dark under ugly, black clouds. "It is an old conflict," Carlos told her. "It is a conflict of the ages." The rain came spilling down, now, and the chickens retreated beneath the colonnade.

Magdalena sighed. She was growing mellow as she drank. "I do not understand," she said. "But who am I? A whore only, Carlos. I live to please men, not to cure their troubles. About you, Carlos, what now do you plan to do?" She crossed herself again as a bolt of lightning glowed in the sky like a red hot fish hook.

"I do not know, Magdalena. For certain I do not know." Carlos spoke through a roll of thunder.

"You will not be a priest?" she asked.

Carlos shook his head. "I have saved money," he told her. "I shall prepare for the University."

"What, Carlos? What will you study?" The tequila had brought a warm glow to her face, and she was feeling young again.

"On the railroad, at times, I thought to be an engineer."

Magdalena scowled. "Engineer! No, Carlos, no, not an engineer."

"To build is good," protested Carlos, "and it is a great satisfaction for the soul."

"Engineers have slept in my house," Magdalena said. "They have slept with my girls and with me, also. I know engineers, Carlos. You would not be happy."

Carlos watched the gathering of rain water in miniature lakes and torrents on the patio floor. "At times I thought to be one," he reiterated, "but again, I thought to study law. There were nights I did not sleep for thinking. There were nights of building roads and bridges, and there were also nights of law. I think this, I think that, I dream this, I dream that. I build a bridge, I try a case, I fall upon my knees and pray. I tear my soul, Magdalena, all my life I tear my soul. This way, that way, night and day I tear it."

"Even the hoofs of a mule point in one direction," Magdalena sniffed.

"Which direction?"

"Law," said Magdalena firmly. "You must study law, Carlos."

"Why?"

"I do not know why, I feel only." She searched the calm brownness of his eyes. There was more of sureness in them than she had seen before he went to work. There is tearing inside, she thought, but there is also more of strength.

"I need a reason."

Magdalena sighed impatiently. "What are reasons? I do not understand reasons. But men I know. All my life I am dealing with men. Rich men, poor men, good men, bad men. You would be surprised, Carlos, at the men I have known. With men I talk, with men I weep, with men I laugh, with men I sleep. Men are happy, I feel their joy; men are sad, I feel their sorrow; men are afraid, I feel their fear. You see men upon the street, you see men within their clothes, you see them behind a desk. I see men upon my breast. I see them like tiny babies upon my breast."

"You were wrong about Ronca," Carlos chided. "And about Don Ricardo, too."

"I never slept with Ronca," Magdalena answered sharply. "Nor with Don Ricardo, neither."

"Must you sleep with men to know them?"

"A man making love is a flute playing a tune," Magdalena explained impressively. "There is music."

"And the tunes are different?"

"Yes, there is simple music, over and over, the same, always the same. There is music that is sweet and soft. There is music that scratches the ears. There is sad music, too, and music that stirs to fight."

"In me there must be discord," Carlos said.

"Did you ever hear a madman play?" Magdalena asked. "Did you ever hear a madman play upon a flute?" Her eyes grew large and soft.

"Never."

Magdalena placed a hand on Carlos 'wrist. "Let me tell you this," she said with mawkish solemnity. "In the village where I was born a madman lived. He had seen the devil himself. When he was a tiny baby only he had seen the devil himself, and the fear was in him and would not come out. When he was a man, he was yet a little boy, and he ran wild upon the streets." She stopped as a gust of wind blew rain

beneath the colonnade. Carlos moved their chairs and the table close
in against the house.

"He cut himself a reed," Magdalena continued, "and from it he made
a flute, but the holes were wrong, and there was no proper spacing.
He sat in the plaza by a fountain and blew upon his flute. Screech-
ings and squeaks, and growls and snorts, and there was no music in
him. It sliced the ears, and the glassblowers drove him away. His
high notes smashed their ware, and they drove him away from the
shop. You see, Carlos, what his soul had become? It was — it was — "

"Discord?"

"—the flappings of a rooster that has lost its head," Magdalena said
with emotion. "Yes, he was only a madman, and the people laughed,
and the people stoned. For many years he was a madman blowing a
flute, and then a miracle happened. He was in a pasture among the
rocks and trees, and he had lost his way. There he was in woods
alone, and darkness came down out of the sky and fitted him tight
all around. He wandered through the night, and just with the rising
moon he came upon a woman weaving. She was an ugly woman,
Carlos, and she was sitting against a rock and weaving. He saw a
serape upon the frame, and it was a precious thing. The colors were
bright, and the colors were soft, and they blended in together. The
madman looked upon this thing, and he was overcome and wept.

" 'Why do you weep?' the old woman asked.

"The madman pointed a finger at the serape all clean and colorful
in the moonlight. 'It is this,' he said. 'It is this.'

" 'Do you know why it is beautiful?'

" 'No,' blubbered the madman, 'no, no!'

" 'It is the weaving of a pattern only,' the woman explained. 'I take
a bright thread here, like this, and a soft color there, like that, and I
weave them so.'

" 'It is precious,' the madman exclaimed. 'It is precious so.'

" 'Would you like to weave this pattern upon your flute?' she asked
the madman.

" 'Oh, yes, I would like!'

" 'Then blow upon your flute,' she said. 'I will take a thread, and
you will take a note, and together we shall weave a pattern.'

"The madman put his flute to his lips, and the woman took a thread.

It was a soft thread, and the note he played was likewise soft. She took another thread, and the thread was bright, and he played a note to match. So she wove her threads, and he wove his notes, and all through the night they worked together. When the sun rose, each had finished.

"Upon the serape was a pattern, and in it were all the colors and all the designs the world has seen, and they made an image. Upon the serape was a pattern, and in the air was music. And in the music was every note the world has known, and they were blended.

" 'Look upon my serape,' the woman told the madman, 'for I must go. Look upon it, and remember well the pattern.'

"The madman looked, and he played the pattern upon his flute until there was no forgetting. As he played, the fear left his body, and the devil's image with it, and there was peace within his breast.

" 'Remember well,' the woman said, and she gathered up the serape. 'Remember well the pattern.' She gathered up the serape, and before his eyes she rose above the earth, and her face was young and lovely to behold, and the madman recognized Our Lady as she rose among the clouds.

"The peace grew within his breast, and he returned to our village, playing upon his flute, and when the people awoke, they heard him. It was not music only. It was wind among the trees, and it was children laughing. It was rain upon the roof, it was grasses rustling, it was the whisper of a mother to her baby dying, it was thunder, it was swift water running, it was angels singing. Softness, shrillness, a bird flying in the sky! No one had heard. Never before had anyone heard. Flowers bloomed, although their buds were small; cocoons burst, although it was not their season.

"Men heard and came, and they looked upon the flute, and it was the same. The holes were wrong, and there was no proper spacing, but they looked upon the madman, and he was no longer mad.

"He was soft, like his music, he was strong, like his music, he was gentle, like his music, he was sky-reaching.

"People would have him play. Day and night they would have him play. They could not live without."

"What happened to him?" Carlos asked. "Did none of the world ever hear?"

"He went away, Carlos. With his music he blew out his soul. In each note was a bit of his spirit, and it passed out through his flute and travelled away on high. His soul went through the flute and left only his body behind. You can hear his music, though, if you listen at night."

"About the serape," wondered Carlos. "What was this pattern, this image he saw? Did he ever tell?"

"Yes, Carlos!" Magdalena said. "It was the face of God."

VI. Shaft and Sphere

THE UNIVERSITY OF SAN RAMON de Cuautak is sixty years older than Harvard, but it is not as large. When Carlos began the study of law there were three main buildings of adobe, and these were built around open courts. The largest was for Arts and Science, and it was located a block from the Central Plaza, not far behind the Cathedral. There were classrooms and a lecture hall with benches for a hundred, and there was a scientific laboratory with stuffed birds arranged on shelves and snakes of tropical coloring suspended in jars of alcohol. There was also a live condor in a cage. That was the School of Arts and Science in the days of General Ronca.

Engineering was another block to the south. The building was almost the same; yet it was rumored that new quarters would soon be built. Through the generosity of General Ronca a new building would soon be built of stone and steel. There would be a lecture hall to seat a thousand and there would be a model railway and an oil well complete.

Law was like Arts and Science, but somewhat smaller. Situated on the Avenue of the Bees five blocks east of the Cathedral, it was a low adobe building with a court inside and a fountain which watered the flowers planted there. Within was a lecture hall, smaller than that in Arts and Science, and there were classrooms and a library of a thousand volumes.

During each day Carlos listened to lectures and studied in the law school and library. At siesta time he returned to the house of Magdalena, where he had a room, and in the late evening he also returned and stayed the night.

One Friday after dark Carlos lounged near the fountain, breathing

deeply of night air. The patio of the Law School was deserted and
silent except for the tinkle and splash of the fountain and a rustling
of breezes among banana trees and rubber plants. He had been studying all afternoon, and now he stretched his arms and legs and his
fingers that were stiff from note-taking. He was resting thus when he
was startled by footsteps close behind. He turned in time to see a
dark, slender figure move up against the fountain.

"Good evening!" Carlos called.

The dark figure returned the greeting. "This is not a night for
study."

Carlos agreed. The stranger lighted a cigarette, and in the glow
of the wax-stemmed match, Carlos recognized the face of a fellow
student whom he remembered as a tall, nimble-witted mestizo who
had made a name for himself as a speaker and debater.

The stranger flipped his match into the fountain where it died with
a short hiss. "I am Francisco Fernández," he said. "We have heard
good things about you, Carlos. You were arrested in the house of
Don Ricardo a year or two ago."

This startled Carlos. "Yes, that is true."

The cigarette glowed brightly as Francisco inhaled. "There are
other matters that we have also heard about you," he said. "If they,
too, are correct, then we would like to know you better."

Carlos was tempted to ask who "we" might be, but he held his
tongue, deciding that it was better to let Francisco do the talking.

"Are you busy tonight?" the mestizo asked. "Do you feel obliged
to study?"

There was something in Francisco's tone that roused one's curiosity.
"No," Carlos replied. "I am stale enough already."

"Then come along with me," Francisco suggested, "and we shall
pay a visit that you will not regret."

Carlos accepted quickly. Francisco flipped his half-smoked cigarette
into a gutter of the fountain, and the two students set off together.
From the Avenue of the Bees they turned westward into La Calle
Florida which they followed into the Central Plaza. Just south of the
cathedral rose the steel frame of the city's first projected skyscraper.
This was the new Prettyman building. For months Ronca's railway
had been hauling in cement and rivets and girders to give it sub-

stance. When completed, the structure would tower fourteen stories above the Plaza and cast its morning shadow well over toward the Market Place, but this evening it was a black skeleton against the night time sky.

Francisco paused near the curb and stared across at the shadowy framework. "There you have it," he said harshly. "Old Prettyman seizes our country like a fistful of mud and squeezes and that's what columns upward — a monument of blood and muck and sweat and dead, decaying human flesh."

Carlos did not answer. After a moment Francisco turned abruptly, and the two of them made their way across the Plaza and beyond the new Cine Rex to the Market Place. There Francisco turned into a narrow, dingy street and stopped in front of a hardware store. He sidled up against the front to light a cigarette, and as the match flared, Carlos saw a brass plaque with the name Heinz Eidelman etched upon it. He had a momentary feeling that something similar to this had happened long before, and then he remembered another brass plaque which Pepillo once had spit upon.

Francisco dropped his match on the sidewalk. "Here you have the city's second tallest building," he told Carlos. "One day it may be the tallest."

Carlos backed away toward the curb and looked upward. The Heinz Eidelman shop had only one story. "It is a low building," he said.

"Very low," Francisco agreed.

"You speak in riddles," complained Carlos.

Francisco took his arm and led him back into the Market Place, and from there they moved on toward a dismal section of the city that lay beyond La Calle de las Mujeres. "That building is only a hardware store," Francisco said as they hurried along, "and Heinz Eidelman is a chubby, bald-headed merchant with thick spectacles. Yet that little, low building casts a shadow as black as that of a fourteen-story concrete column, and Heinz Eidelman in his own way represents a danger as great as Mr. Prettyman does in his. Your little bald-headed merchant, Carlos, is undercover agent for Hitler's Reich."

Carlos stopped. They were beyond La Calle de las Mujeres, now, in the section of the city known as the Barrio of the Spiders. "How do you know these things?" he asked.

Francisco examined him with an amused, slightly patronizing expression. "You don't know much about politics, do you?" He peered over one shoulder more from habit, it appeared to Carlos, than because he really expected to see anything. "It seems quite safe to talk. Let me explain a thing or two, amigo." Speaking rapidly, in short, precise sentences, the law student described the world situation as he saw it. Falangista and similar rightist elements sought to block progress, using force to prevent any kind of change, while other groups were fighting for a people's world.

"Many important leaders today are afraid to take a stand against men like Hitler and Franco and Mussolini," he charged, "and now they are leaving the small and helpless nations to their fate. Only one nation has taken a clear position."

"Which one is that?" Carlos asked.

Francisco ignored the question. "Have you ever read the works of Marx?"

Carlos shot a startled glance at his companion's face. "Marx? Karl Marx? No, I never have."

"I thought that one should warn you," Francisco told him, "because our host tonight is sure to speak of Marx. A strange man, Carlos — a drunkard, yes, and perhaps a genius."

Carlos was interested. "A drunkard? Oh, I did not know, I thought — "

Francisco cut him short. "No, no, cabrón, I do not speak now of Marx. I speak of Doctor MacNeill, our host. Doctor Rory MacNeill. I tell you, he is a remarkable stallion. He's lived in every hole from Bierut to Colon, mind you, not to mention our own San Marcos. In Port au Prince he took up with a Haitian dancer and had himself a daughter by her. A tasty apple, you will see, that daughter Sapho."

The street was lined with pawnshops, junk yards, and livery stables. Tango music blared from a corner cantina, and as Francisco and Carlos came near, they heard shouts and raucous laughter within. The slatted swinging doors flew open and disgorged a lurching youngster of thirteen or fourteen, his sombrero cocked low over one brown cheek. He screamed a gutter word as he collided with Carlos, and then broke into an hysterical cackle. His breath carried a sour-buttermilk stench. Gently but firmly Carlos pushed him away.

The youngster danced lightly over an open gutter and into the rough cobblestone street. There was a strange, loose-jointed rhythm in his every movement as he stumbled airily over a pile of paving stones, defying gravity with every step. Francisco quickened his pace.

"You spoke about a certain country —" Carlos reminded his companion.

Francisco's eyes burned with repressed excitement. "Bien, but first a word or two about this Marxism. It is a marriage, I think, of Hegel's dialectic and Feuerbach's — no, no, that is a poor way to begin. Doctor MacNeill would laugh at that and tell me it doesn't matter. He scoffs at books, and reads them day and night."

Two soldiers and a shrill-voiced girl were arguing under a street lamp. Francisco waited until he and Carlos had passed them before he began again. "Let me put it this way," he said quickly. His words came tumbling out, now, one on top of another. "Means of producing things require that men live in a certain manner, shepherds this way, fishermen that way, and so on. Bueno, and when men develop new ways of producing things, they must also develop new ways of living. But the truth is, Carlos, that those who have benefited most from an old way of living, those who have won power from it, those men are afraid of change."

They were coming, now, to the outskirts of the city. Francisco turned into a street that was cobbled, but pitted with deep holes of mud. There were open lots where goats and sheep were picketed, and Carlos recognized the acrid odor of gardens fertilized by nightsoil. As they moved along this dismal street, Francisco explained more about the philosophy of Marx. In the Middle Ages there had been a feudal way of living, and for those times, it served a purpose. But when men's way of producing began to change, there were certain classes who tried to keep living ways the same.

Francisco seized Carlos' shoulder as they walked along. "Men's ways of producing changed," he said fervently, "but the lord liked his serfs too well, and in a land like ours, he has them still. So there you have a struggle. In Europe it was serf against his lord, and here it is peasant against the hacendado, which is really all the same."

They stopped before a narrow door cut through an adobe wall that flanked the street. A rope protruded through a hole in the panelling.

Francisco grasped it, but he did not pull. His eyes burned clear and bright. "Peasant against hacendado," he exclaimed. "That is a feudal struggle. In forward nations it is a different matter. In those countries the factory lord has long since replaced the lord of the medieval manor, and industrial labor supplants the serf. The machine owner's living ways have brought to life and trained a whole new working class skilled in wealth-creating. Well, give them time — " Francisco yanked the rope, and somewhere beyond the wall a sheep bell tinkled.

"What has this to do with Heinz Eidelman and his hardware store?"

Francisco spoke impatiently. "Don't you see, Carlos, when the industrial lord realizes that the established order is not strong enough to preserve the old time ways, he then casts about for some new order, some stronger method of freezing things the way they are?"

Carlos considered this, and as he did so, a number of stray events fell into place and began to form a vicious pattern. There was the revolution in his boyhood, the looting of Santa Marta. There was Blas forming a railway union. There was Pepillo with his talk of Hispanidad and a new order. There was Mr. Prettyman accepting Il Duce's decoration.

Carlos found these thoughts disturbing. But there was something about Francisco that disturbed him even more. "This dialectic," he ventured, "this struggle of classes — isn't that Bolshevism?"

Francisco's teeth gleamed in the murky night. "And what if it is?" he challenged.

2

CARLOS HEARD the patter of bare feet within and the rattle of a sliding bar. The door opened a crack.

"Chitón! Miguel, it's Francisco Fernández!"

The door opened wider, and Carlos saw an old Indian in white shirt and pantalones, an ancient man with scrawny, billy-goat beard hanging from the brownness of his chin. Francisco stepped into a passageway between two adobe walls. Carlos followed, and the Indian padded close behind. It was dark, and the two visitors felt their way along until they had reached a small court that was full of plants growing from empty gasoline tins. Straight ahead was a kitchen shack where red glowed in a charcoal stove. There was an aroma of peanuts roasting.

Francisco turned onto a narrow stairway that rose out of the court, while the old Indian disappeared inside the kitchen shack. Halfway up the stone steps was a landing where an oil lantern hung from a rusty nail. Francisco paused. "This Doctor MacNeill, he is a very beast to look at," he warned. "So do not be surprised." They made their way up to the second story.

The whole house was built around the patio which they had left below. Carlos saw that they were now upon a balcony which circled above the court and that there were many numbered doors. Francisco paused at one of these and knocked. Tacked on the panel was a name card which in the semi-darkness Carlos could not read. The floor beyond the threshold creaked under heavy footsteps but to Francisco's knocking there was no response.

He rapped again.

"Pase, pase, porr la Madrrre de Dios!" shouted a voice in a sort of Spanish Carlos had never heard even among Yanquis on the railroad. "For the love of Chrrist, won't ye quit your pounding and come on in!"

The room had about it a strong scent of boiled cabbage. As his

eyes became accustomed to the yellow glow of a kerosene lamp, Carlos
saw a floor with a thick but tattered carpet, an easy chair that was
fat and worn and bulging with excelsior, a table strewn with papers
and books, and a tottering brass bedstead covered with a bright
serape. A pipe rack was nailed to one adobe wall, a brace of pistols
hung from another, and a third was decorated by a surrealistic dream
done in water colors.

The floor of an adjoining room creaked as under a heavy weight.
"Sangrre de Crristo, Frrrancisco, and must ye stand there like a con-
stipated penguin?" bellowed the same bull voice from beyond a half-
closed door.

After testing the bedstead with one hand, Francisco sat down
cautiously, while Carlos sank into the overstuffed chair. A newspaper
lay on the floor. It was *Las Noticias,* the daily which Don Ricardo had
owned before his exile. Carlos picked it up and scanned the front
page idly. According to the headlines, Adolph Hitler had accused
Czechoslovakia of persecuting the Sudeten Germans; the San Marcos
Falange had held a review in honor of the new Spanish minister; Air
Águila, a subsidiary of Luft Hansa, had included Ronca's capital in its
new Central American spur line.

The bull voice let out another bellow from the adjoining room.
"Damn bastarrdly buttons!" Carlos shot a quick glance at Francisco,
but the law student seemed not to have heard.

On the second page of *Las Noticias* was the story of a ball given at
the Strangers' Club to celebrate Mr. Frank Nash's thirtieth year with
Prettyman Enterprises. Carlos read how the famous Yanqui had risen
from a clerk in the Buenos Aires office to become one of Mr. Prettyman's senior field executives, how he had been to a large extent responsible for the remarkable expansion of the San Marcos headquarters, how he was now considered an outstanding authority on
Central American affairs. There was also a picture of Mr. and Mrs.
Nash in their reception line, greeting his Excellency, General José
Ronca, President of the Republic.

The floor creaked again, and over his newspaper, Carlos saw a red-
faced hulk of a man standing in the doorway. It seemed that the
body was overstuffed, like the chair in which Carlos was sitting, and
the tweed suit that clothed it bulged about the pockets in such a

manner that one half expected to see kinks of excelsior sticking out. Carlos dropped his newspaper and stood up as Francisco made the introductions. The huge man had a knuckle-crushing grip.

Doctor MacNeill seemed to know a number of things about Carlos. "Frrancisco tells me that ye were arrested." He stood with his back to the wall where the water color was, and it was not easy for Carlos to decide which was the more grotesque. There was this giant of a red-faced man, and behind him in the painting was an angel with silver wings, and in the middle of the Madonna face was a nose, round and button-shaped, a hoggish snout. Doctor MacNeill stared down at Carlos through watery eyes. "Frrancisco says ye were arrested in the house of Don Ricardo."

Carlos admitted this. He was trying hard not to stare. In a land of small-framed Indians and mestizos it was not common to see such a head on the shoulders of a human being. The skull was massive, the skin of the face bordered on purple, the hair was white tinged with yellow near the roots, the eyes were blue and watery. It seemed to Carlos that the man's brows stuck out at least an inch, while white hairs grew in tufts from his nostrils and ears, and the stubble on his chin and jaws was stiff and had a scaly look. There was a purple pouch of skin beneath each eye. The nose was red and porous and swollen.

"Frrancisco tells me ye had with ye a number of books," Doctor MacNeill observed. Carlos edged away from the bulging chair, and the huge man lowered himself between the two overstuffed arms. "I was wondering to myself — sit down, sit down, the both of ye — I was wondering to myself how ye came to get away."

Carlos, on his part, was wondering how Francisco came to know so much. Sitting down on the bed, he tried to explain about Pepillo, but as he spoke, his voice sounded thin upon the bull roar of Doctor MacNeill, his story scarcely credible.

"I've seen otherrr men that were caught with books," Doctor MacNeill said shrewdly. "T's from trrees I've seen them hanging. Where were you borrn, boy, where have you lived, how came ye to know Don Ricardo?"

Carlos told something of his boyhood, his keeping of Don Ricardo's gates, his years upon the railroad.

"What was the purrpose of leaving your village?" Doctor MacNeill shot out.

Carlos felt warm blood flooding his face. "There was trouble," he stammered. "I —"

"You went away for your health?" suggested Doctor MacNeill. "Well, I've had a bit of the same trouble myself." He turned to Francisco. "Tell me, what have you been doing with yourself since last ye were here?"

Francisco was sitting close to Carlos on the battered bed. "I study," he said, "or argue sometimes with Bernardo Cabrera."

Doctor MacNeill snorted. "Faith, now, I'll wager old Bernarrdo has got ye stuffed with dialectic," he grumbled. "Well, let me tell you, Bernarrdo is an ass. The dialectic is a name for a process, a system of change. It causes nothing, crrreates nothing, brrings nothing to an end. No, no, look to miserry in the nearest alley. There's your cause for revolution."

"Bernardo calls dialectic the central force in Marxism," Francisco said.

"Class strrruggle!" cried Doctor MacNeill. "There's yourr dynamic, boy. Always has been. Slave against his masterr, plebe against patrician, serrf against his lorrd, jourrneyman against the guildmasterr. Incompatibility, boy, incompatibility of interest, there's yourr cause of rrevolution."

With a knowing wink at Carlos, Francisco said, "but according to Bernardo Cabrera the dialectic —"

"Dialectic, hell!" the huge man cut in. "That's Marrx the philosopherr, Marrx between the coverrs of a book." He glared at Carlos. "T's another Marrx I'll show ye, boy, a Marrx that Bernarrdo will neverr know." He pushed his gigantic body out of the chair and started a search about the room. "Dialectic, hell! Can a man that's starrved eat dialectic? Can a man that's sick get curred by dialectic? Can a poor devil drrink it? Can he wearr it like a coat when the wind blows cold? God damn it!" he broke into English. "God damn that bastarrdly sonofabitching bottle!" He tore back the serape from one end of the couch, searched under the mattress, stomped over to his table and pawed through stacks of papers and books. "God damn that — Sapho! Sapho!"

He bolted back into the room from which he had come in the first place. There was the sound of his mumbled curses mingling with the softness of a woman's voice, and Carlos felt ashamed for what he had seen and heard, and he was afraid to face Francisco.

In a moment the bear of a man was back with a bottle. He eased himself into his battered chair, poured a drink into a water tumbler, downed it quickly, and grimaced as though it had scorched his throat. "I do not ask ye to join," he apologized in a strangely gentle voice. "For to drrrink with a drrrunkarrd is not a pleasure. Well, let me tell you, boy, Karrl Marrrx believed that human naturre could betterr itself, and that's morre than some of yourr pious faced theologians will admit. Laborr, he said, and the naturre of its social orrganization, yes, and its tools, all these, says Marrrx, create envirronment, and envirronment, he says, larrrgely shapes the naturrre of man."

Carlos' interest jumped. "Then if you change our environment," he suggested, "you change our nature."

"Therrre ye have it, boy!" agreed Doctor MacNeill. "A slave acquires a cerrtain naturre with his chains. A man borrn and rearred in a stink hole carries some of the stink. Envirronment! Ah, but man can change it. Unlike the beasts, man can shape his historry."

Carlos looked doubtful. "I have heard it said that human nature never changes."

Doctor MacNeill glowered. "The man who says that," he declared, "has a rreason for wanting things to rremain the way they are. Rrremember, Carlos, whatever is to the interrest of those who rrule is seldom to the interrest of those who do not. Only a people's government will rule in the interest of the people."

This perplexed Carlos. "It appears to me," he said, "that as long as there is government there will be a ruling class. Revolution merely overthrows one class and tries to substitute another."

"You miss the marrk," Doctor MacNeill told him. "As long as there arre classes, therre will be a strruggle, as you say. But the Marrxist would abolish classes, and give all men a common interest in production. Then there is no conflict."

Carlos considered this. "How would one bring an end to classes?"

Doctor MacNeill raised a long and heavy finger. "Industrial laborr will overthrrow its masters," he explained, "and, worrking in its own interrests, will develop a classless state."

This aroused Carlos. "Does that mean that Marx would use class conflict as a weapon against itself?"

"Marrx would do that," Doctor MacNeill agreed.

Carlos flushed. "I do not believe that evil can be overcome by evil."

The huge man shifted his body impatiently. "The struggle cannot be avoided!" He explained how industrial lords would hasten their own destruction by failing to prevent inflations and depressions and other sorts of crises, by exploiting backward countries, by resisting even the most necessary kind of change. "You can see the conflict here," he cried. "Just considerr Misterr Prrettyman! Do you doubt that one day the people will turrn against him?"

Doctor MacNeill's arguments disturbed Carlos. There was no doubt in his mind that they contained a degree of validity; yet he could not quite accept them. Perhaps they were too convincing, too — too made to order. "Do you really think that industrial labor can bring about a perfect state?" he asked.

The doctor raised his bushy brows. "Oh, neverr! The classless state is only another stage in human living, a stage where furrther prrogress will be planned by all, where struggle will be reduced to frriendly crriticism."

Carlos shook his head. "I doubt that men can do it."

Doctor MacNeill gulped another drink. "T's a sick worrld of brrotherly hatrred," he admitted. "I've seen it in Dublin and Bombay and Singapore, in Shanghai and Cairro and Cuba, and in Yanqui Frreedom Land. We've all seen it here in San Marcos. Each day you see men upon the strreets in rrags, and women, and childrren, too, the little ones with their pot bellies full of gas. You do not pass a stinking hut that you do not hearr the coughing and the spitting. And then you see your Prettymans and Ronquistas waxing fat. That's not just San Marrcos, either. That's India, China — all the places where people starrve."

Doctor MacNeill slumped in his chair. Francisco tamped a cigarette against his wrist, stuck one end between his lips, and struck a wax-stemmed match. There was a long silence during which Carlos heard only the rasp of the doctor's breathing, the piteous bleatings of a goat somewhere outside in the night.

After a time Doctor MacNeill stirred. "Now ye'd better be going, the both of ye," he said. "It's getting to be a time of night when things are bad, and I'd not be for making you wish you'd gone the sooner. But firrst I'd like you to meet my daughter, Carlos, that I would!" He got to his feet, calling, "Sapho! Sapho! Will ye come to me, Sapho?"

There were light footsteps in the adjoining room, and a girl appeared upon the threshold. She was slender, Carlos saw, and her hair was black and tightly curly, and her skin was smooth, the yellow of a ripe banana. She smiled at Francisco, and Carlos saw her teeth, white and even.

At her father's introduction, she held out a hand to Carlos. Their eyes met, and Carlos saw that hers were jet black. There was a bottomlessness about them, too, like the bottomlessness of a deep well, and it seemed to Carlos that far down in the depths were fires burning.

Carlos meant to speak. He meant to, but he did not. He stood there only, holding her hand, and when she took it away, he felt an emptiness in his own.

Francisco moved toward the door, and Carlos moved with him.

Doctor MacNeill spoke. "Make no mistake," he said to Carlos. "I am not a Bolshevik. I am old and tirred, and I am drrunk most of the time. They want young men, strrong men, men of will and self-contrrol. You know the Jesuits, Carrlos, you know the men they are. It demands the guts of a Jesuit, Carrlos, rrememberr that."

Carlos nodded, scarcely aware of what the doctor said.

"And rrrememberr also, Carrlos, the Bolsheviks may not be rrright, but they prrresent a hope. To the rrragged and the hungrry and the sick of hearrt they prrresent a hope!"

Francisco and Carlos stepped through the door, and Francisco closed it behind them. But it opened again, and Doctor MacNeill poked his leonine head into the passageway.

"I like you, Carrrlos!" he said. "I'll be wanting ye to come again!"

3

IT WAS EARLY EVENING when Carlos left the School of Law and made his way across the city toward the Barrio of the Spiders. Only a few years had passed since the arrival of Ronca's railroad, but already he could see its effects upon the city. The old lamps had disappeared from the Central Plaza, and electric bulbs glowed yellow where thin gas flames had formerly flickered. South of the Cathedral towered the Prettyman building, a high, many-windowed structure of steel and concrete, and the Gran Hotel San Marcos was crowded every night with engineers and contractors and well-stuffed men of business. The outside world was pressing into Ronca's capital.

Carlos still found it strange to see low-slung limousines parked along the gutters of the Plaza, to see uniformed chauffeurs, to hear the whine of beggars drowned out by noisy beep-beep horns. He found it stranger still to see a long, sleek chromium-plated marvel stalled in a traffic jam of burros. Yet there they were, slender muzzled cabriolet and plebeian donkey, brought nose to nose by General Ronca's railway.

An amplifier atop the Plaza bandstand screamed out an hysterical diatribe from a radio in the lobby of the Gran Hotel San Marcos. Carlos paused momentarily to listen. There was a harsh, familiar voice screaming German, there was the soft, monotonous voice of a Spanish interpreter breaking through. . . . "I saw to it that a change was brought about . . . between Germany and Poland . . . that insures henceforth . . . a peaceful existence. . . . There is our struggle . . . for living room . . . and peace in Europe . . . under a new order."

Carlos moved on across the Plaza. He was confused about this new war in Europe, even though he had discussed it with Francisco and with other students at the law school. Certain of his friends were in favor of Hitler simply because the Yanquis were said to be against him. Others appeared to oppose him because Nazism was so similar to Ronquismo. But whichever side one took, it was safer not to talk too loud; for the federal police were reputed to be much interested in anyone who expressed himself politically.

As he left the Market Place, Carlos paused to read a recent proclamation pasted on a lamppost. PATRIA! IGLESIA! FAMILIA! "Through the grace of God and the determination and foresight of our Great President, General José Ronca," the placard stated, "the magnificent railway which pierced our mountains a few years ago will soon be extended to Cocamba on the Pacific Coast. Yet for loyal Ronquistas, that is but a small beginning. Let us gird our loins and set to work! Let us build a powerful nation! Let us erect a Temple of Progress beneath the sun!" That was the beginning of the proclamation, and the rest was text, and it explained how all the workers of the nation were about to organize with their employers to form what the proclamation termed a mighty keystone in the new Ronquista corporate state.

This was the boldest proclamation that Carlos had yet seen, but he realized, now, that Ronquismo had been steadily growing in confidence during recent months. There were whispered rumors that Ronca was very close to certain governments in Europe and that if Hitler won the war, Falangism would take over the Americas altogether. But there were so many of these stories being passed about that Carlos remained skeptical.

As he read the proclamation, a trooper rode near and reined his horse. There were those who insisted that it was dangerous to be seen reading one of Ronca's placards since even an expression of the face might easily be misinterpreted. So Carlos moved on as quickly as he dared.

Doctor Rory MacNeill's dingy flat was already filled with students when Carlos arrived. Francisco was there, and Carlos recognized four or five from the School of Law, and Francisco introduced three others as "good chicos, but misguided engineers."

Carlos squeezed down on the bedstead between Francisco and one of the engineers and looked for Sapho. He thought he heard her voice in the kitchen, but the door was half shut, and he could not be

certain. Waiting hopefully, he pretended to be absorbed in the conversation, which was mostly about the European war and the pact between the Russian Bolsheviks and Nazi Germany. The general opinion
seemed to be that England and France had proved themselves both
unwilling and unable to join with the Soviet Union in maintaining
security through the League of Nations. " 'Tis but another capitalistic
warr," Doctor MacNeill maintained. "Stalin has no choice but to act
alone."

The voices were louder in the kitchen, and Carlos was certain, now,
that he could hear Sapho. The war in Europe seemed far away and
difficult to comprehend, and, although he had no particular sympathies for either side, he found himself somewhat shocked by Doctor
MacNeill's defense of the Soviet pact with Hitler.

"Your capitalist leaders in London and Paris were always hoping
that Hitler would attack the Soviet Union," Francisco charged. "That
is why they refused to negotiate with Moscow reasonably. That is
why — "

The kitchen door swung open, and something like a fish flopped in
Carlos' stomach as Sapho appeared. He forgot all about Francisco's
defense of Bolshevik policy as he watched her pause a moment on the
threshold, a tray of hot chocolate balanced in one hand. He gaped
at the smoothness of her skin, at the ripe banana hue; he saw the
blackness of her eyes and a flash from the fires that burned behind
them. She passed around the chocolate, and at her heels was another
student whom she called Luis, and Carlos felt a twinge of jealousy
and hated him at sight.

He was tall and slender, this Luis, and his skin was dark, his hair
short and curly. He was speaking to Sapho in rapid Spanish, and his
accent was not Nacheetl or anything that Carlos had ever heard. "Oh,
I have seen it danced in Havana," Luis was saying. "Baya, baya, hein,
hein!" His hands clapped a rhythm. "Some night I'll bring my radio
over so we can try it."

Sapho laughed, and her black eyes sparkled as smoldering charcoal
does under a bellows. "Moin vo dit, my mother was a mamaloi," she
told Luis, "a real Congo dancer." She spoke in a soft, slightly nasal
tone that Carlos found intriguing.

She moved along before the bed, passing a tray of chocolate. Carlos could not take his eyes from the white, embroidered blouse, the peasant skirt cut short, the slender, amber legs tapering to her high-heeled slippers. She paused in front of Carlos. "Pues ça y est!" He smiled, discovered too late that it was Luis to whom she had spoken.

Doctor MacNeill pried his ursine body from the easy chair, hunted up a bottle, and poured himself another drink. When he had gulped it down, he continued with his talking. "Adolph Hitlerr is only the tool of capitalist bosses in Berrlin," he grumbled, "just as Rronca is only the tool of Prrettyman. They are the men who make these warrs, not the people. Faith, now, if ye are wanting to see how it works, ye need only to look about ye."

"Patria! Iglesia! Familia!" snorted Francisco. "For imperialism — law and order, for the workers — work, work, work!"

"And for the peasant — taxes!" Doctor MacNeill added, " 'Tis a combination that can't be beat. Well, if the Nazis ever get over here, they'll have a base to worrk from, and the Yanquis can thank their own Mr. Prrettyman for brringing it all to pass."

Thus they talked about the capitalist war and about Ronca and about Mr. Prettyman, and Luis talked about forbidden programs which he had heard over his radio at night. Carlos, meantime, could only drink his chocolate and gaze at Sapho while the evening wore away. Gradually Doctor MacNeill's face grew redder with drink, and eventually it was time to leave. The guests slipped away one by one, lest a group might cause suspicion. Francisco left, and the engineers, but Carlos hung back, waiting for Luis to go, hoping for a word with Sapho.

Doctor MacNeill's tongue got heavy, and his voice was coarse to hear. "Those God damn bastarrrdly Rrrrronquistas," he growled. "Those sonofabitching — "

Sapho looked at Luis and at Carlos, too, and her eyes were pleading with them to go. Luis picked up his cap and moved toward the door, and Carlos followed. They said good-night to Sapho, and Luis stepped out.

Here was the moment that Carlos had wanted, the moment he had waited for. But what was there to say? Nothing at all that he could hit upon. "Good night!" he mumbled again. "Good night, señorita!" He backed through the door, collided with another person.

"Señor doctor! Señor doctor!" It was a barefooted boy dressed in rags. He squeezed between Carlos' legs and stood before Sapho in the lamp light. "Oh, señorita doctor, come quickly, please, Beatriz, she hit my papacito hard-hard with her little hoof!" From broken Spanish he burst into San Marcos Nacheetl.

"Wait, wait, chiquito, I do not understand," protested Sapho. "What does he say, Carlos?"

"He says that Beatriz — that's his family's mule — Beatriz hit papacito hard-hard with her little foot and broke his leg," Carlos explained, "and he wants Doctorcito to please come mend it."

"Where, chiquito, where did he break the leg?" asked Sapho.

"In the courtyard," wailed the youngster in Spanish, "near the well only."

"No, no, where did he break the leg, what part?" demanded Sapho. "Down here, up here, where, chiquito?"

The youngster touched his femur. "Here," he said, "where it takes root from the body."

"Very well, chiquito, we shall fix the leg," Sapho said, "Will you help me, Carlos?" She kicked off her high-heeled slippers and replaced them with sandals, and from the adjoining room she brought a medicine kit and a rebozo which she threw about her head and shoulders, and a serape for her father.

Doctor MacNeill appeared to be asleep. The massive head was slumped upon his chest, and his breathing came in ugly gasps. Sapho wrapped the serape about him, grasped his right arm firmly, motioned Carlos to the other side. "Come, mon père," she chided softly, "get up, Papaloi, you must mend a broken leg."

"God damn bastarrrdly sonofabitching Rrrrrronquistas," he grumbled. "Lemme alone."

Together Carlos and Sapho lifted. Immediately the bearish arms shot out.

"Careful!" warned Sapho.

Doctor MacNeill fastened upon his daughter with a watery stare. "Lemme be, you bitch!" he screamed. "Lemme be, you f —— bitch!"

The youngster backed through the door, wide-eyed and terrified.

"Try another time," Sapho said to Carlos. "All right, Papaloi," she told her father, "let's go catch Ronquistas!"

Doctor MacNeill looked up, pushed himself out of the chair. "Why'n hell dinye say it in the firrrst place!" he roared. "Ho! Catch Rrrronquistas! Catch 'em? Hell, we'll castrate the pimping bastarrrds with a carrrving knife. Where's my bag? Eh, Sapho, where's my God damn bag? Now how'n hell'r we gonna castrate Ronca without my bag?"

"Right here, Papaloi," Sapho whispered. "I have it here. Oh, the lantern!" She turned to Carlos. "In the kitchen, please."

Carlos found the lantern and lit it, and together he and Sapho propelled the doctor out and down the stair and through the passageway to the darkness of the street.

"Go along, chiquito," Sapho told the youngster, "and we shall follow."

They made their way by lantern light, passing into a maze of alleys, the youngster leading. It was a black night, and in the whole sky there was not a star. The alleys were narrow, and there were smells. Rats scampered into holes when they saw the light, or hid in shadows, their eyes gleaming red. The youngster went ahead, squashing barefoot through manure and mud, and startled pigs bolted away, their shrill squeals echoing back and forth through the alleys.

"Here we are," the youngster said at last. He pushed open a narrow door that squeaked on wooden hinges. Carlos saw a muddy yard sliced with hoof marks, and in the center was a wooden covered wellshaft, and near it a small boy was passing water.

"Lorrd have merrrcy on these people!" the doctor grumbled. "And teach them where to pass theirr water."

Carlos saw that there were bare adobe chambers built about the court, and some were stalls for beasts, while others were dwelling places. The youngster who was guiding pointed to a doorway that was jammed with people. "Papacito," he said. "He lies in there."

"What's in there?" demanded Doctor MacNeill.

Sapho stooped and picked up a length of board. "The man with the broken leg," she said.

"Brrroken leg! Who has a brroken leg? God damn it, Sapho, why didn't somebody tell me there was a brrroken leg?" The doctor plowed through the crowd, Sapho and Carlos following in his furrow.

There was a dirt floor, and stretched out upon it was a young peasant, and the right leg of his pantalones bulged just below the hip. Near him squatted a frightened woman who seemed to be his wife. Doctor MacNeill dropped down upon his knees, took out a pocket knife, and slit the trouser leg. A sharp lump disfigured the smoothness of the man's brown thigh, but the skin remained unbroken. Doctor MacNeill looked back over his shoulder. "Clear out, you people!" he roared. "Vamos! Get!"

Fearfully the onlookers backed away, and Carlos closed a pair of wooden doors that separated the room from the yard outside. Sapho set down her father's bag, flipped a catch, and the mouth flopped open.

The youngster who had guided stood close to the squatting woman, and two smaller boys stood next to him. The injured man smiled and pointed at the boys. "These are my sons," he said. "And my wife."

Doctor MacNeill grunted, looked about the room. In a dark corner another figure lay outstretched, and it coughed and moaned and passed wind in sputters and blasts. "What is your name?" he asked the injured man.

"Pablo Valles."

Doctor MacNeill took the board which Sapho handed him, and from his bag he took tape and strips of heavy bandage. Gently he ran his fingers along the leg, first with his right hand, then with his left. "Who is the otherrr?" he asked Pablo. "Who is that who lies in yonderrr corrrnerr?"

"Oh, that is Mamacita," the peasant explained. "She is very — oh!" He grunted as Doctor MacNeill pulled, twisted, reduced the fracture. "She is very old."

Sapho laid the board down beside the broken leg, and her father bound it as a temporary splint. She turned to Carlos. "Take down a door," she said quietly. "Any door that is smooth and flat."

"Hell, yes, any doorrr!" cried Doctor MacNeill. "And slap on a set of legs, Carrrlos. Any old legs, so it's thrrree or fourr feet off the floor."

Carlos stepped into the yard in search of a door. All the neighbors were crowded close, peeking through the cracks to see what went on, but they moved back respectfully to let Carlos pass.

Inside, Sapho and her father worked together, and they sent the eldest son after a hammer, and the watchers gasped. "Pues!" they exclaimed. "He wants a hammer!"

The second son was dispatched to find some nails.

"Caray!" whispered the crowd among themselves. "The doctor now wants nails!"

"And you!" Doctor MacNeill told the youngest. "You, boy, go get us a saw."

Full of importance, the youngster pushed outside, and the crowd fell back in consternation. "A saw!" they gasped. "Oh, pobrecito!"

At this point Carlos returned with a door he had ripped off the stable. He took it inside, and Doctor MacNeill explained about the building of a bed. Next the nails arrived, and then the hammer, and finally the saw. Sapho shut out the crowd again, to the great disappointment of the people. In vain they squeezed against the doors and peered through cracks; it was impossible to know what went on within. But there was plenty to hear, for Carlos went to work, and he hammered and sawed and ripped, and Mamacita lying in the corner took fright and raised a howl.

Squeezed against the doors, the neighbors listened and winced and crossed themselves, breathing extra prayers for Pablo's soul.

Carlos put legs on the door, and when he had finished, he had a bed that was hard, but flat and firm, and Doctor MacNeill nailed an extension from the foot. Then they lifted Pablo off the floor and placed him gently upon the bed, and Carlos felt his fingers touching Sapho's beneath the body of the man.

"Now some rope is needed," Sapho told him. "About four feet. And a small sack, also, and about twenty pounds of stones."

The neighbors stirred. "Rope?" they muttered. "A small sack? Twenty pounds of stones? Oh, madre! What a broken leg!"

When all the materials were together, Doctor MacNeill taped a wooden stirrup to Pablo's ankle and attached the rope, and he ran the rope along the extension and through a ring so that it dangled toward the floor. Then Sapho filled the sack with stones and tied it on the loose end of the rope where it dangled.

The sack now hung ten or twelve inches above the floor, pulling at the injured leg.

"Now off with the splint!" exclaimed Doctor MacNeill. He and

Sapho untaped the board. "Pues, therre you arre in trraction," he told Pablo, "but don't slide down, don't everr slide down or let the stones rrest upon the floorrr."

Sapho gathered up tape and bandage and knife and scissors and put them in the doctor's bag.

Together they left Pablo to the mercy of his neighbors, but as they crossed the yard, the patient's eldest son ran after. "Doctor! Doctor!" he cried. And then, in a lower voice he asked, "Do you not wish some money?"

"Money? What the hell do I want with money?" snapped Doctor MacNeill. "Why, if I charrrged ye money, yourr papacito would worrrk a yearrr to pay forr a mended leg."

"But we wish to do a thing," the boy said, "to make you joyful."

"You want to make me joyful?" demanded Doctor MacNeill.

"Sí, señor."

"All rrrright, then!" thundered Doctor MacNeill. "Just stop pissing in the well!"

4

CARLOS SLEPT at the house of Magdalena, but took his meals elsewhere, usually at a café on the Avenue of the Bees not far from the
School of Law. There was a small, low-ceilinged dining room with
a kitchen behind, and there were five square tables spread with red-
checked tablecloths, and in the center of each stood bowls of grated
cheese, meat sauce, and tiny red peppers, a jar of toothpicks, and an
ashtray advertising Cerveza Volcán.

On this particular night he was eating arroz con pollo while a radio
on a shelf behind him blared an overseas broadcast which Berlin was
piping directly to Central America. First came a newscast.

*According to a DNB dispatch, the French Army is in a state of
panic, their flight impeded by hundreds of thousands of refugees
who, even now, are jamming all possible roads of retreat. German
forces, meanwhile, are pressing forward in their irresistible drive
toward . . .*

It was soft, assured, convincing, this voice from far-off Berlin.
Carlos noticed the accent. It was not Castilian Spanish, but a Central
American dialect scarcely distinguishable from that of San Marcos.
The newscaster predicted an early surrender in Paris and spoke
glowingly of the new Europa even now arising to spread order across
the globe.

Carlos beckoned the waiter, a barefooted Indian in a spotted black
jacket and shiny trousers. "Can't you get another station?"

The waiter grinned. "This is the very best music, señor, sí, pues!"
He made no move to adjust the radio.

A program of rhumbas and tangoes followed the newscast. The
orchestra was undeniably good. Carlos had almost submitted to it
when a ghoulish-looking man sat down across the table from him and

ordered a bowl of chili. The stranger's body was short and small
with a startling combination of rounded shoulders and pigeon breast.
His face might have been modelled from dirty greyish clay, his sharp
nose stuck on, perhaps, as an afterthought. He wore foggy, thick-
lensed glasses which he took off, as he sat down, and rubbed with a
soiled handkerchief. Without the spectacles, his eyes shrank to actual
size, looked somehow rodential beside the pointed nose, while the
lids were red and wrinkled and strangely foetus-like.

He replaced his glasses, looked cautiously about the nearly empty
room, and leaned across the table. "Pardon the intrusion," he said in
a booming whisper, "but are you not Carlos Chichayan?" His voice
sounded as though he were speaking from within a sepulchre.

A blast of static from the radio drowned Carlos' answer. Chimes
announced a change of program. The next feature from Berlin consisted of two comedians who composed scurrilous jokes about the
Yanquis and sang a ribald song dealing with the adventures of President Rosenfeld and Mr. Morgenthau. Carlos got up and adjusted the
volume.

"My name is Bernardo Cabrera," the stranger announced. Each
word seemed to rise full-blown from deep in the pigeon chest. "Are
you not he who was arrested in the house of Judge Cervantes?"

Carlos started. He wondered how so many people had come to
know so much about him.

"I would like to see you in my quarters when we have eaten,"
Cabrera confided.

When the Berlin comedians had finished their chatter, a Doctor
Schmitt gave detailed accounts of Yanqui imperialistic activities in
Central and South America. It appeared that New York Jews had
been entirely responsible for the seizure of Texas, California, Puerto
Rico, Cuba, and the Panama Canal Zone.

Carlos shared his bottle of red wine with Cabrera and tried to main-
tain conversation. But the stranger appeared to be uninterested in
Law School gossip, and when Carlos expressed concern over German
victories in Europe, he merely shrugged and muttered something
about "stupid imperialist wars." It was a relief to Carlos when, having
paid their checks, they left the café and set out for Cabrera's flat.

After making their way southward to the Calle Bolívar, they turned a corner and entered the lodging house where Cabrera lived. It was an old building that had once been a mansion, but Carlos noticed that the tiles upon the floor were cracked, the iron grillwork rusty. An oil lamp lighted the court which was overgrown with weeds. A stench announced the location of an ill-kept latrine.

"Lasciate ogni speranza voi ch'entrate!" Cabrera quoted — a bit pretentiously, Carlos thought. "It is cheap, there is that much to recommend it." They climbed a flight of steps to a wooden balcony, and Cabrera opened the door of a dark and narrow room. When an oil lamp had been lighted, Carlos saw that there was no window at all, but the door onto the balcony admitted air and, by day, no doubt, a degree of light. "There you have it!" Cabrera cried with a dramatic gesture. "Lares et penates!"

Table and bed were littered with books and papers. Cabrera sat down in the only chair, leaned back, thumbs hooked into the waistband of his dark serge trousers. "Here," he announced importantly, "it is safe to talk. La propietaria is deaf, and my worthy fellow tenants are all students who dedicate their nocturnal hours to the city's more disreputable cantinas. Well, tell me now, how do you make out at law?"

Carlos made a place for himself amid the clutter on the bed. "Well enough," he muttered, uncertain whether to be annoyed or amused.

Cabrera jerked a forefinger impatiently. "How did you happen to let them catch you in the house of Don Ricardo?"

There was an implication in Cabrera's tone that nettled Carlos, but he was careful not to betray his annoyance.

Cabrera chuckled good-naturedly when he had heard the story. "Ho! So they caught you with your books in a bundle, fragrante delicto!" he exclaimed amiably. "In any case," he added, "you were well out of the whole mess. Let me tell you, that Don Ricardo is a fool. I know because I studied under him. Oh, a brave enough man, but an utter fool!" He jumped to his feet, stood staring down at Carlos through foggy lenses. "Don Ricardo knew some law," he conceded pompously. "Roman Law, Common Law, Cannon Law — Don Ricardo knew that sort of thing well enough, and he spoke out, too."

Carlos bridled. "Yet you call the man a fool," he snapped. "How is that?"

Cabrera stood holding his coat lapels, his head bowed as though deep in thought. "Don Ricardo was a reformist," he charged. "Don Ricardo mistook the chancre for the spirochete. He tried to make this country a better place by overthrowing Ronca only."

Cabrera sliced the air with his palm. "A-a-a-ah! That Ronca is a gumboil," he said contemptuously. "What books did you carry on the night of your arrest?"

Carlos had an impulse to resist this questioning, but along with his condescension, Cabrera exhibited a friendliness that was difficult to turn aside. "There was the *Social Contract*," Carlos said, "and Benjamin Constant, and Locke's *Treatises*."

Cabrera grimaced. "Locke!" he cried with scorn. "There you have it! Don Ricardo always quoted Locke. What else have you read?"

Uneasily Carlos outlined the reading he had done under Don Ricardo's influence and under Father Timoteo, too. He expected a disdainful remark from Cabrera, but the lawyer made no comment. "I read also Jefferson," Carlos added, "and Thomas Paine."

Cabrera scowled. "And Doctor MacNeill, I suppose, gave you nothing to read?"

This was too much for Carlos. "Does someone spy?" he asked irritably. "Everything about me seems well known to all."

The lawyer chuckled importantly. "It was I who told MacNeill about you in the first place," he said. "As for me — well, I have my ways of finding out. But never mind that. Don't tell me anything about this matter of books. I know that MacNeill saw fit to give you none. He's non compos mentis, anyhow, and a half-baked Marxist." Cabrera strode over to the bed, flipped back the mattress, and pulled three volumes out of the stuffing. "Marx and Engles," he said. "Take them along, but under the shirt like this."

As he prepared to leave, Carlos asked Cabrera about the dialectic. This appeared to please the lawyer greatly. Pacing the floor with long strides, he loosed a jargon about ontological structures of development and empirical change that defied comprehension. When Carlos confessed this, Cabrera ran his fingers through the unruly tangle of his hair. "Let us say with Marx, then, that all things, from the tiniest grain of sand to the mightiest planet, from the simplest animal cell to man himself, is always coming into being and passing away according to the laws of change."

Convinced that Cabrera's explanation would serve for the present, Carlos broke away as soon as an opportunity presented itself and, hugging the books against his ribs, went home to the house of Magdalena.

Night after night, thereafter, when he had finished with his studies, he read by candlelight and thus discovered that Marx was no easy matter. He found words tumbled one against another in German fashion, and many of the meanings were difficult to figure out. When he had found one, he would try to explain it to Magdalena as a means of fixing the meaning in his mind and sometimes as a way of teasing.

There was the theory of surplus value. "It is a manner of thieving," he told Magdalena. They were sitting in the court while two of Magdalena's girls were entertaining soldiers in upstairs rooms. He explained how, in the market place, all things had a value. "A serape, let us say, will sell for twenty pesos. That value is a lifeless thing. But in all the world there is one thing men sell that is still alive and creates a value greater than itself. That thing is labor."

Magdalena laughed coarsely. "That sounds like crazy talk to me."

Carlos persisted. "Suppose I have a shop for making pots of clay. I give you clay and a wheel to work upon, and you labor twelve hours a day. In six hours you have created the value of your wages, that is, a living for you and your family. But you do not stop. You work another six hours, and thus create double the value of your labor. The point is this. Who gets the surplus value that you have made?"

"You do!"

"Then I make my profit by filching value which you have made."

Magdalena remained indifferent. "Pots, serapes, value — what silly things to talk about."

Carlos grinned. "Then let's talk about you!" he teased. "Suppose you sell yourself for a peso."

"I never did," protested Magdalena. "For a peso I never did."

"Well, then, five pesos — it is a small matter. For five pesos you sell your labor for a night. The result of your labor has a pure value — five pesos. That is the price of your product."

"And a fair price always," maintained Magdalena. "Never have I made a false profit, never. Let any man deny that Magdalena was always worth her price. Let any man deny —"

"There is another aspect," Carlos added slyly. "There is the aspect of the middleman, the exploiter of labor. Let us say a certain woman buys a house, and girls come there to live. At night the girls sell their bodies, and this certain woman collects the pesos. Now there, you see, is exploitation — exploitation pure and simple."

"But I pay them!" Magdalena protested. "More than they are worth I pay them!"

"Then for what does the customer pay his pesos if the lesser amount you pay your girls is still too much?"

Angrily Magdalena tossed her head. "But that is different, Carlos, that is different. My house — is it worth nothing? All that you see here — my flowers, the food in my kitchen, the tip for the police — is it worth nothing? All my life I work hard, Carlos, and now the wrinkles, they are ditches in my face, and I am sick, Carlos, and men do not like."

"It is exploitation," Carlos insisted. "Pure and simple."

"I do not like your book," Magdalena stormed. "It is a book of lies!"

5

SAPHO LIKED COSMETICS. She liked the brilliant colors, and when she put them upon her face, it was a kind of portrait painting according to her mood. Today she stood before the cracked glass of her mirror, and on the grey metal washstand beneath she spread her colors. This was a fiesta week, and all San Marcos was ribbon-decked, and, choosing her brightest harlequin hues, she drew sprightliness upon her face.

She was working on her lips when Carlos came. She heard his rap upon the door, she heard her father's bear-like shuffle. "Carrlos! Come in, come in, my boy!" The pleasure in the doctor's greeting brought a smile across her mouth and disturbed her making-up. Old Papaloi liked this Carlos, and Sapho was beginning to believe that she liked him, too. At first she had thought him cold and hard; indeed, his face was so, almost like a witch doctor's wooden carving. Yet there were also tiny signs of something else that Sapho had recently begun to notice. She had seen a delicate quiver about his lips, while in his eyes was a certain softness, almost a look of pain, that made her think that deep inside there must be a kind of hurting.

Her glass told her that she was nearly ready. She stood back a bit and examined critically what she saw. Her face was slender, her cheekbones high. The nose flared a bit too wide, perhaps, but a man like Carlos wouldn't care. She had plucked her eyebrows just thin enough and had arched them some, and they looked slim and curved and satiny black against her skin's soft yellow. Her hair fell long and curly upon the red muslin shoulders of her peasant blouse. As for the lips, they were full, sensuously full, but delicate, too, and with brilliant scarlet she had drawn a mouth that was pert, nearly impish. Her eyes she examined last of all. She knew well that there was fire deep within their blackness; she knew also how a touch of shading made the fire look deeper.

There were so many Saphos, she thought as she added coral pendants to her ears, and each one was real. There was Sapho, the daughter of a Haitian mamaloi, a lighthearted Sapho with dance drums throbbing in her heart. This was a rhumba, congo-dancing Sapho who rose out of drumbeats like a wicked jinni whenever syncopated music played. But only stop the music, and the demon jinni disappeared, and Sapho became something else. She might be the poetry-scribbling Sapho, or Rory MacNeill's daughter who could quote Byron or François Villon, or again, she might be the nurse who held a splint for the setting of a bone. Sapho knew each one of these, and she also knew a Sapho that was soft, like far-off organ music, that was fragile like a tear drop, and this Sapho was as real to her as any other.

All these Saphos lay hidden within a single body, each one ready to rise up in a moment and take possession, and she liked them all, and what was more, each one was free and able to communicate itself to other persons, especially men, and it was this fact that Sapho thought of when she considered Carlos.

Her thoughts, like her passions, flowed and ebbed like the impulsive movements of a seemingly chaotic dance that moves with violent steps within a well-traced pattern. Much of her thinking was in brilliant imagery that moved about in the colorful stage setting of her mind, but sometimes she left those images for words in Spanish or Portuguese or English or the strange patois of Haitian French. She was humming to herself in the latter now.

> Tous les joli belle-belles
> Dansants dan la tête!

Taking one more look into the cracked mirror above her washstand, she accepted what she saw. With a swish of her red and blue striped skirt she passed through the doorway into the room where Carlos and her father were talking. She was watching Carlos, and she saw how his Nacheetl eyes flickered slightly as she entered. He rose, and she held out her hand as an old friend might.

Doctor MacNeill spoke to her wistfully as they prepared to leave.

"Faith, now, ye'll be taking Carrlos away," he sighed, "and I'll have to arrgue with myself alone."

Sapho kissed him lightly, patted his massive shoulder with her slender hand. "Never mind, Papaloi," she reassured him. "You can be thinking up some good points for when we come back tonight."

She and Carlos went out the door and down the stair, and in the dirty court she stopped for a word with Miguel about her father. "Pues, do not worry, señorita," the old Nacheetl said. "Like a sheep dog I will watch."

They made their way through the narrow passage to the street, and they headed toward the center of the city. "What did my father talk about?" Sapho asked Carlos.

Carlos smiled. "About the dialectic," he replied. "The Marxist mind thinks dialectically, your father said, and sees all things in a constant state of change. Thus there is no static truth, but only truth in evolution. The world cannot be all this or that because this is always changing and hence is already partly that."

Sapho took Carlos' arm. "Poor Papaloi," she sighed. "What a Don Quixote! If only he were younger, Carlos, strong enough to be a real Bolshevik! Oh, he would be a leader!"

Quizzically he looked into Sapho's eyes. "You mean that?"

"Of course I mean it!"

"To me he is a wild bird locked up in a cage," Carlos said, "and the customs of the world shut him in. He wants his freedom, Sapho, and in Marxism he thinks he sees it. But real Bolshevism would be only another cage. He speaks of Jesuit discipline among the Comunistas. Well, I do not think that he would like it."

She shook her head. "It is not freedom my father needs, Carlos, but a cause in which to believe and lose himself, and he could find it, too, in a Marxist state."

Carlos remained unconvinced. "Your father is a rebel," he said, "and an idealist. He could lead a revolution, but he would not like the newly created world any better than the one destroyed."

Sapho gave Carlos a coquettish look which did not reveal her searching interest in what he said, but she told herself that she had hit upon at least one phase of an inner conflict. "Are you also a rebel, Carlos?"

She saw in his eyes the slightest glint. "I fight for nothing," he told her, "nor do I rebel. I merely wander through a darkness, striking matches."

Sapho made no answer. In silence they pushed through streets that were crowded, now, with throngs of men and women and burros and mangy, yelping dogs. As they came closer to the city, there were long, sleek autos, too, crowding through streets already clogged, pushing heavily laden men and women and beasts against adobe walls on either hand. Under her breath Sapho cursed in Haitian French as a shiny mechanical monster plowed through a mudhole spreading brown slime upon all who were close about. "Diputado!" she spat. "A zopilote from Ronca's National Assembly!"

The limousine charged forward through the narrow street, scattering man and beast with the hideous beep-beep of its chromium horn.

The Market Place was jammed with peasants. There were shooting galleries set up among the booths, and for ten centavos each Carlos and Sapho potted at wooden ducks and geese moving across a blue horizon. Sapho won a doll in Nacheetl dress, while Carlos came off with a piggy bank of greyish clay. They took their prizes and gave them to a pair of ragged urchins playing in a near-by gutter. "See, she has never had a doll," Sapho exclaimed when she saw blank amazement on the face of the little girl. "Mon Dieu, the poor grow that way in a place like this. They cannot understand good fortune, and sometimes, even, they are very much afraid."

Arm in arm Carlos and Sapho moved along to a pavilion where musicians played, and when a dance began, it was easy for them to join in. They danced the Guajalote together, and the Chacalaneca, and Sapho felt the music as it spread through her body to fingertips and toes, and she tripped and flounced and fluttered according to the pattern of the dance.

Moving through the figures, Sapho flirted with each partner as is the peasant custom, but always she was watching Carlos. One learned nothing from his face, she knew, but his eyes were like stained-glass windows for seeing through, not transparent, but sensitive to lights and shadows. They could be all brown and dark, and then somewhere far behind a tiny candle flared briefly, and as quickly died. She watched closely whenever the dancing took her near, and once or twice she brushed against him softly and was aware of sensuous response.

Now they were drinking pink pop while the musicians rested. Carlos stared at Sapho with frank admiration. "You dance well," he told her. "Better than any person I have known."

Sapho fluffed out her skirt and dropped a curtsy. "Merci," she said. "Yet, after all, I should. My mamaloi taught me to dance when I was very young, and even now if Papaloi should buy too many bottles I could dance for money — flamencos, rhumbas, anything you wish." She felt Carlos' gaze fixed upon her, and she suspected that he was both stirred and shocked. "With flared-out skirts," she added impishly, "I can really dance!"

His eyes burned bright. "I would like to see you — dance." His voice was husky.

This Carlos is not altogether wood, she thought.

When, at last, they were tired of dancing, they strolled to a far corner of the Market Place where a ferris wheel was spinning to sprightly music. It was an old wheel, creaky and rusty, and there was only a sputtering engine to turn it, but no one in San Marcos was critical of that. In fact, before the coming of the railroad, ferris wheels were only wonders that one heard about from far-off Santa Cruz.

Carlos and Sapho took their places in a line and waited for their turns to come, and while they chatted, Sapho considered all that she had so far learned about this young Nacheetl. In certain ways he is like a hardwood tree, she thought, with a fire burning somewhere deep in the trunk. She could be wrong, of course, for he might be all wood and bark, sturdy, dependable, completely like his stolid outwardness, but she hoped for more. She hoped to cut through that outer trunk and see red flames come licking out.

Now it was their turn to have a gondola on the ferris wheel, but just as they moved up, a trooper and his girl crowded in ahead. Sapho gripped Carlos' arm. "We are next!" she hissed.

Carlos said nothing.

Sapho gave him a quick, appealing glance. "Carlos!"

His eyes remained unperturbed, but she saw a tiny quiver of his upper lip. The trooper and his señorita sat down within the gondola and secured the strap. The gasoline engine popped and sputtered, and the wheel began to turn while an amplifier blared "Valencia." Sapho felt anger creeping up her neck and across the softness of her face. Carlos made no move.

Unpleasant thoughts raced through her mind. Was he afraid? It was hard to believe. Through the corners of her eyes she watched his face for some expression, but the eyes were soft and calm, the features stolid. She drew away, and her upper lip was a tiny, scornful curl. "Why did you stand there?" she demanded. "Why did you do nothing?"

A startled expression crossed Carlos' face. "It was a small matter," he protested.

She stood apart from him. Her anger spread upward and across her temples as blood pounded at her head. No longer did she hear the tinny music, the pop and sputter of the engine, the creaking of the wheel. She tossed her long, black curls and bit at the redness of her lips.

The tempo of the music slowed, the engine coughed, a gondola stopped before them. She drew away when Carlos touched her to help her in, and she sat on the far side of the seat with as much space as possible between them. Once more the music jangled as the wheel began to turn. Up, up they went, high above the Market Place, and all the people below were sombrero tops or rebozos brilliant in the sunlight.

For Sapho there was no more pleasure, while Carlos sat, stiff and uncomfortable, gripping the safety belt. Up they went and over and down, and up and over and down, and up and over and —

The engine coughed and sucked and died. The wheel squeaked to a stop. High in the air Carlos and Sapho sat in uneasy silence. There was a long wait, a wait so long that the trooper shouted down from the next gondola. "E-e-e-yah, cabrón! What goes on down there?"

A fat man who had tended the engine peered up, spread his palms wide and shrugged. "No hay gasolina!" he wailed. "The tanquecita, she is empty!"

The trooper glared back. "Well, go get some gasolina, you lazy pig."

"Oh, yes, señor!" the fat man exclaimed. "Pronto, pronto, sí, señor!"

He started off in one direction at a waddle, thought better of it, and headed in another.

This was too much for Sapho. From the bosom of her blouse she pulled a handkerchief and used it to cover a smile, especially the side toward Carlos.

Like a frightened duck the fat man wobbled across the Market Place in search of gasoline. He was very much afraid of the trooper, as Sapho could see when he peered backward over his blubbery shoulder.

The trooper shouted down again. "Hurry up, you pig." Like Sapho, his girl was holding a handkerchief against her mouth, but not for hiding laughter.

Sapho stole a glance at Carlos. Cramped against the gondola side, he was looking miserable. Her anger had seeped away even more quickly than it had come, but the silence was awkward, and she could think of nothing worthwhile to say. She looked upward at the sky above. There was blueness broken only by two clouds just below the zenith.

She touched his arm. "Look at the sky," she said, "and tell me what you see."

With boyish relief, Carlos looked above him, stared at the clouds he saw. His forehead wrinkled. "There is nothingness," he said. "And out of the nothingness rises a shaft of hard, white stone. It rises straight up, and near by, but reaching only half as high, I see a sphere that is also hard and white."

Sapho looked into his eyes still staring upward. "Tell me what you think it means."

Carlos half closed his eyes. "Well, the shaft — that is a reaching upward," he murmured. "And the sphere — I think that must be a holding back."

Sapho caught her breath. "I like that," she said. She moved closer, touched Carlos with her fingers. His grip upon the safety belt loosened. He looked at her with warmness in his eyes, and he took her hand in his.

In a moment the fat man came waddling back with a tin of gasoline. He punched a hole in the top, and Sapho saw liquid splashing into the empty tank. Soon the engine sputtered, the music started, and to the jangling of "Valencia," down to earth they came.

From the Market Place they pushed toward the Plaza, and when
they reached it, feathered Nacheetls in ceremonial dress were performing the Dance of Tana's Nuptial. The whole square was a garden
of brilliant flowers. There were arches of bougainvillea and clusters
of heliotrope and white gardenias. On every lamppost were delicate,
wax-like orchids enshrined in sections of banana stalk, and the very
cobbles of the streets were strewn with red and yellow and purple
blossoms. Carlos and Sapho moved closer to the dance.

Only men were performing now, brown, smooth-muscled men in
carmine capes, with red and white and green plumes rising high above
their heads. Their belts were spangled, their loincloths embroidered,
and about their slender Nacheetl wrists and ankles were woven
feathers and brass bells that tinkled with the dancing.

It was a sedate dance, forward and back, forward and back, in tight
formation, around and around in concentric circles, all in rhythm to
the pulsing of Nacheetl drums and the strumming of mellow guitars.
A hundred men were dancing, stately figures in feathers and carmine
capes, and bells strung about their ankles tinkled as they moved.
Here was something that Sapho's body knew. These were not voodoo
drums before Dumballa's altar; the tempo was far more measured,
more dignified in its solemn pulsing. Yet she felt their booming, and
her blood picked up the rhythm.

The dancers moved forward like the comb of a lazy surf, then drew
back again against a flowered wall. The ranks broke, opened to either
side, and from a gaping hole among the flowers there advanced a
stately, dancing figure. It was twice as tall as a Nacheetl man. Robes
of golden yellow hung loosely from his shoulders, while a burnished
crown upon his head caught the sun and spread its gleaming, coppery
rays. The face was masked.

Carlos breathed in Sapho's ear. "Chan!"

The crowd fell back in awe as the great god moved across the
center of the dance. The drums throbbed on, and their rhythm, together with the splendor of the dancers, transported Sapho, and she
was dancing with them even though her body stayed among the en-
chanted crowd.

Once more the ranks moved back against the flowered wall and
broke, and Tana came out, a white-draped maiden figure borne on a

bed of gardenia petals. Female attendants in white robes carried her to the very feet of Chan, who received her as the Dance of Passion began.

The drums beat loud and soft, loud and soft, and it seemed to Sapho that she could feel the mounting passion of the dancers. She watched as Chan knelt at Tana's bed and drew back a coverlet of filmy white.

Carlos seized her arm. "The Nuptial!" he whispered, and she felt the warm moisture of his breath. "One does not view the Nuptial!"

As Sapho looked away, she saw that all the crowd had turned its back. The drums were beating softly, now, and she welcomed the touch when Carlos took her hand. The music nearly died, and she could feel the calmness of a long and reverent moment followed by a crash of drums. She felt the pressure of Carlos' fingers about her hand.

Turning about, she saw that the dancing place was empty.

6

DURING WEEKDAYS Carlos, being busy with the study of law, had no time for visiting, but on week-ends he often gathered with certain of his law-school friends in a cramped flat or a garret room to discuss politics or listen to foreign news over Luis' radio. Among his friends there was still no agreement about the war. Some were certain that the Germans were going to beat the British and, ultimately, the Yanquis, too, and that conditions would be no worse, even if they did. After all, the Germans were no more fearful than Yanquis; in fact, they were less aloof, more inclined to accept and take part in local ways of living.

Another group argued that, since the British and Yanqui governments were in a measure democratic, the world would suffer from their defeat. Those who held this view did not overlook the evils for which both Englishmen and Yanquis had been responsible; they merely maintained that Anglo-American domination was the lesser of two evils. This contention was strengthened one Saturday night when, huddled in an attic room, they picked up a certain transcribed broadcast.

They heard the bold, clear-ringing voice of a man who was not satisfied with the world as it then existed. Unlike Mr. Prettyman, this Yanqui wanted the same freedoms not only for his own people, but for all human beings everywhere, in every corner of the earth. He also wanted a broader kind of freedom: not just freedom of speech and worship, but freedom from fear and want as well.

The words were simple, but they brought hope and admiration surging in the throat, and when the speech was over, there was an impressive silence in the little attic room.

The inspiration of this Yanqui voice left Carlos impatient to talk with Sapho, to describe to her the powerful effect which the words of this man had exerted.

Almost every Sunday he found some excuse for a visit to the Mac-Neill flat. Sometimes he called to borrow or return a book. Again, he might feel compelled to ask the doctor some question in regard to Marxism. But whatever the excuse, he never admitted even to himself that he could not live in peace without these frequent calls. They were always far too short, and when he had come away, Carlos found himself tortured by the fact that he could not remember every expression that had hovered on Sapho's face, every word that she had uttered.

It was easy to remember the doctor. That redness of the bloated face, the pale blue eyes that seemed to float in sockets full of water, the purple pouches directly beneath — all these left an impression that one could not forget. Sapho, on the other hand, was a more subtle vision. Carlos could recall her yellow velvet skin, her hair that was so jet black and tightly curled, the depth of her eyes. But when he strove to put the parts together, when he tried to fit her nose, with its high bridge and flaring nostrils, against her face, the result was disappointing.

During weekdays he tortured himself with thoughts about her, and the hurt was greater because he told himself that she was far beyond his reach. Surely many men had sought her, and probably she had already made a choice. Perhaps she loved Luis. Carlos had heard them talk and laugh together, had seen her hand in his. Yet even as he told himself to forget this Sapho, he thought and talked about her.

It was remarkable how a conversation concerning any subject whatsoever had a tendency to lead toward Sapho. If he were talking politics with Francisco or with Bernardo Cabrera, Carlos invariably found a reason for mentioning Sapho. Or if he merely chatted with Magdalena about weather or taxes or the price of food, he found himself leading up to Sapho.

Magdalena was growing tired of this. "Will your Sapho be good to sleep with?" she asked coarsely. "When she is as old as I, will she still be good to sleep with?"

Carlos flushed beneath the brownness of his skin. "I do not think such things of her." He was beginning to be annoyed by Magdalena's increasing slovenliness. "She is the daughter of a friend."

"She is ugly, then?"

"She is not," Carlos snapped. "She is precious, she is — "

"The daughter of a friend only," Magdalena snickered. "Have a care, Carlos, and find out how she sleeps."

Carlos pushed such unpleasant recollections from his mind as he made his way through the Barrio of the Spiders on the morning after the transcribed Yanqui broadcast. He was having dinner with the MacNeills today, and he was fancying that he might grow bold enough to find out how Sapho felt about him. Not being certain how to go about it, he created fantastic plans each of which he eventually damned and cast aside. If only he had Luis' glibness! If only he could talk about Havana and the fiestas there!

It was not that he felt ill at ease with Sapho. On the contrary, they had talked and laughed and danced together. But what Carlos wanted was some smooth and easy road to a more intimate level, a road that he could follow and, if necessary, retreat upon without trespassing where he was not wanted. His greatest fear was that, having advanced too far, he would cause Sapho to close the gates completely, whereupon he would find himself doomed to an exile which he could find no courage to face.

Such was the disturbing nature of his thoughts when old Miguel opened the door and let him in. "Oh, señor, you are just in time!" exclaimed the ancient Indian. "There is a precious sight to see, let me tell you."

Sapho met them in the court where various of the tenants stood about the kitchen shack, gaping through the door. "The cat had kittens in the stove," she explained to Carlos. "Has Miguel told you?"

The Indian pushed through the knot of curious watchers. "Let me through, let me through! Señor must see the gatocitos!" He beckoned to Carlos. "Come, come, señor, here they are!"

Cat and kittens lay curled in the firebox of a charcoal range. "Bien, let me begin again!" begged Miguel. "The sun was about to awake, as I told these people. The sun was about to arise from its sleeping pallet when I heard a song. It was the song of a gatacita giving birth. E-e-e-e-e-ya-a-a-a-a, e-e-e-e-e-e-e-ya-a-a-a-a, that was the song. Hearing it, I left my pallet and came into the cooking house and listened. E-e-e-e-e-ya-a-a-a-a, e-e-e-e-e-e-e-ya-a-a-a-a-a-a, the song of my gatacita. But where? I look here, I look there. No gatacita. Where is she? In the stove, caray! On the warm charcoal is la gatacita. On the warm charcoal with seven teeny leetle gatocitillos. Brr-brr-brr-brr, seven teeny leetle gatocitillos, brr-brr-brr-brr."

The brown faces peered and nodded. Young and old, the brown faces nodded wisely.

Brr-brr-brrr-brr.

Old Miguel had a sudden thought. "Oh, señorita, about the stove. We cannot cook today. Look! On the warm charcoal, my gatacita. Señorita Sapho, my gatacita! A-a-yeah, let me tell you, the sun was about to wake. From its sleeping pallet the sun —"

"Since morning he has been saying that," Sapho whispered to Carlos. "No one is allowed to cook, and so we have no dinner."

"I will buy something from a vendor," Carlos offered. "Enchiladas, a chicken, perhaps." He found Miguel's excitement infectious, and deep inside himself he felt a gayness which he almost showed.

"I'll go with you!"

They went through the front passageway and forth upon the street. "More over there," Sapho directed. "More over there is a little market."

From a vendor they bought a chicken spiced and cooked, and a basket for it, and they bought roasted peanuts and corn steamed within its husks.

Sapho sensed the lightness in Carlos' heart. "We should go on a pic-nic," she suggested. "Did you ever go on a pic-nic, Carlos?" She watched him closely. I love that man, she thought, whatever he is like inside.

"No," Carlos replied. "Never." Sapho's nearness roused him almost as though their hands had touched.

"Then we shall go, Carlos. I know a place! There is a stream, and pepper trees for shade. A little way only, Carlos, and the chicken will still be hot."

Back in the flat Sapho told Doctor MacNeill about the plan. He was searching for his bottle. "A picnic!" he stormed in English. "A picnic! Why should we be going on a picnic?"

Sapho found his bottle and poured him out a drink. He gulped it down and shuddered.

After a time he felt better and began to beam. "A picnic!" he declared. "Sapho, now, it's been yearrs since we went upon a picnic!"

He fumbled around, buttoning up his breeches and searching for a cap. "My tweed cap," he wailed. "Indeed, that tweed's the very thing for a picnic!"

Sapho found it, and she put it upon his head straight, and she helped him with his buttons.

"A book!" he exclaimed. "A picnic calls for poetry!"

They agreed upon a book and packed it in the basket.

"My walking stick!"

"Voici, mon père!"

They were off.

This was a strange sight for a city like San Marcos. Sapho, walking between, linked arms with Carlos and her father — a thing that no local woman would ever do. Dressed in a Nacheetl skirt and blouse, she moved with panther grace, her head held proudly high, like a Nacheetl head, as though she had carried earthen jugs upon it. Her hair was loose, without rebozo, and it blew freely about her shoulders. On her left, Doctor MacNeill strode forward, stiff and straight in tweeds, the visor of his cap pulled low to shade his eyes. His free hand grasped a heavy cane which he swung in rhythm with his strides, and the silver tip glittered in the sunlight.

Carlos, on her other side, was describing the Yanqui broadcast. He had worn his best today, a black sack coat passed on long ago by Don Ricardo. The matching trousers were long at the waist and tight about the ankles. His shirt was lavender, with a black string tie. His hat was black and low of crown, his shoes pointed and buttoned up the side.

"Freedom from want — think of what that means!" Carlos exclaimed.

Doctor MacNeill did not seem impressed. "I have heard that kind of thing before," he said. "Yanqui politicians get their votes that way."

Carlos felt disappointed and somewhat hurt. "This man is different."

"A reformist," the doctor grunted.

Feeling the pressure upon his arm from Sapho's hand, Carlos changed the subject. Now they were following a dry and dusty road stretching westward from the city, and after a kilometer or more they came upon a stone bridge that spanned a stream. As they turned into a path that disappeared through a stand of eucalypti, Sapho took the lead. Women were doing laundry in a shallow place, scrubbing clothes upon rocks in greenish water and beating out the dirt with paddles.

The trail followed close along the bank to a grove of pepper trees a hundred yards or more above the laundry place. There Carlos spread a thin serape on a grassy spot beneath the trees, and the three of them began their picnic.

They tore the chicken apart and ate with their fingers. The meat had been crusted brown to hold in the juices, and it was spiced and nipped the tongue. From ears of corn they stripped the husks, and the kernels were yellow and fat and flavored with lime, and the kernels held their heat.

When the chicken was gone, and the corn as well, they shelled peanuts and ate them and quenched their thirst from a calabash of water, while Doctor MacNeill had a nip from his bottle.

"We have fed the belly," he sighed, "and it is content. Shall we proffer a bite of food to the soul as well?" He opened the book which he and Sapho had selected, and he leaned against a pepper tree and began to read.

It was the *Luciad* of Camoëns, and the words were Portuguese, which Carlos scarcely understood. "The storry of the firrst grreat imperrialist," Doctor MacNeill said, "but good to listen to."

The words were Portuguese, and the sounds were soft and lush, and they were music to the ear. Doctor MacNeill read in an Irish lilt, and Carlos listened, stretched upon the serape, with Sapho close at hand.

Carlos watched her, and he sought to memorize her face, and he sensed the lines of her body beneath her blouse. She was listening to her father's reading, to the words of Camoëns, and yet Carlos could feel her womanness. It stirred him, it aroused a hunger, it made him aware of maleness.

A canto here, a verse there, Doctor MacNeill read on. The words grew drowsy, but Carlos did not hear. The words died sleepily away, and Carlos did not heed. He was watching Sapho.

Doctor MacNeill could read no more. His hand, holding the book, dropped, and his fingers lost their grip, and the book slid away to rest upon the ground. His big lids closed, and he fell asleep, breathing heavily.

The sun shone bright and warm, and they went together to the water's edge. She waded out where the water was still and green over a smooth, gravelly bottom, and she tucked up her dress as she waded, drawing it between her legs and looping the edges over her belt in such a manner that Carlos saw the length and slimness of her legs, the banana yellow, the smooth thigh curve.

She called to him, and he removed his button shoes, hoisted up his trouser legs, and waded out. She took his hand, and they moved about, slowly, and felt the roundness of tiny pebbles beneath their feet and she leaned over to watch the minnows swimming. Her blouse fell away a bit, and Carlos saw her breasts. They were high and firm and pointed, like yellow mangos, Carlos thought. He felt a stirring, deep within his loins, a vicious stirring, an anguish, a joyous pain. He slipped an arm about her waist. She looked up, and her black eyes blazed.

They crossed the stream and climbed the bank where reeds grew high around a plot of feathery grass. They lay there close, and the blouse came off, and the skirt and the sack coat and the long-waisted pantalones. There in the greenness of the grass, in a patch of brilliant sunlight, they embraced, these two fine bodies, one so tan, one such a gorgeous yellow.

VII. Tiburon

When Carlos awoke on this strange morning, he was lying in a tremendous bed, and he saw the clay-brownness of his skin against a white sheet beneath him, while another sheet was tucked up under his chin, and a feather pillow supported his head. He lay sunk deep in the softness of a bed, and warm rays of sunlight were streaming through doors that opened out upon a balcony. This was the Gran Hotel San Marcos, and he remembered —

In momentary panic he looked for Sapho.

She was there asleep beside him.

He raised upon an elbow in the softness of their bed, and he saw her there, her black hair spread wide and wild upon a pillow, her shoulders peeping from between the sheets. He touched her with his hand. She flinched a little, still asleep.

This was difficult to believe!

He settled back upon his pillow, allowing himself to dream a bit. Awake, he allowed himself to dream of what had happened, and, dreaming, he relived it all. . . .

They were lying in the grass by the stream, and they were naked and tired and content, and after a time, they talked. Carlos spoke of Uncle Vicente, of Santa Marta and Don Ricardo's gate, of his years upon the railroad, while Sapho told of Haiti and Havana and a stinking cantina in Port au Prince, of Rio and Colon, of Buenaventura and Mérida and Vera Cruz. She spoke of cafés where her mother danced, of bars, rum soaked, of rhumbas and samba music, of naked bellies and twisting hips.

Speaking of her mother, she told of cantinas, and speaking of her father she told of books piled helter-skelter on broken-down beds,

of Rimsky-Korsakov played on café pianos out of tune. She told of
books and music, and she told of back rooms and her father's week-
long drunks, of whores in labor and brawls and broken jawbones set,
of syphilitic sores and gunshot wounds, of appendectomies performed
upon a bar.

They lay there in the tall grass, naked in the sunlight, and there
were warm breezes rustling through slender reeds, and water gurgled
among rocks in the stream bed near at hand.

"We shall have a bed tonight in the Gran Hotel San Marcos," Carlos
had promised, "a big, wide bed with sheets, and they will bring our
breakfast in the morning."

A cloud crossed Sapho's face. "Madre, Carlos, what about my
father? We cannot leave him alone even a single night."

Carlos showed his disappointment. "I had not thought."

Sapho ran her fingers through his hair. "I want a big, wide bed
tonight, Carlos. Perhaps —

Carlos hesitated. "There is Magdalena," he said doubtfully. "Would
that do?"

She laughed gaily. "Indeed, Carlos, Papa will feel quite at home."

Things had come about that way. . . .

Now Carlos lay sunk in the softness of a bed, and Sapho was close
beside him. He could hear her breathing, and the sound made him
feel secure and happy. He dreamed about their future. He would find
a flat today, and that would be their home until he was admitted to
the bar. Within a few months he would be a lawyer, whereupon he
would find another place, a house like Don Ricardo's, only smaller
and in a poorer part of town.

There would be a court with flowers and a study for his books. He
saw his practice grow until he could buy a second-hand piano for
Sapho and rent an office near the plaza. He would have to be careful,
of course, in order to build a reputation. No politics, no dangerous
books, no controversial cases. He could attend to this man's deed and
that man's will, and while he might not get rich that way, he could
make a living and avoid trouble with the government.

There might be some difficulty about Doctor MacNeill. If the au-
thorities discovered that a Marxist was living in the house, they might
deprive Carlos of his right to practice. The doctor was an old man,

however, a harmless alcoholic, and the whole matter might easily be explained away so long as it was generally known that Carlos himself was reputable and safe.

It was true that Carlos himself had studied Marx, but so far he had not become sufficiently convinced to consider Bolshevism seriously. The Communist goal, he thought, was admirable in concept; he, too, would like to see a classless state where all men and women were mature enough to administer their lives without resort to force. But he doubted whether class war would ever bring about the result that Marx predicted.

In any case, he did not intend to allow Marxism to intervene between him and his happiness with Sapho. Of course, one did not need to be a Communist to find oneself in trouble under Ronca's rule. He had not forgotten those men hanging from a tree in the courtyard of the Provincial Prison. But Carlos was certain that there must be a way of avoiding trouble altogether.

He remembered how, in railroad-building days, he had dreamed of a career in politics. He had gone forth among the people, making speeches, stirring them up against Ronca, and when the proper moment had arrived, he had led them against the government. Well, those dreams were good enough when one was young and had no family. But now he had a wife; he hoped to have children in years to come; and consequently he had no more wish to act so rashly.

Yet it would not be easy to live in the midst of San Marcos' misery and do nothing to make things better. One did not have to be a Marxist to realize that Ronca should be overthrown. A handful of the people owned all the land, while peons grubbed for grains of corn. Most of the population could neither read nor write; more than half of all the babies born were doomed to die before they were five or six; the nation was plagued with every kind of sickness. Knowing this, could one buy a house and a second-hand piano and rent an office and never think of others?

Carlos considered Don Ricardo, and as he tallied all that the judge had given up, he realized for the first time the full stature of his old benefactor. Had he not sought to fight a revolution, Don Ricardo would even now be enjoying his huge house with all its gardens and stables and corps of servants. There would be gatherings in the parlor where the Señorita Dolores' wedding had taken place, there would be tables heavy with food, there would be music and laughter on fiesta days.

These were but a few of the pleasures and comforts that Don Ricardo had exchanged for exile. Now, no doubt, he was living in some far-off, lonely place. Had he accomplished enough to balance this sacrifice? Carlos was afraid to weigh the issues. If Don Ricardo wished to make himself a martyr, that was his affair. The judge was old, in any case, and had lived an abundant life for many years previous to his exile. Carlos, on the other hand, was young and had not yet tasted enough of the good things that life could offer.

He felt twinges of guilt as he remembered a bold, clear-ringing voice as it had come over Luis' radio. "Freedom of speech and expression — everywhere in the world," that Yanqui voice demanded. "Freedom of every person to worship God in his own way — everywhere in the world; freedom from want — everywhere in the world; freedom from fear — "

The voice haunted Carlos this morning. There was a Yanqui who wanted good things of life for every man and woman and child throughout the earth. He had spoken from far away, but his words had defied distance and the barriers of Ronca's censorship and had sounded firm and fearless in a land where common men had none of the freedoms that he called for.

Could Carlos or any other man ignore such words? The whole of Ronca's nation stood as a mocking challenge. Yet what could a single person do? A great leader, perhaps, could call a million men to arms, but Carlos had no power, no influence, no inspiration to stir a hopeless, broken people. Bien, he would go ahead and build his happiness, and later on, when he had prestige, he would do something for his country.

Thus he dismissed the Yanqui voice with its call for freedom and turned his thoughts upon the present. Shifting gently in the softness of his bed, he studied Sapho's hair. Rays of warm sunlight streaming into the room showed a tinge of redness in her curls that he had never noticed before. She stirred slightly. He waited hopefully for her to waken, but she only gathered the bedclothes closer to her and continued sleeping.

Steps sounded on the stairs outside. They were hurried steps that brought to Carlos a twinge of premonition. But they would go by, of course. No one knew where he and Sapho were except Magdalena, and she would not come so early in the morning to disturb their rest.

The steps stopped just outside the door, and someone rapped.

Carlos knew there was some mistake. He had told the man behind the desk that they were not to be disturbed.

The rap sounded again, and it seemed to Carlos that there was fear behind it. He reached for his sack coat, the one inherited from Don Ricardo, but before he had it on, he saw the door fly open. Magdalena stood there upon the threshold.

"They came to get you," she gasped breathlessly, "but they took him instead."

Carlos reached over to awaken Sapho. Perhaps they could reach the mountains, he thought, and hide away. His hand had just touched her shoulder when a picture flashed across his brain. He saw a chair, an old chair, an easy chair with the excelsior coming out. He withdrew his hand, and the future melted. "There is Pepillo," he whispered to Magdalena. Quickly he began to dress.

2

CARLOS WENT THROUGH the Viceregal Palace to the gate of the Provincial Prison, and asked the trooper on duty for Captain Lopez. This sentry turned him over to a runner who escorted him immediately to the room where long before Pepillo had made his proposition. But the officer behind the desk today was not Pepillo. He was a soft-eyed, boyish-faced mestizo with a very thin mustache, precisely trimmed, and lips that were red and full.

Carlos gave his name.

The officer stood up, bowed slightly and clicked his heels. "Captain Alvarez."

Carlos asked about Captain López.

"A shame!" exclaimed Captain Alvarez. "Your friend has recently been transferred. Not without advantage, may I add, not without advantage!"

Carlos paused, uncertain how to continue. He had a proposition rehearsed for Pepillo but what could he say to this youngster of a captain? "I came in regard to Doctor Rory MacNeill," he said at last.

Again Captain Alvarez bowed slightly. "Your servant," he murmured.

"There was a slight mistake," Carlos continued. "When Doctor MacNeill was arrested — "

Alvarez indicated a chair. "Please sit down!" A copy of the newspaper *Las Noticias* was lying on his desk. He handed it to Carlos. "Read this," he said, "and you will understand why it is necessary that we detain Doctor MacNeill."

The headline was thick and black: HITLER DECLARES WAR ON BOLSHEVIKS. Carlos ran his eyes rapidly over the story beneath. Already German armies were rolling across the plains of Poland into Russia; already German pilots were bombing Russian towns and cities; and Bolshevik troops were falling back in every quarter. Hitler had spoken. "I have decided today again to lay the fate and future of the German Reich and our people in the hands of our soldiers."

Captain Alvarez was sitting on the corner of his desk, watching Carlos closely. "The world did not listen when Hitler warned against the Bolshevik danger, Señor Chichayan! On the contrary, the British and the Yanquis turned on Hitler. Bien, now Hitler fights two wars. But the time will come when our well-fed friends in London and New York will realize that Adolph Hitler was right about the Bolsheviks."

Carlos tossed the paper back upon the desk. "How does this concern Doctor MacNeill?" he asked.

Alvarez turned one palm in a helpless gesture. "We have been checking on Doctor MacNeill for many months. We know where his sympathies lie."

"We are not at war with the Bolsheviks," Carlos countered. "We are not at war with anyone. In any case, Doctor MacNeill is not a Bolshevik."

"The second point is open to question," Alvarez contradicted. "As regards the first — Bolsheviks, as you well know, are always at war against us. They even boast about it."

Carlos examined the captain critically. This was no hale adventurer like Pepillo. This was a young man of inborn prejudice and conviction with whom it would be no easy matter to make a deal. Carlos was inclined to place Alvarez as the son of an hacendado, the sort who had probably gone to school in Spain. "Doctor MacNeill is a sick old man," he said, "a sick old man with a curious mind and a tongue-unhitched. There is no harm in him."

Alvarez raised an eyebrow. "Doctor MacNeill had a room full of proscribed books."

"It seems strange to me," Carlos observed, "that the State is so terrified of books."

The officer disregarded this. "We are trying to persuade Doctor MacNeill to answer certain questions," he said. "Our treatment is necessarily harsh. If you would answer some of these questions for him, Señor Chichayan — "

Carlos considered the implications. "What sort of questions, Captain?"

Alvarez stood up. "Suppose we go to see the doctor."

After leaving the office, they walked across a court and through an iron gateway where a trooper presented arms. Carlos recognized the original wing of the Viceregal Palace, a sixteenth-century building of fortress-like proportions to which other, more luxurious sections had been added later. They passed through a dark stone corridor and into the famous Court of Lions which the first viceroy had built as a botanical garden. It had been the nobleman's ambition to plant here at least one of every plant and tree native to New Spain.

The court now consisted of an hectare or more of desert and jungle and temperate forest transplanted in miniature. There were pines and rubber trees, oaks, rosewood, mahogany and Spanish cedar, tall pitahayas and tunas and corpulent organ cacti. There were banana trees and zapote chico laced together with a tangle of vines that stretched from treetop to treetop. Giant ferns grew in impenetrable clusters, while sword-bladed jungle grasses prevented would-be trespassers from leaving the narrow footpaths.

Crossing the court, Carlos and the captain skirted a pit which Indian serfs had dug to satisfy another of the viceroy's whims. Alvarez paused at the edge. The top was like the mouth of a huge well, guarded by a wall of stone, but the excavation became larger with depth, being in the shape of a bell. The floor, about twenty feet down, was a tangle of plants and grasses, while thick jungle creepers lined the sides, pushing upward after sunlight.

Alvarez slapped the stone wall. "No more lions!" There was a legend which asserted that in viceregal times a prisoner had been cast into the pit each day to be devoured by half-starved beasts.

The path led to another historic wing of the palace. "One day this will be opened to the public," Alvarez said, "and people will pay a peso to gape at its relics." They passed through a narrow doorway into a stone chamber the walls of which were partially hidden by heavy tapestries. Woven into the fabric were scenes of another age. One depicted judges of the Church gathered behind a tribunal. They wore blood-red robes, while their mitres were black, and before them stood a prisoner in chains.

That was one tapestry, and a second showed three victims being burned at the stake, and woven into a third Carlos saw the figure of a man walking on hot coals, his feet already consumed to the ankles. As they moved through an adjoining chamber hung with even more blood-chilling scenes, Carlos marvelled that so much misery had ever been inflicted for Man's salvation. There seemed to exist in human nature, he thought, some innate tendency to enforce good with evil.

Alvarez ushered Carlos down a flight of stone steps that dropped away in a tight spiral. There was the sound of water dripping, and Carlos, touching the cylindrical walls with his fingers, felt a smooth, hard surface that was cold and wet. The staircase bored down into the bowels of the building and opened into a dungeon chamber lighted by an oil lamp. A strange machine stood in the middle, its shadow gross and misshapen upon the floor. Carlos recognized this as a torture wheel. There was a rack just beyond, while close against the farthest wall were a number of other mechanical monsters created for purposes which were not apparent.

Alvarez proceeded through a stone corridor that eventually opened into a chamber similar to the one they had left. Walls, ceiling, and floor were of dark basalt. A gasoline lantern hung from an iron hook overhead. In the most distant corner Carlos saw the backs of two guards who were so occupied with some object between them that they were not aware of intruders.

One of the troopers turned and straightened as Alvarez came close. "He is a stubborn man, Capitán!"

There was a chair in the corner, and slumped upon it was the naked, ponderous body of Doctor Rory MacNeill. The head, battered and pulpy, had sunk upon a chest covered with rope-sized welts. A single thin stream of blood had trickled down across the navel.

"Is he conscious?" Alvarez asked, his voice high pitched and tense.
"No, Capitán."
The officer kept his eyes downcast. "Bring him to."

From an assortment of tools upon the floor one of the guards selected an hypodermic syringe and jabbed it into a bruised bicep. Carlos felt the heaviness of his own body as the plunger yielded slowly to the guard's thumb. "In a little moment," the trooper said.

Alvarez tried to light a cigarette, but his hands shook, and the match went out. He did not strike another. The trooper who had administered the hypodermic watched Doctor MacNeill closely. "El viene," he whispered.

"Poco-á-poco!" muttered the other trooper. He stepped close and lifted the massive head with gentle fingers. "Hombre!" he said sharply. "Hombre, it is time to waken." Doctor MacNeill's body made a con-vulsive effort, slowly subsided. "Amigo, I think you gave too much!"

The first trooper held the syringe high in lantern light. "This much only," he said, indicating with a thumbnail.

Alvarez glanced at Carlos, quickly looked away. "Well, in any case, you see how matters stand." He removed the unlighted cigarette from his mouth and dropped it on the floor. "It would go easier with him, Señor Chichayan, if you would give us a bit of information."

Carlos swallowed. There was a dry, coppery taste deep in his mouth and throat. "What — what kind of information?"

The captain tugged violently at his right ear. "A list of names."

Carlos shook his head. "If Doctor MacNeill wished to tell, he would tell."

Alvarez turned on Carlos sharply. "He is your friend, Señor Chicha-yan. You would not want matters to go much worse with him."

"If he wished to tell," Carlos repeated, "he would tell."

The young officer touched Carlos' arm, and his upper lip quivered slightly as he spoke. "It will go much worse — "

There was a long silence. Carlos heard the hard, uneven pounding of his own heart, a soft moan from the victim, water, somewhere, dripping. Doctor MacNeill stirred, raised his head, stared dumbly about. The trooper who had used the syringe gave Alvarez a ques-tioning look. "Now, Capitán?"

The officer was watching Carlos. "The information is very small."

Carlos felt blood draining from his face. He turned toward Doctor MacNeill and searched the pulpy face. There was no expression, no hint of recognition; the eyes stared dumb and swollen.

"A few names?" Alvarez asked.

Carlos shook his head.

At a nod from his captain, the waiting trooper selected an instrument from among the assortment upon the floor and bent over Doctor MacNeill. Lantern light projected a hideous pantomime upon the stone wall behind. The victim's throat loosed a rattle followed by a gasping shriek. The young officer's face turned sickly green, but the guards worked coolly, with efficient dispatch.

3

THE TRAIN from San Marcos labored up the last of the grade to La Cumbre and dropped over the continental divide. It was a tren mixto; following the engine and tender came a baggage car, two freights, and three passenger coaches. It was a tren mixto, and it was bound for the oilfields and the port of Santa Cruz.

In the baggage car, in addition to the mail clerk, there were two passengers. One, a trooper of the federal police, lounged in a straight-backed chair in one corner of the car, while the other, a prisoner, lay propped against a payroll lockbox, shackled legs stretched before him, handcuffed wrists resting hard upon his aching femurs. From time to time the trooper whistled snatches from native folksongs or hummed a verse of the "Virgin Whore," but the prisoner made no sound. His body was badly battered, his face swollen and covered with purple bruises. Despite the prisoner's helpless condition, his trooper guard had chained and locked the leg irons to a ringbolt in the baggage car wall.

Brakes squealed almost continuously on the down grade, couplings rattled, and the locomotive whistled for curves and tunnels. Through the open door of the baggage car one could see cliffs dropping off sheer for a thousand feet and more, and deep within the gorge wound a river, brown, like a length of hemp cordage threaded through the mountains.

After a time, when the mail clerk had finished sorting the mail, he left his bench and struck up a conversation with the trooper who seemed eager to talk.

"This man," he announced with a nod toward the prisoner, "this man goes to Tiburón!"

The mail clerk whistled. "He must be a bandit."

The trooper shrugged. "The orders read Tiburón," he said with importance. From an inner pocket of his powder-blue blouse he drew a paper, three times folded and bearing a large, red seal. "It says here," he continued, unfolding the paper, "that the prisoner has been transferred to the federal prison on the island of San Luis de Tiburón."

The mail clerk peered over the trooper's shoulder. "Carlos Chi — Chichayan," he read aloud. "A strange name — Chichayan." He examined the paper carefully, forming each word with his lips as he read. "Political — it says here political."

"So it does!" agreed the trooper who was trying to hide the fact that he couldn't read. "A revolutionist, more or less. Madre, but we gave him a going over!"

They chatted on, and while they chatted, Carlos stared dully through the open door of the car. The shacks were gone from the edge of the grade, but the cuts were there, and the tunnels, and the culverts which made a hollow sound beneath the train.

There were many changes. El Prado was now a station, and the train stopped for water. Carlos couldn't see the meadow; it was above the tracks. But the grade had been widened, and women walked along the side of the train selling enchiladas.

Thus through aching eyes he was aware of landmarks as the train moved along. The brakes were squealing when darkness fell. The stars came out, and here and there in the canyon far below were lights twinkling, open fires, or perhaps a torch blazing.

A brakeman went through the train, lighting coal-oil lamps.

The mail clerk closed the baggage door and settled down to a game of craps with the trooper. Carlos tried to sleep.

Stations came more frequently now, and there were mail bags to load. At each stop the clerk opened the door, and men outside tossed in a bag, or a dozen hens with their legs tied together, or a shoat, securely hobbled.

As soon as the train was again in motion, the mail clerk went back to his dice, but finally, when he had lost all his money, he rolled up in a serape and fell asleep. The trooper stuffed his winnings into a leather bag about his neck, removed his blouse, hung it on a nail, and wrapped himself in the folds of a military cloak.

He yawned. "Tengo sueño!" he told Carlos, not unpleasantly.

On the floor of the baggage car Carlos stretched his battered, pain-ing body and dropped into exhausted sleep while the brakes squealed and the couplings rattled and the tren mixto looped and zigzagged out of the cordillera into the foothills and savannas far below.

When morning came, the trooper got up, brushed the wrinkles out of his breeches and cape, and washed in the gasoline tin which the mail clerk used for a basin. At the next station he sent the mail clerk off to find a can of coffee while he bought an enchilada for himself and one for Carlos.

Through the baggage car door Carlos saw a town which in grade-crew days had not been there at all. It was a town of frame buildings, such as he had never seen, and there were rows of board dwellings, low and squat, each painted white and looking exactly like the others. There were tar and gravel streets, and there were cars — dilapidated taxis parked beyond the station, a quarter-ton truck, an immense tour-ing car with the top rolled back.

To the rear of the town loomed a gigantic refinery, and Carlos could smell — or taste — the sickening odor of oil. It was more taste than smell, he decided, because it brought saliva to his mouth and made him want to spit.

"This town, how is it called?" he asked when the trooper had brought the enchiladas.

"It is called Usoco," the trooper replied.

"Usoco? That is a strange name, Usoco," Carlos said.

"It is a Yanqui name," explained the trooper.

"A Yanqui name?"

"Yes, in the Yanqui language," elaborated the trooper, proud of his erudition, "in the Yanqui language it means those-who-deal-in-oil."

The train pulled away and continued its journey into the hot low-lands. The baggage clerk opened both doors of the car to let the air blow through, and yet even the wind in one's face was hot, as though it were an oven blast. The trooper removed his blouse and hung it up. His face dripped sweat, and his shirt was soaked.

The air was hot, and Carlos felt his wrists and ankles swelling. They grew puffy beneath the steel of his shackles, and the flesh bulged out on either side of the metal cuffs. The trooper loosened them a notch.

There were more towns like Usoco, all the same except that some lay deep in a forest of derricks and pumps. They had strange names, these towns. There were places like Adiós and Manuela Johnson and Paraiso, Aceite and Royal Flush, Number Sixteen, MacDonald's Folly, and Happy Hooligan. There was Filadelfia, and ten kilometers down the track lay Piccadilly.

All day long the train bored deeper into jungles, and there was no break in the greenness except where the oil fields lay. All day the train bored deeper, and through the night as well.

At daybreak of the third day the train was approaching Santa Cruz. When Carlos awoke, they were in marshalling yards at Kilometer 10, now called Empalme. They were on a siding, and on either hand stretched acres of track. There were flatcars loaded with tractors and trucks, mining machinery, pumps, derricks, well-drilling rigs, and cranes. There were masses of machinery for uses which Carlos could not so much as guess.

Busy little yard engines puffed back and forth, marshalling cars, and swarthy switchmen moved from track to track.

There were the yard engines and the switchmen, the marshalling yards, the flatcars loaded with machinery, and off beyond were the stacks of a refinery, the first refinery of all, the refinery of Kilometer 10. It lay off beyond, and its stacks reached high above the jungles on either hand.

It was ten kilometers to the docks of Santa Cruz, to the end of the line. In the beginning, when Carlos had gone to work, those kilometers were swamp and jungles, they were fill, a narrow dike across the marshlands.

How they had changed!

Santa Cruz had pushed outward from its center almost to the switchyards of Kilometer 10. As the tren mixto rattled toward the end of the line, Carlos saw drainage ditches and acres of fill, and on the fill stood factories and warehouses and rows of shacks roofed with gasoline cans, flattened and laid on like shingles. The shacks stood in rows, and there were muddy streets between, and in the mud children were playing. Black children, brown children, entirely naked, they played in the mud and splashed about in oily pools.

When the tracks were laid, Carlos remembered, they skirted the city, but now they seemed to go through the center. The tin-roofed shacks gave way to two- and three-story tenements; the streets were paved with asphalt; there were trolley lines.

Naked children swarmed the streets here, as well, but, having no mud, no oily pools, they rolled auto tires upon the pavements or made their own pools by damming gutters.

As the train swung around to approach the docks, Carlos could see the real center of the city, the old center, the area of public buildings. There was a new customs house of stone with a massive dome, and there were wings on each side. Supporting the wings were Doric columns, and atop the dome stood a statue of Justice, her scales neatly balanced.

There was the customs house, and there was a boulevard, a new, central boulevard stretching seaward from the very foot of its impressive steps. It was so wide that four cars could pass abreast, and there were palm trees along each edge, and gardens and in one place a circle with a fountain. This much Carlos saw before the train entered the dockyards and the city was shut from view.

He could see the harbor, now, and it was full of ships. From the docks out seaward to San Luis de Tiburón were ships lying at anchor. There were tankers, dingies, low-slung freighters, a liner. There were tugs, like the yard engines at Kilometer 10, plying back and forth, kicking up greenish wakes, there were lighters, there were dug-out canoes with colored sails.

The train pulled up at a platform. On the inland side, beyond the platform, stood a station; on the seaward side was dock space, and there was a fruit ship loading. Stevedores, brown and black, barefooted, naked above the waist, passed up and down a gangplank, loading bananas.

"Bien, aquí estamos!" the trooper told Carlos. "We go out upon the platform, now."

When the trooper had unlocked the ringbolt chain, Carlos stood up and began to move. There was a shackle about each ankle, and there was a steel bar to which each was fastened. The left shackle was fixed to one end of the bar, but the right slid back and forth like a ring upon a curtain rod, and thus, right foot first, step by step, the prisoner could inch along.

Right foot first, left foot follow, right foot first, left foot follow —
that was the rhythm. There was also a sound, a kind of dismal song.
It was the slide of leather, the clank of metal, the slide of leather, the
clank of metal — sl-l-l-l-l-l-l-l — clank! Sl-l-l-l-l-l-l-l — clank! That was
the sound, that was the song.

As Carlos moved from the baggage car onto the platform, a baggageman stopped to watch, and three or four small boys, and soon
there was a semicircle of curious spectators. Sl-l-l-l-l-l-l-l — clank!
Sl-l-l-l-l-l-l-l clank! There were barefoot boys and a baggageman,
there were two tall men in Panama suits and straw hats, speaking
English, there was a barefoot Indian woman with a huge market
basket.

They watched him inch across the platform. Sl-l-l-l-l-l-l-l — clank!
Sl-l-l-l-l-l-l-l — clank! They watched him — and whispered.

Carlos made his way across the platform, his guard a few steps
behind. Across the platform, step by step, and down a ramp. There
they waited until the train had backed away, and then they crossed
the tracks and inched along the docks beyond the bow of the fruit
ship.

There was a guard shack built upon the dock with an army sergeant
in charge. The trooper showed him the orders with the big, red seal.

"Un momentito," the sergeant said, "there will be a little boat for
San Luis de Tiburón."

Carlos sat down upon the dock, while the trooper got out his dice
and began playing with the sergeant.

The day wore on, and no boat appeared. In the early afternoon,
after the trooper had won all his money, the sergeant spread a ragged
serape upon the floor of his shack and slept.

In the midafternoon it rained. The skies opened up and loosed a
downpour that sent little rivulets gushing across low places in the
dock. Carlos went inside the shack with the trooper. Within an hour
or so there were branches of trees and hanks of tropical grass floating
in the harbor.

The sergeant woke up briefly, yawned. "At this hour it always
rains," he said.

"When comes the little boat?" asked the trooper.

"Un momentito," replied the sergeant. He yawned again and went
back to sleep.

The trooper cleaned his fingernails with a pocket knife, lighted a yellow cigarette, and squatted on the floor, eyes half closed, smoke curling lazily from his nostrils.

Carlos stretched flat upon the floor of the shack, and after a time, he fell asleep.

The trooper woke him with a rough shake. "The little boat comes."

Carlos got to his feet. It was already dusk.

A lighter was warping up to the dock. It was manned by soldiers. The trooper stood in the door of the shack. "I have a prisoner," he shouted, "for San Luis de Tiburón."

"Un momentito," the soldier at the wheel of the lighter called back. "We must wait for another."

The sun set. There was no sound but the scrape of the lighter against the dock, the occasional chatter of the soldiers who manned it. After dark the sergeant lighted a lantern and hung it from the door of the shack. Aboard the lighter, crewmen showed their masthead lights.

After an hour or more a quarter-ton truck chugged onto the dock and stopped behind the shack. Three men jumped down from the back, and as they walked in front of the headlights, Carlos saw that one was handcuffed.

"Is this the boat for Tiburón?" asked one of the men from the truck.

"It is," replied one of the soldiers aboard the lighter. "You have a prisoner?"

Carlos was hoisted aboard by two of the soldiers, and the trooper followed.

"We can take charge," one of the soldiers said.

"I have my orders," grumbled the trooper.

The other prisoner stumbled aboard, but his guards remained behind. The lighter backed away from the dock. In the darkness of the harbor there was nothing to see but the black outlines of ships at anchor, the red and green of their masthead lights; but behind, the city was ablaze.

As the lighter chugged out toward Tiburón, Carlos saw the high hulks of anchored ships, like rocky cliffs in the gloom, and he heard the slap of water and the grind of anchor chains against their hawses. The watch on a freighter struck a match to his cigarillo. For a brief moment soft light illuminated a face which disappeared in darkness when the match went out.

Out of the blackness loomed the bulk of San Luis de Tiburón. To Carlos it looked like a sombre mesa, a Lost World rising out of the water. He could hear surf pounding against the castle's lower base; sea caves among the rocks caught every sound and echoed it in a deep crescendo. Each cavern was booming, and it was the boom of a bass viol many times magnified.

As the tender rolled near, Carlos saw the main tower of San Luis, a black Babel mounting into the sky. Soon the gunwales scraped against a landing at the foot of an iron gate. Carlos heard a rattle of chains and the rasp of bars sliding out of place. The trooper prodded him out of the lighter. The other prisoner and two soldiers followed. As he stepped upon the landing, the gate swung on rusty hinges.

They entered, and the gate closed behind. Carlos heard the bars slide back into position as prison guards with lanterns appeared on either side.

4

EARLY EACH MORNING a guard came down the cell block, unbolting doors. Early each morning Carlos stumbled into the dim prison corridor and took his place in ranks. Early each morning a second guard marched them all away in a tight lock step. There was the sound of many sandals scuffing on flagstone floors; there was the constant hawking of men who sought to clear their throats of nighttime phlegm; there were the shrill, yapping commands of the guard who marched them.

Just outside the prison galley they peeled off in a column of files to the left and shuffled through a narrow passageway. There was a hole in the wall like a post-office window, and through this hole a trusty passed out tortillas spread thick with frijole paste and rusty condensed-milk tins filled with lukewarm coffee. Each prisoner took his food and moved into a prison yard that was grey and cold in the early morning. There were no tables. Men squatted on the hard-packed earth or, if the weather was bad, they huddled close under the eaves of stone buildings that surrounded the yard.

Thirty minutes were allowed for eating. After that the prisoners rinsed their coffee tins in a drum of greasy water and handed them back at the galley window. From there they filed by a tool shack where another trusty handed out crowbars and twelve-pound sledge hammers which they carried with them into the quarries.

The island of Tiburón is solid limestone with only a few mosses and hardy bushes growing on its surface. Before the middle of the sixteenth century early Spaniards had already put Indian slaves to work with sledges and crowbars, hewing and drilling into stubborn rock, shaping blocks, and smashing or grinding smaller chunks into dust for the making of lime and cement. In later years, as the Fortress of San Luis became a dungeon, prisoners replaced common slaves in the quarry pits.

For three centuries all manner of men had served their sentences with sledge and crowbar. Some had been ordinary criminals — murderers and thieves; others had been Protestants and free thinkers who had run afoul of the Inquisition; no small number had been English buccaneers captured on the Spanish Main. But after 1800 the majority, aside from the criminals, were men whom the State had condemned as traitors, although there was scarcely one of these who, in his own mind, did not serve his term and probably die a patriot and a martyr to his conscience.

The political complexion of those in the quarry pits at any given time depended, of course, upon the nature of the government in power. For the traitor of today is likely to be the magistrate of tomorrow, and he who judges runs the constant risk of future judgment imposed by the very man he now condemns. Thus, in the early decades of the last century those who crushed lime were mostly black republicans, but they were followed later by the royalists who had sought to crush them out. Most of the latter died on Tiburón, but several of them lived long enough to share their sledges with black republican victims of a mid-century reaction.

In modern times the selective process had been less doctrinaire. Ronca never bothered to ask what a man called himself. If a citizen owned an hacienda that Ronca wanted, he gave it up cheerfully or took the quarry pits. If a citizen were a writer, he became a Ronquista writer, unless he wanted to exchange his pen for a crowbar. If a citizen were a priest, he confined his criticisms to things spiritual, or found himself addressing a block of stone instead of an altar. In consequence of this, the men who labored with Carlos were of many sorts.

It was not easy to discover who or what they were. For as soon as they had their sledges and crowbars in the morning, they were formed into platoons and marched down into the quarries that gashed deep into the flanks of Tiburón. There they went to work under the muzzles of machine guns emplaced in nests around the rim of each pit. Sometimes they worked in pairs, one with a hammer, one with a bar; often they worked in gangs under the supervision of a guard well-armed, of course, with a short-barrelled shotgun. But however they worked, there was not much chance for talk. Because of this, no one ever asked a newcomer who he was, what he stood for, why he was there.

Rather, there was an exchange of short, penetrating glances; there was the lift of an eyebrow; there was the slightest quiver of a lip. These came first, and it was not until much later that words were spoken. Even then the words were short and isolated one from another.

Carlos gradually found out how it was. Two of them were working in a pile of rocks and rubble that had been blasted out of a cliff by an army explosives squad quartered on Tiburón for that sole purpose. He had probed under a boulder with his bar and was just setting his weight to pry when the first word came.

"Courage!" a low voice said.

Carlos shifted his eyes just enough to examine his companion's face. He saw brownish-ruddy skin, a high, Spanish nose, blue eyes searching his. The rest of the man went about his work, seeking to budge the limestone block, but his gaze remained fixed on Carlos. In those few instants a bond was forged between them. Carlos grunted softly. Together they worked upon the rock, edging it out of the rubble onto a spot where they could demolish it with sledges and drills.

A guard moved near, shotgun barrel gleaming in the early morning sunlight. Carlos lowered his eyes upon the rock, and he did not look full upon his companion throughout the rest of the day. Thereafter they were careful never to seek one another out, but usually every week or two it chanced that they were paired for work, and gradually each came to know about the other all that was essential.

The stranger was Andrés, he had good friends outside, and he intended to escape. He was formulating a plan, but two were needed to carry it out. He had selected Carlos. By helping one another, they would both have a good chance of getting off Tiburón alive.

Those were the more important of their communications. Carlos learned much else from him, however, and as the months lengthened into a year it was evident that Andrés had some sort of contact with the outside. Much of what he passed along concerned events that were taking place in the world at large. There were great rumors, of course, that travelled widely through the prison. The first that Carlos remembered hearing was about a victory in Africa. Andrés called it by name and told in five or six words what the battle meant.

Little by little Andrés passed on further news: Pearl Harbor, Stalingrad, Guadalcanal.

In a sense, these were not matters of great concern. Carlos told himself that they were, but he did not really believe it. Tortillas and beans were of greater concern, and so were aching muscles and limestone dust clogging the throat. So were thoughts of Sapho.

Those were the thoughts that tromped across one's brain — those thoughts of Sapho. They were the ones that marched in at night and passed on in endless review across the parade ground of consciousness. Those were the thoughts in hobnailed boots that tore up the sod and left deep scars across the smoothness of the turf.

Such were the matters of great concern, while Pearl Harbor and Stalingrad and Guadalcanal were only words breathed across the threshold of lips that dared not move.

Pearl Harbor and Stalingrad and Guadalcanal meant nothing for a long, long time, until one particular morning when the labor platoons were lock-stepping down a slope toward the pits. The sky was dark grey in every quarter except the east, which was crimson with dawn. The guards were yapping as usual, and the hundreds of sandal soles made the same shuffle and slap that they always did when a dozen or more platoons were marching down the powdery, limestone slopes.

Carlos was in the front rank of his platoon, and he could see below him the edge of Tiburón Island and the leaden waters of straits beyond. While he looked, the sun rose out of the Caribbean horizon and sent long, golden shafts of light across the water. At that same moment, too, a vessel rounded the island and moved through the straits before them. It was long and slender and rode low in the water like some snaky, poisonous thing waiting for a chance to strike.

The sunlight grew more intense, and Carlos saw men upon the decks and a flag fluttering above the stern.

It was a shimmering, silken flag with a swastika in a field of red.

The vessel slid along through the straits, and after a few moments, the decks were cleared and the flag hauled down. Then Carlos saw the bows sink into glistening water; the decks followed; and soon there was nothing left but thousands of dancing white caps and the faintest sort of V-shaped wake where once a long, slender, pointed thing had moved.

Carlos carried each tiny detail with him into the pits, and this time he made certain that he was working with Andrés. They scarcely spoke that day, but each knew well what was on the other's mind.

It was a hot, seemingly interminable day, as all days were, but throughout those many hours, Carlos found that whatever his thoughts explored, they came back at last to the submarine with all the crew upon its decks, with the swastika rippling in the sunlight above Ronca's Bay of Pearls. That night, after a guard had locked him in his cell, he pulled from its crack the stub pencil which he had found in the prison yard many months before.

In the dim light of a lantern that hung in the prison corridor he examined the chronological table that he had scratched upon the cleanest wall. There was a listing of each event, dated by the day upon which Andrés had passed the news along. At the bottom of a long column Carlos scribbled the date followed by the words: *sub with flag flying scornfully.* Then he put his pencil carefully away.

The German vessel remained vigorously alive in his memory during the days when Andrés was smoothing out details for their escape. There was an intricate plan which Carlos was memorizing step by step. Since they dared not be seen together often and since they dared exchange only the fewest words while they were close enough to speak, the process was slow and agonizing.

On a certain evening just at sunset a canoe was to come out of hiding from one of the marine caves that pocked the base of San Luis de Tiburón. It was the responsibility of Carlos and Andrés to be there when it slipped away. Point by point the two prisoners had worked out their plan. Andrés did not yet know the date, but he judged it to be near at hand, and he warned Carlos to be ready. That was the stage which their plotting had reached when disaster struck.

The platoons had come in from the pits, and a column of files had broken off to pass in front of the galley window. Carlos saw Andrés take his tortilla and his can of coffee and move toward the prison yard; he also saw two guards slip up behind and pin his friend's arms from behind.

Andrés was dragged away, struggling, and Carlos never saw him again.

The column filed past the window. Carlos gulped his supper without any sense of taste. He washed his coffee tin and passed it through the window. Somewhat later he was marched down the prison corridor as usual and locked in his cell. He was not aware of time, but lanterns were still burning in the block when two other guards unbolted the door and motioned him out.

They marched him along a narrow and dismal corridor to a series of steps. They were stone, and they spiralled downward through wells cut in solid rock. There was another corridor, a tunnel cut through limestone. Torches carried by the two guards behind sent his shadow leaping ahead. The sound of his own footsteps boomed in his ears.

At length he was shoved into a dungeon keep which had been carved out below the level of the bay. Salt water oozed through cracks and pores and formed stalactites which hung down like gigantic icicles. Globules of brine gathered constantly at the lower ends, enlarged, and dropped to the rock floor with an echoing *spat*.

The guards backed out, closed a solid iron door, and turned a key in the lock.

The darkness of the chamber was complete. For a few moments Carlos heard the hollow echo of footsteps shuffling along the corridor, ascending stone steps in the stair wells. Then there was silence, save only for the dripping of water, the *spat* of each drop upon the floor of his dungeon.

5

ONCE A DAY the door opened and let in light. Once a day a guard held a blinding lantern while a second guard left tortillas spread with frijole paste and a can of water. Once a day they emptied the slop bucket into another pail which they took away. Once a day the door closed, leaving darkness.

Between openings of the door Carlos paced his cell or sat upon his haunches, waiting, or slept, stretched out on the damp rock bottom of the chamber. There was neither day nor night, but only darkness ticked off by the spat of water globules upon the floor. At first they were only drops of water dripping, but with time the resounding smacks grew louder, and the emptiness of the chamber, magnifying the sound, led Carlos to believe that the globules were much larger than they should be.

The chamber was dark, and yet in his mind he came to see the drops of water forming. Each one began as a small bead on a stalactite tip and grew steadily larger, bloating fat and round like a transparent sphere of glass at the end of a blower's tube, until it reached the size of a human head. Then, like an overgrown soap bubble, it would sway back and forth, as though on the point of detaching itself. But no, it would continue swelling until it was at least as large as the dome on Ronca's customs house, and sometimes Carlos wondered if it were not larger than the world, a kind of crystalline planet suspended from the stalactite tip.

Eventually, of course, it broke away and dropped through space to crash to pieces at his very feet.

That was finished, but already another was bloating fat and round. Minute after minute, hour after hour he saw these globules forming and heard them come smashing down upon the floor. Sometimes he threw himself upon the bottom of the chamber and stuffed his ears with fingertips, but even then he knew that another gigantic sphere was forming.

There was neither day nor night, but there were globules bloating, and there was always thinking. Most often there were thoughts of Sapho. She was standing on the threshold of her father's flat, slender, her hair black and tightly curled, her skin ripe yellow. She was holding out her hand to Carlos, and their eyes met, and he could not look away. They were black, jet black, and about them was the bottomlessness of a deep well, and in the depths were fires burning. She was standing on the threshold, and then they were buying a chicken in the market, she and Carlos, and when she laughed, he watched her teeth, and they were even and white.

Or they were walking along a dusty road with Doctor MacNeill. Barefooted, Sapho was, and dressed in Nacheetl skirt and blouse, and her head was high, like a Nacheetl head, as though she had carried water jugs upon it. Her head was high, but without rebozo, and her hair blew free. He saw her there, walking at his side, or he was lying close beside her in deep grasses among the reeds or in the whiteness of a wedding bed.

There was Sapho, and there were thoughts of childhood. "He looked upon her hair and saw its blackness," Uncle Vicente said. "He looked upon her shoulders and saw that they were smooth and full." So Uncle Vicente spoke through time and space, and his words echoed in the chamber. "Breezes blew warm upon their bodies," he was saying, "and the stars shone, and nighttime saw creation."

Carlos could see Uncle Vicente clearly in the blackness, and sometimes the old man was sitting upon a rock above La Perla, smoking his pipe in the sunset, and sometimes he was standing in the village square before the council house, and sometimes a runner came from the Barrio of the Frogs in the great city beyond the mountains. "People of Zalapec!" shouted the runner. "José Ronca has seized the government in the name of the Democratic-republican Party. Long live the new government!"

Now they were climbing to Santa Marta, and Carlos felt important because he was directly behind Uncle Vicente and Jesucristo Salvador. They were directly behind the presidente; they were at the gates of the hacienda; they had passed inside; they were gaping at the tables

and chairs, the tapestries and paintings, the mahogany sideboard
with its cruets and goblets and ladles of silver and gold.

There was Uncle Vicente alive, and there was Uncle Vicente dead,
buried deep in the hard brown earth of the campo santo. There was
the new father, Lorenzo Reyes, there was his son Diego of the grabbing hand.

They were together in the pasture, Carlos and Diego. "Whore-son,
whore-son," taunted Diego. Carlos stamped his foot helplessly.
"Whore-mother, whore-son," chanted Diego. Carlos ran a few steps
down the hill, stopped abruptly. With one hand he unwound the
sling from his belt, while he scooped up a large, round pebble with
the other.

"Whore-mother, whore-son," yelled Diego from down the hill.

Carlos swung his sling and loosed the pebble. He was certain that
he had overshot. He was certain, and yet — and yet — it was falling
fast, that pebble, it was coming down, straight down — down — down
SPAT!

Carlos was in a dungeon, and the water was dripping. Carlos was
in the bowels of San Luis de Tiburón, and a globule had crashed
upon the stone floor of the chamber. Carlos was in a bottom chamber
of General Ronca's medieval pyramid of stone. There he lay buried
in a bottom cell among all the cells of stone, and he dreamed of freedom.

What was freedom? It was light and air, a perfect end to darkness.
It was hope, the tearing away of Ronca's pyramid, the building of
Don Ricardo's kind of government. Freedom was a contract government depending upon the consent of the governed. Freedom was a
civil compact with checks and balances to restrain the power of the
governing. It was freedom of speech and press, freedom from unwarranted arrest, the guarantee of a speedy trial by a jury of one's
equals.

Freedom was letting be.

There was neither day nor night, but there were globules bloating,
and there was thinking. For just at that moment Don Ricardo and a
blondish gentleman came out of the house and dallied about the
gateway. The judge looked at Carlos quizzically, then turned to

Frank Nash. "This is the boy I was telling you about — the one who wants to become a priest."

The Yanqui extended a hand genially. "So you want to become a priest, eh?"

Don Ricardo took a book down from its niche in the wall, spread the volume open on one palm, and held it for Mr. Nash to examine.

Mr. Nash squinted at the page before him. "What's this — Saint Jerome, eh?" He faced Carlos. "Are you — certain that you wish to become a priest?"

"Yes, sir."

Don Ricardo replaced the book, clapped his friend across the shoulder. "Bueno, Frank, time for a little copacita, eh?" The two men moved out of the gateway.

There was neither day nor night, but there was the crash of globules against the floor of the chamber, and there were ghosts of long ago. Don Ricardo flicked the ashes of his cigar onto the rug of his study. "So you see, Carlos, rebellion is our only choice. After that we can make a government, a constitutional, democratic government, and then we'll modernize. With Yanqui help we'll build roads and factories, we'll give people jobs and wages and things to buy, we'll set up schools and hospitals and — "

Carlos rose on one knee among the papers which he had been sorting. "With Yanqui help? But you spoke only now of Marines in Santa Cruz!"

Don Ricardo was amused. "Do not judge a people," he warned, "by an individual or by a faction or even by the government in power. It is true that Prettyman channels a monstrous part of our national wealth into his private reservoir. It is also true that Yanqui Marines have landed in Santa Cruz. But that policy is done for, and most Yanquis know it. We must win their confidence, Carlos, for our destiny is bound tight to theirs. That is why it is so important for us to found a democracy in the Locke tradition."

There was neither day nor night, but there was blackness. It was not the darkness that comes with night, nor was it the darkness that a blind man knows. This was a dimensional blackness five steps long and three steps wide. Those were two of the dimensions, and there was another that he knew at first as height. This dimension was important because it marked a limit of blackness beneath his feet and another limit an arm's length above his head, but it was less real than length and breadth.

Such were the limits of his blackness. It was not the endless dark of a cloudy night, but a finite blackness that was his existing space.

He recognized this space as space, he knew its limits, but it meant less to him than blackness. For his eyes were blind to space, while they registered blackness. Throughout his conscious existence he felt himself submerged in blackness, and even his waking dreams were summoned out of blackness.

For great lengths of time he did not think of space, but when he did, he saw it as a cube of blackness.

Five steps of length, three steps of breadth, and height that was a short arm's length above his head — that was his living space, his cube of blackness, his great reality. The walls had a certain realness when he touched them, but he no longer conceived of them as walls. They were merely the utmost limit of his cube of blackness. He even forgot that they were stone, knowing them only as hardness and dampness, as the immovable limits of his living space.

Hardness and dampness were limits, and they were also a pressing up from below. When he sank upon his knees, when he lay outstretched, they became an upward pressure. The hardness pushed against his flesh and reached for bones, while the dampness sought his blood, and he seemed to feel osmosis.

For great lengths of time he lay upon the hardness and upon the dampness, and at first his lengths of time had a realness. From one opening of the door to the next opening of the door was at first a length of time. Five steps were also a length of time, being longer than three steps, but not twice as long. These were lengths of time, at first, because they could be measured and were in turn a measure.

Five steps were a length of time, but a dream was not. Occasionally he tried to measure a memory of long ago or a thought of Sapho according to the spats, but dreams were fluid things that did not lend themselves to measurement, while five steps were five steps and could be counted off precisely.

After a time, even his steps began to lose their meaning. At first he thought that his mind was slipping, but slowly he came to realize that the spats were what confused him. Originally, they had formed themselves apart from him, but now he felt them growing in his head. They began as small, metallic beads clinging to his cranium dome, and there they expanded, filling the cavity of his skull, pressing against his temples and eardrums, exploding with the violence of a thunderclap.

The moment came at last when he could no longer suffer these explosions. Seizing his slop bucket, he charged the stalactite where the dripping had been before it started in his head. There was a clang of metal resounding against hard stone, and the noise spread out from the stalactite tip like expanding, concentric rings of shiny metal. He waited for the spat, but it did not recur.

In its place he heard a drip — drip-drat.

For a great length of time the dripping went drip — drip-drat. Carlos was not sure how long. It might have been a week; it might have been a month; it might have been a year. Then it went DRIP — DRIP-DRAT, interfering with his steps when he paced his cell.

One-two-three-four-five steps, turn, one-two-three steps, stop. One-two-three-four-DRIP-steps, turn, DRIP-DRAT-two-three-DRIP-one-two-DRIP-DRAT-four-five-DRIP —

He jammed his fingers into his ears and tried to walk, but he could hear the dripping. It jangled his steps until he found himself stumbling over his own feet and pitching head foremost upon the floor. Thereafter he found that he was safer upon the hardness where he could lie and wait until an airiness came to lift his body up and provide a softness upon which he could float away. Gradually he discovered that by lying very still he could bring the airiness sooner. Like a stiff, firm breeze it pressed against his supine back and lifted him into blackness where he could float about through space a million miles or so, soaring high and low and swooping like a hawk.

Once while he was floating in the blackness about a thousand miles below the top he came upon Don Ricardo's head suspended in a globe of light. Carlos reached out his hand to touch it, and his fingers found the beard, and the hairs were stiff like wires. The lips moved, speak-

ing words that rose up like bubbles toward the top of blackness.
Carlos reached out to catch a word or two, but each one burst at
touch, and there was nothing left.

Eventually the head moved away and passed through an outer
wall of blackness leaving a hole behind. Carlos tried to follow,
squeezing through, but beyond the hole was a blinding light that
jabbed pain needles in his eyes. Then, as he hid behind his arms,
a powerful hand reached through and seized him and dragged him
out into a tank of light where words came whining down like bombs
to crash inside his ears.

As his eyes became somewhat accustomed to the light, he saw two
men, and they were standing over him, shouting questions. Sometimes he could see the words like black clouds in the lightness, but
they had no meaning, and since he did not answer, the two men beat
him. After that their words were more than ever blackness, and so,
after another beating, they dragged him away to his cell where there
was no more light.

For a time he could not hear the dripping or even see the blackness. For a time he heard only pain which was a kind of siren screeching. For a time he saw only pain which was a bolt of lightning in the
eyes.

But the pain went away, and then he heard the dripping louder
than before. The dripping returned, and after so much dripping, he
did not know whether they had come to get him and had beaten him,
or whether he had been there all the time. Later on he seemed to
remember that they had come a second time, but maybe they hadn't
because he wasn't even sure about the first time.

He also seemed to remember that Pepillo had been there the second
— the first — no, the second time. He seemed to think so, but he
could not be sure, and after a while he thought that it was a dream
or something that had happened long, long before. No, he could see
Pepillo, and so he knew that Pepillo had been there. He could remember very clearly, now. Pepillo had been there in the stabbing
light. He was seated behind a desk in a room that was large and
bare, and when Carlos came in, he appeared to be writing. Carlos
walked toward the desk, stopped a few paces off, and waited, feet

apart. "Why do you not sal —" No-no, that was another time, that was — that was —

Perhaps he had never left his cell. Perhaps they had never come to get him, to ask him questions, to beat him.

It must have been the devil.

The devil came often at night to squat in Don Ricardo's gateway and talk with Carlos. He was no longer the devil of the pastures back of La Perla, but the devil of Abraham and Isaac and Jacob, the devil of Father Timoteo's teachings. He was all of these, and yet his face was a face that Carlos had always known. It was loose skin hanging in folds, and it was a pair of green slit eyes, and it was curling horns.

The devil snorted. "You remind me of Cain."

"I did not mean to do it," Carlos muttered. "I wanted to frighten, only."

"I'll tell you about that Cain," the devil said. "He *dared* to frighten only, but I tell you the truth, he *wanted* to kill."

Carlos swung his sling and loosed the pebble. He was certain that he had overshot, and yet — and yet —

"He *wanted* to kill," repeated the devil, "and so I came to help. I gave his hand a push, a precious leetle push!"

Down — down — the pebble was falling fast — it was coming down — straight down — it struck Diego's head.

Carlos saw it strike Diego's head. He saw Diego fold quietly into a small heap.

Carlos ran down the hill. He ran down the hill to Diego's side, and the devil was sitting astride Diego's body.

"That Cain was the same as you," the devil said.

"Get out, get out!" Carlos screamed.

"Very well," answered the devil, and he melted into the dark, merging with blackness, and Carlos was alone with the drip — drip-drat of water falling.

For a while the devil stayed away, but eventually he slipped back again. Carlos tried to ignore him. Carlos sat on his haunches in a corner of his cell, and he pushed back the matted hair that fell about his neck. He stuffed his ears and closed his eyes, hoping thus to shut the devil out.

The tempo of the music slowed, the engine coughed, a gondola stopped before them. Sapho drew away when Carlos touched her to help her in, and she sat on the far side of the seat with as much space as possible between them. Once more the music jangled as the ferris wheel began to turn. Up, up they went, high above the Market Place. But the engine coughed and sucked and died. There was a long wait, so long that the trooper shouted down from the next gondola. "Cabrón! What goes on down there?"

The man who was tending the engine peered up, and his face was the devil's face —

Carlos leaped out of the gondola and floated off through space, and now he lay in a tremendous bed, and he saw the clay brownness of his skin against the white sheet beneath him. He lay sunk deep in softness, and warm rays of sunlight were streaming in from a balcony. This was the Gran Hotel San Marcos, and he remembered —

He looked for Sapho. He raised upon an elbow and he saw her there beside him, her black hair spread wide and wild upon a pillow. She was there beside him, and her two shoulders were peeping from between the sheets. In wonder and admiration he touched her skin. She flinched a little.

This was difficult to believe!

He brushed aside her hair.

There she — no-no, that wasn't Sapho, that was the devil's face. Slit eyes, grey skin hanging loose in folds, that — that —

He must keep the devil out! He flailed the darkness with his arms. He couldn't keep the devil out.

For the door of the cell opened, and Carlos saw the devil standing there on the threshold with a lantern in his hand. Carlos backed away because the light blinded his eyes, and he covered his face with his hand, but the devil was still there emptying the bucket. Carlos lowered his head and charged to drive the devil out. Like a mad bull Carlos charged, but he was no match for the devil who raised a hoof and caught Carlos in the groin and spilled him over backwards into the far recess of the chamber.

VIII. Release

It WAS LATE AFTERNOON when Colonel López stepped into the private limousine which he always kept in readiness outside Constabulary Headquarters in the San Marcos suburb of Chacala. The chauffeur, a well-armed sergeant, pressed a dashboard button to start the almost noiseless motor.

"Executive Palace!" the colonel ordered as he settled back in the deep upholstery.

The long, sleek blue car pulled away from the curb, streaked eastward to the Avenida. As they glided along the smoothness of the asphalt between rows of slender palms, Colonel López stared thoughtfully through the bullet-proof transparency of polished windows. In his mind he was straightening out his thoughts, deciding exactly what to say to General Ronca.

Short of the Viceregal Palace they whisked into the Calle General José Ronca and then, almost in the shadow of the Viceregal Palace, they eased to a halt before the Presidential Mansion. The chauffeur hopped out and opened a door.

"Wait!" Colonel López ordered.

The chauffeur saluted.

From across the street one might well mistake Ronca's residence for a gloomy fortress. The rusticated sandstone walls were weather-darkened and thick and massive, the lower windows small, like grated loopholes, with pediments above and brackets below the openings. Windows of the second floor were double, with Gothic mullions. Crowning the whole structure was an imposing cornice with Roman mouldings where flocks of pigeons roosted.

Colonel López approached the narrow doorway with military briskness. Two dismounted troopers, like stiff wax models in tiny sentry boxes, presented arms as though moved by clockworks within their bellies. The colonel saluted.

Beyond the doorway opened a marble court where slender columns supported arcades too light for the heaviness of the vaults above. The colonel's heels clicked along the shiny hardness of the cloister paving.

Two more troopers guarded the entrance to the waiting room outside President Ronca's private study. Few human beings ever passed between them without challenge, but for the colonel they merely presented arms. In the waiting room an aide in the uniform of the National Army saluted. "The General is expecting you," he told the colonel. "A moment please."

He disappeared beyond the heavy door. When he reappeared, it was to usher the colonel in.

The general's long and narrow study had once been a refectory with tables for a hundred people, but the tables had been removed for him, the walls hung with battle flags, the marble floors burnished to reflect like polished metal.

Down the length of this room marched Colonel López, his eyes fixed upon the bemedalled chest of President Ronca who sat like a squat, clay god behind a flag-draped desk on a dais that raised it up like a heathen altar. At his right stood an upright pike with the national standard, while on the wall behind hung the old scorpion banner of Ronquista partisan hordes.

Just short of the dais Colonel López stopped, clicked his heels, and saluted, arm and hand extended. "Viva Ronca!"

The little god behind the desk returned a similar salute. When these formalities were over, however, he grinned broadly, showing a dozen or so mud-brown teeth. "Sit down, Pepillo! There is a chair around here behind."

Colonel López took a folding chair from its hiding place back of the desk and set it up on the dais facing General Ronca. "Cabrón! To be back again is a precious matter, General."

Pepillo watched General Ronca closely as he spoke. "Our spy reports were true," he said. "In every town and village they plan a revolution to say nothing of what they do here in San Marcos. Don

Ricardo's old Liberales make it, but our agents know every move."

There was no expression on Ronca's baked-clay face. "Sí, pues."

"They join the militia," Pepillo explained. "Oh, those Liberales, they are precious soldiers, now. They seek to take San Marcos, first, and then fight on from there."

General Ronca opened a silver box that lay upon his desk, took out a plug of black tobacco, bit off a quid, and replaced the plug. "Sí, pues."

From a pocket of his blouse Pepillo took out a map of national territory and spread it flat upon the desk top. "All the time they keep in touch with Don Ricardo. He is up in the United States, now, talking with important Yanquis. When the right time comes, he will be close at hand, and zup! Those Liberal goats, they sneak him across the border. Oh, they count on Don Ricardo. He is their leader, their horseback general, and he will be their president. They have plans even now to elect deputies for their assembly."

The President grunted. "Sí, pues."

Pepillo spread his palms in a depreciatory gesture. "Mostly lawyers, you understand, and keepers of shops, landless nanny goats with pesos buried in the garden. Well, so much for them. But there is another matter." Even as he smoothed the hair of a bow-shaped mustache that graced his upper lip, his eyes were watching Ronca's. "There are Comunistas that also make a plot."

There was only the slightest flicker in Ronca's eyes. "Sí, pues?"

Pepillo pointed to La Cumbre on the map. "They keep a headquarters here on charcoal slopes," he said. "With sooty faces they are hiding out as carboneros. That is a beginning only. They are working in every city and town and village. In Santa Cruz, in Tumaco, on the Río Mosca, under our noses here in San Marcos, in Chacala, in Cocamba, El Monte, Usoco, pues, in every place. They are working in the oil fields and on the railroad, sí, in coffee plantations of Puerto Colon and in banana groves on the Río Mosca. They are in the Peasant League and in the Unions, too. They teach the peasants how to read and write and other dangerous matters. Cabrón! They have made a deal with the Liberales."

Ronca spat a brown stream of tobacco juice into the spittoon. "You know this Comunista thing yourself, Pepillo?"

Pepillo's strong white teeth gleamed. "I know these things myself," he said, "from a very Comunista!"

There was a sparkle of interest in the general's eyes. "Sí pues?"

Pepillo chuckled. "Cabrón! You should see this Comunista! Oh, the very precious devil of a Comunista is my new amigo!" He touched Ronca's sleeve. "My Comunista feeds on books. Believe me, for many years he has eaten nothing else. He claims to know all about this Comunismo, so, pues, he thought himself to make the revolution. But no, there comes from across the sea a fighting Comunista, a veteran of Guadalajara and Madrid and Teruel. He comes from across the sea to make the revolution, and after that they do not listen to my cabrón. No, no, pues, they even make a joke! So he is very mad, and hate is a poison lizard thrashing in his belly, and after many months, a year, maybe, he comes to us. Oh, precious!"

Ronca eyed Pepillo with critical shrewdness. "It is not a trick?"

Pepillo checked himself. A sly instinct told him that in front of Ronca his enthusiasm had gone too far. "We watch for that," he assured the general soberly.

The president shifted the tobacco quid into the pocket of a cheek. "Sí, pues."

"Well, there it is," he said. "We have ten months to go. The revolution is made for then."

Ronca turned in his chair so that he faced Pepillo squarely. "Well, Pepillo," he asked, "do we wipe them out?"

These were the words that Pepillo had expected — and dreaded. He returned Ronca's searching glance. There was a paternal anxiety in the general's eye that Pepillo had come increasingly to know, of late, and he was rather certain what it meant. He was not old in appearance, this President Ronca; indeed, he looked younger, more well-fed, than when the twelve-year-old Pepillo had first fallen in behind the scorpion banner. But he was old, very old, as Pepillo had convinced himself by many countings. If anything should happen — in a crisis —

Pepillo had his words well-chosen. "One could do that," he admitted, "but —"

There was the tiniest gleam of pleasure, Pepillo thought, in the brownness of the old man's eyes. "Sí, pues?"

Pepillo leaned forward tensely. "There is another path," he said. "Crooked, perhaps, but — I like it better."

Ronca settled back in his chair. "Sí, pues."

"I do not see our country only," Pepillo told the general. "I see the world. Five years ago it was a different place with a new order growing, but now — well, one needs the slyness of a mountain fox. Our friends across the the the sea, they cannot help us now. Everything is up to us — so we take the crooked path."

Pepillo saw that the general's eyes were shut, but he knew that the old man was not asleep. "After those fighting years in Europe, most Yanquis do not like us much, and even Prettyman is a little cool. Nowadays they like Don Ricardo better. We do not have so many friends, perhaps, but on the crooked path we shall soon have so many more. Here is what we do. We let them make the revolution. Liberales and Comunistas, we let them work together and start the fight. We watch their every move and let them go so far, oh, just so far, and then we strike. A war against Comunismo, pues! Then we shall have friends enough. That way we get plenty help and do away with the Comunistas and the Liberales, too, and save our Corporate State for the good of all the people."

Eyes still closed, old Ronca smiled appreciatively. "Sí, pues," he murmured. "Sí, pues!"

Pepillo relaxed against the straightness of his folding chair. Matters were going well, he told himself. There was no more need to fear. He gathered up his map as though to leave. "Bien!" he said. "General, su servidor! With your permission — "

The old man stirred as Pepillo had been certain that he would. The eyes opened and turned on Pepillo with an expression of craftiness and hope. "Is that all?" he asked. "After your trip, Pepillo, you have no other matter?"

"Cabrón!" exclaimed Pepillo, "almost I forgot! There is indeed one other tiny matter."

Ronca leaned forward, and Pepillo saw a trembling in the old man's hand. "Yes-yes?" he demanded eagerly.

Pepillo had waited long for this single thing. "At last we have found a truly precious apple!"

About the old man's jaw was a peculiar limpness. He placed tremulous fingers upon Pepillo's knee. "What this time, boy?"

Pepillo waved a casual hand. "There is no need to speak about this one," he said. "For you only, General, I have found a truly luscious dish. I send her over in my car."

"Tonight?"

Pepillo nodded. "Tonight!" he promised. He stood up quickly, replaced the chair, and stepped backward off the dais. There he stiffened with a click of heels and saluted, arm and hand extended. "Viva Ronca!" There was a touch of gaiety in the precision of his voice.

2

MAGDALENA WAS DETERMINED to try one more house on La Calle de las Mujeres. Two months had passed since the sale of her own place for unpaid fees and taxes, and her body was sore from sleeping in doorways and damp alleys, and her stomach was hungry for food. It was a hot day, and sun-heat pressed downward upon her head, and she felt as though a wire had been drawn tight around her skull. She walked unsteadily, tripping her bare toes on loose cobbles, and in her knees was a weakness that felt liquid, like water.

She found the door of a house where she had once worked when she was young, and she beat upon the door. It was opened by a small boy of seven or eight, and when she asked for the proprietor, he took her through a court to a back room where a fat man was sitting on the edge of a bed, yawning. He had trousers on and an undershirt which fitted tightly over rolls of fat, and he grunted when he saw Magdalena.

"I search for a place," she said.

He looked her up and down with his bulging eyes, and he spat upon the floor. "You have the body of a goatskin bag," he sneered.

"I have much experience," Magdalena contended. "For giving men pleasure I know many tricks."

"Men don't want an old nanny goat," he said, "even if she does know tricks."

"I am hungry only," Magdalena sighed. "A little food, and I shall be all round like ripe melons."

"Bien, if it is food you want, I shall find a place," he said. "Can you make exhibiciones?"

Magdalena hawked and spat. "I want none of your exhibiciones," she snapped. "All my life I work for men, all my life I make them pleasure. They seek their joy, and I give it, and when they tire, they sleep upon my breast, and they are babies in my arms, and I feel gladness. That I do with pleasure, but exhibiciones — never."

The fat man shrugged. "You spoke of hunger — ?"

"I will go suckle a filthy hog, I'll eat balls of horse dung, I'll — "

"Bien, go ahead!" He waddled into the court. "Pedro!" Like a little dog the boy came running. "Toss this garbage in the gutter, Pedro."

The little boy picked up a stick. "Nyaaaaa! Get out," he snarled. He poked her between the legs. "You stinking old bag of hog droppings."

As Magdalena passed through the door, he kicked her from behind, and she fell forward in the slimy mud of the street. For a time she lay there sobbing, and she was alone except for a scrawny pig that was rooting in a gutter. Then she climbed painfully to her feet and dragged herself down the street in the direction of the central plaza.

There was one hope.

Through the heat of midday she made her way to the cathedral, and she climbed the steps, and went inside. It was dim and cool, and there were only a few praying, and they did not notice Magdalena. She crept forward along the aisle until she was as close to the chancel as she dared to be. There she sank upon her knees.

Red and yellow light, filtering through the stained windows, fell upon the altar. She saw Jesucristo Salvador looking down from his cross, and she saw María Madre, also, and she prayed. "O, Jesucristo, O, María Madre, this is just Magdalena, a poor whore, sabe, and perhaps you do not remember her. She has done many wrong things. In her life she has made many sins. She has told lies, and she has not gone to Mass, and you know all the other wicked things she has done. Her clothes are dirtied with mud and garbage filth, and her soul is dirtied with badness. She is not fit to enter your holy little house, but she comes because she has no other place. She comes upon her knees, and she hopes that you will be kind to her. She hopes you will forget the bad things she has done, and will remember only how to many men she has given pleasure. Please, Jesucristo, please María Madre, thank you, Amen."

That was Magdalena's prayer, and she looked up at Jesucristo, and she saw his head turn. He smiled a small, kind smile, and she was very grateful. She looked at María Madre, who also smiled, and Magdalena knew that they had heard. So she arose from her knees and left the cathedral and sat upon the steps outside.

She sat in sunlight, and the rays were no longer cruel and scorching, but soft and warm, and as she sat there, a young priest came by. He smiled and gave her a peso, and thus she knew that Jesucristo and María Madre had really heard.

There were vendors across the square, and she went over and bought an enchilada that cost ten centavos. When she had paid from her peso, she tied the change into her kerchief. Then she returned to the cathedral steps to eat. She sat in the sun, and its warm rays seeped into her body to her toes and to the very tips of her fingers. She finished the enchilada, and the warm contentedness of her body brought drowsiness that turned into sleep.

It was nearly sundown when she awoke. She looked about, and a beggar woman had come to the steps of the cathedral and had squatted there, and the beggar woman whined to those who passed. "For the love of God, señor, for the love of God, señor, have pity, señor, upon a poor woman have pity, for the love of God, señor, for the love of Jesucristo, for the love of María Madre."

The beggar woman held out a hand to those who passed, and her voice was the sound of a dog whining. Magdalena watched, and after a little while the same young priest came out of the cathedral. He stopped by the beggar woman and gave her a coin. "Peace be with you!" he said.

Magdalena felt a sharp bite of bitterness at her throat. She drew her skirts tight about her as the young priest passed, and when he was gone, she jumped to her feet in fury. With trembling fingers she tore at the knot in her kerchief until she loosed the coins. Seizing them in her fist, she ran to the edge of the cathedral steps and hurled the money out among the grass and flowers.

"I am not a beggar!" she cried. "I am not! I am not!" She stumbled down the steps and into the plaza, and she headed toward La Calle de las Mujeres, muttering to herself. "To the fat man I'll go, to the house of exhibiciones."

Already it was dark as she made her way across the city, and there were sombre shadows. As she dragged along, she saw herself working in the house of exhibiciones.

Then she saw the faces of the men. She saw their bulging eyes, their drooping jaws, the saliva drooling out. She saw them leaning forward, she saw the veins stand out blue upon their foreheads, she saw the beads of sweat, she saw the look of sex-guilt upon their lips, and she heard the laughter, the low, brutish laughter, the idiot giggle, the mocking snicker — she heard them all.

She stopped, loathing herself, and she turned about with a taste of vomit in her mouth, and she headed back toward the plaza.

She struggled along through the mud of La Calle de las Mujeres, crossed the Market Place, and reached the plaza again.

There was an orchestra playing now upon the bandstand, and the scarlet jackets of the musicians had buttons that gleamed gold in the lamplight.

The city's gentry had come to the plaza for an evening stroll, and while they strolled, there were waltzes played, and there was flirting. For the men circled the plaza in one direction, while in the other direction the women moved. There were army officers in uniforms of blue and gold, and the plumes upon their shakos rippled in an evening breeze.

There were army officers, and there were troopers in powder blue, and there were caballeros in colored jackets and breeches tight about the legs. In one direction they moved, and in the other strolled the women. There were señoritas in satins and long mantillas, señoritas hiding behind their fans, señoritas flirting with the men who passed.

The musicians were playing waltzes as Magdalena skirted the square. She sneaked through shadows until she reached the cathedral, and she went beyond the steps to the spot where she had thrown the coins. She glanced about to see whether she were watched, and then she dropped upon her knees and searched for what she had cast away.

3

SAPHO SAT before a gilded dressing table while a maid combed out her long black hair. "The beautiful ones come here," she was telling Sapho. "Always the beautiful ones come here. For men, some say, he has no feelings, but women, beautiful women — madre! He can't resist."

In the mirror Sapho saw the maid's pretty, childish face just above her own. Behind the maid were plush-upholstered chairs with gilded fringe, a bloated divan, a square, canopied bed with silken sheets and coverlet of rich brocade. There was a wooden washstand with a marble top, and on the walls were paintings of fat-faced saints and Italian cherubs hovering in mid air. Two arching windows opened over the central courtyard of the Presidential Palace.

Sapho shifted her gaze, studied herself critically in the glass. Years in prison and informal house confinement had taken the glow from her banana-colored skin, but the basic hue was still the same, perhaps even more alluring. She considered Ronca. "What is he like, Juana?" she asked the maid. "As a lover what is Ronca like?"

The maid sighed enviously. "Oh, they say he is a perfect stallion."

They were looking at one another's images in the mirror. "You do not know?" asked Sapho.

Juana paused in her combing. "Oh, señorita, you are making fun!"

Sapho raised slightly her arching eyebrows. "On the contrary, querida, I thought surely he had — "

The girl flushed. "I am very plain," she protested. "Yet I think, perhaps, I dream sometimes, that he will see and — and — "

Sapho smiled at the reflection of the pretty, pouting face. "I think he will."

The maid fluffed Sapho's curls. "Yet it is three years I am here," she said. "You would never believe what it is like. There have been so many women. There was even a gringa señorita, let me tell you. Oh, madre mía, this one, she was a real Yanqui, she had such golden hair — " so Juana babbled on. There was this woman, and there was that woman. Some were prisoners, and others had come of their own free will to beg, but it was all the same. If they were beautiful, it was all the same.

Sapho heard vaguely. Indeed, she could not yet believe that at last her chance had come. It had taken her so long to reach the house of General Ronca!

"Do you think he will like me?" Sapho asked.

The maid bent low over Sapho's shoulder and gazed with admiration at what she saw reflected in the mirror. "Oh, señorita, but observe only!" she protested. "Your glass will not lie."

Sapho inclined her head, studying her mirrored image. "I think I am not really beautiful," she said.

The maid began pinning up the thick, black hair. "Guapa, señorita, puramente guapa," she explained, "y sexual! You will drive him mad."

Sapho winked, "Thank you, Juana!"

"Madre! he has brought you here," the maid protested. "He would not do it if he did not like."

"He took so long!"

"Señorita?"

"Nothing." Sapho said. But it *had* been long. There were the months of waiting after her arrest, the months in the Provincial Prison. Qué linda! the trooper had said, qué linda! That was the trooper, and next it was the sergeant. A-ha! Qué preciosa! exclaimed the sergeant — until the captain came. He had rubbed his hand, this captain, this Alvarez. What a magnificent apple! simpered the captain.

From the trooper to the sergeant, from the sergeant to the captain, up through channels, always up through channels — what a long way, Sapho thought, what a long way to here!

She turned her head sidewise, examining her image through the corners of her eyes. "I must look my best," she told the maid.

"Do not be afraid," Juana soothed. "You are not like the others."

"Oh?" Sapho breathed. "How not?"

"But señorita," shrugged Juana, "I do not know, I have no words. It is the skin, perhaps, soft, like yellow velvet, or it is los pechos, so sweet and round, I do not know, but he will like!"

From the trooper to the sergeant to the captain she had been passed along, and then that Colonel López. After three years they had moved her to the house of Colonel López. Five years, altogether, and through them all, she had been glad of what she knew of men. She had been glad of the cantinas of her girlhood, the cantinas of Havana and Port au Prince, the cafés where her mother had danced, the back rooms and brawls, the rhumbas and samba music.

For they were all men — the trooper, the sergeant, the captain, they were all men, and so was the constabulary colonel, this López. They were all men, and Sapho knew about them. She knew about their brutishness and how to meet it, she knew what to say, how to act, when to laugh and joke. She knew about men, and they liked her, and they passed her on, whereas they would have killed another. They would have raped and killed a prude, and that would have been the end.

"Is he passionate?" Sapho asked. "Does he burn fast or slow?"

"He will burn fast if you allow," Juana explained. "Like ocote pine he will burst into flame and be all burnt out, and you are through. Pfft! He wants no more, and he is angry, maybe, and he will kick you out. I have seen it so. If you do not allow, if you handle right, he will be like charcoal, smoldering only. Then he is yours, señorita, for a long, long time, he is yours."

Sapho smirked enticingly into the mirror. "I will tantalize," she promised Juana.

The maid giggled. "Precious, señorita!" she exclaimed. "And las cejas, señorita, I make them thin, I make them arch, like this, señorita! Oh, he will be in torment!"

"What happens when one is through?" Sapho asked. "When he has tired and wants another?"

Juana shrugged. "I do not know, señorita, but he will like. For a long time he will be mad."

"And if one ran away?"

"Ran away, señorita? Why should one run away?"

"I don't know, but suppose one ran away before he was tired."

"What a silly thing!" Juana exclaimed. "Why, he would catch and bring back. He would tear one apart like a tiger. Las pestañas, señorita, I make them thick and curly? Oh, he will like!"

"And if there were a thing one wanted, Juana. What then?"

"Mande? I do not understand."

Sapho hesitated. "If —if there were a thing, an important thing that one wanted, when would be the time to ask?"

"A pair of earrings, señorita? A necklace, maybe?"

"A very great thing that he would not wish to give," Sapho tried to explain, "a monstrous precious thing, when would be the time to ask?"

"Soon," Juana advised. "When he begins to smolder." She bent down and whispered. "Hold him off, señorita, tease him only! Not to make him angry, sabe, but just to tease. A tiny wiggle, perhaps, señorita, or the dress up like this! Ouf! He will go mad, I tell you. He will give, believe me, anything he will give!" She winked wickedly. "Los párpados, señorita, I shade them so."

"I will tease him," Sapho promised. "I will make him give."

"Verdad! You will make him give!" Juana giggled. "And now your gown, señorita."

"Let me see it," Sapho said. She held it up before her. "O-o-o, Juana, did he have this made?"

"He had it made. It is wicked, no?" Juana helped while Sapho put it on.

It was made of white silk and it was cut low, and the fit was tight. Sapho turned about on her toes before the mirror, and she saw the richness of her skin beneath the whiteness, and she saw her own shape to which the cloth clung tightly. "What do you think, Juana?" she asked the maid.

"That precious thing you want," Juana answered, "señorita, I think you surely get it!"

4

CARLOS CROUCHED in the corner of his cell, and he was like a wild beast with his hair matted about his neck, his muscles twitching. He was crouching there in the blackness when the door opened, flooding his chamber with lantern light. He shrank away, hiding his eyes with his arms, and he kept his lids shut as protection against the blinding glare of the lantern.

"Bueno!" a voice sounded. "Ven acá, you are going out!"

Carlos drew back against the wall, deep in a corner.

"Dios! He wants to stay!" exclaimed a second voice.

"They all do," explained the first voice. "He is afraid of the light. Bueno, hombrecito, vamos!"

Powerful arms seized his shoulders, and he was dragged from the cell. He was dragged out of the rock chamber and along a stone corridor. He kept his face covered with his arms, and he stumbled, unable to keep his feet, and when he came to the stone steps in the well, he was too weak to climb. The guards pushed him upward, and somehow he reached the top.

He was taken before an officer. "Madre, a corpse!" the officer exclaimed. "How long is he here?" He studied a book of records, took down another volume, ran through the pages. "Hm! Fifty-two months and three-four-five days." He made an entry. "Bien, take him down to the launch."

It was a relief to be in nighttime darkness, but the air stung his throat, and he was afraid of the bigness of the space about him.

Guards tumbled him into the launch moored outside the iron gate of San Luis. He lay hunched against a gunwale, and bilge water sloshed over his bare feet. After a time a motor coughed, and the launch slid away and bucked a choppy sea across the harbor.

His mind remained confused, and already he could not be certain how he had got where he was. He could remember the blinding light of the lantern, he could remember the prods of the guards as he stumbled along the corridor, but that was all. He remained in half a stupor.

He was confused, and yet he was vaguely aware of voices in the boat. "It does not happen often." The words sounded small and far away. "Caray, he had a friend, no doubt." The words grew louder. "A powerful friend!" Like thunder, the words rolled near, and then receded far off into the distance and died away. "Quién sabe, it sometimes hap —" There was no sound now, but he felt the wind. It tore at his neck and shoulders, and he shrank from it.

There was a sound of wood grating against stone; there was no more sense of motion. "Get out!" a voice shouted in his ear. "Get out, hombrecito, you are free." He was pulled to his feet, lifted out of the boat, and tossed upon the dock. "Hombre, you are free!"

He raised his head. He was lying flat upon the dock, the lights of Santa Cruz stabbing at his eyes. He felt weak and sick, and he was afraid of the bigness about him. It was a small place that he wanted, a rock chamber, a hole where he could hide. He staggered to his feet upon the dock, swaying like a drunken man, and covered his face with his arms.

Making his way along the vast openness of the dock, he came to a string of freight cars upon a siding. With one hand outstretched, he felt about, running his fingers along the rungs of an iron ladder.

This car was low and flat and loaded with machinery. He got his arms through the ladder and tried to hoist himself upward, but his feet were heavy, and he lacked the strength. He hung there, until his right hand found by chance a higher rung, and with its help, he inched the rest of his body upward until he flopped upon the flatcar deck. There was an opening in a piece of machinery, the hopper of a cement mixer, and he crawled inside. The cavern that he found was small, and he curled up within it, and the greatness of the world was shut away.

In a state of exhaustion he lay curled within the belly of the hopper, and he was asleep when a crew made up the train.

An engine was coupled, and the cars were made into a train with a caboose attached. Switches were thrown, and the locomotive moved away from the docks, and the whole freight began threading its way toward Empalme. Carlos was not aware of the rattle of couplings, the jolt of cars, the short, piping whistle of the engine as it neared a crossing. He saw neither the bright lights of Santa Cruz dropping away behind, nor the red and green-lit switches coming up, the shadowy roundhouses, the marshalling yards, the arc of a lantern signalling, the black bulk of the Empalme refinery beyond.

The freight rattled through the yards of Kilometer 10 and headed across the swampy lowlands of la tierra caliente. . . .

The brakeman was Esteban Cruce.

With leather cap and ragged serape, he stood in the caboose, a lantern in his hand, and he was drawing on a pair of canvas gloves. "You soldiers have it easy," he chided the train guard. "Jesus, what do you do? You ride the trains. Back and forth you ride the trains, sitting on your ancas. Now take me — observe all that I must do."

"Not much," grunted the guard. He was making coffee over a wood burning stove.

"Oh, no? Then come with me, amigo! Come with me to the tender only, along the tops of the cars, only."

"I have other matters," grunted the guard.

"Oh, here it is nothing," Cruce continued. "But up in La Cumbre, where the frost forms on the gangway — I invite you to come along with me."

"You apply the brakes," snorted the soldier. "I protect your life."

"Ho! Protect my life! In the puke of a sick sow! Have a care, amigo, that your anca grows not too fat beneath you. Oh, what a cushion it is, what a precious cushion. Tell me, amigo, how do you protect my life?"

"I inspect the cars, brakeman, I — "

"You inspect the cars! When? Drawn up in a station, perhaps. Tell me this thing, who inspects the cars a hundred times? From caboose to tender, rain or frost or wind, who inspects the cars? I spit upon your offal!" Esteban Cruce left the caboose, and he swung upon the roof of the first car and made his way along the catwalk. There was warm wind in his face, and he liked it, and he sang a song.

> On the back of my train,
> My little train,
> I ride the wind, like a hawk.
> On the back of my train,

> Like a hawk,
> I ride the wind.
> Trenecito, halconcito!
> I ride the wind.

He moved along atop the cars, singing his song, and he swung his lantern, and he laughed at the feel of wind.

> On the back of my train,
> My little train,
> I ride the wind —

He swung down onto a flatcar loaded with machinery, and picked his way. He thought of the soldier back there in the caboose, and he laughed, and he added the soldier to his song.

> O-o-o, soldado
> Sitting on his anca,
> He rides the wind,
> Sitting on his anca!

He picked his way along the flatcar, singing his song, and he climbed the cement mixer.

> O-o-o, soldado
> Sitting on his Eeyah!

Esteban Cruce had stepped upon something soft. He drew back, cursing, and he swung his lantern low. It was inside the mixer — this thing. Cautiously he stooped and looked, and for a moment he was terrified at what he saw. A corpse, he thought, a corpse dug out of its grave. He had seen long, matted hair like that on ancient Nacheetl mummies.

But no, the corpse moved.

He held the lantern closer. The body stirred, raised its arms about its face. Esteban Cruce hung the lantern on a projection of the mixer and got down upon his knees and felt the body cautiously. It was a man, alive, but very weak.

"Holy Mother!" he muttered to himself. "From the mines, perhaps, but how —" He considered a moment longer. "San Luis! San Luis de Tiburón of course!" He felt the wrist. The pulse was strong. He seized his lantern. "Un momentito!" he promised. "Stay there, un momentito only!" He hurried back over the machinery, swung himself onto the roof of the next car toward the caboose.

The guard was snoozing. So much the better. To think that he had tried to shame this useless soldier into coming along! He tested the coffee on the stove. It was boiling. He poured a half-litre or so into a tin can, and from a shelf above the stove he took down a tortilla and a cold drumstick.

When he returned to the mixer, he found that the sick man had not stirred. He squirmed his head and shoulders into the hopper, being careful not to spill the coffee.

"Pobrecito!" He held the ragged head high and put the coffee can to the blistered lips.

The sick man drank gratefully.

Esteban Cruce nursed him along and helped him with the tortilla and the cold drumstick. The sick man nibbled, but he appeared too tired and weak to eat.

"Enough, for now that is enough," the brakeman said. He removed his grimy serape and wrapped it about the man to keep him warm, and he set the coffee tin within reach, and what was left of the tortilla and the leg of chicken. "Stay there only," he said. "And do not be afraid. . . ."

It was daytime when Carlos awoke, and sunlight was streaming into his hopper. He unwrapped the serape from around his body and hung it across the hopper opening to keep out the brightness. He looked about. There was a can of coffee close beside him, a leg of chicken, and a cake of cheese. He was not sure where all these things had come from, but he had a faint recollection of someone bending over. He drank off the coffee and nibbled at the cheese.

He felt weak and drowsy. He shifted his position, stretched out his legs, and soon he was asleep again. When next he woke, his bladder was swollen from the coffee, and his stomach was wracked with pains. He edged around so that he could relieve himself beyond the rim of the hopper.

The coffee can had been refilled, and there was a tortilla covered with honey. He drank, and he tasted the honey, and it was soft and smooth and easy to eat. He finished everything that was there and went back to sleep.

The freight train rumbled through another night, stopping briefly at towns along the way. It stopped at Piccadilly, at Happy Hooligan and Number Sixteen and MacDonald's Folly, at Royal Flush, Aceite, Manuela Johnson and Adiós — to take on wood or water, to cut off a car, to let a fast train pass.

During the night it clattered through lowland jungles and across savannas, and then it began to climb among foothills of the great cordillera. When Carlos next awoke, the air was cool and fresh. He drew the serape close about him and drank another can of coffee that was waiting.

He felt strength beginning to return. He shifted his position within the hopper so that he could see beyond the rim, and he listened to the engine. It was laboring on a grade. There was a curve, and he could see ahead, and the engine was spitting sparks, and a crack in the firebox gleamed red.

He saw a light moving back from the tender. Instinctively he cowered back within the hopper.

The brakeman held the lantern high, peered inside. Carlos covered his eyes.

"Dios! I forget," the brakeman apologized. He hung the lantern outside. "Com' 'stá, amigo?"

Carlos looked up, but said nothing.

"How would you like to wash the face and hands and cut the hair? I'll bring a bucket." The brakeman took his lantern and went away.

When he returned he had a gasoline tin with a wire bail, a shirt, and a pair of pantalones. He leaned inside the hopper. "Now we wash, eh?"

He stripped off the filthy rags that Carlos wore. "E-e-e-yah! Those lice!" He tossed the clothes outside. "You will pardon me, amigo, but I do not like your stink." He dipped a cloth into the water and began bathing Carlos' face and arms and neck.

Carlos felt better.

"Tiburón?" the brakeman asked.

Carlos nodded.

"Pobrecito! You are the first I ever saw. From Tiburón you are the very first." He scrubbed the chest and trunk and crotch, the long, spindly legs, the feet. "Qué caga! Pues, a man covered with his own caga — I have seen that!" He chuckled at his little joke.

He finished the washing, tossed out the water, and helped Carlos into pantalones and shirt. "There, now, you are clean," he said as he attacked the matted hair with a pocket knife. "Only remember this, my friend, there are no more pantalones, so keep them white."

With his knife the brakeman chopped and hacked at Carlos' hair. "Caray, what a barber," he exclaimed when he had finished. "One could do better with an axe. Pues, no matter! I'll be going now, or the soldier will wonder what passes on up here." He eased out of the hopper, then stuck his head back in. "Did you ever hear of Cuerno?" he asked. "Felipe Cuerno?"

Carlos shook his head.

"You will, amigo," the brakeman assured him. "Listen a moment! He is in San Marcos now, but you would not be safe there. I'll roll you off at La Cumbre. At dawn, more or less, I'll roll you off, and Jorge Bronco will find a place. Among the carboneros he will find a place. Comprende?"

Again Carlos shook his head.

"It is a small matter," the brakeman said. "You will be safe with Jorge Bronco. And later on — Felipe Cuerno!"

IX. Carboneros

THE FREIGHT PULLED into La Cumbre just before dawn. A light, cold mist hung over the pass and all but obscured the glow of charcoal pits scattered here and there on the slopes above. Cramped in his hiding place, Carlos saw an electric bulb hanging from the red-tiled eave of an adobe station. A figure in high-crowned sombrero and red serape stood motionless in the yellow light. Esteban Cruce swung off the car ahead onto the gravel in front of the station. "Hola! Jorge Bronco-o-o-o!" said the brakeman. "Com'stá, camarada-a-a-a-a?"

The figure before the station raised an arm which, in the serape folds, looked like a red-feathered condor wing. "Cabró-o-o-on! 'steban, qué se pasa-a-a-a-a-a?"

Lantern in hand, Esteban stood close to the man called Bronco, and the two of them talked together, and clouds of steam came from their lips when they spoke. Meanwhile, the train guard, yawning widely, stumbled onto the rear steps of the caboose, rifle slung.

The brakeman and the station master still were talking together, and Cruce placed an arm about Bronco's shoulder as they moved slowly toward the waiting train. In his cold steel hopper, Carlos felt the chill of high mountain air, and his teeth chattered.

The engineer was peering back from the cab of his locomotive. Esteban arced his lantern. "Vamos!" he shouted as he swung aboard. "Nos va-a-a-a-amos!" To the station master he cried, "A-ye-e-e-yah! You make it cold here, Jorge Bronco-o-o!"

The station master threw back his head and laughed, and Carlos saw the whiteness of his teeth. "Ho! For a swamp pig like you, 'steban!" he shouted. "For a swamp pig only."

The train jolted into motion. Agile as a lowland monkey, Esteban ran along the edge of the flatcar, reached in the hopper, and seized

Carlos by a skinny shoulder. "Now," he hissed as the freight train slowly gathered speed. "Quick, before we go too fast." He yanked Carlos out of the hiding place, pushed him over the edge of the jolting flatcar. "Hola, Jorge Bronco-o-o-o-o!" he shouted. "Cuidado-o-o-o-o, un vagabundo, Jorge, un ratoncito-o-o-o-o-o-o!"

Carlos pitched forward onto the hard gravel where he felt the sharpness of tiny stones grinding into the flesh of his face and shoulders and arms. On the flatcar Esteban was peering back anxiously. Jorge Bronco ran forward, seized Carlos, jerked him to his feet. "E-e-e-e-e-yah, I've got him," he shouted, "I've got the ratoncito-o-o-o-o-o!"

The engine driver pulled his whistle, and the shrillness of it echoed and reechoed among the mountains back of La Cumbre. Click-clack, click-clack, the freight cars rattled past. "What goes on?" asked the train guard as the caboose rolled by the spot where Jorge Bronco held Carlos by the collar. He swung out from the steps of the moving car, stretched a leg forward as though to get off. But by this time the train had gathered too much speed.

"A vagabond, soldado, only a vagabond!" Jorge called out good-naturedly. "What shall I do with him?"

The guard retreated onto the platform, slapped a half-crooked arm. Steadily the caboose withdrew into the darkness beyond La Cumbre until only its red lights were visible. Jorge released his grip, and Carlos stood unsteadily, shivering in the coldness of the night. The station master looked him over. "How goes it, comrade?"

"Well enough," said Carlos weakly.

"I'll take you in," suggested Jorge. The station master started to lead Carlos along the tracks, but seeing his weakness, he leaned over, swung him across one shoulder as a hunter would sling a deer, trotted easily toward the door of the station. "Like a sack of feathers!" the station master chuckled. He carried Carlos into the adobe building, eased him gently onto a brass-knobbed bed.

Carlos heard the clickety-click-click of telegraph on a hewn pine table across the room. He looked about. It was a simple chamber of whitewashed adobe with fare and records books upon a shelf and dispatch slips skewered upon a nail. On the floor was a brass spittoon, and the place smelled strongly of stale cigar smoke.

Jorge disappeared into a back room, returned with a tall tequila bottle. "Una copacita," he said. "A little drink to fire your blood."

Carlos downed the drink gratefully. It burned its way into his stomach, and immediately he felt a liquid warmth oozing through his arms and legs, to his fingertips and toes. The tequila was quick to act upon his weakened stomach, and in a moment he felt a pleasant giddiness seeping through his head. Jorge Bronco, meanwhile, had filled a tin basin with soapy water, and he set about bathing Carlos where the gravel had cut his face.

"Turn over now, comrade!" the station master said. "Lie on the belly while I fix the back."

Carlos did as he was told, but as he settled on his stomach he saw a sight that made him jump. There before him stood a naked woman. Violently he shook his head to clear it, but the woman stayed. There she was, tall and curved in the yellow twenty-watt light. Then Carlos saw that she was only painted on the whitewashed wall, a lithe figure of vivid brownish, earthy colors.

The station master laughed, slapped Carlos across the buttocks. "Ho, now, how do you like my desnuda?" he inquired. "Muy guapa, eh? E-e-e-e-e-yah, and I thought you would be too weak to like!"

"Did you paint it?" Carlos asked.

"That I did!" admitted Jorge Bronco. "Between trains, so to speak. Oh, I have painted many pictures on that very wall. I put one there and live with it awhile, and when I no longer like, whish! The whitewash takes it away." While he spoke, he worked on Carlos, washing off the bruises. "Caray, what sharpish bones! Were you working in Ronca's mines?"

"No, Tiburón," Carlos told him.

Jorge whistled. "A-a-a-a-yah, welcome, comrade! You are very lucky to get away. Pobrecito, you must be hungry, but wait a moment only. In a very little moment there will be a thing to eat, and then, comrade, you must sleep for a few hours and gain some strength because before the next train comes — whoosht! You must go above among the carboneros, camarada, for it is safer there. Smeared with charcoal, all men look alike, and already on the slopes there are many like you."

"Gracias!" Carlos murmured. When Jorge brought tortillas and beans and coffee, Carlos ate and drank, and when he had finished,

Jorge put him to bed and covered him with sheepskin robes and the red serape. "Lie there now and sleep," the station master said, "and do not dream about my pretty desnuda. No, no, you are still too weak to think of her." He tucked Carlos in as he would a tiny child.

Carlos slept too hard for dreaming, and it was nearly noon before Jorge woke him. By his bedside Carlos found a basin of water, and on the table near the telegraph were terra cotta pots of steaming food. "Coffee, eggs, potatoes, tortillas, go to it, comrade," Jorge said, waving a paintbrush, "while I tickle the nipples of my precious nude!"

Carlos ate while Jorge worked upon his painting. When he had mixed his colors on an old tin plate, the station master stood back and squinted; then with his brush he touched between the breasts. She was brown and lithe, with strong body and slim Nacheetl wrists and ankles. She stood straight, with a tall olla balanced on her head.

"As soon as Henrique comes," explained Jorge Bronco, "we shall start for the carbonero slopes. He is my assistant, sabe, and all last night he was out a-whoring. I think he sleeps with this one," he added, indicating the nude. "I do not know, but I think he sleeps with her who models. He was out all night and came home late for finding horses." Jorge stepped back again and squinted at his painting, and Carlos watched.

In the early hours of morning he had been too tired and weak to notice much about Jorge Bronco, but he watched the station master now. The man was short and stocky with broad face and nose, and there were crinkles about his mouth and eyes from laughing. He stood with feet apart, and his shirt was open low upon his chest, and his pantalones ended high above open Nacheetl sandals. "I used to paint social matters only," Jorge explained to Carlos. "But I had to cover them when the trains came through, or else the guards would see."

"Social matters?" questioned Carlos. "I do not understand."

"About the revolution!" Jorge grinned.

"What revolution?" demanded Carlos.

Jorge Bronco spun upon his heel. "Madre, comrade, how long were you in prison?"

Carlos swallowed a mouthful of coffee. "I do not know," he said. "There was only blackness."

"You have heard of Felipe Cuerno?" the station master asked.

"From the brakeman," Carlos said.

Jorge went back to his painting. "Pues, 'steban and I are friends," he told Carlos, "and Felipe Cuerno, too. We belong to the same union, comrade. We piss on Ronca. This Cuerno, he is engine driver, a real stallion, you will see. About yourself, comrade, how did you arrive in Ronca's prison?"

Carlos told of Doctor MacNeill, of Sapho and his marriage, of Magdalena rapping at the hotel door. He spoke also of the prison in the Palace of Lions, of Alvarez, of the doctor's death, of his own transfer to Tiburón. Jorge put down his brush and listened, and moisture settled in his eyes as he heard what Carlos had to say.

"Oh, the poor señora!" he exclaimed as Carlos finished. "Oh, the poor señora!" He sat upon the bed with his hands folded. "Now you do not know where she is! Comrade, I hope you spoke of this to 'steban."

Carlos shook his head.

"Oh, you should have told!" Jorge exclaimed. "He might find out, that 'steban. He might find the poor señora somewhere in San Marcos." There was the sound of hoofs outside. "Bueno, here is Henrique with a mule." He helped Carlos to his feet, steadied him through the back room to the door where the mule was waiting.

When they had hoisted Carlos into the saddle, Jorge led the animal away from the station to a path that rose steeply upward from the mountain pass. It was an ancient trail that had been worn deep by generations of men and beasts. In places there were mud holes where the animal picked its way, while other stretches had been neatly cobbled and the rain water channelled off. All about rose mountain slopes which were thickly wooded with pines and stunted oaks. Myrtles grew close beside the trail and feather-veined magnolias bloomed lavender on every hand.

"You see the clearings?" Jorge pointed. "No, Carlos, more down there, beyond the ravine, and off here to the left as well. Those are charcoal pits, but they are not burning. Later, your nose will tell. Long ago these people started making charcoal, comrade. Not these very people, but their fathers, pues, and their grandfathers, too. They started down below, and they are working upward. Always they are working upward. Someday, perhaps, there will be no trees. They will reach the snow on the Fire Mountain, and there will be no trees."

"They do not turn one in to the police?" Carlos asked.

"These people? No, camarada, they hate Ronca. They are waiting, only."

"Will there be fighting, you think?"

Jorge Bronco shook his head in astonishment. "You have been buried a long time, Carlos. The whole country is ready to blow up. Any day, verdad."

"There were those who tried in San Marcos," Carlos recollected. "I saw them hanging from an oak tree."

"This time it will be Ronca who hangs," Jorge promised. He sniffed the air. "We come to a pit, now. One smells the smoke." A few steps farther along he turned off the trail along a smaller footpath.

Carlos could see smoke rising from a conical pile of saplings partially covered with leaves and sod. There were voices and the sound of chopping.

"A-a-a-a-a-yah, Jorge Bronco-o-o-o-o!"

"Hola, Leonarrrdo-o-o-o-o, qué tal, amigo-o-o-o?"

Jorge Bronco ran ahead and shook the hand of a grey-haired man who was leaning on an axe, an aged peasant whose white blouse and pantalones were streaked with soot.

The mule picked its way more carefully, and Jorge was already deep in conversation with the old man and with a younger man when Carlos reached the pit.

It was clear that Jorge was explaining about Tiburón. "You know how it is, Leonardo, deep in the rock below the sea. You have heard, amigo. Well, this man here, this Carlos, he was there. Buried like a corpse." Jorge described each detail. He explained about the rock chamber, about the slop bucket, about everything that Carlos had told.

Leonardo nodded, and when he had surveyed Carlos from head to foot, he stepped forward and touched the spindle legs and arms. "Pobrecito!" he exclaimed, and Carlos saw that there were tears in the old man's eyes.

"You will take him in?" Jorge asked.

"My little house is his," Leonardo said with a slight bow to Carlos. "Will you come?"

He led the way, and Jorge took the mule by the halter and guided it toward a pine-slab cabin among the trees.

2

LEONARDO'S HOUSE was made of pine boards, sawed out by hand, and it was roofed with axe-hewn shingles. There were four small rooms in one of which the walls and timbers were black, and that was the kitchen.

Old Leonardo was head of the family, and he shared a room with his wife, María. There was also Fermin, who was Leonardo's son, and there was Fermin's wife, Rosita, and they slept in a room with their five children. The fourth room they gave to Carlos.

The board floors were clean, swept by a willow broom, and it was the duty of the eldest daughter, Bertita, to keep them so. She was nine years old, and it was she who was chosen to nurse Carlos. She placed two sheepskins upon the floor, and over the sheepskins she spread a large serape. Carlos stretched out upon this bed, and Bertita covered his skeleton body with a second serape to keep out dampness and cold. She brought in a pottery brazier for burning charcoal, and she fed it with coals from the kitchen until it glowed red in the dimness of the tiny room.

"See that our amigo has always tea," Rosita told her daughter, "and see that it is hot."

Bertita brought a clay teapot from the kitchen and nestled it among the coals of the brazier. In it she brewed a tea of sarsaparilla.

Here in Leonardo's cabin on the mountainside Carlos lay and slept and ate and gained in strength. During the day he was alone, save for Bertita who cared for him, for Leonardo and his son went out upon the slopes to cut palings and to tend their charcoal pits, and hour upon hour he watched the trail for Jorge Bronco.

If it were a day for Jorge's coming, Carlos would hear him shout as he neared the cabin. "Hola, Carlos, camarada-a-a-a!" In a moment the station master would appear astride his mule.

Squatting on the board floor, he would talk with Carlos. "Sturdy as a goat you'll be, comrade, in another month or so."

Still thin and weak, Carlos would lean upon a trembling elbow and ask a question. "Has Esteban Cruce been through on a train?"

"Tonight he will be through, I think," Jorge answered one day.

"You will tell him of my wife?"

"Of course, Carlos, I will tell." Jorge promised as he had before.

"In San Marcos he can inquire from Magdalena who has a house on the Calle de las Mujeres," Carlos said. Again he explained about the place and how to get there.

"'steban will find it," Jorge chuckled. "Esteban can always find a whore house."

Thus Jorge promised to help in the finding of Sapho, and Carlos waited. Day upon day he waited, and he watched the trail for Jorge to return with news. Often Jorge came, but week followed week, and there was no word of Sapho.

During each day Carlos lay and slept and ate and waited while Leonardo and his son were at work upon the slope. But at night, unless there was a pit that needed watching, they returned and sat about the charcoal stove and talked with Carlos. They talked about the weather, and about births and deaths and sicknesses upon the slope, but they asked no questions.

When Carlos spoke, they listened, and they were anxious to hear, and they discussed his words. They wanted to learn of Santa Cruz, of the oilfields and the refineries in jungle country down below, of the prison in San Marcos, and of the dungeon of Tiburón. They wanted to learn of the federal police and of Ronca's government and of the thinking of those who lived in San Marcos and in the country beyond the mountains.

For Carlos there were days when memories slept, and living was for the moment only. But the past was alive within him, if sometimes dormant, and when it aroused and stirred, it was a foetus in his belly, and he was pregnant with recollection. At such times he talked, and he spoke bitterly of what had happened.

As he spoke bitterly, Leonardo and Fermin listened with respectful silence. They sat in the darkness of their cabin while a reddish glow from the charcoal stove spread across their faces, and Carlos saw their eyes glitter in the light.

When Carlos had finished talking, Leonardo spoke. "They have taken men from these very slopes to work in Ronca's mines," he said. "And a few have returned alive. But I've met no living man from Tiburón."

"It is blackness," Carlos explained. "All blackness."

Fermin coughed, spat into the brazier, and his saliva sizzled there on the hot coals. "This Ronca's day is near," he said, "and then —" He drew a finger across his throat.

Old Leonardo dipped his pipe into a leather pouch and filled the bowl with coarse strings of tobacco. "That is true," he agreed with his son. "Why, even in the old days we stood for less. I remember when all these slopes were on a single hacienda. It belonged to the family Tortosa who owned from San Marcos all through here and down to the very jungle. It all belonged to one family, and from each three litres of our charcoal Señor took two. A-a-a-a-a-yah, we yelped like beaten dogs, and when the revolution came, we joined it. All through the country it was Ronca riding on a burr-tailed nag. The land to those who till it, Ronca shouted, and we listened, I and all the other men along the slopes, and we marched to the Hacienda of San Ramon and burned it to the ashes. Now the slopes belong to us, we said, and out of three litres of charcoal, three belong to us."

A pine shaving dropped onto red coals in the brazier, caught fire, and lighted the cabin room with a flare of amber. Carlos saw a wood spider hanging from the roof by a thin thread of web. It swayed a little just in front of Leonardo's face. The shaving burned away into a curl of grey ash, and the room was dark again. Once more Fermin spit. "Three litres out of three," he said reflectively. "That's how it was for a time, too."

"For a time, yes!" Leonardo agreed. He drew deep drafts on his pipe, and the tobacco blazed red like the charcoal in a blacksmith's forge. "For two or three years there were no complaints. Then Ronca feels a rat gnawing at his belly, and he grows hungry for power, and he gets it. How? Quien sabe, I am an unlettered man. But power he gets, and then he sends his police to collect new taxes."

Fermin snorted. "Oh, that Ronca, he is a very pig for taxes. In the market place we got a peso for a hundred kilos. A peso in San Carlos for a hundred kilos. On foot that is very far, amigo, and we cannot afford the railroad. In a year, perhaps, one makes two hundred pesos. And then for taxes, amigo, this Ronca demands a hundred or a hundred and fifty pesos."

"More!" cried old Leonardo. "Sometimes even more! I know taxes that were even higher than all the sale of charcoal. Oh, we could not pay. So then came the federal police, and they took our land away by paper and collected rent."

"Not in charcoal," Fermin explained. "Like taxes, we pay our rent in pesos according to the land we use. In the old days it was charcoal, sabe, and we paid to the family Tortosa. We paid according to our yield, two kilos out of every three, two kilos out of every three. But today, pfft! If my father here gets sick with a snake coiled in his belly, or if I am bitten in the foot by my axe, or if in our wood there is an excess of water, it makes no difference. The rent is still the same."

In silence they sat huddled about the charcoal brazier. Outside in the night an owl hooted, and somewhere a dog barked in answer. Fermin reached into a corner for a sack of charcoal, scattered a handful on the greying coals. Tiny star-like sparks shot out as the fire took hold.

"The owner of the land?" Carlos asked. "Who is he?"

Leonardo shrugged. "Ronca, perhaps, I do not know. Anyhow, we lose our right of use if we do not pay the rent. If the amount is small, that is. If it is large — the mines, amigo!"

"It will not be long," Fermin insisted. "It will not be long. We peasants have formed a League. There are many grimy faces upon the slope, amigo. There are men with faces covered with soot who never before made charcoal."

"Who?" Carlos asked. "What men are these?"

"Lettered men," Leonardo said. "Men from the cities, from San Marcos and Santa Cruz, men who read and write and know the laws."

"Yes, and there are also those of the Railway Union," Fermin added. "Men like Jorge Bronco, only these ones have stepped into trouble. They have spit upon a soldier, perhaps, or have talked against Ronca. They are like mad foxes, amigo, they are wild, and their teeth are small, but sharp. There are others from the hot country who have worked for the Yanquis and know how to suck oil out of the earth."

"Oh, that Peasant League," Fermin exclaimed, "it will be the end

of Ronca." Already they had explained to Carlos about its forming.
The peasants of Chacala had organized it first, building about the
Village Council. They belonged to the Barrio of the Hornets, those
Chacala men, and their runners had carried word of the League to
the Hornet Barrio within San Marcos. There other Barrios had heard
about the League and had joined in organizing. Then, carried like an
itch by Barrio runners, it had spread from village to village throughout the mountain country.

Thus at night the two peasants sat around the charcoal brazier and
smoked and chatted with Carlos. Usually they spoke about the slopes
and the people living there, but now and then there was talk about
the great, mysterious world that lay far off beyond the mountains.
Neither Leonardo nor Fermin had a clear notion of what it was, but
they had seen pictures of magic cities like Nueva York where all the
buildings rose high above the earth, poking holes among the clouds,
and Shee-cah-go where the gangsters lived. During recent years they
had also heard much about the war across the seas, and there were
men upon the slopes right now who had seen the fighting, but it was
finished, now.

"Sí, pues, those Yanquis, they drop one little bomb," Fermin explained to Carlos. "There is a great big city, oh, big, big, like San
Marcos, and those Yanquis drop one bomb only, and pfft! every man
is dead! Believe me, amigo, that is the end of fighting. Madre, in all
that great big city there are no men left to fight."

Carlos listened soberly. He was pleased to hear about the war's
end, but he wondered what it might mean for his own country.

Fermin and Leonardo sank down upon their sheepskins with their
wives, coughing incessantly, while Carlos lay alone in the night with
only his thoughts to divert him. Increasingly, as his strength had returned, old thoughts had come trooping into his mind. These were
the unfettered, joyful memories that came with freedom. Sometimes
Sapho was lying close beside him in their tremendous bed in the Gran
Hotel San Marcos. He raised up on an elbow and saw her there, black
hair spread across a pillow. Again, she was walking with him upon a
dusty road, or lying close to him in reeds beside a river bank.

But tonight, as Carlos lay upon his sheepskin and thought of Sapho,
the devil came and dragged him into the darkest corner of the cabin.

Eyes gleaming wickedly, the devil squatted near Carlos and talked of pastures above Zalapec, of Diego, of Cain and Abel. Breaking into a feverish sweat, Carlos finally dropped into an exhausted sleep, only to find the devil waiting for him in a nauseating dream.

They were back in Tiburón, imprisoned in a rock chamber beneath the surface of the sea. The devil was squatting in a corner watching, and Carlos saw his eyes and heard his heavy breathing. There was neither night nor day, but there was blackness ticked off by the spat of globules upon the floor, and there was the devil waiting in the corner, watching.

3

WHILE JORGE BRONCO was visiting Carlos one evening he launched into the horrifying details of Hiroshima and Nagasaki.

Even as Jorge Bronco told it, the story was not a thing that one could hear and wholly comprehend. Second-hand disasters are unreal at best, but to talk about the mangling of a hundred thousand people was entirely too fantastic. It was like discussing a trip to the moon or a Martian battle or a collision between the earth and Saturn. Listening attentively, Carlos tried to visualize what had taken place on those far-off Pacific islands. He managed to picture a small, deceptive package floating downward; he managed to picture an initial explosion that was something like a ton or two of dynamite touched off at once; he managed to sense the atmosphere charged with unleashed, uncontrolled, destructive energy that was like the vital center of an electric storm intensified a million times.

So much he managed to comprehend, but he knew well from Jorge Bronco's story that his comprehension fell far short. He tried to visualize a city like San Marcos in total ruin; he tried to visualize a hundred thousand men and women and children torn apart and baked.

Jorge Bronco was watching Carlos. "One does not believe a thing like this in a short-short moment," he said. "It is big like the sky. One sees a little patch directly before the eyes, and one considers that. Then one moves along to another little patch and tries again." Carlos asked Jorge further questions, but the station master was preparing to leave and did not seem disposed to discuss the matter. Carlos was perplexed by this. Was it possible for any man to ignore the implications of this monster? Or had human imaginations been so stunned that they had ceased to fear?

Carlos chafed at his own weakness and incapacity. Yet his strength was returning, and with faithful nursing he was able, after a time, to leave his sheepskin bed and move about the cabin, and later he went with Leonardo and Fermin to the charcoal pits where they were working. There he watched them cut pales into proper lengths and arrange them on end in the shape of a cone. Later, he even helped them to cover each cone with sod and dirt and to light a fire inside. The labor gradually increased his appetite and made his body stronger.

It was while he was working among the pits that Esteban found him. There had been a broken piston, and Esteban's freight lay upon a La Cumbre siding while another locomotive came up from San Marcos. Jorge Bronco had suggested a visit with Carlos. "Go on up, camarada, and tell him about Magdalena," the station master told the brakeman. "Tell him also what has happened to her house. Pobrecito, he thinks only of his señora, and he makes himself sick through waiting for word."

Carlos was gathering pales when he saw Esteban approaching along the trail. With a yell, he dropped his load. "You have news for me!"

The brakeman shook his head. "No, Carlos, I could not find your wife, or Magdalena either," he admitted regretfully. "Oh, I went to Magdalena's house, amigo. But she is gone." He explained that Ronquistas had seized her house because she had not kept up with taxes and the license fees.

"That was her own property," protested Carlos. "She had bought it."

"Now it belongs to Ronca," Esteban told him. "Ronca, or Alvarez, it is all the same. Oh, that Alvarez is a slick coyote. He runs La Calle de las Mujeres. He runs every house up and down the street. Pues, Carlos, he makes much money. You see how it is. The tax is raised, raised, until one cannot pay, and when one does not pay, the government takes, and then Alvarez buys."

"The girls in the house?" Carlos inquired. "They knew nothing about Magdalena?"

"The girls were new," Esteban replied. "They did not know. But about your wife, Carlos, you have no cause for sorrow. I shall search again in San Marcos. We have friends in other places, too — among oilfield workers and on the Río Mosca where bananas grow, on coffee plantations of Puerta Colon, pues, in the government under Ronca's very nose. Do not worry, amigo, we shall find her."

"She may be in prison," Carlos said.

"If she is in prison, we shall discover that, too," Esteban promised. "This Felipe Cuerno, Carlos, his reach is long. Prison bars are nothing. Let me tell you a thing, amigo. You know the docks at Santa Cruz?"

"I know them."

"Bien, I went there with Cuerno," Esteban said, "last week only. We were to see a man in regard to arms. It was secret-secret. Well, Cuerno took me along to fire, and when we reached the docks in Santa Cruz, we climbed out of the cab and went aboard a foreign ship. We went right past the guards, Carlos, right by the Customs. Oh, it was precious, all fixed, you understand. Have you ever been aboard a ship, Carlos?"

"Never."

"Pues, let me tell you, it was like a palace," Esteban narrated. "There was a room with tables, and the seats were leather with softness inside, and we sat upon them. We had our greasy clothes, sabe, two railwaymen only, but we sat upon those seats, and a mozo brought us drinks, and there was ice floating in them. Real ice, Carlos. It was like chunks of glass, but it bit the tongue, and it floated, too. One drank, and it brought pain to the throat, and one felt coldness sloshing in the belly. Bien, about the arms. You have seen a Yanqui, Carlos?"

"I have seen many Yanquis."

"Well, this man was more or less a Yanqui as to looks. He wore a suit, Carlos, with coat and trousers both the same. He was dressed like a político or a banker in San Marcos, and yet it was not the same. The cloth was grey, and his tie was yellow. That is true, amigo, his tie was yellow. He had no hair upon his head; it was shiny like a cobblestone, and he kept polishing it with his hand. As he talked, he polished. Well, he had a leather bag, not pregnant fat, but skinny only, and he took many papers from it.

"Bien, says he to Cuerno, I have got your invoice, Mac. He called Cuerno Mac. Tell me, Carlos, what is Mac?"

"It is like comrade," Carlos said.

"Well, Mac, says he, I've got your invoice. For Puerto Colon, he says, to go ashore at night in small boats, one thousand Springfields, two thousand Lee-Enfields, and twenty-five mortars, together with fifty thousand round of ammunition and —

"A moment, cuts in Cuerno. What kinds of ammunition? I don't want stuff that won't fit. You played that trick before.

"No, no, says he to Cuerno, it is all here, see, I've put it down on paper — and he reads off many figures.

"Will it shoot? asks Cuerno.

"Well, you know, Mac, he says, maybe not each one, but —

"Is it as good as what you sell Ronca? Cuerno asks.

"Why Mac, I don't —

"Yes you do, says Cuerno. Well, what else?

"To be shipped to Acme Mining Company, San Marcos, through this port, two thousand Mannlicher —

"Don't want them, Cuerno says.

"Listen, Mac, maybe you think —

"Don't want them, Cuerno says.

"Well, maybe we could make it Winchesters.

"All right, what else? Cuerno asks. Well, Carlos, you see how it went. So many for Santa Cruz, so many through Puerto Colon for the Río Papagayo, so many across the border by canoe on the Río Mosca. That was how the invoice was, and there were guns and bullets and mortars I never heard of, and Cuerno knew them all. We want them right away, Cuerno says, and the man in the grey suit says, bien, we drop them when you say, and they fixed the date."

"Where does this man secure the weapons?" Carlos asked.

"I also wanted to know that," Esteban acknowledged. "After we left the room in the ship that was like a palace, we went back down on the dock, and we walked away, and believe me, I felt my tail twitch, but Cuerno says do not fear, I have fixed the whole matter. Then I ask about the guns. He says, oh, that man buys and sells guns for the whole world. Wherever is revolution, that man buys and sells. He deals with both sides, so he makes plenty. But I worry, Carlos. Maybe he will tell Ronca, I say. Ho! says Cuerno, if he tells, then he loses half his business, and that man could not live without business. But where does he get the guns, I ask. And Cuerno says, oh, in capitalist world are big wars every so many years, and they make many guns, and when war is over, this man buys for very small price, and then he sells at very high price."

"No one troubled you?" Carlos marvelled. "Getting on and off the ship?"

"I speak to Cuerno about that, too, and he says look, 'steban, in a country like this, revolution is very easy because every man has a price. Ronca has a price, everybody has a price. The whole capitalist world has a price, and it eats into timbers like white ants and makes the toughest wood like dust after one hard push. That is because each man works for himself only, Cuerno says, while Comunistas work for the good of every man who works."

"Comunistas!" exclaimed Carlos.

. "Si, pues, amigo, that is how the matter is," Esteban said as he got up to leave. "We have friends in every part, in the prisons, even, and so I say this, Carlos. In a short time we shall learn about your wife."

4

FREQUENTLY, NOW, Carlos ventured forth upon the slope, visiting various pits and talking with the carboneros whom he met. One day he climbed somewhat higher than before, laboring upward a few rods at a stretch, resting often in the thinness of the mountain air. It was warm in sunny spots, and magnolia bushes blossomed lavender beside the trail, and rosemary lent its fragrance to the wood-smoke scent carried by all the breezes. But where pines grew thickest the air was chill from altitude and from cold winds blowing off the snowy slopes of the Fire Mountain which lay hidden beyond western ridges.

Once he rested beneath a myrtle shrub and watched a ruby-feathered hummingbird feeding on its flowers, and he looked at La Cumbre down below. He could see the red tiles of the station roof and sunlight gleaming on the smooth curve of rails. There he lay in tall green grass and caught his breath, and when he had rested, he made his way a few rods higher where he stretched out again.

As he looked down upon La Cumbre he saw two sights. He saw the slopes and pass and station roof and curving rails as they really were, and he saw them as they might be in the ruin of atomic devastation. He realized, of course, that no one would waste a bomb upon a place like La Cumbre; but there were other peaceful countrysides here and there throughout the world that might one day be targets, and that was a matter that concerned men everywhere.

Carlos wondered if men were great enough to control this bomb. Or had scientific knowledge outstripped human judgment? Had men created a monster that could turn upon them and wipe them out? Only time would tell.

He found himself worrying about this revolution which Liberales

317

and Comunistas were plotting against the Ronca Government. Could human beings afford to indulge in war at all? Abruptly he told himself that he was oversensitive, his body weak, his mind confused and susceptible to morbid suggestion.

This war against Ronca was no ordinary war; this was a justified revolt against a feudal despotism; this was a universal demand for simple justice; this was force for a good purpose.

Carlos told himself that he must forget the Yanqui bomb. After all, there was nothing he could do. It would be better to cast his thoughts away and concentrate upon the slopes. Pines and myrtle and hummingbirds, sunlight and the scent of burning wood — these were fitter subjects for present contemplation.

Rising quickly to his feet, he shook his head as though ridding his mind of the last vestige of atomic speculation.

There was much to see upon carbonero slopes.

In one place he found a small adobe hut, one of the few that he had seen upon the slope, and a youngster was daubing paints upon the whitewashed wall. When Carlos came near, he saw the likeness of a peasant with a load of charcoal on his back. The lines were clean and graceful, and there was hardship in the sooty face. "Where did you learn to paint?" Carlos asked the youngster, a lad in his middle teens.

The boy stood back and squinted at his work as Carlos had seen the station master do. "Oh, Jorge Bronco taught me," he explained to Carlos. "He showed me how to mix colors from the earth, and he gave me a brush to paint with."

"How do you know about the drawing of the lines?" Carlos asked.

The lad gazed appealingly with eyes that were soft and sensitive. "You think it is not a carbonero?" he asked anxiously.

Carlos reassured him. "I am wondering how you do it."

The boy looked relieved. "One puts down what one sees," he said. "There are also tricks which Jorge Bronco shows."

For an hour or more Carlos chatted with the youngster and watched him paint. Then he set out again and climbed the trail, and after a time he came to a pineboard cabin situated at a springside in a clump of windswept pines.

Sitting out in front upon a stump was a sooty carbonero filing a saw. As Carlos came near, he seemed to notice something oddly familiar about the roundness of the man's shoulders beneath his dingy serape, the deep expanse of chest in front. The carbonero looked up from his work, file poised above the saw, and Carlos was startled to see a pair of thick-lensed spectacles streaked with soot, a tuft of black whiskers jutting straight out beneath a pointed nose. "E-e-e-e-yah! Bernardo!" Carlos shouted as he recognized his former acquaintance.

Cabrera examined Carlos furtively from beneath his heavy soot-blackened brows. "I don't remember you," he said cautiously. "What do you want with me?"

Carlos was so pleased to see a familiar face that he forgot his old dislike for Bernardo. "It is I!" he exclaimed. "Carlos Chichayan!"

Cabrera gaped. "I thought that you were dead," he breathed. He took the hand that Carlos extended. "By Jove, now, but you gave me a turn. For two years, I am a hunted man, ergo, I take no chances. Tell me, Chichayan, out of what grave have you arisen?" He indicated the doorway to his house. "My present quarters!" he explained. "*Simplex munditiis!*" Beyond the doorway was a table littered with books and papers.

They sat together in the narrow doorway where warm sun played upon them, and Carlos asked about Sapho.

Cabrera tugged at his beard with grimy fingers. "She was arrested, that is all I know." He smiled ingratiatingly. "We left San Marcos, of course, all of us who had known MacNeill. One by one, mostly at night, and we hid among the mountains, becoming peasants. Well, there you have it. I would not be worried about Sapho. If any person can handle those Ronquistas, it is that — she!" He stared at Carlos with an expression of amiability mixed with self-satisfaction. "You, my friend, how did you get out?"

Carlos told his story, and when he had finished, Cabrera said, "Well, you have found a place for hiding. One stays here almost *aequo animo*. A litle soot upon the face — half the law school lives upon this slope." He talked on about the coming revolution. From San Marcos to Santa Cruz there was organizing, from the Río Negro to Puerto Colon. Why, Francisco Fernández — yes, Carlos remembered him — Francisco was with banana workers on the Río Mosca. In mountain villages the Peasant League was getting ready, and the day was not far off. "We Comunistas are now co-operating with the

Liberales in San Marcos, and the Liberal underground is in touch
with Don Ricardo." He adjusted the saw between his knees, teeth
pointed upward.

"Are you — are all men upon the slope, then, Comunistas?" inquired
Carlos.

"A few only," Cabrera told him. He peered cautiously about as if
afraid of being overheard. "They call themselves Comunistas here."
He straightened up and pointed the file at Carlos. "All my life I have
studied Marx," he said, "and I have read Lenin, every book! These
coyotes here, cabron! Half of them have never been to school and do
not know enough to understand a word they read." He set his file
against a saw tooth and rasped angrily.

Carlos was confused by the things that Cabrera said. "You Comunistas," he hesitated, "you work with Don Ricardo?"

Cabrera waved his file. "It is a tactic," he explained, "against imperialists and their Ronquista tools. I have no use, of course, for Don
Ricardo's politics. He is a reformist, sabe, a fuzzy liberal. But we
work together against imperialism and against Ronquismo, too. It is a
tactic Lenin used."

"I know very little about this Lenin," admitted Carlos.

Cabrera laid down his file. "Lenin put teeth in Marxism," he told
Carlos. "He gave us a doctrine of revolt. We destroy capitalism in
industrial nations, and then comes the dictatorship of industrial
labor." He explained about the Party. It was a vanguard of industrial
labor, a small group of picked men, highly disciplined and devoted to
the cause. "They will lead the people," Cabrera said, "through peasants' and workers' soviets, and reason shall be their guide. The dictatorship of industrial labor will form a socialist state. From each
according to his ability, to each according to work performed — that
is your socialist state. The dictatorship of industrial labor will educate
the people to live together, and gradually through many decades the
state will wither away, and the world will reach a higher, communistic
stage of peaceful classlessness. From each according to his ability, to
each according to his need — there is communism."

Cabrera resumed his filing, but he talked to Carlos as he worked.
He explained how soviet was a word for council and how bolshevik
meant the greater part. He emphasized that, as true communism was

brought about, the dictatorship of industrial labor would disappear, and the world would have no classes. "The dictatorship is a period of tutelage only," he concluded. "It is a temporary matter."

"All I know," Carlos said, "is what I heard from Doctor MacNeill and what I found in the books you lent me back in San Marcos."

Cabrera paused again. "The Party is a different thing," he told Carlos. "A large group may be all right for your parlor pinks, but we are finished with that kind of Marxist chatter. This is not an evening in MacNeill's flat. He was a brilliant man, but what did he accomplish? We have no time for dreaming. Teacup Marxism is an utter waste. No, my friend, this is Bolshevism."

Carlos frowned. He was trying to digest all that Cabrera had told him. There was an appealing logic in this Communism, and yet there was also some unnamed element that he found disturbing. What about these unlettered leaders that Cabrera so mistrusted, where did they fit in? Was this Party already split in two?

Bernardo stood up with arms folded across his pigeon chest, and he looked down at Carlos. "One does not join the Party *sponte sua*," he warned, "but I think that I can get you in. We need a few good Leninists to set the Party straight."

Carlos was cautious. "I am not so certain about this Communism," he said with independence. "I shall want to study more about it." He stood up, face to face with Bernardo, as if to stop the downward flow of condescension.

Cabrera stroked his scrawny beard. "I tell you what," he suggested. "You come to my hut each day, and we shall talk it over. I shall explain to you about true Bolshevism, and I shall give you books to read."

Carlos was noncommittal. He was confused, and there was something about Cabrera that he didn't trust. "I must think about it first," he said.

Bernardo shrugged his rounded shoulders. "The Party is very small," he repeated unnecessarily. "We look only for a few picked men."

With difficulty Carlos swallowed the irritation that mounted in his throat. "I've got to go," he said. "I shall see you some day later, and we shall talk again." Thus he made an abrupt departure and hastened down the trail. Almost immediately, however, he regretted his animosity. Cabera was, after all, an amiable and kindly sort, despite his pompous ways.

Carlos was about to shout back a friendly quip when Bernardo called down the slope. "When you have thought it out, just let me know, Chichayan, and I'll get you in." He resumed his seat upon the stump and continued filing, and the rasp he drew out of the saw followed Carlos down the trail.

5

WEEKS DRAGGED BY after Esteban's visit, and there was no word from him in regard to Sapho. Jorge Bronco had sent the brakeman word of the little which Carlos had learned from Cabrera and had suggested a search through all the prisons, but Cruce had not stopped off in La Cumbre since.

Carlos waited impatiently, and during each day he went out upon the slope. Often he spent a night with Leonardo and Fermin beside some pit that needed watching; again, they might all return together to sit around a brazier and eat and chat until it was time to sleep; but increasingly, of late, Leonardo and Fermin would set out after supper for meetings of the Peasant League in the Barrio council house. On such occasions Carlos would lie upon his sheepskin bed visiting, perhaps, with Bertita or with her mother or with Leonardo's wife, María, or lying alone in the darkness where he could think of Sapho and make fantastic plans for finding her: he would set out for San Marcos very soon; he would go down the trail to La Cumbre in a night or so, and he would catch a freight; maybe Esteban would be aboard and hide him; in any case, he would catch a train for San Marcos, and there he would search for Sapho.

By the hour he would make and remake these plans, and often he was deep in thought when Leonardo and Fermin returned from the Barrio council house. There was a mystery about their movements that increased his restlessness.

One day as he was helping near the pits, Carlos asked about these meetings of the Peasant League. "What goes on?" he inquired. "What do you do so late at night?"

Leonardo straightened his back above the pales that he was cutting. "Oh, now we have this Pablo Macho," he explained. "He has come to make us soldiers, pues, and he knows how. Why, even I will be one.

He is Comunista, sabe. He came to us from Santa Cruz to turn us into soldiers. Asturian, they call him, from across the sea where he dug in Spanish mines and fought a war. He has worked for Yanquis in the lowlands, sucking oil from out the earth, and he knows their coyote tricks. He can manage an auto, pues, I have heard that he can make one go."

Carlos gathered up a load of pales and carried them to Leonardo's newest pit. "What brought Pablo Macho here?" he asked Fermin.

Fermin was arranging the pales into a conical heap. "Felipe Cuerno sent him to make us into soldiers," he told Carlos. "Oh, those Comunistas, everywhere they help the Peasant League. Now at night we crawl upon our bellies, or maybe make an ambush. It is for the learning only, you understand. This Pablo Macho, he makes a precious ambush."

Carlos went back to Leonardo for another load of pales, and when he returned, Fermin had more to say about Pablo Macho. "He has no fear at all. He handles dynamite with naked hands. There is nothing to fear, he says. In dynamite there is nothing for a good man to fear. It is like a woman, he says. For a firm hand, dynamite is obedient like a woman. But in the fingers of a trembling hand — pues, it explodes against the face!"

Leonardo came up with an armful of pales and dropped them on the growing heap. "Like a woman!" he cackled. "Dynamite is like a woman."

"E-e-e-e-e-e-yah! Like a woman," Fermin shouted. "It is like a woman."

Old Leonardo winked at Carlos. "We can handle, can't we, son?"
Fermin laughed. "Si, pues, we can handle both!"

They continued with their work. When they had built a cone of pales, they covered it over well with sod and mold, and deep inside they built a fire and arranged it in such a manner that the wood charred slowly. A cloud of grey smoke arose from within the pyre, and Carlos liked the heavy scent. They moved off, then, to another spot, and lazily they began to clear away the undergrowth and brush.

"I know about that dynamite," Carlos volunteered. "When the steel was laid, I worked upon the railroad. I was on the grading crew."

"No! You did not tell," protested Leonardo. "Then you know La

Cumbre from long ago. I remember when they laid the steel. It reached La Cumbre — that was Christmas — and a train came up the grade. It was loaded with federal police. Horses, too; they had their horses on the train. I was there that night. I saw it all."

"I, also," Carlos said.

"Madre! If you can handle dynamite," Fermin exclaimed, "you should come with us tomorrow night. Pablo Macho, he would like your help. Among those on the slope there are not many with a hand for dynamite. As I was saying, that Pablo Macho, he explains about it. He takes it in his hand and explains. It'll blow a train off the track, he says. It'll blow the station, it'll smash the council house. He says that, and then he puts it on a flat rock on the table, and he takes a hammer and pounds it like this."

"A-e-e-yah!" yelped old Leonardo, "you should see the chicos scatter! That Pablo Macho, he is a fox, verdad!"

"And you and Fermin?"

"We have a steady hand with women," Leonardo boasted.

"Yes, and that is not all," Fermin added. "That Pablo Macho has other tricks. He takes gasoline and pours it into a tequila bottle. He stuffs cotton in the neck and lights it, and he throws it at a pig. A-e-e-e-yah! What a sight that was!" Leonardo was excited. "It roasted alive. Let me tell you, that pig was roasted alive. It was still squealing, and you could smell it cooking."

"A Ronquista won't smell so sweet," Fermin said. "There you have Pablo Macho. What a stallion!" He picked up a flat-sided stone and began honing his axe blade.

"Is that all he teaches?" Carlos asked. "Only dynamite and roasting pigs alive?"

"No, no, he makes soldiers," protested Leonardo. "Completement he makes a soldier. Out of anybody, out of an old man like me. We learn also to read and write a little, and drive off sickness, too." He squatted down on his haunches, took out pipe and tobacco pouch, and filled the bowl.

"Do you have rifles also?" Carlos asked.

With a lighted match above his pipe bowl, Leonardo paused. "Only Pablo Macho," he replied. "He has one, and we learn about it. We take it apart and put it together, and we make the cartridge." He put the pipestem in his mouth and drew, and the flame from the burning match disappeared into the bowl, popped out again, and licked at his calloused fingers.

"A cartridge?" inquired Carlos.

Leonardo tossed away the match. "Yes, from charcoal," he said. "We make powder from charcoal."

"There is the adding of other things," Fermin qualified. He tried the new-ground axe edge with thumb. "There is sulphur and — and other things."

"Now we make the cartridge," Leonardo boasted. "Next we shoot it."

"Every one must kill," Fermin added. "A Ronquista for every cartridge."

"We are not really soldiers," Leonardo explained. "We are guerrillas, Pablo Macho says."

Fermin dropped to his knees, held the axe head to his shoulder like a rifle butt. "We fight at night like this," he said further. "When the enemy is asleep, we creep up so and strike. When he is tired, then we strike. When he is lost in the marsh."

"And when he is strong?" asked Carlos.

"Then we hide in the woods," Leonardo chuckled.

Thus they worked and chatted and rested. Thus they worked upon the slopes and cut pales and tended their pits. Thus they chatted about Pablo Macho and the fight that was coming.

Slowly Carlos was gaining in strength. He helped them to cut and carry pales; he helped them to cover the pits with sod and dirt and to light a fire inside. He worked, and he listened to their talk, and also he thought of Sapho and made his plans, until it happened one night that he could wait no longer.

He had planned for many years, and he knew exactly what to do. He would go this night, he would catch the first train for San Marcos. But he would not tell Jorge.

Impulsively he explained to Leonardo and thanked the old man and all his family. Then he slipped away in the darkness and headed down the trail toward La Cumbre.

It was night, and he could easily catch a freight, unnoticed. He would climb aboard and hide and take a chance.

Such were his thoughts as he stumbled down the slope.

Suddenly he came face to face with a man who was coming up the trail. They almost collided in the darkness.

"Who's that?" It was Jorge's voice.

"It is I," Carlos admitted.

They stood there in the night. Both, at first, were too embarrassed to speak. Already a damp fog was closing down upon the slope, and Carlos felt the cold and wetness. He shivered.

Jorge struck a match and held it beneath a cigar clamped between his teeth. The corners of his mouth twitched a little as he drew a draft through the rolled tobacco. "You, Carlos!" he exclaimed. "What a sturdy goat! You come to see me, eh?" His eyes were twinkling in the match light.

Carlos hesitated. "Well, no," he contradicted as the match went out. "No, Jorge, I do not come to see you. I —" He left his sentence hanging.

Jorge's face was lost in darkness, now, and he was a voice behind a red spot of fire. "That is unimportant," he told Carlos. "The truth is I was on my way to you. There is another important matter. Shall we go up the trail, or down?"

"Down," Carlos said.

Jorge turned and felt his way along the trail, the red spot of his cigar bobbing like an enormous firefly. "The truth is," he said, "that Felipe Cuerno comes this week, and there will be a meeting in the Barrio council house. Not for all, you understand, but for the leaders only."

"So?" Carlos felt his heart pounding.

They continued on in silence. Somewhere down below a dog was howling. A branch of myrtle scraped across Carlos' face. The leaves were wet with dew, and they left a coldness on his cheek. He breathed deeply. The air was dank and carried a moldy scent like the aroma of rotting leaves. Carlos tripped over a small, round cobble, and it went bounding down the trail ahead.

"There is a further matter," Jorge said. "You know about our Party, Carlos. It is small, comrade, very small, but there is an important place for one like you. I intend to speak of you to Felipe Cuerno."

"Yet there is another thing," Carlos told him. "I have not come to a decision, Jorge, about this Communism."

Jorge Bronco stopped, and they stood facing one another in the darkness. "Why not?" he asked. "What is the trail fork in your thinking?"

Carlos groped for words of explanation, but even in his own mind he was not yet certain about the nature of his thoughts. Doctor Rory MacNeill flashed across his memory. Unlike the beasts, he said, man can shape his history. Faith, yes, man can plan, organize, shape the courrse of future historry and thus transforrm his nature. Doctor MacNeill had said those words, and here was an opportunity to make them live. Why not seize it? Carlos did not know what it was, but an unformed objection held him back.

There was something about the Party that he did not like. Perhaps it was Cabrera rather than the philosophy itself. Perhaps if Jorge Bronco had explained about the Bolsheviks, about the dictatorship of industrial labor, perhaps then he would not be suffering from this uneasy doubt. No, he was certain that his objections were more concrete. Was it distrust of Comunista methods? Perhaps — but he could not be certain.

"You must study more about communism," Jorge Bronco said, "and you must talk with Felipe Cuerno. Only tell me this, Carlos. Do you believe in this revolution which we now prepare to fight?"

Carlos laughed nervously. "The last five years have left me very much convinced," he assured the station master. "When the time comes, I shall be with you on that, at least. For tonight there is another matter. I am leaving the slopes for a while, Jorge. I shall climb aboard a freight for San Marcos. That is the reason for my stumbling down the trail in darkness."

"Why do you go, Carlos?"

"To find my wife," Carlos replied. He felt uneasy standing there in the blackness, face to face with Jorge. He moved a few steps along the trail, and the station master, taking the hint, followed close behind, his lighted cigar glowing like a will-o-the-wisp in the night.

Jorge did not speak at once. Together they continued down the trail in sombre darkness. When the lights of La Cumbre appeared twinkling through the pines and oaks, Jorge grasped Carlos' arm. "Wait," he suggested, "let us talk here alone."

"Very well."

"Listen, Carlos, you must not go to San Marcos."

"It is a personal matter," Carlos told him.

"On the contrary, comrade, you cannot think of yourself only," the station master contradicted. "If anyone can find your wife, 'steban will do it. He knows where to go, this 'steban. We have members in every place, Carlos. We have told you that. Among the soldiers we have a friend here, a member there. We have a member in the household of Ronca. We have a friend among the guards in almost every prison. It is an easy matter for 'steban. He asks a question here, he asks a question there. But for you, Carlos — no, no, that is a waste of time, and it is also dangerous."

"The danger is no matter," Carlos said.

"It is an important matter," Jorge disagreed. "It is not yourself, Carlos, it is the whole movement. If they find you, they will investigate. If they investigate — who knows? No, Carlos, we want no martyrs, we want no dreamers, we want no man dying for no purpose at all. We need discipline, we need a plan. Bueno, Felipe Cuerno gives them to us. You must be here, Carlos, to take part in all the planning. I have in mind speaking to Felipe Cuerno about you. I shall recommend that he give you some important job to do."

"You do not know me," Carlos protested. "Felipe Cuerno knows me even less."

"I am ready to speak to him about you."

"All right, Jorge, I shall be there," Carlos conceded reluctantly.

"Bueno, Carlos!" exclaimed the station master. "I think your job will not be a small one. Now let us continue to the station and have a copacita, comrade, a tiny nip of fire!"

They made their way down the trail toward La Cumbre, and Carlos could see the amber lights of the station and the red and green lanterns where the switches were.

6

As THE OILFIELD WORKER told his story, Carlos felt the growing of a tenseness in the Barrio council house where leaders of the Party had gathered. Feet apart, the stocky mestizo stood at one end of the white-washed room, facing all the others, and a lantern hanging from a rafter cast his shadow against a whip-sawed wall and distorted his squat body into a monstrous shape. As Luna spoke, Carlos gathered that he had infiltrated Ronquista meetings in San Marcos and had thereby assembled the intelligence which he now reported.

Carlos shifted his gaze from Luna's face, and he studied the expressions of other men who sat on wooden benches and listened there in the council house. Near the front was Jorge Bronco, leaning slightly forward, his eyes fixed on Luna, and on his other side sat a railwayman named Flores, and behind, in rows, were a dozen or more Party leaders. In the very rear, near an open door, Cabrera sat, his eyes magnified enormously by his thick-lensed spectacles. Carlos moved his gaze from member to member until he came to the man known as Felipe Cuerno.

He was seated on a bench across the room, this Felipe Cuerno, and he had leaned back against the white-washed wall, blue eyes half closed, as though he were about to fall asleep. He had a face that was square and bony. The cheekbones were high, the nostrils narrow, and there was a ruddiness beneath the brownness of his skin that suggested years of sun and wind and rain. Carlos wondered if the man were listening.

Luna was speaking of a new Ronquista tactic. "Whether or not their goal has changed," he told his listeners, "I leave to you. Their slogans are no longer quite the same. One hears less about the Prot-

330

estant-Jew Colossus up in Washington, but very much about the Comunista in San Marcos, less about the mob-beast of democracy, very much about the Marxist Menace. Let me tell you what it means."

Carlos glanced across at Felipe Cuerno. He seemed to be sound asleep.

"The end of European fighting," Luna explained, "made matters difficult for the Ronquista. The new order, you know, fed on action only. It could not live on peace and prosperous times, and so there was need for movement. But where to get the needed help — the arms, the goods, the money? In this part of the world there is but a single place. Bien, how to win support? Well, comrades, you know that answer as well as I — FIGHT THE COMUNISTA! So there it is."

Luna went on to tell how old-time Ronquista action squads had been reformed and were being trained by troopers. "The big support," he said, "comes from the hacendados, but they organize among the peasants, too, and among those who have no work. Pues, let me explain a further tactic. They watch the planning of the revolution, and they will let us go so far until even Don Ricardo can be accused of Marxist stink. Then they strike. Ronquismo, can't you see, is then a lonely champion against the Bolshevik."

Jorge Bronco stirred. "How do Ronquistas come to know so much about our revolution?"

Luna faced him. "There has been a leak. Most of you know, I think, exactly where it is."

Carlos noticed a tiny flicker in Felipe Cuerno's eyes.

"There is one thing in our favor," Luna added. "Even Ronca does not know our strength. He does not believe that we can take San Marcos. He is not prepared for a real revolt. There is also another matter. Between ourselves and Don Ricardo's Liberals, General Ronca expects many disagreements, and he has ways to help them come about. Well, if Ronca drives a wedge like that, he can win."

That was the end of Luna's report. He sat down and the chairman of the meeting, a lanky mestizo with mournful, hound-dog eyes, took his place upon the floor and called for questions. Immediately Flores, the railwayman sitting next to Jorge Bronco, raised his hand.

When he was recognized, Flores stood up and faced the others. "I think we make a mistake," he said, "to deal with Don Ricardo.

They say he and his Liberales speak big words how they are going to give back to the peasant lots and many lands and care for the old and sick and pay more wages and tie big churchmen's hands behind the back. Those Liberales say big words about all that, and also about taking oil wells away from the Yanquis, and the mines, too, and make them national. Well, I think Don Ricardo and those Liberales are after all only capitalist masters. I think we do not trust them."

There was a strained silence in the Barrio council house. Carlos noticed that Felipe Cuerno's eyes were wide open now, although he still lounged back against the whip-sawed wall.

Jorge Bronco turned on Flores. "What do you think to do?" he asked.

There was a simple earnestness in Flores' manner. "Fight Ronquistas, yes," he said. "But as for Don Ricardo —" he drew a stubby finger across his throat. "His son was killed in Spain fighting Comunistas, pues!"

One heard the sound of bodies twisting on wooden benches, the scrape of sandals on the wooden floor. One by one each pair of eyes in the room came to rest on Felipe Cuerno. He did not rise, but he leaned forward a trifle, sitting there on his bench, knees apart, feet planted firmly on the floor. From his pocket he took a pouch and a porcelain pipe, short stemmed, with an enormous bowl. He blew through the stem once to clear it, and then he filled the bowl. When he had tamped the tobacco well, he looked up at Flores. "Who told you these things?" he asked sharply.

Flores appeared bewildered. "I-I don't know," he faltered. "Some things I think up myself, and Comrade Cabrera, he —" The railwayman stopped short, somehow aware of the mounting tension.

Carlos darted a glance in the direction of the door. The bench where Bernardo had sat was empty, now. He looked back at Felipe Cuerno in time to catch a glint of understanding between him and Jorge Bronco. The station master left his bench, exchanged a word with Cuerno. Then Jorge Bronco slipped out the door.

Felipe Cuerno lighted his pipe, and as soon as it was drawing, he turned back to Flores. "It is an old time tactic in backward nations," he told the railwayman, "to support liberal democrats against the imperialist foe. You see, we, too, seek democracy. For the hacendados and the Ronquistas are a tiny part, while the peasants and the workers and honest thinking men of letters are a great majority. But our democracy cannot permit conspiracies of the smaller part for we cannot forget what they have done in Spain and other countries."

The porcelain pipe was out again. Felipe Cuerno relighted the tobacco in the bowl, broke the match, and tossed it away. He would look like a Nacheetl, Carlos thought, if his skin were darker and his bones smaller, if his eyes were not so blue. But he was not Nacheetl. He could be a Basque, perhaps, or a Moor — Carlos didn't know.

Cuerno spoke again. "We co-operate with the Liberales," he said, "as long as they are truly revolutionary. When they make a deal with the Ronquistas or when they cease to fight imperialism, then we fight them, too. Otherwise they need not fear us. To give land to the peasant makes a busier market for the small maker of things-to-sell. To give to the worker bigger wages and a better way of work means better machines and means of working. We help the small maker of things, but the big refineries of Usoco and other places along the tracks — they give their owners too much wealth and power and send too much wealth abroad. We must take them for the people."

The crack of a pistol a distance down the slopes brought silence to the council house. Cuerno leaned back against the wall, and his pipe went out. The meeting continued with other matters. By the time Jorge Bronco had returned, there seemed to be nothing further to talk about, and the chairman was about to adjourn the session.

At that moment Felipe Cuerno spoke again. "Who has been among the Xlalaks?"

Flores faced Cuerno uneasily. "I went to Xlalak country," he said. "I went all the way to Pavón. It is no use. They cannot understand politics. They are friendly with no one. They steal and kill because it gives them joy. If they help us, they will turn against us."

Cuerno pointed his pipestem at the railwayman. "You think these Xlalaks are dangerous warriors?"

Flores nodded vigorously. "They are beasts, comrade, I have seen. In all the country there are no men like those Xlalaks. No one ever tamed them. The Españoles, the first government of Republicanos, neither could tame them. Even Ronquista police do not touch the Xlalaks."

"They control our rear," Felipe Cuerno pointed out. "Have you thought of that, Comrade Flores?"

"They are very dangerous," the railwayman admitted.

"If I sent you to pacify the Xlalaks," persisted Felipe Cuerno, "how many rifle companies would you need?"

"Companies!" exclaimed Flores. "This is no matter for companies. I think one needs brigades. They are riders, those Xlalaks. They are mighty horsemen."

Felipe Cuerno puffed on his pipe for a while. "Brigades, eh? Well, tell me this. How many brigades do we assign to our rear when we advance toward San Marcos?"

Flores had no answer. Jorge Bronco shifted on his bench. "We have no brigades to spare, Comrade Cuerno."

"How do you plan to eliminate this challenge to our rear, Comrade Flores?" demanded Cuerno.

"It will be protected by the most and biggest forces we have," Flores said weakly. There was sweat oozing from his forehead.

"You waste our time," Felipe Cuerno charged. "Let me tell you this. If the Xlalaks fight *with* us, they cannot fight *against* us. Have you considered that?"

"They will not join us," Flores insisted. "They are savages."

Cuerno's eyes shrank into small, hard beads. "Have you been to see their chief?"

Flores shook his head. "No, comrade." A red flush spread beneath the clay brown of his skin, and he lowered his eyes. A tense hush fell upon those who listened. Cuerno's cold, hard gaze had not relaxed. At length, Flores took a deep, gulping breath, squared his shoulders, and faced the assembled Partymen. "I wish to say I make mistakes," he stated firmly. "I did not understand about working with the Liberales. That is one mistake. I did not go to see the Xlalak chief. That is another."

With this confession, the railwayman sat down, and Carlos saw that his head was high, his eyes clear and unafraid.

Cuerno moved his eyes about the room, searching faces. "Does anyone here know Xlalak country?" There was no reply.

Jorge Bronco leaned forward. "There is Chichayan," he said. "He is the man of whom I spoke to you, the man from Tiburón." He indicated Carlos with a puckering of his mobile lips.

Felipe Cuerno examined Carlos with a measuring stare. "All right," he snapped, "you are the man I send. The Chief of the Xlalaks is known as El Casco. He is said to live high upon the slopes of the volcano. I shall expect no fewer than a thousand horsemen. We shall provide them with arms and ammunition. You must start at dawn."

7

A LANTERN BURNED in the Barrio council house long after the meeting had broken up. Carlos and Jorge and Felipe Cuerno had dragged the chairman's table to a spot where the light was brightest, and there they talked about Communism and what it stood for. Cuerno spoke while Jorge cleaned the pistol. In his hand Cuerno held his porcelain pipe, and its smoke curled upward, and just below where the lantern hung, it mingled with smoke from Jorge Bronco's fat cigar.

"We are not concerned about a government of industrial labor," Cuerno told Carlos. "There you have Flores' error. Our backward country must develop capitalism and a larger body of industrial labor before it is ready for a socialist state. No, no, what we seek is an end to this imperialism, a new restricted capitalism controlled for the good of the greatest part."

It seemed to Carlos that he could still hear the pistol shot. "I understand all that," he answered shortly. "But there are phases of this Communism that I do not like. You use violent means to reach your goal, while I believe that improvement must take place in the hearts of men." His eyes were on Jorge's holster.

An expression of drollness played about the corners of Cuerno's mouth. "You want an evolutionary change," he suggested. "Revolution by ballot, maybe?" He chuckled. "Well, you might begin by voting Ronca out! Oh, make no mistake, we do not believe in revolution for the sake of revolution. No, no, only when the state disregards what the people need and want — then only is revolution right."

Carlos shook his head.

Cuerno was watching him. "We do not deal with palace revolutions," he told Carlos. "They accomplish nothing. We fight for the great majority." He explained that three conditions were essential for a truly popular revolution. It was necessary first of all that the masses of the people should reach a point where they could no longer tolerate the old ways of living. It was also important that the government be diseased and corrupt and out of sympathy with the needs of the many. Finally, there must be leaders with an understanding of human needs, with courage to fight, with ability to organize the millions.

"Bolsheviks do not make revolutions," Felipe Cuerno added. "Inequality is the cause of revolution."

Carlos felt the appeal of Cuerno's simple explanations; yet he knew that his skepticism remained. It was not the overthrow of Ronca that troubled him. That phase of revolution was justified against any government that oppressed its people. Carlos was more concerned with what was to come about after the fall of Ronca. "There is your dictatorship," he mentioned. "That does not seem democratic to me."

Cuerno pointed his pipe stem at Carlos. "You confuse the meaning of a word," he said. "Dictatorship to us is not necessarily a matter of one-man rule. In the Communist sense, dictatorship is any force which a state may use to instrument its laws. Armies, prisons, police, all these imply dictatorship. Of course, we do not expect a proletarian dictatorship to develop right away in a backward country like this. It may take many years before the people are ready. In any case, whatever sort of government we have, it will be a dictatorship in a Marxist sense. The important matter is, in whom resides this force, in all the people or in a small minority. Our dictatorship is not undemocratic. On the contrary, we use it to expand democracy."

There was force in Cuerno's words; yet they did not answer for Cabrera's summary execution. "You believe in a single party," Carlos protested. "I do not call that democratic."

Cuerno slapped a mosquito that had lighted on his ruddy cheek. "We believe that in an industrial nation one party serving the people's needs is more effective than two parties serving capital. It is an instrument for the democracy of industrial labor, the first, socialist stage of development. When communism is reached — pft! No party at all!"

Carlos leaned forward across the table. "With one party there is no legal opposition," he pointed out. "I call that a loss of freedom."

"Freedom from what?" demanded Cuerno. "The bourgeoisie is always screaming to be free from something, but it is impossible to live in a society and yet be free from it. The dictatorship of industrial labor is for the good of the vast majority, so why should anyone wish to free himself *from* it? No, no, the important thing is that each man and woman be free to participate *in* it without any regard for his race or creed or color or economic status. There is the basis for our freedom."

Carlos could think of no rebuttal. It all seemed logical, and yet — Or was there justice in Cabrera's death?

"In your bourgeois democracy," added Cuerno, "there is a fetish called free speech. Well, the capitalist can buy a string of newspapers, while the poor man shouts on a street corner. Who is heard by more? Or there is education. The rich man's middling son goes to a university while the coal miner's son of genius is free to go to work. I do not call that freedom. Along the left hand trail, our state would guarantee for any man or woman the means to achieve those ends. We go further. We insist on freedom to participate in the future of our way of life. That means a job, a guaranteed, socially useful job, for every person who is willing to work and the right — the duty — to help decide what sort of jobs must be done. Those are the matters which we call freedom."

A long silence followed Cuerno's words. The truth was that Carlos had no ready answer. He sat nervously fingering his lower lip, and inside himself he felt a tearing apart that he had not known for many months. It was not easy to best this Felipe Cuerno.

Abruptly Jorge Bronco pushed back his bench. "In a few hours there will be a train," he said. Carefully he refolded the map of Xlalak country and handed it to Carlos. "Will you have the strength to climb steep mountains?"

Carlos shrugged. "I have climbed these slopes," he pointed out.

Jorge winked. "There you have this Cuerno," he chuckled. "Sick men, cripples, he drives them all like slaves."

Cuerno stood up, too. "When they forget themselves," he said, "they feel much better."

Jorge took down the lantern and moved toward the door. Carlos got to his feet and followed the others out. They left the Barrio council house together, and made their way down the narrow trail. The night was dark, but the lantern spread a round spot of light around them and showed them where their footing was. From the rear Carlos watched the foreshortened squatness of Cuerno's shadow upon the ground. There was power in it, he thought, as there was power in Cuerno, a compressed kind of power like dynamite in a short, hard-packed stick.

The slopes dropped away before them, and Carlos saw here and there the red glow of smoldering charcoal pits. Tomorrow night he would be far away on the edge of Xlalak country, alone, without a word of Sapho. Secretly he hoped for some delay. At first, of course, he had been flattered by Cuerno's confidence, but now a strange irritation stirred within him. To help Don Ricardo, yes, or even Jorge Bronco, he would do a thing like this. But to be assigned the job by a total stranger, to risk his life for communism — that was another matter.

He could not overlook the value of an alliance with Cuerno for the purpose of overthrowing Ronca. But Esteban might come through tonight with word of Sapho and — well, there were other ways of fighting Ronca.

"About a horse," he ventured. "It may take some time to find a good one, Jorge."

"That is a matter for my doing," Jorge said. He swung the lantern as though he were flagging down a train. "You sleep. I will find the horse and provisions, too, and everything else that you will need." He whistled a jaunty tune.

A frosty wind blew down upon them from the west. Jorge shivered and drew his red serape tight about his throat. "It will be cold on the slopes of the volcano. It will be snowy-cold. I have just the thing for that. There is a serape I have, a wool serape that is very thick. You will take that, Carlos, and leather gloves. Oh, I shall forget nothing. Not the smallest thing."

Jorge's enthusiasm was infectious.

"There will be snow?" asked Carlos. "Where the Xlalaks have their houses even?"

"Quien sabe? E-e-e-e-yah, snow! Have you ever felt it, Carlos?"

"Here in La Cumbre I have felt frost."

"Snow is another matter," Jorge said. "I have heard. It falls heavy upon the ground, and one wades up to the knees, like walking in a load of cotton. You will need boots, Carlos. I have just the ones, a pair of Yanqui boots, and they will keep out the snow, eh, Felipe?"

Cuerno only grunted.

They had come to a fork where Carlos would turn off from the main trail toward the house of Leonardo.

"Come at dawn," Jorge said, "and all will be ready. Oh, and another little thing, Carlos, that I meant to tell. 'steban comes through to-night. If he has word, I will send a message. Until morning, Carlos!" He and Cuerno disappeared in the darkness down the trail.

As Carlos entered the cabin, old Leonardo roused himself, left his bed and stirred the coals that were greying in a charcoal brazier. "With age one does not sleep," he told Carlos. "What passes with the revolution?"

Carlos explained his mission to the Xlalaks.

"A-a-a-a-a-a-yah, amigo, I would not go with you," Leonardo exclaimed. "I would not go among the Xlalaks."

"They are wild?"

"Dios, those Xlalaks, they are worse than wolves," Leonardo said.

Carlos was not thinking of the Xlalaks. "Tomorrow I go," he said.

"With care, Carlos!" Leonardo warned. "Have Jorge Bronco give you a pistol."

They sat about the charcoal brazier and brewed sarsaparilla tea, and Leonardo talked. Thus they passed the time until the old man grew sleepy and was ready for bed.

Carlos stretched out upon his sheepskin bed. He was wrapping his serape about him when he heard a shout. He sat up and listened. It was Jorge calling from down the trail. He jumped to the door of the cabin and whistled back. He could see a lantern moving as Jorge made his way along the trail, and he heard voices in the stillness of the night.

"Hola-a-a-a-a-a-a, Carlos, camara-a-a-a-a-a-a-da, hola-a-a-a-a-a-a-a-a!"

Again Carlos whistled shrilly.

"Viene-e-e-e-e-e-e-e, Carlos," Jorge sang. "Vie-e-e-e-e-e-e-ne ah-o-o-o-o-o-ra la señori-i-i-i-i-ita Sa-a-a-a-a-a-a-pho-o-o-o!"

X. Xlalaks

THE TRAIL DROPPED away from La Cumbre and zigzagged downward through thinning pines and oaks into a country that was arid and open, and after a time there were only dry washes and buttes and slopes covered with mesquite. Carlos knew the country, having been over it on foot years before, but to Sapho, who had seen it only from Esteban's train, it was strange and fascinating. She saw where pack trains during previous centuries had worn the trail deep into volcanic soil, and Carlos explained how even before the white man's coming, Nacheetl runners had beaten a path.

Their horses were fresh and carried them quickly downward through a juniper belt into a land of pitahaya and organ cacti, and a dry wind blew hot in their faces. Lightheartedly Sapho hummed a song. It was Jorge Bronco who had suggested that she go along. He had brought her up the trail to Leonardo's hut by lantern light, and he had seen them reunited. "And now I go," he told them. "There is much to do. I must find another horse for the Xlalak journey." He left them alone to go to bed together.

This time it was not a tremendous bed in the Gran Hotel San Marcos. It was not white sheets with pillows beneath their heads. It was not two bodies sunk in softness, nor was it a wedding night. This time it was a sheepskin bed on Leonardo's wooden floor, it was coals in a terra cotta brazier dying away and going out, it was man and woman with a serape wrapped about them. It was all these, and it was sleeping together after five years apart. It was two joined in one.

Wrapped in one serape, they had fallen asleep, exhausted. Wrapped in one serape, they had slept until the cocks began to crow upon the slopes, until Carlos wakened. He shook Sapho. She stirred, and her

341

eyes opened, and Carlos kissed her. "It is dawn," he had whispered. "Jorge will have the horses."

"Two horses, Carlos!"

"Two horses, querida! Jorge promised two."

She sat up, naked and shivering in the morning air. "If there is only one," she said, "I'll go on foot."

Carlos drew her close. "There will be two."

"Then dress me, Carlos," Sapho teased. "Dress me, and we shall go."

She was wearing the same clothes now, riding down from La Cumbre, the same white shirt which Carlos had buttoned over the fullness of her breasts, the white cotton pantalones, the Nacheetl sandals which he had tied upon her feet. She was wearing these clothes now, but in saddlebags were others, serape and woolen shirt, a pair of Yanqui boots for use in snow.

They talked as they rode along across a desert valley in the direction of Zalapec and Xlalak country beyond. There was joy in what they said, and there was also sadness. There was joy of being together, and there was the sorrow of years between. There was the sorrow of Sapho's father. Gently Carlos spoke of him. He told of Doctor MacNeill and Alvarez, of the Viceregal Palace, of the dungeons beneath.

She gazed into the blueness of the sky. "Poor Papaloi," she sighed. "He would want to die that way, for a cause — that must have pleased him."

Carlos was silent. In his mind he saw the dungeon chamber, and he had a frightful vision of the death which Doctor Rory MacNeill had met there. "The Bolsheviks may not be rright," he had once told Carlos, "but for the rragged and the hungrry and the sick of hearrt they prresent a hope!" A hope, yes, Carlos admitted now, but was it a belief worth the kind of death that Rory MacNeill had suffered? Carlos did not think so. As they rode down toward the great plateau, he considered communism in all its aspects, and in his mind he sorted out the points that he had heard Jorge Bronco and Felipe Cuerno make.

Poverty and excessive personal wealth were real enough, and so were disease and ignorance, and he himself had seen the wells where Yanquis sucked out all the oil for shipment across the sea. All those evils he was ready to fight against, but he was not yet certain that Felipe Cuerno's way was the only one. Is Bolshevik freedom real, he asked himself. He did not think so. Don Ricardo's books had taught him that every man should have a legal means of opposition against the state regardless of who controlled. Otherwise any system, however well intentioned, could grow into a tyrant and destroy the individual man.

In his mind he saw a picture of the Ronca state, a pyramid of cells, and he shuddered, feeling walls and blackness closing in tight about him. Might not any state become the same if there were no legal opposition? The government, he thought, must make sure of certain freedoms — the freedoms of which the Yanqui voice had spoken so long ago. All good men would agree on these, Carlos thought. The question was — What system could achieve them best?

When they had ridden a distance, he mentioned these matters to Sapho. "One is torn between what Nacheetls know as I-ness and we-ness," he told her. "There is no good man who does not believe in we-ness, but until it springs like water from a fountain, freely from the spirit, there is need of stiff compulsion. Very well, the state provides it, let us say, and in the course of this providing, it becomes a machine without a soul and tramples I-ness altogether. I do not like that. I prefer a degree of letting be."

Sapho had been watching Carlos while he spoke, and suddenly, more than ever before, she was sensitive to the conflict raging in him. A tinge of redness appeared in her face. "Every kind of state uses force," she told him, repeating Felipe Cuerno's argument. "The important question is, who uses this force, a few powerful ones or the great mass of people? When Ronca uses force against the people's needs, then it is time for revolution."

"It is not revolution I oppose," Carlos answered shortly. "I want to be sure of what comes after. So far, I prefer the kind of government that the Liberales stand for."

Sapho wrinkled her nose. "You must be careful of your Liberales, Carlos. They speak fine words about democracy, but some of them, I think, want it for themselves only. They are against Ronca now, but when they see workers and peasants seeking democracy, too — then, perhaps, it will be a different story."

Carlos resented this. "Don Ricardo has spent his life opposing Ronca." It was not easy for him to control his irritation. "I wish to understand all sides," he told her.

She gave him a shrewd glance. "He who sits upon the crossroads, pondering, is not likely to travel far."

The road wound through deep ravines and skirted buttes, and the cliffs were red and yellow and brown. Gradually the horses moved along the desert valley where still, hot air shimmered just above the sands. It was a stretch of vastness broken only by thorny shrubs and twisted cactus. Carlos stared, and before his eyes a mirage formed, an oval blue lake in the center of the sands, and around it in a shuffling dance moved gigantic, bird-like figures with drooping zopilote wings and distorted avio-human heads. There seemed to be a rhythm, at first, but gradually the figures all went mad and stumbled drunkenly about, colliding in acute disharmony.

Sapho reined her horse, her eyes mesmerized by the sight before her. "Magnificent!" she breathed.

Carlos scarcely heard. Here in the hot and thirsty desert was a frightful panorama of what went on within him. Sapho felt a measure of his repression as they rode along.

Five years was such a time! Sapho found herself telling Carlos about them, seeking thus to fill the gap, but words were useless.

Carlos broke in. "I do not understand that Ronca. He throws us in prison and keeps us there and then suddenly he turns us loose. How did you get out?"

Sapho reined her horse. "I made a bargain, Carlos. Shall I tell you about it?"

Carlos nodded. The horses moved slowly, finding a way through cactus and heavy mesquite.

"I did not wish to talk about these things so soon," Sapho confessed. "But now I must." She told about her arrest and imprisonment, about the months and years of waiting; and then she described herself turning before a gilded mirror in Ronca's palace. The maid was dazzled by the richness of her skin against the whiteness. "The precious thing you want, señorita, I think you will surely get it. . . ."

Sapho tried to explain to Carlos. "In exchange for you, it was a very small thing."

Suddenly Carlos comprehended. "You gave yourself away to Ronca!" He seized the reins of her horse. Both animals halted.

Sapho's eyes burned passionately. "Think, Carlos, was that a gift?"

"I would rather be in prison."

"That is silly," Sapho retorted. "What good is life within a dungeon? Pfft! Aren't we better here? Look, Carlos, look about! We have the world, Carlos, we have one another. You are you, and I am I, and we do a job, and Ronca will soon be dead, perhaps. Tell me, Carlos, did I not do right?"

Carlos shook his head. "You slept with Ronca!"

"Yes, querido, several times!"

"You talk like a slut," Carlos told her. "To have slept with a beast like Ronca!"

"It meant nothing," Sapho insisted. "Don't you understand, querido, I gave my body only?"

Carlos felt her nearness adding to his inner turmoil and stirring strange, sadistic impulses which he had never known before. He felt obsessed to assert his man-ness, to hurt her somehow. So strong, so real became this impulse that he was frightened of himself, of what he might in fury do.

Sapho watched him, and at once she was half terrified, half joyous to see his passion breaking through. "You are only jealous," she charged. "I did what I had to do, and you are jealous."

"You make me into a cuckold, you —"

"Is your manhood pricked, Carlos?" asked Sapho sweetly. "Bien, go find yourself a woman. Sleep with her as I slept with Ronca. Sleep with her until we are even, and after that come back to me. Go on, Carlos, it will heal your wounded manhood, it will —"

Anger surged in his chest, hot and uncontrolled. He gripped her arm. "You low whore!" He twisted until she winced with pain, and he slid off his horse, pulling her with him, and he threw her on the alkaline sand. He seized her by the shirt and shook her until the fabric ripped. She sank back, whimpering softly.

"I'll get everything," he muttered. "I'll get everything that Ronca got." He rolled her on the sand.

Panting, she gave passionately, and she knew that no man had received so much.

2

THE TRAIL LED over a ridge and steeply down the other side, and it was worn deep by hoofs and by the feet of shepherds who for many generations had driven their sheep to pastures above Zalapec. As he and Sapho neared the village, Carlos saw adobe huts that he remembered from his boyhood and cactus fences and tuna just turned red. He saw naked children playing in the yards, and he heard the slap-slap of tortillas being kneaded, and he smelled the smoke of ocote pine. He saw patches where drooping stalks of corn bowed over earth that was hard and parched. He saw the boulder where Diego once had hidden.

Soon they entered the village, passing close about the shores of the lake called La Perla. There were small boys trudging home with gasoline tins and earthen ollas full of water, and there were men going off to work with wooden hoes. Carlos stopped one of the latter and asked him in Nacheetl about his corn.

The peasant shook his head. "It is bad-bad," he mourned. "The earth is tired and sick at heart and thirsty and does not feed my corn."

"There is water," Carlos stated. "Off yonder is a stream. I remember clearly." He could almost see Diego in the pasture just beyond.

The villager shook his head. "In former times there was indeed," he admitted. "There was water running happy-free and singing in the sunlight, and village men worked upon the sluices and turned it into water roads leading to the fields. But some years back a big político came and, with a piece of paper, he took the lands about Santa Marta. Then from the stream he gathered all the water up above and ran it through a pipe, and light came out the other end on wires for lighting up his house."

"That is a simple matter," Carlos said. "One could turn the water back. It is not used up." Shifting in his saddle, he turned his back upon the pasture.

The villager nodded. "Pues, the Comunista said that thing. Now the water runs down another valley, and we cannot get it back."

Carlos looked at the peasant closely. "What Comunista?"

"Why, the soldier-teacher. The man who came to us to make a revolution."

"What does he do here?"

The villager leaned upon his hoe. "He helps us in the Peasant League, that is one thing he does. He also brings to us a rifle and shows us how to take it down and how to make it back. He also —" the man stopped short and surveyed Carlos suspiciously.

"It does not matter," Carlos reassured him. "I am a mountain man myself. Tell me this, do you know the family Morelos?"

The peasant hesitated. "Well, there is Pepe Morelos, and there is Pancho Morelos who was killed by the troopers and —"

"Juana Morelos who was named Flores?"

The villager crossed himself. "May the good Dios rest her soul!"

"She is dead?"

"In the sickness three years back."

So there the story was! Carlos felt a sharp yearning. He remembered dreams in which he ran away to the great city and became a soldier or a mule driver and returned, eventually, to bring comfort to his mother. Well, he hadn't done it. "Who is presidente of the village now?" he asked the peasant.

"Miguel Flores. You wish to speak with him?"

"Thank you, no, we have far to travel," Carlos replied. He touched his animal's flank with sandal heel. Zalapec, he told himself, was better left behind.

The villager raised a straw sombrero. "'diós!" he called out to Carlos and Sapho. "May you have many years of health and pass again this way."

They followed the trail downward through the village toward the river where the willows still grew just as Carlos had remembered them. Women were washing clothes along the bank, and small boys splashed about and skipped stones across a still stretch of water.

From the valley bottom Carlos and Sapho rode their horses up cactus slopes to a ridge covered with oaks and pines. As the sun reached its zenith, they came out upon a promontory from which one could see in three directions. "Carlos, look!" Sapho exclaimed. "The Fire Mountain there ahead."

The great volcano seemed to rise straight out of buttes and washes there before them. The slopes, glistening white, mounted to a perfect cone, and over the exact summit a cloud was glowing faintly red. Inside her Sapho felt a strange confusion of the Sapho who was organ music with the dancing, flirting Sapho, and from that strange confusion she felt a delightful, sensuous pain. She wanted to speak of this to Carlos, but he spoke first. "Somewhere far up those slopes lives El Casco."

"The Hoof — what a strange name!" she mused without knowing what she said. She wanted to tell Carlos how she felt, and she wanted him to share her feelings. But he remained preoccupied.

Within another hour of riding, they found the canyon where years before the Xlalak horsemen had been encamped. It was small, and there was a waterhole near the center of a grove of stunted oaks. They allowed their animals to drink sparingly, and Carlos replaced the water which he and Sapho had drunk from Jorge's goatskin bag.

"They brought me here," Carlos remembered. "They had a fire in this open space, and the third Xlalak was sleeping there."

It seemed to Sapho that, like a victim of amnesia, he was trying to feel his way back to some solid moment in the long-forgotten past.

The trail took them steeply upward to the rim above the canyon. There they found themselves on the edge of a cactus tableland that sloped in a gentle curve and finally merged with the side of the volcano rising before them. Toward noon they saw the mesquite giving way to grass and clumps of acacia, and there was a fresh dampness in the air. They came to a fork in the trail, and as they sought their bearings, a horseman overtook them.

"A 'onde va?" he asked.

Startled, Carlos and Sapho looked up. The stranger had a thin, dark face with thick brows and an enormous black mustache. His serape was short, and one could see the pearl grip of a pistol at his belt, and the curved scabbard of a long machete. He wore his sombrero tilted at a cocky angle, and there was a jaunty chin strap reaching just below his lips.

"A 'onde va?" he repeated. Carlos recognized the sprightly lilting way of talk that the Xlalak horsemen had used before.

"To the pico!" Carlos explained. He gestured toward the snow-white cap of the volcano.

"Come with me," the horseman said in singsong Spanish. He touched his horse with silver spurs, and the beast set off smartly up the right hand fork.

This trail was well cut up by horses' hoofs, and there seemed to be a village ahead. Carlos spurred forward until he was close behind the Xlalak.

"Where do we go?" he asked.

"To Pavón to see El General!"

"Who is he?"

The Xlalak made no answer.

"Who is this general?" Carlos asked again.

"You find out," the Xlalak told him.

Carlos reined back to be near Sapho. "We are going to see El General," he relayed.

"Who is he?"

"Quien sabe?"

"This one looks like a bandit," Sapho shuddered. "Yet he is handsome, too."

After an hour or more upon the trail they came abruptly to Pavón, a cluster of adobe houses well hidden in a lush ravine. There was a cobbled street perhaps a hundred yards long, and as they entered the lower end, Carlos saw a figure lurch out into the center and stand with folded arms. It was a squat man with a huge sombrero and a serape that reached below his knees. A lock of black hair covered one eye, and he swayed as though half drunk.

"El General," announced the rider in an undertone.

The stranger reached out, as Carlos approached, and seized the bridle of the horse. "Buenos días!" He grinned widely, and Carlos saw that the upper teeth in front had been replaced by round pillars of gold. He held out a knotty hand. "Buenos días!"

Carlos shook the General's hand, returned the greeting, and presented him to Sapho.

The General moved as though to click the heels of his sandalled feet, and he bowed, and he took Sapho's hand and kissed it with tobacco-stained lips. "Señora! Welcome to Pavón!"

Carlos dismounted and helped Sapho to the ground. Immediately the Xlalak horseman seized both bridles and led the animals away.

"My house is yours," murmured the General with another bow. He indicated a tile-roofed adobe that was somewhat larger than the rest. "Allow me!" He struck off across the cobbled street, swaying like a drunken sailor, and he spat tobacco juice continually.

There had once been a picket fence around the house, but most of the pales had rotted away at the base, and chickens and squealing shoats were running wild in what had been a garden. With another bow the General ushered them in, and they found themselves in a bare, white-washed room not unlike the Barrio council house above La Cumbre. There was a rough-hewn table, and there were wooden benches, and on one wall was a colored poster that depicted the effect of alcohol upon various organs of the human body.

"Be seated!" begged the General. He had removed his hat, but the lock of hair still covered an eye. "In a moment we shall dine." He spat a yellow stream onto the red tiled floor. "I watched you coming up the trail. The señora has a precious seat!"

Sapho smiled. "Gracias, General!"

"I told them in the kitchen to prepare a meal. It should be ready." He turned toward a doorway and bellowed. "Oh, María, bring the food!"

There was an obedient patter of feet, and a string of little girls entered the room, carrying pots of food.

"Are these your daughters?" Sapho asked.

"Good God, how should I know?" answered the General jovially. "Daughters, granddaughters, great granddaughters, nieces, caray! One has so many."

"Great granddaughters!" Sapho exclaimed. "You can't be that old."

"Pues, I'm not a youth. Why, babies born in my soldier days are grandfathers. I might be a hundred years old, who knows?"

"Your hair is black," Carlos said. He was beginning to feel encouraged by the General.

"That's not all, either!" The old man bared his colossal golden teeth.

"I'm all right with the women, too. E-e-e-e-e-e-yah, a regular old billy goat with women. Why, I can make a baby between belches. Pues, let us eat!"

There were eight little girls, and each carried a steaming pot, and they set them about on the table. There was a chicken roasted, and there was a mutton stew. There were enchiladas, freshly cooked, and frijoles and tamales and chili and arroz con pollo. There were tortillas, neatly stacked, and there were slabs of cheese. There was corn on the cob.

"Eh, eh, why do you wait?" demanded the General. "Reach in, señora, reach in and eat. No forks here, none at all. In Xlalak country, not a fork!" He pulled a drumstick out of one of the pots and handed it to Sapho. "Vamos! Let's eat." He tore into the back of a chicken with his golden teeth, chewing noisily, and the wad of tobacco still bulged in his cheek.

While they were attacking the food which the little girls had placed before them, the Xlalak horseman entered and sat down at the table without bothering to remove his hat. "Eat, Luis," ordered the General. He shoved a bowl of chicken under the horseman's nose. "Eat!"

As soon as a pot was empty, one or another of the little girls pattered in and refilled it. The General turned to Carlos. "Why do you come to Xlalak country?" he asked over an ear of corn.

"To see the pico," Carlos told him.

"Eh, eh! To see the pico?" With a thumbnail he removed a kernel of corn that had lodged between his teeth. "Pues, I heard there was a revolution starting." He watched Carlos shrewdly.

"You eat well," Carlos evaded. "Nowhere in the valley of San Marcos have I seen such food."

The General waved an arm expansively. "They bring it to me," he explained. "The people of the volcano bring it to me. They are old soldiers, and they would not forget their general. Si, pues, they are all soldiers."

"Are you a Xlalak?" ventured Carlos.

"Ho, now, and what does one call a Xlalak?" demanded the General, pointing the ear of corn at Carlos. "If one means an Indian tribe, then I am not a Xlalak. But let me tell you this, amigo, many men have fled to volcano country, and the Xlalaks have taken them in. Sí pues, in that regard I am indeed a Xlalak." He stared thoughtfully at Sapho. "You are Cuban, señorita?"

She shook her head. "My mother was Haitian, General."

"Eh, eh, I thought you were Cuban, perhaps. I fought in Cuba. Years ago I fought against the Yanquis in Cuba. Havana! Oh, qué linda! What cafés, señorita! What cantinas!" He dropped the ear of corn and pounded out a tempo on the table top. Sapho caught it, moving her shoulders in rhythm.

"E-e-e-e-e-e-e-yah! señorita," shouted the General, "you know the Congo dance, señorita?"

"Yes, yes, General!" She snapped her fingers like castanets.

"E-e-e-e-e-e-e-e-e-yah!" screamed the General. "Dance it, señorita, dance it!" He jumped to his feet and swayed over his beating as a rhythm came thumping out of the table.

Sapho sprang lightly to the middle of the floor. "Eh! Eh! Baya, baya, hein, hein!" she chanted. "Eh! Eh! Baya, baya, hein hein!" She spun once about on the tips of her toes, stood poised a moment, absorbing the rhythm, and as her body caught it, she swung into motion with her feet and hands, with her shoulders and hips, with every muscle of her supple body.

Eh! Eh! Baya, baya, hein, hein!

"E-e-e-e-e-e-e-e-e-e-e-e-e-e-e-yah!" shrieked the General. "E-e-e-e-e-e-yah, Luis, take the drum, Luis, come and beat, Luis!" The Xlalak leaned over the table and felt for the beat, and as it came, he pounded it out upon the table top.

"E-e-e-e-e-e-e-e-e-e-e-e-e-e-e-e-e-e-e-yah! Baya, baya-a-a-a-a-a-a-a-a-a-!" The General leaped over the bench onto the middle of the floor and joined Sapho dancing.

Serape flying, his aged body went wild with rhythm and lost its age, and it was young and fluid. He danced in front of Sapho, and his arms and legs were like the muscles of a snake, and his mouth drooped in a loose grin.

Sapho whirled and twisted, her body flowing smoothly beneath the whiteness of her mended shirt, beneath the flimsiness of her cotton pantalones. Her teeth flashed, and Carlos saw the deep fire of her eyes blazing to the surface.

The General lost himself in the abandon of the dance. He stomped and swayed and grimaced, arms and hips caught in swift gyrations. He howled and screamed, joining with Sapho in a chant with meanings long ago forgotten.

> Eh, eh, baya, baya, hein, hein!
> Congo malia me
> Congo daume fe ne
> Congo ji!

"E-e-e-e-e-e-e-e-e-e-e-e-e-e-yah!" He shrieked at the end of the last beat, and he staggered back to the table. Sapho followed. "Eh! Baya!" He sank down on a bench and wiped the sweat from his face with a corner of his serape.

"María!" puffed the General. "Bring water!" He pushed back the lock of hair that had covered an eye, and Carlos saw that the socket was empty.

There was a scuffle of feet as one of the little girls brought in a terra cotta carafe.

"Ah, señorita, what a dance!" exclaimed the General, leering at Sapho with his good eye. "You are muy elegante, you are muy sensual!"

"Gracias, General!"

"And now we eat!" shouted the General. "With new appetite, we eat."

He yelled for María. "Hot food! Hot food for new appetites. What a dance! Eh! Eh! Not since I was in Cuba have I danced such a dance. Not since I was a soldier in Cuba. Eh! Not since I fought the Yanquis."

"How did you come to fight in Cuba?" Carlos asked as soon as he had recovered from watching the dance.

"Pues, I wanted to be a soldier, but here there was no war, so pfft! I went to Cuba."

"How did you become a general?" Sapho asked.

"Just before the days of Ronca I was living here," the General explained, "and I heard there was a revolution."

"But you were already an — you were not a young man!" protested Sapho. "In the days of Ronca's revolution you were not a young man."

"Eh! Eh! One needs something to do in one's aged days!" the

General said. "Sí, pues, in my army were my own grandsons! It was not a real army, sabe, I heard of Ronca's revolution, and so I got out my gun, and I saddled my horse, and I rode around the volcano. Right around the volcano, eh, Luis?"

"Sí, pues," agreed the Xlalak.

"There was a man here making shingles," continued the General. "Come with me, says I, and join the revolution. So he sticks his axe into a stump. Sí, pues, says he. He comes along, and we ride a little farther, and there is a man hoeing corn. So he comes, too. Around the volcano we ride, and when we get back, we have a thousand men. Oh, a Xlalak will always fight against the government, eh, Luis?"

"Sí, pues!"

"So I go to Ronca, and I say, here are a thousand men. And he says, good, I make you a general!"

"Then you are a Ronquista," suggested Sapho.

"José Ronca can drink my urine," growled the General. "Come, señorita, you do not eat. You will think I am mean, you will starve. Come, eat!"

Sapho shook her head. Her stomach was already stuffed, and it was upset from the dancing, and she had become fascinated by the poster on the wall which showed the effects of alcohol; there was a picture of a human liver, and it had grown bloated and green. "No, no," she protested. "Gracias, I have had enough."

The General pressed her with an enchilada. "Eat," he insisted. "Come, señorita, you must eat."

She took the enchilada and nibbled on it.

"Ronca started a revolution," continued the General, "but he was like all the rest. Look at the country, amigos! Everyone is hungry. Only El General does not starve. Another enchilada, amigo, another enchilada!"

"Is it far to the peak?" Carlos asked.

"Three days, amigo," replied the General. "More or less three days." He eyed Carlos quizzically. "You will visit El Casco on the way. Eh! The señorita starves!" He pushed over the plate of enchiladas.

Sapho, still fascinated by the poster, declined. "Gracias, no more liv — no more enchilada!"

"Then you will have a cake, señorita. E-e-e-yah, María, bring the cakes!"

María appeared with a plateful, and the cakes were cookies cut in the shape of kittens with tails curled over their backs.

The General passed the plate to Sapho. "A little cake, señorita."

Sapho declined.

"Oh, eat, señorita, eat! Caray, in my house you will starve."

"Gracias, General," Sapho pleaded, "but already I have eaten too much."

"Eh! Señorita, only observe these cakes!" the General confided. "My great granddaughter made them for you only, señorita! See, they are little cats! They are precious little cats!"

Sapho was desperate. "Gracias, General, really, but I never eat cat!"

"Ho!" chuckled the old man. "Ho! Ho!" He nudged the Xlalak with his elbow. "Did you hear that, Luis! The señorita never eats cat! Ho-ho! Ho-ho-ho!" He threw his head back like a dog howling. "E-e-e-e-e-e-e-e-yah! The señorita never eats cat!"

He roared out his laughter, and the silent Xlalak joined in, and they slapped their bellies and pounded the table, and all the little girls of the kitchen crowded the doorway to see the señorita who never indulged in cats.

3

WHEN CARLOS AND SAPHO mounted their horses, the General was stuffing the saddlebags with tamales and fried chicken and cookies cut in the shape of kittens. "Luis will show you the way," he told them. "He will take you to El Casco."

"Whence comes that name — El Casco?" Carlos asked.

"You will learn," replied the General. "Eh! Eh! Luis, are you ready?"

"Listo caminando, General!"

"Bueno! Adiós, amigos, adiós señorita!" He stood swaying in the middle of the cobbled street, a squat figure in a huge sombrero and a serape that reached below his knees. The lock of black hair covered his empty eye socket.

From Pavón the trail led sharply upward through a series of steep ravines, and stump-scarred cornfields covered the slopes, and there were farmers working in them. They waved at Luis as he passed, and some of them shouted words of Xlalak.

"Those fields!" Sapho exclaimed. "They are almost cliffs."

The trail was about a metre wide, and it was paved with cobbles, and Carlos saw that repairs had been made wherever rains had begun a wash. They passed over a saddle, and below them a canyon dropped away. Luis reined his horse at the edge of the chasm and pointed across. "You see the village there?"

Carlos and Sapho saw a cluster of adobe buildings on a promontory that overhung the gorge.

"That is Kalshayu," Luis explained. "With a sling one might almost send a stone and reach it, but horses do not fly." He pointed out the trail, and it zigzagged down the near face of the canyon, crossed the stream below, and climbed upward again to reach the village. "They see us come!"

A number of men gathered on the other side of the chasm. More men appeared at the cliff's edge, and women and children as well.

"E-e-e-e-yah!" Luis sang out. "Sl'ma-a-a-a-a-a-a-ooooo li-i-i-i-i-i!"

Those on the far side of the gorge waved back.

Luis headed down the trail, and Carlos and Sapho followed.

"My horse!" Sapho exclaimed. "It walks always on the outside rim." She peered over the edge of the cliff, and it dropped straight down toward the roaring rapids of the river below. She clung to the pommel.

"Give the animal rein," Carlos advised. "He will pick his own place to step."

The bank that rose on the inner side of the trail was moist with ground water, and there were grasses growing luxuriantly, and once Sapho's horse shied as a tiny green snake slithered off a vine and crossed their path.

As they descended into the gorge, the roar of water was echoed, re-echoed, and amplified by the rock walls, and there was a constant din that beat against the ears.

"How do we cross the river?" Sapho shouted.

Carlos pointed up the canyon where a suspension bridge was strung from bank to bank. Sapho felt sick as she saw how it swayed in the wind. When they had zigzagged closer, she saw that it was made of sticks and ropes, and it seemed impossible that a horse could cross.

"I get off," she said when they had reached it. She dismounted, but Luis and Carlos rode their horses across.

Carlos returned to ride Sapho's horse. The animal moved slowly, slowly, step by step, and the bridge swung dizzily from side to side. Sapho followed. Once she looked down, but when she saw the angry waves of the rapids below, the eddies and the massive rocks, she quickly raised her eyes. Step by step they made their way.

When they had crossed the middle, Sapho vomited.

The trail on the other side was even steeper than the one they had descended, and they had to stop from time to time to breathe their horses.

"I'd rather not look back," Sapho admitted, but Carlos leaned over the edge and spat, and he watched the slob of saliva drop away.

"It is far!" Luis exclaimed, and he grinned, and for the first time Sapho noticed that his teeth were filed.

Nearing the canyon's rim, they could see no one but they heard the shouts of villagers and the bark of dogs. "Kalshayu!" Luis said. "We are almost there." The horses caught wind of fellow beasts and whinnied and quickened their ascent.

The trail broke over the edge of the chasm onto a small tableland where the adobe houses of the village were scattered. It seemed that all the people of the place were gathered on a greensward, and they were standing in a circle, watching something that took place in the center. As the three horses appeared, a number of Xlalaks left the crowd and came out to meet Luis, and there was an exchange of greetings.

Luis turned to Carlos. "There is excitement," he said. "The people of Kalshayu have caught a prisoner." He urged his horse to the edge of the crowd, and Carlos and Sapho followed.

In the center of the crowd in an open space stood a prisoner, and his wrists and ankles were bound. He was naked above the waist, and sweat streamed down his chest and back in grimy rivulets, but his trousers had not been removed, and they were powder-blue, and Carlos recognized them as part of a uniform of the federal police.

The crowd was undoubtedly Xlalak. There were lean, long-legged men with white shirts and pantalones. Pistols hung from their belts, and their feet were covered with cowhide boots, hand-sewed, and they wore their sombreros at a jaunty angle. Those were the men, and the women were tall and slender, and like the men, they held their heads straight and high. They wore bracelets of silver and gold about their wrists, and rings hung from the lobes of their ears. There was not a chubby face in all the crowd; even the children were spare, almost weedy.

Beyond where the prisoner stood, a break was made in the crowd, and they shouted as an old man drove a yoke of oxen into the center of the circle.

Luis tapped a spectator on the shoulder. "N'blao shik?"

The answer was a stream of Xlalak, and as the man spoke, Sapho recoiled at the sight of the pointed teeth.

"A Ronquista," Luis explained to Carlos in Spanish. "In the foot-hills they have caught a Ronquista on Xlalak lands."

Again the crowd broke beyond the prisoner, and the people shouted as a second yoke of oxen appeared in the center. "Hrrrrr! Hrrrrrrrr!" It was a younger man who drove this yoke, and he turned them about, and he hooked them to the shackles that bound the prisoner's feet. Carlos seized Sapho's arm when he comprehended what the Xlalaks were about to do.

"We go this other way!"

As he spoke, a young Xlalak approached Luis and spoke a few words in his native tongue.

"Come," Luis said to Carlos. "The Village Chief is waiting for us."

The young Xlalak led them toward an adobe building which proved to be the council house, and he stepped aside to let them enter, and Sapho was overwhelmed by the strong aroma of mutton stew.

An old man was sitting in the center of the room, and before him was an iron kettle covered thickly with soot. He greeted Luis and rose to his feet as Carlos entered. "B'nos dí's!" he said, and he extended a hand.

Luis spoke at some length in Xlalak. The old man nodded. "Sit down," he said in Spanish. "The Village of Kalshayu is yours!" He added words in his native tongue. "He asks that you forgive the meanness of this food." Luis indicated the kettle as he interpreted. "He says the corn is sad and does not grow, and even the grass is sickly weak and gives no flesh to grazing sheep."

Carlos and Sapho squatted close about the kettle, and Luis dropped to his haunches a bit behind them. The Chief resumed his former position, and Sapho noticed that he held a kitten in the crook of one arm, and as he talked, he stroked it and fondled its ears.

A woman glided in to remove the lid from the kettle. Sapho felt nauseated by the herb aroma released.

The old man reached into the kettle and selected a cube of meat. "Eat!" he said. "Reach in and eat."

Carlos helped himself, and he nudged Sapho with his elbow, and reluctantly she obeyed the Chief.

The old man ripped into his stringy meat with dog-like teeth, and for a time the only noises were the smack-smack of his chewing and a low buzz from the crowd. Then there was a commotion outside, and Sapho chilled at the sound of an agonized shriek.

It was short, however, and after that she heard only the hrrrrr! hrrrr! of those who managed the oxen.

Across the kettle from Sapho the Chief continued to eat with one hand, while he stroked the kitten with the other.

There was a second shriek.

The Chief smiled. "My people amuse themselves with the Ron-quista," he said proudly. He helped himself to another piece of mutton. "Eat!" he urged Sapho. "Eat, señorita, eat!"

Hrrrrrr! Hrrrrrrrr! went those who managed the oxen.

The kitten in the Chief's lap purred contentedly.

4

WHEN THE LAST SCREAMS had died away, five more aged Xlalaks entered the council house and sat in a ring behind Carlos and Sapho and the Village Chief. For a while no one spoke, and then one of the oldest nodded toward Sapho and said, "Señorita m'dim gao kak!"

The Chief chuckled. One by one the other men laughed, too, and finally there was an uproar in the council house. Luis grinned as he explained to Carlos. "They say the señorita wears pantalones!" Turning to the Chief he began a long harangue in Xlalak. One by one the others stopped their laughing and listened soberly. Luis pointed at Sapho, rubbed his belly, illustrated every point of his story, and at the end he finished up in Spanish. "The señorita says gracias, General, but I never eat cat!"

There was an explosion of laughter. The Village Chief bent forward almost double and pounded the floor in glee.

"The señorita says gracias, General, but I never eat cat!" Luis repeated as though his words were tastier the second time.

"Ho! The señorita never eats cat!" roared the Village Chief. "Never eats c-ca-a-t!"

Luis said something more in Xlalak.

With great effort the Village Chief stifled his laughter. "Why do you come to Xlalak country?" he asked Carlos.

"To see the pico."

"And the señorita, why does she come?"

"Also to see the peak," Carlos said.

There was a murmur about the room.

"I, too, would like to see the peak," said the Chief. "I shall go along." He called to a young Xlalak outside. "Saddle a horse, Luk!"

Three other old men decided that they, also, would like to see the

peak, and, when their horses were ready, the procession made a remarkable cavalcade.

They set off, and as they crossed the greensward, Sapho noted
where shavings had been spread to sop up the stickiness of coagu-
lating blood.

The trail soon reached slopes that, like La Cumbre, were covered
by oaks and pines, and there were charcoal pits, and there were also
stumps where Xlalak woodsmen were hewing shingles. Wherever a
man worked there was always a horse grazing somewhere near.

Luis led the way, while the Village Chief brought up the rear. As
they travelled upward, Luis composed a song.

> La señorita-a-a-a-a
> Never eats gatita-a-a-a-a-a!

When he had made up the words, Luis sang them off, and the
others joined in.

> La señorita-a-a-a-a
> Never eats gatita-a-a-a-a-a-a!

The Village Chief, bringing up the rear, added his own lines to the
song.

> In pantalone-e-e-e-es
> Rides la señorita-a-a-a-a-a-a!

Luis thought up some more.

> To see the pico
> Came la señorita-a-a-a-a-a-a!

As they climbed, they added verses to the song. They sang about
Carlos and about the horses, about the sun in the sky and the wind
in the trees; but mostly they sang about Sapho. Whatever she did,
they put it in the song. If she laughed, they sang about it; if she
sighed, they composed a mournful verse; when she stopped by the
trail and went behind a tree, they sang about that, too.

They climbed higher, and the pines and oaks got smaller. Toward
nightfall they stopped in a village that was even tinier than Kalshayu.
There they ate more stringy mutton, and they spent the night, sleeping
on the wooden floor of the council house.

In the morning four more horsemen joined the cavalcade to see the pico.

As the procession started out, Sapho saw how the trail climbed higher. The pines and oaks became smaller and fewer, and there were fields where stunted potatoes grew, and turnips and rutabagas, and in the fields were Xlalaks working. There were also springs of cool, clear water, and there were close-cropped meadows where wiry horses and scrubby sheep and cattle grazed. Junipers and wild cherries grew thick along the path. Sapho listened to the hum of bees about a magnolia bush, and from afar off she heard the shrill notes of a shepherd's flute. The land, she thought, was like a magic place.

They came at length to a number of frame buildings with corrals about. In the corrals were scrawny burros and mules and horses, and there was a hunchbacked Xlalak in charge.

"The air grows weak," Luis explained. "High on the peak it has no force, and lowland horses will not function. These are mountain beasts. They were born upon the pico, and their chests are big. They have never been below this place."

When they had started again, Luis made up another verse for their song, and it was about air that was weak and air that had force. To their lowland horses it was a melancholy farewell, to their mountain mules a welcome.

"E-e-e-e-e-e-e-e-e-e-yah!" screamed Luis at the end of a verse. "Now we climb like birds high into the sky. On the backs of our mountain hawks we soar about the peak!"

He stroked the mane of his mule, and Sapho laughed to see him. The beast was small, while Luis had legs that were long enough to scrape the ground, and he kicked at pebbles in the trail with his boot toe, laughing deep in his belly. "It is turn about," he chuckled. "When my little mule gets tired, I get off and carry him a while!" He liked his joke, and so he rearranged the words, making them a verse in his song.

The trail grew precipitous in places, and Sapho was astonished to see how the mules dug in with their hoofs and climbed step by step. They needed no guiding, and she was quite willing to give full rein while she clung to the saddle horn and hugged the beast's ribs with her knees.

"One takes a mountain goat," Luis explained solemnly, "and breeds it to a jackrabbit, and pfft! Out comes a mulacita!" He winked. "Do not tell. It is a Xlalak secret." He looked at the sun. "Before night," he said, "we shall see El Casco."

"Why is he called El Casco, Luis?"

The Xlalak shrugged. "You will see."

During the course of the day they stopped at three more villages, and at each village there was a mutton stew, and everyone was fed. By evening, there were, by Sapho's count, thirty men in the cavalcade. "Is there always food?" Sapho asked.

"What they have they give," Luis answered. "In former times it was better. The crops were bigger, then. Our earth is getting tired, señorita. It rebels. So we climb higher, closer to the sky. Pues, we shall soon reach the snow, and there will be no further place to go. There will be starving then, I think."

They spent the night in the third village, sleeping on the floor of the council house, all thirty men — and Sapho. She lay close to Carlos, and for a time she could not sleep because of the riotous snoring, the many coughs and spittings.

When first the sun appeared, they were already on their way, climbing always upward. Once they stopped at a tiny village where two more horsemen joined them, and toward noon they came upon a man digging potatoes from a scraggly hillside patch. "E-e-e-yah! Pancho, may the potatoes grow with joy!" Luis sang out. "C'm'stá, amigo?"

The man straightened from his digging, spoke rapidly in Xlalak. Luis slid off his mule, went over to an open hill, and dug out a handful of marble-sized potatoes. "See, señorita," he said to Sapho, "they are tiny, tiny like our mules. But they grow so close to Dios that he never forgets to water, and they are precious sweet."

With eyes on Sapho, the potato digger spoke rapidly to Luis. "He wants to know where we go," Luis explained to Sapho.

Sapho's eyes danced mischievously. "Tell him, Luis! Maybe he, too, would like to go along."

Luis translated.

The potato digger grinned, tipped his straw hat to Sapho. "Gracias, señorita, I come along." When he had leaned his wooden hoe against a tree, he disappeared into a near-by thicket from which he emerged shortly with a bridled pony.

Sapho had not expected this. "Does he have no house," she asked, "no wife, no —"

"Oh, yes, he lives yonder half a pipe smoke distant," Luis replied pointing toward a deep ravine. "He won't be back tonight."

"Why not?"

Luis looked puzzled. "Well, you ask him does he want to come along and see the pico, so pues, señorita, he comes along!"

Thus the potato digger joined the procession, and they pushed on up the mountain trail. Soon Luis had added the newcomer to his song, together with Sapho's invitation and all that she had said. In his mellow voice Luis sang out the verse for all to hear, and up and down the trail other riders picked it up and added new words to suit their fancies.

The day wore on, and Sapho began to feel the thinness of the air. No single breath gave her lungs enough. Watching Carlos, she was astounded to see how easily he laughed and joked with other riders, how to him the altitude did not appear to have a meaning.

Carlos laughed and joked with various horsemen, but always he was watching, listening, learning how they thought and acted. So these were the Xlalak bandits, the vampires that sucked the blood of babies! Well, he liked them hugely, but he sought to understand what lay beneath the songs and shouts and banter, to probe the sentimentality that allowed the Chief of Kalshayu to stroke a kitten while oxen tore a man apart. He watched and listened and decided in his mind what words to use upon him who led them.

Win the Xlalaks on the merits of the revolution, Felipe Cuerno had said. Bien, what phases of the struggle would appeal to such men as these? It was clear enough that their soil was overworked and that they could not climb much higher in search of virgin fields. Eventually they would be in need of help. That was one reason for supporting a new government. A second was that they could not remain in isolation more than a few years longer. Sooner or later federal police would extend control throughout all the mountain country. But there was a third appeal which Carlos thought would be the most

effective. Here was a revolution coming, and he suspected that
few of the younger Xlalaks would miss an opportunity to fight
Ronquistas.

Carlos did not foresee great difficulty in winning Xlalak fighters,
but in marshalling his arguments, he wondered whether a Liberal
government could offer much to men like these. He was sure that
Bolshevik leaders were looking much farther into the future than
most Liberales ever had. "It is an old-time tactic," Felipe Cuerno had
said, "to support the liberal democrats against imperialism. We co-
operate with the Liberales as long as they are completely revolutionary. When they make a deal with Ronquistas or when they cease
to fight imperialism, then we fight them, too."

There was at the moment a single revolution, Carlos decided, but
for Liberales it meant one thing, while for Communists it meant another. Don Ricardo was fighting to reform the old order; when he
had accomplished that, he would seek no further change. Felipe
Cuerno considered this revolution merely a stage, and his support for
Don Ricardo was temporary, a tactic in a larger struggle. How long
could Liberal and Comunista work together? Carlos did not know, but
he was sure of this: neither one alone could win from Ronca.

Every man was needed against Ronquismo, he told himself. That
was the immediate objective, the only objective with which Don
Ricardo and Felipe Cuerno were now concerned. He breathed deeply
of the mountain air. It was thin, but there was vigor in it, and his
mind felt keener, as though the climb were lifting him ten thousand
feet above the confusion of his anxious thinking. He rose slightly in his
stirrups and loosed a long-forgotten Nacheetl whoop. It seemed that
at least a dozen echoes answered.

Shadows had already lengthened across the trail, and Carlos could
smell the faint scent of supper cooking somewhere up above.

Just at dusk Luis raised a shout. "Conejo! We come to Conejo-
o-o-o-o!"

The trail wound upward against the sides of a narrow ravine, came
out upon a mountain promontory where Sapho saw corrals and pine-
slab cabins. There were men and women and children moving about
in the twilight, carrying ocote torches, and there was a mountain mist

that hung over the slopes, forming a prismatic halo about each open flame.

A small boy opened a gate, and Luis led the whole cavalcade into a corral, and men came out of the darkness from all sides to hold bridles and to help unsaddle.

"Come!" Luis said to Carlos and Sapho. "They will take care of the mules. Come with me to El Casco." He led the way toward a pine-slab cabin.

There was a projecting roof under which a man was standing with a lantern in his hand. His poncho was small and barely reached his waist. Sapho saw that his torso was a Xlalak torso, long, and well shaped, but the legs were short, too short for his body. A shadow from the wide-brimmed hat obscured his face.

Luis spoke a number of words in Xlalak. "This is El Casco," he added in Spanish.

The Xlalak chieftain bowed slightly to Sapho, shook Carlos' hand. He was not more than thirty, she thought, but there was an assurance in his bearing that made him seem much older. "Come in," he said. "My house is yours."

It was like the cabin of Leonardo above La Cumbre, but somewhat larger. There were the same board floors, freshly swept, the same charcoal braziers, the sheepskin beds. El Casco clumped across the floor to hang the lantern on a peg, and as he did so, Sapho started.

His leather-clad feet were the size and shape of a mountain pony's hoofs.

5

EARLY IN THE EVENING a score or more of Xlalak leaders trooped into the Conejo council house to hear what Carlos had to say. It was a long, low building of whip-sawed lumber, and the roof was covered with hand-hewn shakes that gave to the interior a strong, fresh scent of cedar. An ocote torch sputtered at one end of the meeting lodge, and a thin wisp of smoke rose straight up to mushroom against the blackened ridge pole. One by one the Xlalak chieftains pushed through the narrow doorway, paused inside the threshold, hat in hand, and glanced about with eyes that glinted in the half-light.

When a man had spotted a particular friend, he raised his head in casual greeting, moved near, and squatted on the pine-slab floor.

Carlos and El Casco sat under the ocote torch, while Luis posted himself near at hand so that he might interpret. As the room filled up, there was a new aroma of leather and pipe smoke and fresh tobacco. The Xlalaks had ranged themselves in irregular ranks, and Carlos noticed that their weathered faces blended into the dimness of the room, while their cotton shirts stood out clean and white and their eyes caught flashes from the ocote torch.

When the last Xlalak had found a place to squat, El Casco rose to speak. The chieftain spoke deliberately, a sentence at a time, and once or twice he paused so long that Carlos imagined that he had finished. The other Xlalak leaders listened attentively and with obvious respect, and the only disturbing sounds were sibilant suckings on a score of pipestems and an occasional hacking cough. Carlos was fascinated by them sitting there, row upon row of immobile faces.

Since he could not understand the language, Carlos did not know the precise moment when El Casco approached the subject which they had gathered to discuss, but gradually he felt the pull of many eyes upon him, and now and then El Casco turned in his direction. Once there was the slightest stir of excitement, and a number of heads nodded gravely. A few moments afterwards El Casco changed into singsong Spanish which Luis translated monotonously.

"Carlos Chichayan is Nacheetl," El Casco said, and he waited for Luis to turn the sentence into Xlalak. "Carlos Chichayan has been to school and knows the ways of the great city down below. Carlos Chichayan has spent many years in the prison known as Tiburón. Carlos Chichayan is a leader among the enemies of Ronca. Carlos Chichayan has come to us with an important message."

El Casco stopped abruptly and sank down, tailor fashion, upon his hoof-like feet. Carlos, remembering the ways of his own village, did not rise immediately, but sat motionless, eyes fastened upon a knot in the flooring directly before him. One Xlalak shifted his position; another relighted his pipe; the rest seemed lost in ponderous meditation.

After a dignified interval Carlos arose and began to speak as El Casco had spoken, slowly, sentence by sentence, allowing Luis time to translate, allowing his listeners time to consider his words. "Greetings to the Xlalak chieftains," he began. "Greetings to all the people who live upon these slopes. Greetings to the aged men whose heads are heavy with wisdom. Greetings to the young men who are skillful with horses. Greetings to those who till the soil, and may the earth sing joyously and give bounteous crops."

He spoke about the sun and wind and rain, about the sky-splitting pico, about bubbling springs and streams gurgling with fresh, sweet water. He spoke about soil and crops and harvests and other matters of importance.

While he spoke, he watched the Xlalaks, and he saw that they were listening. He saw smoke curling upward from a score of pipes, and sometimes he saw a head nod slightly, and he knew that they considered his words worthy of grave attention. There was a magic in the air that gave him confidence, and when the moment was right, he spoke about Ronquista rule and about the coming revolution. He spoke of carbonero slopes, of Felipe Cuerno, of Comunistas, and of Liberales plotting in San Marcos. He described the general plan for overthrowing Ronca, and he talked at considerable length about the kind of government which Don Ricardo and his Liberal Party would bring about. He tried to suggest all that liberty and freedom meant, and he explained how every man and woman would have a vote. He spoke slowly, sentence by sentence, and he thought that he was making very clear why every able-bodied Xlalak should join the fight.

When he had finished, he sat down, and the council house was quiet except for the coughings, the suckings on pipestems, the sputtering of the ocote torch.

After a long silence an old Xlalak arose. He was small and wizened and toothless, and his face reminded Carlos of a dried apricot. A few grey, silky whiskers hung down from his chin. He spoke a number of words, paused long for consideration, then spoke again, and when he spoke, one saw the redness of his gums. "Let us not forget," he said, "the days of our ancient gods. For in those times the soil was fertile, and it gave forth bountiful harvests of maize." He stopped and cocked his head like an old and weatherbeaten sparrow. Luis translated tonelessly.

There were no sounds other than the coughs of those who had gathered to listen. The old man closed his wrinkled eyelids dramatically, and said, "Xlalak men thrived in those days and saw that life was good. Each man protected his neighbor, guarding his hut when he went to market, cultivating his corn when he was sick, caring for him when he was old, and feeding his aged widow after Dios had laid his hand. Those were our ways in ancient times, and it was filling storehouses according to one's harvest and drawing according to one's needs. It was saving in time of plenty and using when the corn got tired and wouldn't grow."

The old man stopped short to glare down upon the upturned faces. "Now what has happened to our days of plenty?" he croaked. "I tell you, they have gone with our ancient gods and customs. What man now thinks of his neighbor? None! Nowadays each one hoes his corn for himself alone, feeds his own family only. So the earth is angry and gives forth less and less. The day will come when it will give no more at all, and Sky will hold back rain, and we shall die." He pointed a trembling finger at those before him. "We shall die, every one, and be like dusty earth."

His whole body shook as though he had caught a chill. For a

moment he closed his eyes, gathered strength within the frailness of his withered frame. "What man now considers Sun?" he demanded, spitting out his words. "For Moon-Woman who now remembers to slaughter a suckling lamb? None, save some old croaking cricket about to die. One goes to meetings, yes! One hears about making revolution, yes! One talks about liberty and freedom, yes! But the old ways — pfft! They are not good enough. Have we made our choice? Have we turned our backs upon the past? Then be ready to die and be like dusty earth!"

He sank back upon his haunches where he was hidden from sight as though shadows near the floor had swallowed him up. He had spoken, this old, old man, and he had scattered many words that had to be considered. Carlos pondered along with all the others, and it seemed to him that he had heard Uncle Vicente talking once again.

As soon as the ensuing silence had lasted long enough, a young man sprang to his feet. His skin was smooth and hairless except for the very beginnings of a soft mustache. He had broad shoulders and fingers that were strong and sure. "The words we have heard," he said, "are words from long ago. They are words whispered by dying winds at night, words that rustle among the leaves of our minds while we are deep in sleep, words felt in the hush of sleep. Venerable words they are, Xlalak words, rising from the bottomless pits of our Xlalak souls. But I tell you this — " he squared himself upon his sturdy feet — "in these days they are no use."

While Luis translated into Spanish, Carlos heard a restless ripple through the council house.

The young man spoke again, and with each spit of words, he lunged forward like a striking snake. "What are these ancient gods? What are their customs of long ago? What is this neighbor-helping neighbor? Just old men's legends, a brew of herbs soothing for an empty belly. Well, it is too late for that kind of medicine. I ask you this: will old-time ways bring vigor to our tired soil? Will old-time ways put the strength of manhood into hungry bellies? Will old-time ways make markets for our corn? Will old-time ways cure sickness or show us how to read and write? Will old-time ways teach tricks to confound the police of Ronca? Will old-time ways make men out of hamstrung dogs?"

A young man among the listeners half rose from where he squatted. "No, Bal, no!"

The speaker clenched a fist and shook it at those before him. "No, the old ways will not do these things. That is our answer to old men's pleadings. Now I ask the stranger a question." He turned on Carlos. "Now I ask this Nacheetl from down below the clouds to speak in words that all can understand. What is this Liberty, Stranger? What is this Freedom that you talk about? What will they do for us? Will they make a market, Stranger? Do they cure the sick? Do they enrich the tired-out soil? Do they feed the starving?"

Bal swept his eyes triumphantly over those who had come to listen. "There you have the answer," he said, levelling a finger at Carlos. "You see it in the Nacheetl's face. Liberty, Freedom, they do not do those things. Well, my belly aches for food, my child is sick, my soil is tired of growing corn. Let me tell you this. I am back from Río Macho, and there I met a man who answered all these questions. Your soil is good, he said, but it needs a certain feeding. Beans and corn are good, he said, but they are not enough for a manly body. Sickness is not los aires, he said, but a mosquito or pissed-in water. To read and write, he said, are easy tricks to learn. By what God-handed-down right, he asked, does the Ronquista rule? Here is a rifle, he said, let's go find out. I like that talk. It is clear to understand."

E-e-e-e-e-e-e-e-yah! The young men screamed. Several sprang to their feet, fists clenched, and all were speaking at once. El Casco raised a hand, and the noise subsided, but Carlos felt excitement like air that crackles before a mountain thunderstorm.

El Casco spoke softly. "It is the stranger's turn to speak," he said. "Let us listen to his answer."

Carlos rose to his feet and stood silent, for a moment, gathering up his many thoughts. When at last he spoke, his words were soft, coming from deep within, and they were his own thoughts, his own grave doubts, his own searchings for a proper trail. Perhaps the old gods and customs were indeed a legend that never lived except in old men's minds. In any case, the wooden hoe was now as old-fashioned as the bow and arrow, and a sacrifice of turkey blood or a suckling lamb would give no lasting strength to depleted soil. Against almost world-wide famine the village storehouse was not enough; and for the widows and orphans of the great, broad earth, for the millions of sick and crippled and aged, village care was not enough.

So the old ways were perhaps a legend, a story told to children, a golden age to sigh for. Yet they did exist in good men's minds and were very much alive, and that was no small matter.

As a legend, as a memory for sighing, they had no use, but as a vision for the future —

There was that much to say for tales of long ago. Now about Liberty and Freedom and the living ways belonging to them. These could be empty words, memories for sighing. One could laugh at them and tuck them away in a dusty corner with all the other wornout gods, and one could spend one's time feeding empty bellies and curing sickness and enriching depleted soil. That was one way. Another way was to build a great, high altar of stone and place Liberty and Freedom at either end like snow-white candles to flicker in the tempest and light the darkness of the world with two tiny orbs of pure, pale gold. One could do this, and the sick and poor and starving could fall upon their knees and worship, shoulder to shoulder with their well-fed brothers.

These were two ways, and each had been tried. There was also a third way which Carlos now sought to describe. His words came slowly, and lines eating deep into his face showed how painfully real his thinking was. As he spoke, he saw Magdalena there before him. "The ugly woman took a thread," she told Carlos, "a soft thread, and the madman played a note, and it was likewise soft. She took another thread, and he played a note to match. Thus she wove her threads, and the madman wove his notes, and a pattern grew."

That was what one did, and Carlos described it to the gathered Xlalaks. One made a warp of Liberty and Freedom and other human rights, and through these one wove stable peasant markets and fair returns for human labor and a useful job for every willing man and woman. Those were three threads, and there were many more. Carlos spoke of treatment for the exhausted soil, of doctors travelling through mountain regions on horseback, of teachers and a school in every village. "A pattern grew, and in it were all the colors and all the designs that the world had ever seen."

Weaving his threads, Carlos looked down upon the gathered Xlalaks.

The torch had burned low; it was dark within the council house; the men's brown faces were difficult to see. As he watched, the features seemed to fade away until he saw only the squareness of their squatting bodies, like headstones, row on row. "There is the pattern I seek to weave," he told them, "but it cannot be achieved without that warp of human rights to bind the weave and give resilient strength."

He forgot the faces altogether and spoke only to rows of white squares upright in the darkness of the room, and he grew taller as he spoke. He was a shaft of hard rock thrusting upward, and the headstones were white squares in the darkness far below. "That is the purpose, that is the pattern, and as each generation hands over the weft, as the cloth comes nearer to completion, may not the face revealed belong to God?"

6

DAWN WAS BREAKING over Conejo when Carlos and Sapho awoke. Shivering, they went to the door of El Casco's house and looked out upon heavy clouds that obscured the entire world below them, and it was as though the volcano were an island in a vast, white sea.

They were putting on the leather boots that Jorge had lent when El Casco appeared from among the mules and horses. "Come out here," he called, "and see the pico." He stood with his club feet wide apart, gazing into the sky behind his house. He had massive shoulders, Sapho noticed, and she suspected that his arms were very strong.

Joining him, Carlos and Sapho saw that scarlet rays of sunlight had painted the snowy slopes of the volcano which rose directly before them.

"That is his red serape," El Casco said. "He changes many times a day."

As Carlos watched the change of colors on the titanic peak, he asked, "How far from here to the edge of snow?"

"You will see."

The Xlalak chieftain stared upward at the massive cone of whiteness tinged with red. Snow crystals had caught the early morning sunlight and were glittering like millions of precious gems. "We climb the pico right away," he said to Carlos. "Highness clears the brain. One is close to Diós there on top."

Inside El Casco's house they sat about a charcoal brazier and ate frijoles that had been fried and rolled in thin tortillas, and they drank sarsaparilla tea and filled leather panniers with food to take along. "It is better to eat a little at a time," El Casco said when they had begun to saddle, "as the stomach requests." While the chieftain tightened up girths, a young Xlalak drove a lean yearling lamb into the corral, hobbled it, and threw it across the horse's croup.

It was still early morning when the cavalcade set out. The trail climbed straight up through a belt of junipers where herds of stunted cattle grazed, and above the junipers were grassy meadows and fields where potatoes grew. Here and there, in ravines, there were groves of low, crippled pines, but most of the slopes were open.

The earth was damp and lush, well watered by countless streams that tumbled downward from the ice cap above. "Drink!" El Casco said. "Taste our mountain water."

Carlos and Sapho dismounted and lay upon their bellies beside one of the streams and sucked up mouthfuls of icy liquid. "It bites the tongue!" Sapho gasped.

"Wait until you have tasted snow," El Casco warned. "It bites-bites!"

As the sun moved higher in the sky, the air grew warm and even hot, and Sapho removed her serape and opened her shirt low about the neck. "It must be far!" she exclaimed. "The air is oven hot."

The lamb that lay across the croup bleated softly. "Yet it is a small distance," El Casco corrected. "A few smokes only."

Sapho noticed how he rode his horse. The saddle had special stirrups to receive his hoof-like boots, but aside from that, one forgot that he was a man deformed. How fortunate, she thought, that he was born in a land of horsemen. He could be a leader here, while afoot, he would be a pitied cripple.

As Sapho rode ahead with Luis, El Casco drew his horse close behind the mule which Carlos rode. "Few men," he said, "have ever come to climb our pico." They rode through a clump of pines where a spring of water gushed from beneath a boulder and cascaded down a grassy slope. With three fingers El Casco rolled a cigarette, and when he had licked the paper, he spoke again. "You have come." The trail moved across an open slope where a tiny girl was tending a flock of sheep. The tinkle of the bell wether sounded loud and clear in the mountain air. El Casco lighted his cigarette. "Do you like our mountain?"

"It splits the clouds," Carlos said. "I find it precious."

They left the sheep behind and climbed steeply upward to a tiny lake that was round and deep and green, an eye of water, El Casco called it. Here the cavalcade paused for a moment's rest. "When one comes from far," El Casco said, "one finds many matters about which to talk."

As the procession moved slowly upward, Carlos spoke again about the revolution, a few words only. El Casco concealed his interest. Carlos waited a proper length of time, then added a few words more. El Casco reined his horse out of the trail and rode close beside.

Even the grass was shorter now. It hugged tight against the slope, and the hoofs of El Casco's horse left sharp imprints upon its greenness. "Are you Liberal," the Xlalak asked, "or are you Comunista?"

"I have no party," Carlos said. "I only search a way."

El Casco flipped the yellow butt of his cigarette into a puddle of water where it hissed and died. "Which do you think is better for a peasant man like me?"

While their animals struggled upward, Carlos explained carefully what Liberal and Comunista each believed. "There you are," he said when he had finished. "You yourself can choose."

The Xlalak pulled his horse back into the trail, and as he rode along he whistled softly to himself.

Gradually the grasslands gave way to cobbled slopes and the cobbles to gigantic boulders. This morning Carlos felt a sense of sureness greater than he had known since railroad days. "Vámonos," he cried, "let's go, mula-a-a-a-a-a!"

The animal moved this way and that, searching for a place, and when he had found an opening between two boulders, he placed a hoof within it, testing. If the footing held, he drew a hind leg forward, advanced his other front one, and then the remaining one behind. Poised between the rocks, the mule searched again, found another solid spot, and placed a hoof upon it.

This was slow work, but the boulder belt was narrow, and soon the trail came out upon smooth slopes of volcanic ash, slick with water. El Casco was ahead of Sapho when his animal slipped and somersaulted backwards. Down the slope they slid, man and horse and lamb, the horse on top. Carlos rolled out of his saddle and snatched for the bridle, but already the beast had dug into the mud with his hoofs and had come to rest. El Casco crawled out from beneath, and a wide grin bared his pointed teeth. The yearling lay among the bushes, crying piteously. The chieftain slung it across the horse's croup again.

"E-e-e-e-e-e-e-e-e-e-yah!" screamed Luis from somewhere ahead. "El Casco-o-o-o, your poor little horse, he asks that you carry him!"

"E-e-e-e-e-e-e-e-e-e-e-e-yah!" screamed the Chief of Kalshayu, "carry him, Casco-o-o-o-o-o! A big man like you should be ashamed."

El Casco lifted the haunches, helping the horse to stand, but the animal held a front hoof high. "Pobrecito!" murmured El Casco. He stroked the shank with his hands. The animal whinnied. Straightening, the Xlalak seized the bridle. "Come, it is better to walk," he said caressingly, and he set out, leading his horse, the sharp edges of his clubfoot boots cutting deep prints in the mud.

"What a stallion!" muttered Sapho. It was indeed a sight to see his stumpy legs and body climb.

Luis shouted back from the head of the column. "The snow! Señorita, we have reached the snow!" The line was jagged with long fingers reaching down from the solid cap.

"That is the fringe," El Casco said, "the fringe on Pico's serape."

A cap of ice and snow covered that portion of the peak that rose above. The cavalcade had stopped in a ravine that was sheltered and had a stream of water near. Luis was scraping snow from an altar-shaped pile of rock. As she came closer, Sapho saw a cross on top, and behind the cross sat a hideous, grinning god of stone, man-sized, with pot belly and barrel chest. For Sapho, however, the snow was more exciting.

She slid off her animal and dropped to her knees in whiteness. She plunged her hands into a fluffy drift and felt the cold. "Look, Carlos, it's like — like — "

Carlos dismounted and touched it with his fingers.

One by one the Xlalaks swung out of their saddles, removed their broad sombreros, and stood reverently before the altar. El Casco lifted the yearling lamb from the croup of his horse and laid it before the grinning god of stone. Sapho looked at Luis inquiringly. "There you see Saint Peter," the Xlalak whispered as he slid to the ground and stood with bowed head. "Here he guards the climbing slope to Heaven-in-the-Sky. For safe passage one leaves a gift."

El Casco stretched his yearling lamb across the stone altar. Its eyes were large and round and dumbly beseeching. He took from his belt a shining knife, and there he stood a moment, blade poised. Little jets of warm breath rose from the animals nostrils and mingled with El Casco's breathing mist. Sapho turned away. There was a short bleat, then nothing but the mountain's stillness. When she looked again, the altar, the cross, the face of the grinning god of stone were purple with steaming blood.

When the sacrifice was over, the Xlalaks left the altar and once again took up the bridles of their animals. "I stay here," the Chief of Kalshayu stated, and the others said that they, also, would stay, and only Luis agreed to accompany El Casco and his visitors.

"It is a matter of feeling," Luis explained to Sapho as they started upward through the snow. "There would be too many people."

"Why too many?" Sapho gasped. There was a tightness across her breasts.

"To Heaven-in-the-Sky is a short distance only," Luis said. "There would be talking and shouting and a great disturbing of Dios in his meditations."

El Casco broke a trail, and Carlos came next, and then Sapho, and Luis brought up the rear. They pushed forward a few metres at a time, and Sapho felt a pounding of the heart, and so did Carlos, now, and even El Casco stopped often. "Slow-slow," he said. "That is the most rapid way." He drew an onion from a bag about his neck, quartered it, and divided the pieces among them. "Chew a little at a time," he directed. "It gives power to the spirit."

The surface of the slope was hard and burnished by the winds, but there were crevasses beneath, and there were bridges of snow which El Casco tested. Sapho felt sleepy, and she lost all desire to climb. Her heart was flopping like a wounded bird.

"Slow-slow," El Casco said.

The sun, nearing its zenith, gleamed against the snow. "It stabs the eyes!" Luis muttered. He was stifling a yawn.

"Slow-slow," El Casco said.

Sapho bit into her piece of onion. It seemed that the fumes revived her. She raised her eyes. There were smooth slopes of whiteness reaching into the sky. She looked behind. They had come but a little distance.

"Look!" exclaimed El Casco. "The clouds fly away." There was a hole through into the world below, and Sapho saw jungle lowlands stretching flat like a bed of moss. "The Río Pongo," added El Casco.

Upward, upward, a step at a time. Slow-slow.

Sapho felt her lids droop, and black curtains seemed to hang about the corners of her eyes. She wanted to lie in the snow and sleep. El Casco was talking, but his voice sounded far away, like words spoken in a dream. She took another bite of onion. There was a rope wound about her body above the waist, and it was drawing tighter, tighter, and her heart was growing bigger, bigger, and there was fire in her lungs.

They came to a hollow in the mountain slope. There were gigantic boulders piled one upon another that broke the wind. Water was running out from under, but the earth was bare of greenness.

"I stay here with the señorita," Luis volunteered.

"I wish to climb," Sapho gulped.

"To remain is better," El Casco said. He was watching her face and eyes. "It is a matter of the heart and lungs."

She exchanged a parting glance with Carlos. There was a lustiness about him that she had never sensed before. She noticed for the first time that his chest was wide and deep, while the vigorous climb had brought a really handsome flush to the brownness of his face.

El Casco pushed ahead, and his hoof-shaped boots, cutting into the crust, made a series of toeholds which Carlos used. Step by step they made their way. The sun was dropping from its zenith. Carlos looked off, and the clouds were so far dispersed that he could see the earth beneath. It gave him a heady sense of power to see the world below.

They came to an overhanging ledge. "We rest here," El Casco said. Carlos squatted in the lee of a naked rock and drew his serape close about his shoulders, while El Casco took a fist-sized lump of sugar and another onion from his bag.

"Is it far to the top?" Carlos asked.

The Xlalak bit into an onion as though it were an apple. "A hundred metres, more or less."

Carlos sucked on the sugar lump that the Xlalak gave him. The atmosphere was calm and restful when one did not move about.

El Casco was staring downward at the far-off greenness of the earth. "Look at all the world spread out!" He moved his palm in an arc to indicate the vastness of the panorama. One could see blue rivers cutting deep into the jungle carpet and a lake set among foothills like a mounted turquoise. The Xlalak turned to Carlos. "You think in this whole world the people can learn to live together and work together as you spoke last night?"

A chill wind blew around the ledge. Carlos rose unsteadily to his feet, stretched to remove the cramps that gripped his muscles. "The future must see all men working together," he said. "Xlalaks and Nacheetls and railwaymen and oilfield workers and all the rest must work together." He paused momentarily. "Don Ricardo and Felipe Cuerno must also work together," he added, more to himself than to El Casco, "and each must accept the good which the other has to offer."

The Xlalak stood up. "About the revolution, amigo — I think Pavón will be the place to gather."

Slowly, deliberately the two men resumed their climb. There was a cold wind that lashed at the face, and Carlos bit into it to breathe. Step by step they toiled upward, and there was frost about the mouth even while sweat ran in broad trickles down the center of the back. Carlos was slipping, now, and his legs were heavy logs, but deep within his belly was a vigor that drove him upward. Facing the wind, he threw back his head and laughed at the pico's challenge.

XI. Revolution

In ravines and on the slopes around Pavón a thousand horsemen gathered. Down volcano trails they came in village troops, each under its particular chief, and they built their fires by night and roasted mutton, and the countryside around the house of the ancient general twinkled with the lights of a vast encampment.

As soon as El Casco had heard from his village chiefs, Carlos had sent estimates to Felipe Cuerno, and within a week long pack trains loaded with arms and ammunition began arriving at the General's adobe house. The old man had directed Luis to move a table out upon his tile-roofed porch, and there the arms were stacked.

For two days, now, while Sapho checked record sheets, Carlos and Luis and El Casco had been handing out grenades, carbines, and clips of ammunition to Xlalak warriors filing by. It was a sight, Sapho thought, to see a swarthy horseman grin when he got his fingers wrapped about the barrel of a shiny carbine. Always he had to try it out, and on the first day nearby ravines rang with shots as though the whole encampment were a guerilla battlefield. Since ammunition was limited, Carlos and El Casco had put a stop to that, allowing only a single shot for the trying out of any given carbine.

Hour after hour the horsemen filed past the table while Sapho checked and Carlos and Luis and El General handed out the weapons. There was laughter and there was much singing of songs, and when Sapho saw how the toughest warriors had accepted Carlos, how they laughed with him and asked him questions and included him in their songs, she came to believe that at last his time had come.

Sapho often wondered about that meeting with Xlalak chieftains in the Conejo council house. Something that had happened that night, or else the climb to the pico's summit, had given Carlos a reservoir of confidence which she had never felt in him before. Now she noticed how he moved all day among Xlalak horsemen, directing, teaching, showing how to handle dynamite, to toss a hand grenade, to cut the timing of a fuse; he was taciturn as ever, she admitted, but he acted with an inner firmness and decision which gave him new strength.

He would soon become a leader among the Xlalaks, the practical Sapho told herself, and through them he could win the confidence of Felipe Cuerno and thus become a peacetime figure. Although she knew that a tiny, backward Central American country like this could not reach a truly Soviet stage for many years, she was certain from all that her father had taught her that the far-off future belonged to communism.

So, when her imagination built up Carlos' greatness, she saw him as a real Bolshevik who would see beyond the immediate present and work upon problems that could not be solved, perhaps, until decades after both he and she were dead. For even the greatest Liberal, it seemed to Sapho, had a snapshot mind which saw only the present.

With such thoughts in her head, Sapho watched her husband by day and encouraged him and built up his sureness and pride whenever chance permitted. During daytime hours she helped him thus, and at night, when they lay down together on mats in El General's adobe house, she felt serene assurance in his touches, and in all their love there grew a harmony which she had never known with him or any other human being.

The thoughts which Carlos harbored were not altogether placid ones. As he handed out arms and ammunition to files of swarthy Xlalaks and while he moved among their campfires in ravines behind Pavón, he worried about the hopes he had expressed that night in the Conejo council house. He had spoken of a warp of Liberty and Freedom and other human rights through which one must weave stable peasant markets and fair returns for human labor and a useful job for every willing man and woman. These were three threads, he had told them, and there were many others such as treatment for exhausted soil, doctors travelling through mountain regions on horseback, teachers and a school in every village.

These words that he had spoken burned against his brain. They kept him awake at night long after Sapho had dropped asleep beside him, and he could not escape the searing. It was not that he had spoken beyond his own convictions. Moving through these mountain areas on horseback, he had seen for certain that, in a backward country such as this, political rights alone were as useless as tent poles without a tent. But could he be certain that Don Ricardo and his San Marcos Liberals had reached a similar conclusion?

He wanted to mention these doubts to Sapho, but when he talked with her, something held his thinking back. Fortunately, he worked day and night among the Xlalak horsemen and had little time to heed these hurting questions. Although he told himself that he would talk further with her, he had not done so when the Nacheetl runner came with Felipe Cuerno's summons.

Carlos had paused under an oak one day to watch a Xlalak blacksmith working. The Indian had a leaf from an auto spring which he was pounding into the shape of a cutlass blade. He worked fast, and it was a beautiful sight to see this crude band of metal leaping into its proper form beneath the hammer blows. Carlos took a mental inventory of the tools which the Xlalak had to use. The forge was merely an oversized charcoal brazier with sheepskin bellows attached. There was a rusty gasoline tin full of water; there were nippers with which the smith was holding his white-hot blade; finally, there were the hammer and the anvil, which was only a section of rail mounted on a stump.

Grinning broadly, the Xlalak stopped to wipe forehead and neck with a blackened rag. "This kind work makes very hot," he said in broken Spanish.

Carlos examined the metal blade with respectful caution. "You make a knife?" he asked.

The smith opened a cloth-wrapped bundle near his feet and drew out a finished cutlass that gleamed dangerously in the afternoon sunlight. Carlos grasped it by the hilt, sliced the air experimentally. It had an easy balance.

As he compared the completed weapon with the raw strip of metal lying on the anvil, Luis came up and touched him on the shoulder. "A messenger from La Cumbre brings important words," he said, motioning to an Indian runner waiting just behind.

The stranger spoke in breathless Nacheetl. "Felipe Cuerno, he says for Carlos Chichayan to come with me and go to a forgotten place near Santa Margarita. Felipe Cuerno, he says an old, old friend is waiting there. Felipe Cuerno, he says the Xlalak chieftain must also come."

The sun was low on the horizon before Carlos and El Casco were able to saddle their horses and get under way. As they rode down the trail from Pavón, Carlos could feel the warmth of fresh tortillas which Sapho had packed into saddlebags and slung across his pommel. The Nacheetl runner led the way on foot. Carlos came next, riding a Xlalak pony, and El Casco took up the rear.

Carlos was certain that the "old, old friend" was Don Ricardo, and as he gave free rein to his mountain pony, he considered the approaching reunion with a mixture of pleasure and uneasy speculation. He felt toward his former patron much of the affection that a son would feel for a father from whom he had long been separated; and perhaps it was for that very reason that certain doubts were now arising. His mental image of Don Ricardo was not a simple one, but a complex portrait of many different shadings. He saw a tall, broad-shouldered, black-bearded man of mental vigor and strong opinions. He saw also a series of genial, kindly lines that crinkled the corners of mouth and eyes. But those, as Carlos remembered, were lines that represented a personal warmth toward those with whom the judge shared common interests rather than any feeling of fellowship with all mankind.

Carlos could see etched on Don Ricardo's face a composite of faults and virtues which, because of his almost filial ties, were now the more excruciating. For the young Indian could not forget that within Don Ricardo's very house there had lived two kinds of people. He could not forget that the inner court had originally included himself as well as Pablo Larra and the blacksmiths and saddlers, the laundresses and maids, and all the other servants of the household, while the persons inside the house had been limited to Don Ricardo and his señora, to the young señorita and her brother, Don Juliano, to Father Timoteo who came to hear confessions, and to others who rode up in magnificent carriages or astride prancing horses and entered through the door in front.

As he rode along in the dusk, Carlos remembered how young Don

Juliano used to look at one with eyes that did not see, and he remembered the loneliness that had engulfed him when, hiding in a pepper tree, he had gazed through a window at Don Ricardo's massive table loaded with more food than he had seen in all the market place. He remembered also the waltzes and the tangoes playing, the polished, gleaming floor, the people laughing.

Most of all he remembered the people laughing. He shuddered as he seemed to hear them now. Yet they were far away in time, and the only real sounds were the clop-clop of hoofs in loose gravel and perhaps the far-off howl of a coyote prowling through the mesquite.

As the Nacheetl runner found a path through what seemed like a boundless sea of mesquite, Carlos gazed about him at the nighttime serenity of the great plateau. He reined in his horse until El Casco had ridden close. "Do you think that your people could learn to live in peace?" he asked.

The chieftain grunted softly. "True men are born to fight." He rolled a cigarette with expert fingers, placed it between his lips, and struck a wax-stemmed match. The flaring light glowed in the darkness and gleamed against the ivory butts of his half-concealed pistols.

The Nacheetl runner was waiting like an impatient bird dog. Carlos urged his horse along the trail, and no one spoke. Clouds hid all the stars tonight, and the darkness was oppressive. They made their way down into an arid country of buttes and dry washes fringed with chaparral, and from there they passed over onto the plateau proper where agave grew in extensive fields and tuna lined the trail. Carlos opened up his saddlebags and shared tortillas with El Casco and the Nacheetl runner.

It was a little after nine, Carlos judged, when their guide stopped near an organ cactus and pointed through the undergrowth. "The railroad is only there," he whispered in Nacheetl. "A certain farmhouse lies just beyond." He bent low and pushed cautiously through to the very edge of the right of way. There he paused, peering up and down the tracks.

Carlos could hear no sound but the steady, liquid hum of telegraph wires. In one direction the tracks were absolutely dark, but in the other he could see green lights of a semaphore and two gleams where the rails reflected. The Nacheetl slipped across the tracks, and the horsemen followed in file. The trail beyond the right of way was little more than a rabbit path, but after winding through a forest of tall and spiny cactus, it came to a pale fence that marked the edge of a clearing. Carlos could just make out the lines of a low adobe building fifty yards or so beyond.

As they rode across the clearing, Carlos caught a strong scent of horses in the nighttime air; a moment later his own pony whinnied softly, and another animal answered from somewhere near the adobe farm house. The Nacheetl runner guided them to a thatch-roofed shed where three horses were already tethered. El Casco slid to the ground and fastened his pony to an oak tree that stood a rod or so away, and Carlos did the same. Then they followed the Nacheetl toward the entrance to the house.

From out of the darkness came a short hiss. The Nacheetl answered with a few words in his native language. Carlos saw a doorway draped with a heavy poncho; a guerilla figure stood motionless in the shadows to one side. Carlos heard his name mentioned by the runner, and after that, the guard drew aside the curtain. Carlos and El Casco stepped over the threshold, and the poncho fell back into place. The Xlalak pressed against a wooden door; it opened into a white-washed room flooded with light shed by a gasoline lantern hanging from a rafter.

Three men sat near one end of a long board table, a map spread before them. One was young and dapper with sparkling eyes and a neatly clipped mustache; another was short and squat and florid-faced, a man of middle age in tailored riding habit. The third was Don Ricardo.

At first glance, Carlos thought that the judge had not changed much. Despite the surroundings, he wore his usual black sack coat with trousers to match. A trickle of sweat ran down each cheek and disappeared in his heavy beard. He looked up from his map and stared toward the door. As Carlos became accustomed to the brightness of the room, he saw a pair of gold-rimmed spectacles riding low on the bridge of the old man's nose. Carlos stepped forward, and Don Ricardo lowered his head in order to peer over his eyeglasses. The oddness of the movement struck Carlos, who remembered when the judge had boasted of his perfect vision.

The lantern overhead sputtered and flared and sent long shadows leaping. Recognition gleaming in his eyes, Don Ricardo rose from his bench, tugging at the spectacles as he greeted his former gate boy. Carlos seized the judge's extended hand. Still grasping the eyeglasses, Don Ricardo laid his other hand upon the younger man's shoulder and stood gazing with pride and wonder into the broad Nacheetl face. Carlos saw now that there were streaks of grey in the judge's hair and whiskers, that face lines had deepened into wrinkles, that the skin had lost its former olive lustre, had grown dull and dry.

He also noticed a dampness gathering in the corners of Don Ricardo's eyes, while his own throat felt a gripping tightness. Impulsively the judge drew Carlos close and enfolded him in a firm embrace.

2

THE LIME-WASHED ROOM of the farmhouse was cloudy with tobacco smoke, and Carlos felt a tension that reminded him of his railroading past when engineers and foremen had gathered for all-night poker sessions. There were seven men hunched about a rough-hewn, oblong table. The stout general was Ramírez, a local mine owner and commander-in-chief of militia, while young Captain de Mayo was serving as his aide-de-camp. They sat between Carlos and Felipe Cuerno. El Casco and Jorge Bronco had found places on the other side of the table.

Each of these might be clever in his own way, Carlos conceded, but Don Ricardo and Felipe Cuerno were playing the decisive cards tonight. They were sitting at opposite ends — a pair of crafty tacticians, stony-faced, shrewd, and calculating. The judge sat with his spine erect, head slightly lowered, and his beard was spread fanwise upon the whiteness of his shirt front. The gasoline lantern hanging above and a little behind one shoulder threw his profile in long relief upon the wooden table top.

At the other end, Felipe Cuerno presented a stocky and imperturbable figure in blue work shirt and leather jacket unbuttoned down the front. Now and then he paused in speaking to stroke his porcelain pipe. His unhurried manner and stubborn, peasant logic contrasted notably with Don Ricardo's more fluid demeanor, but it was too early to determine which one was likely to outwit the other. As Carlos watched them maneuver, he tried to piece together the reasoning behind each play, but already the game was moving fast and he was often left behind.

Each man knew through spies and other channels that Ronca had no intention of scotching early phases of their revolution; each man also knew that Ronca was banking heavily upon a split between them. Both recognized the fact that they were allies through mutual interest rather than common conviction; and neither forgot that the other, given a chance, would maneuver for his own advantage.

Carlos sought to appraise them both. What were Cuerno's chief objectives? There was no immediate way of knowing. The two Comunistas had been the last to arrive, having ridden into Santa Margarita in the cab of a slow freight, and Carlos had exchanged only a few brief words with Jorge Bronco, who wouldn't have divulged significant facts in any case.

Don Ricardo's intentions were somewhat clearer. Carlos had talked privately with the judge for nearly an hour before Cuerno's arrival, and during their discussion it had become clear to the younger man that years of exile had somewhat altered the viewpoints of his former patron. Leaving the stuffy farmhouse, they had sat down together on the tongue of a high-wheeled oxcart in the darkness of the clearing.

The judge, much disturbed by what he had seen and heard during conversations in New York and Washington, had sought to impress upon Carlos how small the world had grown and by what delicate threads the terrible new Yanqui bomb hung suspended over the heads of all mankind. Now, as the young Nacheetl watched each move in this all-night game of political poker, he kept hearing certain of Don Ricardo's words sounding loudly in his ears.

The world is going mad. Let me tell you, there are times when I feel no hope . . .

Don Ricardo looked up from a sheaf of papers which he had placed upon the table before him, peered over his gold-rimmed spectacles. "What is your plan for seizure of the city?" he asked Felipe Cuerno.

The Comunista unfolded a map of San Marcos for all to see. "My thought is that General Ramírez and his militiamen will seize the armory on the western edge of the city just at midnight on the tenth. From that point they will sweep eastward behind the main Ronquista defense line which roughly follows the river." He explained how this drive would be supported by two subsidiary attacks, one delivered by Comunista guerrillas, the other by Carlos and his Xlalak horsemen.

The Comunista assault battalions, he stated, would attack from the north, seizing the San Marcos railway station and the river bridge. These guerrilla troops would then be in a position to join the San

Marcos militiamen in their crucial attack upon the Castillo barracks.

Don Ricardo's eyes narrowed.

. . . The world divides itself into two opposing camps — Comunista and anti-Comunista. . . .

He faced General Ramírez. "Rudolfo, are your troops not strong enough to secure the city and seize El Castillo?"

The militiaman nodded. "Bastante!"

Now the judge turned to Felipe Cuerno.

. . . Many influential Yanquis have already lost faith in the United Nations and are urging preparations for a third great war. They even talk about dropping atomic bombs to preserve the world from Communism. . . .

"General Ramírez and his militiamen are capable and they know the city," Don Ricardo told the Communist leader. "I see no reason for your guerrillas to disperse themselves by crossing the river."

Carlos saw Felipe Cuerno meet the judge's gaze. For a long, still moment they stared at one another, and the hissing of the lantern was loud in the quiet of the farmhouse. Finally the Comunista tipped his head ever so slightly. "I assume that sole responsibility for securing El Castillo rests with General Ramírez."

The militiaman shifted on his bench, and Carlos noted pinhead beads of sweat oozing from his forehead.

Don Ricardo agreed. He was watching the Comunista closely.

. . . Men of science perfect deadly plagues for future warfare. Well, either side can start a holocaust, but neither side can win. . . .

"What is the next phase of your plan?" the judge asked Felipe Cuerno.

The Comunista sucked at the stem of his porcelain pipe. "Since the forces of General Ramírez are sufficient for securing the city, he will have no need of General Chichayan's cavalry."

Carlos was beginning to realize that his thousand horsemen had made him a political and military force which even such men as Don Ricardo and Felipe Cuerno were now concerned with. He felt a momentary surge of self-importance which he hastily sought to check.

General Ramírez cleared his throat. "I could use some horsemen."

Don Ricardo regarded Felipe Cuerno slyly.

. . . Many Yanquis claim that the whole fault lies with the Comunis-

tas, and perhaps it does. But whoever deserves the censure, no nation can absolve itself from seeking some solution. It is the duty of the Yanquis to discover a more positive crusade than anti-Comunismo, to do their overwhelming share toward achieving universal peace. . . .

"Cavalry, like artillery, is considered a supporting weapon," he told the Comunista.

Felipe Cuerno made no comment. The gasoline lantern was burning low. Jorge Bronco took it down from its nail and pumped the pressure up. There was a hiss of air, and the mantles turned hot and brightly white.

Replaced on its nail, the lantern swung slightly, causing shadows to leap across the room. "I suggest," Don Ricardo told Felipe Cuerno, "that a body of horsemen be attached to General Ramírez' command."

It was Carlos who now felt the Comunista's appraising inspection. Did Felipe Cuerno seek to stare him down? Carlos fastened his eyes upon those of the Comunista.

"Bueno!" Cuerno jotted notes in a pocket memorandum. "General Chichayan and one regiment of horse — less two troops — to be attached to General Ramírez' command — and to revert to my headquarters — upon seizure of El Castillo."

As a plan was thus worked out, detail by detail, Carlos began to understand more clearly how the game was being played. Both Don Ricardo and Felipe Cuerno knew that throughout early stages of revolt, Liberal and Comunista interests would remain almost identical; but both men also knew that the positions held by their respective forces when the fighting ceased might be determining factors in their relative post-revolutionary strength.

It was clear that Don Ricardo wanted no Comunista troops in the nation's capital, but Carlos was not yet sure why Felipe Cuerno had accommodated himself so quickly. Was the Comunista counting too much upon the loyalty of General Chichayan? The question troubled Carlos.

Meanwhile, a combat plan took form. In its final draft, the document included not only a detailed order of battle, but also a series of annexes dealing with supplies for both troops and civilian population, with prisoners, with codes, and with a hospital train for taking care of sick and wounded.

"We are short of nurses," Felipe Cuerno said, looking at Carlos. "Jorge Bronco tells me that your wife is capable. I want her on that train."

Although he raised no objection, Carlos felt secretly annoyed — just as he had when Felipe Cuerno first sent him off to work among the Xlalaks. Yet he knew that Sapho would choose to be aboard.

Military plans were eventually completed. Felipe Cuerno cleaned the bowl of his pipe, tamped it full of tobacco, and struck a match which he shielded with cupped palms. The initiative belonged to Don Ricardo.

. . . I have no serious objections to the Comunista goal, but I dislike the road they take and question whether it will lead them where they think. . . .

"A provisional government will be proclaimed," Don Ricardo promised, "as soon as the Viceregal Palace is in our hands. This will function until such time as a constitutional government can be effected." He outlined the policies which he intended to implement as long as he remained in power.

. . . I believe, however, that our real enemies are not Comunistas, but poverty, disease, ignorance, exploitation, and lack of food. . . .

While Don Ricardo described the sort of governmental machinery which he thought could best achieve the ends he sought, Carlos flicked a curious glance about the room. Perched expressionless upon his wooden bench, El Casco rolled a smoke with the fingers of his left hand, licked the paper, and inserted one end of the cigarette between slightly parted lips. Jorge Bronco was leaning back in his chair, studying the gasoline lantern. Felipe Cuerno puffed on his pipe with an air of serene contentment. Lieutenant de Mayo was absently polishing four fingernails against the lapel of his jacket, while General Ramírez stared sleepily at a knothole in the table top.

There was general agreement with Don Ricardo's plan of government, but when he spoke about politics, General Ramírez raised an objection. The judge wanted a progressive program which would include universal suffrage, an eight-hour day, the right to strike, free and universal education, a broad agrarian reform, and a degree of nationalization.

"What kind of nationalization?" General Ramírez demanded.

Don Ricardo peered over his spectacles. "The state should control
our railways," he said, "and the banking system, a few heavy industries,
foreign trade, perhaps."

The militiaman's mouth twitched about the corners. "You go too far,
Ricardo!"

Patiently Don Ricardo explained his reasons. "It will be easier to
begin right now," he said, "than to put these matters off until later."

"You'll never do it," General Ramírez warned. "The assembly will
see to that."

"This won't be Ronca's assembly," Don Ricardo reminded the
militiaman. "This will be a more progressive thing."

Felipe Cuerno pointed his pipe stem at Don Ricardo. "What is
your view in regard to oil?"

Oil! The word jerked the militiaman's attention toward Cuerno,
but Don Ricardo remained unperturbed, exhibiting only the most
casual interest, while El Casco, exuding smoke like a clay incense pot,
seemed not to have heard at all. Carlos waited for the judge to speak.

. . . *As the most powerful state in the world, the Yanquis are under
an obligation to wage through the United Nations an everlasting fight
against ignorance, poverty, disease, and inequality. Yet those who try
are always opposed by certain influential interests. . . .*

Don Ricardo uttered a single word. "Nationalization."

"When?" the Comunista leader asked.

The judge selected a brief from among his papers. "I have a crude
draft here," he said. He outlined a plan for arbitration with foreign
owners, a schedule of expropriation, and a bond issue scheme that
would indemnify the owners over a period of twenty years.

. . . *and for that reason, the Yanquis must accept a large degree of
leadership. No small nation is strong enough, unaided, to resist the
Prettymans. We, on the other hand, must restrict ourselves to lawful
processes . . .*

Don Ricardo cast a shrewd glance at Felipe Cuerno. "The success
of our whole program," he said, "requires rigid protection against
damage to foreign interests."

The Communist leader settled back, eyes half closed, as though he
were on the point of falling asleep.

"Foreign interests include Prettyman interests," Don Ricardo emphasized. "More specifically, they include the refineries and every oil well between La Cumbre and Santa Cruz."

The fire had died in Felipe Cuerno's pipe. He knocked the ashes out and cleaned the bowl with a bone-handled penknife. "You propose to expropriate by legal, peaceful means?"

Don Ricardo removed his spectacles and observed the Bolshevik intently. "I do."

A faint smile flickered across Felipe Cuerno's lips. "You think Mr. Prettyman will agree to that?"

For the first time that evening the judge appeared to hesitate. A train whistled far off down the tracks in the direction of San Marcos. The Comunista closed his knife with a snap and returned it to a jacket pocket. Don Ricardo was tapping the table top with his spectacles.

. . . We must use every lawful means to dislodge the Prettymans and abolish by parliamentary action the evils which the Comunistas attack with bolshevism. We must prove ourselves the champions of a true democracy. Therein lies our greatest strength. . . .

"We do the best we can," Don Ricardo stated. "In any case, we stay within the law."

Felipe Cuerno changed the subject. "What date do you set for an opening of the constituent assembly?"

"It is difficult to set a date," Don Ricardo countered. "Within six months, perhaps."

This failed to satisfy Felipe Cuerno. "My party stands for elections at the earliest moment possible."

Don Ricardo remained obscure. Immediately it occurred to Carlos that the Comunistas, with their superior organization and their influence within the Peasant League, would catch the Liberales at a disadvantage during an early election. This placed the judge in an embarrassing dilemma.

"It is widely known," Felipe Cuerno persisted, "that the Communist Party favors a democratic election just as soon as the machinery can be set up."

Carlos knew that the Comunista had won his point.

"As soon as practicable after organized resistance ceases," promised Don Ricardo.

The train whistle sounded closer. The Comunista leader rose and took a greasy railwayman's cap from a nail in the wall behind him. "How many provisional cabinet places can my party count upon?" he asked the judge abruptly.

Don Ricardo raised his eyes toward the rafters as though he were making careful calculations.

. . . Over the course of years, that system which best serves mankind will be the one to live. In the meantime, I intend to get along with the Comunistas as long as accommodation is possible. Unless . . .

There was an anxious doubt in the judge's eyes. "Labor and Agriculture, I think, are the only portfolios open."

Felipe Cuerno grunted. "An election would give us a stronger proportion," he maintained. "The Party expects War, Interior, and Labor."

Carlos could hear the puff and rattle of a freight train near at hand. Don Ricardo shook his head. "Labor and Agriculture — that is final."

The Comunista considered this. "We might make some sort of arrangement," he said, "if you guarantee Interior."

Don Ricardo shook his head.

Cuerno shrugged. "Bien, we'll arrange this matter when the moment comes."

When the Comunistas had left, Carlos and Don Ricardo stepped out into open air. Dawn was breaking, clouds burned red on the eastern horizon, and birds had already begun to chirp. The freight, having passed through Santa Margarita, was laboring on a distant grade. Don Ricardo stood near while Carlos saddled his pony. "Are the Comunistas strong," the judge asked in a guarded tone, "or does this Cuerno bluff?"

Carlos straightened the saddle on his horse's back, reached for a girth and cinched it tight. Then he faced the judge. "Far and wide, in every village, men and women are ready for revolt," he said. "Felipe Cuerno and his Comunistas know what these people want. That is where their strength is found."

The judge stood still, head bowed in sober thought. His face looked grey and tired in the dimness of early morning. "We must not allow this revolution to run wild," he warned. "If Felipe Cuerno gets too strong, we — " He stopped short as the door of the farm house opened. It was El Casco who waddled toward them on his gnomish legs.

Don Ricardo seized Carlos by the wrist. "I count on you!"

El Casco's pony whinnied. The Xlalak approached the animal, cooing softly. Carlos felt the pressure of Don Ricardo's fingers about his wrist. "Adiós, Carlos! Be careful, hijo!" There was deep affection in the old man's voice.

Carlos felt a heart-wrench as he watched the tall, slightly bent figure disappear within the farm house.

As soon as El Casco had saddled, he and Carlos mounted and set off toward the tracks and Pavón far beyond. The Xlalak grinned appreciatively as they rode along. "That Felipe Cuerno — what a precious stallion!"

3

TIME WAS RUNNING SHORT in the village of Pavón. When they had eaten one of El General's frequent meals, Carlos and El Casco rode out among the horsemen, moving from campfire to campfire, leaving directions with village chieftains. A week had passed since the meeting in Santa Margarita, and Sapho had already left to help equip the hospital train on a siding near La Cumbre. Since the day of her departure, final preparations had been completed at Pavón, and the Xlalaks were ready to start. For several hours one heard shouts and verses of endless songs, the whinnying of horses, the drum of galloping hoofs, and then, shortly after midnight, the horsemen began to move.

Astride his Xlalak pony, Carlos watched while El Casco rode out onto a ridge line where man and mount were outlined black against a star-filled sky. The chieftain threw back his head and gave a shout. "E-e-e-yah! I-la-ka Xlalak!"

From up and down the ravine, from far and wide upon the slopes came answering cries. "Bl'ao ka Xlalak!"

Carlos rode beside El Casco. He turned once to wave at El General, who stood torch in hand on the cobbled street in front of his house, feet apart, swaying drunkenly. The old man waved back, and Carlos distinguished a broad grin beneath the long black lock of hair that hid his eye and cheek. El Casco halted upon a barren promontory. The gentle, lower slopes of the Fire Mountain curved away below them, shadowy slopes covered with grasses and mimosa merging into mesquite far beyond. It seemed to Carlos that every bush came suddenly alive and moved away in the shape of a Xlalak horseman. Or had a mounted army risen out of the earth itself to ride away in the clear, bright night?

El Casco cooed softly to his pony. The animal sprang into motion and streaked off. Carlos rode close beside, and within a few moments they were parts of this gigantic movement toward Zapala and San Marcos beyond.

They travelled throughout the remaining hours of night, and when dawn broke, they were spread across the great plateau, a thousand horsemen — like the migration of a Mongol horde. During daylight hours they bedded down almost unseen among the mesquite and chaparral, and it was not until well after sunset that they began their final, sweeping arc around the western flank of San Marcos.

This second night was darker than the previous one had been and even peasants lighting ocote torches in their huts were scarcely aware of the mounted host that moved swiftly through agave fields and arroyos and cactus-studded pastures. In the blackness of night the thousand riders were merely shadows, and the only sounds they made were owl hoots and cricket chirps by which each village chief maintained contact with those he led.

Carlos and El Casco rode near together with a Nacheetl guide whom Felipe Cuerno had mounted and sent along to show the way. For Carlos it was a powerful experience to feel himself a part of this sinewy Xlalak legion. He sensed an invincible strength, as though all the men of the world were riding in a single body, seething, but under tight control.

They rode throughout the early hours of darkness, then turned southeast in the direction of San Marcos. Just before midnight the Nacheetl guide came out upon a rounded hilltop where a cold breeze from the Fire Mountain touched the brush and tuna. He pointed eastward, and with arm raised beneath his poncho, he looked like a mighty eagle with wing extended. "The Great City is there only," he told Carlos in Nacheetl, "a pipe smoke on ponies fast-fast running, and Chacala is halfway nearer."

Carlos translated this to El Casco. "We stay here a time," he said, "until redness rises in the sky above San Marcos."

There was not long to wait. Close against the earth there was first pink as though a charcoal brazier glowed, and the pinkness grew until it was a flaming bonfire licking at the dark. Carlos saw a jagged city skyline of buildings most of which had not existed when last he had seen the city.

He felt the muscles of his mountain pony tense between his knees. Under the lightest touch of spurs the animal sprang away and raced down open slopes in the direction of Chacala. Carlos reined in; it was too early for a gallop. El Casco moved close beside, and hard upon their backs came a thousand ponies, nervous, straining at their bits.

The redness above San Marcos was the vermillion of a brilliant sunrise, but the hour was midnight, and all the world on either side was sable black. Carlos guided his horse directly toward a blinding whiteness that lay in the very center of the redness. Chacala should be right in line.

They moved through fields of corn, pausing for ditches which the Xlalak ponies seemed to sense, and across a road, and within a few moments they broke out upon open, grassy ground which the Nacheetl guide identified as a drill field for the federal police. Carlos felt his pony dancing taut beneath him. "Now is the time," he told El Casco.

In his cup-like stirrups the chieftain rose, threw back his head like a bloodhound baying. "E-e-e-e-e-yah! I-la-ka Xlalak!"

From far and wide, out of the deepness of the night, came answering cries. "Bl'ao ka Xlalak!"

Carlos felt his pony gather tight, shoot forward like a coil spring released. Behind came a thousand Xlalaks, shouting, screaming, screeching, carbines swinging like clubs above their heads. Carlos charged across the field, El Casco close beside, and redness from the fires ahead gleamed bright on weapon barrels. I-la-ka Xlalak! Bl'ao ka Xlalak! Four thousand hoofs of hardness thudded on the sod.

Straight ahead Carlos saw long barracks buildings outlined against the redness. That was the constabulary. Just this side, a line of crackling fire drew itself across the field. On his right hand he saw the Nacheetl guide pitch sidewise from his saddle. The horse raced on, crowding close to Carlos' pony. From deeper in the darkness came the frightening scream of a wounded beast.

All across the field were little blinking lights, and as Carlos came upon them, he saw naked barrels just behind, fire streaking from their muzzles. There was a sandbag barricade, and now the machine guns were wicked serpents licking with tongues of red. Carlos ripped a hand grenade from his belt, pulled the pin, and listened briefly to the sizzling fuse. Rising in his stirrups, he heaved the missile and saw it blossom red just short of a gunner's face. The Ronquista sagged forward over his weapon. The top of his head was gone, the inside completely hollow. Another figure jumped to take his place.

The new gunner struggled desperately to raise his fire. Failing that, he jerked his machine gun out and backed away, gaping dumbly at the vastness of the horde that charged upon him. As Carlos cleared the barricade, the gunner dropped his weapon, turned, and fled for a horse that was waiting just behind. With one foot in its stirrup, the Ronquista folded up. The horse took fright and galloped off, dragging the rider by one leg.

That was all that Carlos saw, but up and down the line action was much the same. Behind the barricades was a field of wild confusion as troopers leaped astride their horses and galloped toward the city, a thousand Xlalaks in close pursuit.

The fleeing Ronquistas spread out, and soon the greater number were lost among the narrow streets and alleys of Chacala village. Carlos reined in close to El Casco, breathing further orders which the Xlalak screeched out for village chieftains to relay from mouth to mouth. The attacking horsemen pounded through Chacala and soon reached the outskirts of San Marcos where they fanned out across the Avenida and adjacent streets and courts and alleys.

Once within the city, Carlos heard shooting on every hand, and there was the crash of dynamite, and every now and then a wooden shack burst into a mass of fire. Great licks of flame reached high above the tallest buildings, and Carlos heard the crackle of burning wood, the thud of timbers. The redness was most intense over western fringes of the city, and soon a fog came down and held the smoke and heat and spread fumes and hotness through every street and alley, and soot drifted down like black snowflakes on the smooth pavements of the Avenida.

As Carlos rode with El Casco and a swarm of horsemen toward the plaza, he saw a dozen different mobs tramping through the streets. On all sides they charged and screamed and smashed gates of the largest houses along the Avenida. They set fires in the finest mansions, and no man was safe within his house or upon the streets unless he joined a gang.

Carlos and El Casco were moving slowly, now, blocked by senseless, maddened mobs. An old woman lurched out of a gutter. "Down with Ronca!" she screamed. "Gimme a knife and I'll cut his chestnuts out!"

A younger woman with matted hair and face streaked with blood thrust a flail into the old woman's hands. "Here you are, Mamita, go to it!"

The old one seized the flail. "I'll cut his chestnuts out! I'll —" Her eyes gaped wide as she was jostled close to El Casco's horse. "O-o-o-o! Xlalaks!" she rasped. Her eyes lighted on the hoof-like feet. "The devil himself!" With a scream of terror, she dropped her flail and scurried for the nearest alley.

Riding through the frenzied mob was like bucking a stream with all its eddies and many currents. Up and down the Avenida mobs stampeded by the light of a hundred conflagrations, beating their way into the largest houses, killing every living creature they came upon. Through smashed in doorways they dragged their victims out and kicked or burned or strangled according to the moment's fancy. Here they seized a woman in her gown of whitest lace, there, a child with a doll hugged close. A pointing finger and the word Ronquista were a stroke of death.

"Down with Ronca!" They burned a church. "Down with Ronca!" They ripped off clothes. "Down with Ronca!" They slit a throat. "Down with Ronca!" They bashed a head against the nearest adobe wall. "Down with Ronca!" They slaughtered a priest. "Down with Ronca!"

As Carlos and the Xlalaks came closer to jagged buildings that marked the center of San Marcos, they saw fighting of another sort. Here were guerrilla assault squads working southeastward, block by block, shooting, blasting, killing from door to door, and when they saw the horsemen, they raised a shout.

Siren screaming, a touring car sped down a side street, and turned into the Avenida with a squeal of tires. The top was down, and hanging to the sides and hood were stiff-faced men with pistols and scorpion brassards. "Ronquistas!" screamed a ragged beggar, and with nothing but a pitchfork he charged the speeding car. He was left behind. Out of an alley came a Xlalak horseman at full gallop, and for a brief second he moved beside the car. With pointed teeth he pulled the pin of a hand grenade and dropped it neatly into the back seat. A Ronquista fired. The Xlalak folded up and slid slowly off his horse. Simultaneously a cloud of smoke blossomed in the touring car. The vehicle careened wildly and smashed against a lamppost where it crumpled into a mass of black and twisted steel splattered with blood and strips of skin and flesh.

In the center of the Avenida a riderless pony nuzzled the body of its master, whinnying softly.

4

A RIFLE SHOT smashed the nighttime silence. It was followed by a crash of exploding dynamite. Magdalena stirred, cold and cramped within the smallness of the empty keg where she had curled up to sleep. She poked her head out the open end and stared about the muddy wineshop yard.

A hideous shout was raised in the direction of the market place, and Magdalena heard the scrape of leather sandals running on sandstone flags. Curiosity aroused, she eased her arthritic body out of the night's hiding place, climbed upon her feet, and moved with painful steps toward a small and dirty square that flanked the far side of the wineshop.

The sky above the city seemed strangely red, and even the narrow alley where she staggered was dimly lit. She felt sick, and blood kept flooding through the channels of her head. There was a fountain in the square; if only she could reach it, she could drink the water and douse her neck and temples. Moving with shaky steps, she was about to leave the alley when she stopped abruptly. The square was filled with mounted horsemen.

She leaned weakly against the wineshop wall. Men in powder-blue uniforms were tightening saddle girths while their horses watered. She saw that they were troopers and that they had strewn the cobblestones beneath their feet with discarded crusts of bread and salmon tins. Magdalena crouched forward and watched, trembling with hunger and excitement. Impatiently she listened to a click of caulks upon the pavement, a squeak of saddle leather, the soft chuckles and o-o-o-o-o! o-o-o-o-o! of troopers cooing to their mounts.

Someone snapped an order, and by two's and three's the men swung into their saddles and clattered out of the square. Magdalena stumbled forward, pounced upon a crust of bread, and squatted there in mud and horse manure, eating ravenously. Finding food was easy. There were biscuits and lumps of chocolate scattered about. When she had stuffed her mouth, she scrambled on hands and knees to the fountain's edge and drank from the trough in deep gulps.

Soon her stomach grew heavy. As soon as she had gathered all the remaining food into her rebozo, she picked up a cigarette butt, leaned back against the fountain, and smoked, drawing deep drafts. When the stub was too short to hold, she skewered it upon a sliver and continued to inhale until the paper fell apart and the remaining strings of tobacco dribbled down her blouse.

She ran her tongue back and forth across her lips, discovering a salty taste left by the cigarette. She felt drowsy. The city was quiet, now, and she snoozed a little until a hunchbacked beggar woman came to drink. Magdalena stirred.

The beggar woman straightened up from the trough, water dripping down her pointed chin. "Pues, there comes a revolution," she grumbled, "and you lie there and sleep."

, Magdalena found another cigarette butt and lighted it. The hunchback poked about until she had one, too. "What is this revolution people talk about?" Magdalena grunted. "My anca, they are all the same."

Something in the beggar woman's throat wheezed whenever she took a deep breath. "Not this one, dearie! This is Comunista."

Magdalena hawked and spat. "There is no difference. This talk of revolution is only belly wind."

The hunchback made a hissing sound like air escaping from a tire. "Don't stuff me with your stinking beans, precious. The Comunistas have armed the poor folk. Men and women are coming right up out of the ground like ants, and they've all got guns. I'll bet I could get a gun if there was a Comunista hereabouts."

Magdalena pinched her nostrils between thumb and forefinger. "The troopers will make a stop," she snorted. "I saw them leave."

The old woman screwed herself into a more comfortable position against the wall. "Ho-ho!" she cackled. "This is a beginning only. The militia is fighting in the city, too. They help the Comunistas."

"It makes no difference," Magdalena insisted. "They will be the same as Ronca."

The hunchback stuck into her mouth the few strands of tobacco that were left from her butt. "Not those Comunistas! They'll make life a thing to live. No more rich men, sabe, and no more beggars. Pues, a man will stuff his belly, then. I'll grab me a big house on the Avenida and eat hot beans for break — "

A crackle of rifle fire drowned her out. She snuggled against Magdalena like a pus-eyed kitten. "Oh, those Comunistas, dearie, the music of their shooting." She giggled in her excitement, and as the shooting sounded closer, she wobbled to her feet and danced to and fro, cackling to herself and wheezing. Magdalena heard hoofbeats of horses galloping, and a trooper spurred through the square in the direction of the shooting. Three more followed, one behind the other. Almost in their tracks came a careening sedan with a Ronquista action squad clinging to the sides. The firing was in La Calle de las Mujeres sector.

"It will stop soon enough," Magdalena predicted. "There will be no — "

A rattle of small-arms fire came from the direction of the river. The hunchback grinned, baring her gums. "Those police, they will have a busy time, and the soldiers, too. Many little fires, dearie, in a field of dead grass. Oh, those Comunistas, those precious foxes!" She spun around and around in a circle, fluffing out her ragged skirt until it ballooned about her. "Give me a gun, pues, give me a stick!" she screamed. "Give me a big old cobblestone. I'll whale those Ronquistas. E-e-e-e-e-yah, let's go fight! Let's get into the fracas! Vámonos!" She bolted into a westward-pointing alley like a hungry rat, and Magdalena, forgetting her aches, followed.

The whole city was red with firelight. People were streaming out of their rickety dwellings into the streets, men, women, children, and they were waving sticks and stones and screaming and smashing windows and lamps as they charged madly through the streets.

"I'll whale those Ronquistas," the old woman gasped as they scrambled along. "I'll find me a big old house some place and I'll smash in the gates. I'll find me a soft, white bed, and I'll get in naked and wallow in it."

They were close to La Calle de las Mujeres when a bullet whined close above their heads and scared them down upon their bellies.

There was more shooting, and a trooper galloped back toward the Plaza, and after him came a mob with sticks and scythes and rocks and fish spears, and they were mad to kill. They swept along and gathered Magdalena in, and the hunchback, too, and they were like molten lava pouring through the streets and alleys.

Magdalena felt her heart pumping new strength through her body and legs and arms, and it flowed like raw whiskey to her toes and finger tips. "E-e-e-e-yah! Down with Ronca!" The mob swept her into the Plaza and beyond the Prettyman building around which platoons of militiamen had formed a protective cordon. Magdalena was like a stick of driftwood carried along by the current, and since there was no need to think or to make decisions, she opened her mouth and yelled and longed to get a grip on something that she could tear apart and scatter on the ground.

The mob flowed toward the cathedral. "Patria! Familia! Iglesia-a-a-a!" someone shouted. "Down with Ronca-a-a-a-a!"

"Kill the bishop!" piped a squeaky voice. "Castrate him! Burn the cathedral!"

Magdalena found herself near the head of the crowd, and there were the cathedral steps straight in front. Sudden anger gathered in her breast as she remembered herself sitting there on the steps in warm sunlight when first she had become a beggar. On that day a young priest had smiled and had given her a peso. That was the beginning. "Kill the bishop!" she screamed.

Her shrivelled body felt drunk with fury as she remembered how she had come back with her enchilada to find a beggar woman squatting on the cathedral steps. "Kill the bishop!" Magdalena panted.

She pushed ahead of the crowd, reached the steps, and began to climb. Her hair lay tangled about her shoulders, and her mouth was a tight-drawn slit. She remembered now the sharp bite of bitterness that had come as the young priest blessed the hag. "Kill the bishop!" she shrieked.

Magdalena was a rod ahead of the crowd and halfway up the steps when a very old and white haired man appeared on the threshold of the cathedral. "I am the bishop," he said gently. "What do you want with me?" Magdalena stopped where she was. The old man standing before her was Father Timoteo.

⁀aight at Magdalena with soft, reproachful eyes. "What
⁀t with me?" he asked again.

⁀alena shrank away. Overcome with shame and terror, she
⁀ed to escape from Father Timoteo's eyes, to lose herself in the
crowd behind her. But the mob, hearing these soothing words of the
bishop, had already fallen back, and Magdalena was left alone upon
the cathedral steps.

The old man moved forward a yard or two. The red glow of burning buildings suffused his face, and a light breeze ruffled the whiteness of his hair. "Won't you come in?" he asked. "The door of God's
house is ever open for those who knock."

Magdalena felt a tightness below the base of her spine as though
shame were crushing her. Like a frightened beast, she broke and ran,
scuttling through the scattered crowd.

There was more shooting, and a trooper galloped back toward the Plaza, and after him came a mob with sticks and scythes and rocks and fish spears, and they were mad to kill. They swept along and gathered Magdalena in, and the hunchback, too, and they were like molten lava pouring through the streets and alleys.

Magdalena felt her heart pumping new strength through her body and legs and arms, and it flowed like raw whiskey to her toes and finger tips. "E-e-e-e-yah! Down with Ronca!" The mob swept her into the Plaza and beyond the Prettyman building around which platoons of militiamen had formed a protective cordon. Magdalena was like a stick of driftwood carried along by the current, and since there was no need to think or to make decisions, she opened her mouth and yelled and longed to get a grip on something that she could tear apart and scatter on the ground.

The mob flowed toward the cathedral. "Patria! Familia! Iglesia-a-a-a!" someone shouted. "Down with Ronca-a-a-a-a!"

"Kill the bishop!" piped a squeaky voice. "Castrate him! Burn the cathedral!"

Magdalena found herself near the head of the crowd, and there were the cathedral steps straight in front. Sudden anger gathered in her breast as she remembered herself sitting there on the steps in warm sunlight when first she had become a beggar. On that day a young priest had smiled and had given her a peso. That was the beginning. "Kill the bishop!" she screamed.

Her shrivelled body felt drunk with fury as she remembered how she had come back with her enchilada to find a beggar woman squatting on the cathedral steps. "Kill the bishop!" Magdalena panted.

She pushed ahead of the crowd, reached the steps, and began to climb. Her hair lay tangled about her shoulders, and her mouth was a tight-drawn slit. She remembered now the sharp bite of bitterness that had come as the young priest blessed the hag. "Kill the bishop!" she shrieked.

Magdalena was a rod ahead of the crowd and halfway up the steps when a very old and white haired man appeared on the threshold of the cathedral. "I am the bishop," he said gently. "What do you want with me?" Magdalena stopped where she was. The old man standing before her was Father Timoteo.

He looked straight at Magdalena with soft, reproachful eyes. "What do you want with me?" he asked again.

Magdalena shrank away. Overcome with shame and terror, she hoped to escape from Father Timoteo's eyes, to lose herself in the crowd behind her. But the mob, hearing these soothing words of the bishop, had already fallen back, and Magdalena was left alone upon the cathedral steps.

The old man moved forward a yard or two. The red glow of burning buildings suffused his face, and a light breeze ruffled the whiteness of his hair. "Won't you come in?" he asked. "The door of God's house is ever open for those who knock."

Magdalena felt a tightness below the base of her spine as though shame were crushing her. Like a frightened beast, she broke and ran, scuttling through the scattered crowd.

5

CLOSE TO THE PLAZA a fluid, jostling mob gathered Magdalena in as an amoeba might enfold a particle. Here she felt safe from the soft, reproachful eyes of Father Timoteo, safe even from God and María Madre and Jesucristo, too. Gradually she lost her shame in the excitement and adventurous anticipation which had seized the crowd.

A rattle of drums sounded from near the market place. Rrr-tat, rrr-tat, rrr-tat-tat-tat! Magdalena fought her way through a mass of pushing, sweating bodies. As she came to a curbing, the crowd raised a shout, and a column of guerrillas swung into the square. They were peasants in white shirts and pantalones, and their straw sombreros were high, and the rims were broad. These men were barefooted, like most other peasants, but they carried rifles that gleamed in the sunlight. Bandoliers of shiny ammunition were about their chests, while clusters of hand grenades hung from every belt.

Rrr-tat, rrr-tat, rrr-tat-tat-tat. They cared nothing for the crowd, these guerrillas! Magdalena gasped to see how they swept into the Plaza, how the mob parted, how small boys scampered!

Rrr-tat, rrr-tat, rrr-tat-tat-tat! Men and women and children stumbled back upon the curbing while others pressed forward to watch. Magdalena peered and craned while squad upon squad of silent, white figures marched across the fire-lit plaza. The rhythmic pad of feet, an occasional scrape of sandal leather, the rattle of rifle bolts made her forget Father Timoteo altogether, made her squeal with new excitement. She felt a glorious welling in her throat, a tingle up and down her spine.

"Viva!" screamed a man in baker's coat and apron. "Viva los Comunistas!" Others took up the shout.

Rrr-tat, rrr-tat, rrr-tat-tat-tat! The column passed through the plaza, headed toward the railroad station. Simultaneously another column appeared from the university quarter. There were peasants and railway hands in sooty caps and students and grey-haired men who might have been professors. There were women in long skirts and bright rebozos, each with a rifle on her shoulder, each with grenades or a bottle of gasoline fastened to her belt.

Rrr-tat, rrr-tat, rrr-tat-tat-tat! The columns turned into the Street of the Holy Saints of the Cross. "Comunistas!" cried a voice. "Viva los Comunistas de San Marcos!" Magdalena felt the rhythm of drums pulsing through her body, and she wanted to cry. Unable to bear longer the excitement and pain and excruciating joy, she leaped from the crowd and attached herself to the end of the column. "Vámonos!" she screamed. "Let's go, amigos, let's go!"

Rrr-tat, rrr-tat, rrr-tat! Magdalena was old, and the pace was fast, but the drums were like tequila on a dark, cold day. She marched along, straight as she had been when she was young. Her shoulders were back, and her chin was high, and there was music in the cadence of her feet. The column marched down the full length of the Street of the Holy Saints, crossed the bridge, and turned in at the railway station.

There were five or six trains upon the sidings, and each had a locomotive with steam up, and guerrilla troops were loading. Men with rifles slung across their shoulders were shouting orders. Many of them wore greasy, railroad caps, while others were peasants and oilfield workers. One guerrilla seized Magdalena's arm. "Where's your rifle, Mamacita? Pues, go get one quick, over there upon the truck!"

As Magdalena seized a rifle and bandolier, she saw a long freight back onto a siding straight in front. A guerrilla officer snapped an order, and squad by squad the men and women began swarming over the sides of waiting cars. Magdalena grasped the rungs of an iron ladder and scrambled aboard. The car was already jammed with peasant soldiers. She sank into a corner, heart pounding, head weak and dizzy.

An old man with a purple birthmark across one cheek was crowded opposite, and he was watching her from beneath the brim of his straw sombrero. Shortly he unslung a gourd from about one shoulder and offered her a drink. "A bit of fire," he suggested, "to warm the belly."

She gulped down a mouthful of the burning liquid. It oozed through her veins to the tips of fingers and toes, and a great, warm glow settled in her stomach. A flush spread across her face, and gradually her tongue began to loosen. "Oh, what a great gladness!" she exclaimed to the man with the purple birthmark. "You cannot imagine."

"It is a small thing," he told her, "for one who carries such a heavy load of tiredness. E-e-e-e-yah, see, the engine is spitting fire. Now, I think, it gathers strength."

"Where goes the train?" Magdalena asked.

"Why, to fighting, of course," he told her, "somewhere down Cocamba way."

A pixy-faced boy peered over the old man's shoulder. "Eh, Tomás, you have got yourself a woman for sleeping with tonight!"

Tomás seized the boy by the hair and pulled good-naturedly. "No, no, Manuel, I give her a tiny drink only."

"Ah, then perhaps she'll sleep with me!" Manuel teased.

Magdalena spat. "Never with the likes of you."

Manuel looked hurt. "Oh, Mamita! Why not with me, Mamita?"

She eyed him scornfully. "Because the sap does not run yet, I think."

"Ho, Mamita! E-e-e-e-e-e-e-e-yah! Mamita!"

Tomás chuckled. "Then how about me?" he asked. "Will you take an old oak, Mamita?"

Magdalena observed him critically. "You have no woman?"

"I have no woman, Mamita."

"Then I sleep with you tonight!"

Ho, Mamita! E-e-e-e-e-e-e-e-e-e-yah! Mamita!

Magdalena squirmed about until she was close to the old man with the birthmark, and she nestled against his shoulder where the rifle sling crossed, and she let her head fall against his discolored cheek. "I am Magdalena," she said.

"And I am Tomás!" He moved an arm about her scrawny waist and seized one of her hands in a knotty fist. "What a precious revolution, Mamita, what a magnificent revolution!"

The crowd in the freight car roared approval.

Ho, Mamita! E-e-e-e-e-e-e-e-e-yah! Mamita!

The crowd roared, and Tomás raised a closed fist in reply, and at that moment the engine lurched forward, coughing and spitting, and its wheels spun on slippery rails, seeking a grip.

A cry went up and down the train. "Vámonos! Vámonos!"

Forward in the engine cab the firebox door was open, and the flames inside lighted the sooted face of the fireman and cast a red glow over stacks of wood in the tender.

"Vámonos! Vámonos!"

Slowly the train pulled out of the yards, and it rattled away through fields of agave, past meadows fenced with cactus, across a bridge of steel.

Lying close against Tomás, Magdalena felt warm and secure, and she watched the lights of San Marcos recede, and she was not afraid even in the darkness of the night.

Later on a bright moon broke through the clouds, lighting the valley, and Magdalena saw the silvery slopes of the Fire Mountain far away behind, and there were patches of stars here and there across the sky. She heard Tomás humming softly.

Jerkily the train rattled away to the southeast. It passed through Palo Negro and through Salinas, and men came down to the tracks with their wives and children to watch the train, and they shouted and waved and tossed their hats in the moonlight. "Viva!" they screamed. "Viva la revolución!"

Magdalena fell asleep, and when she awoke, the engine was laboring up a moderate grade, and she looked over the edge of the freight car, and down below was a loop of track, and the rails shone bright in the moonlight.

Tomás was singing a song that he had made.

> O, Mamita!
> Sleep with me tonight.
> O, Mamita!
> Sleep with me tonight.
>
> Rest your head upon my shoulder,
> Dream awhile 'til we grow bolder.
>
> O, Mamita!
> Sleep with me tonight.
> O, Mamita!
> Sleep with me tonight.

A brakeman, perched atop a box car directly behind, heard the song and liked it, and he added verses of his own. Brakes squealed on the downgrade, and couplings rattled. Magdalena snuggled back against Tomás and pulled his serape close about her as she listened to his song.

XII. Roadfork

SIMPLE FOLK who screamed and smashed and burned and killed looked upward toward the sky and saw an angry sun born between eastern hills. Daylight spread across the city, and each mobbing man and woman and child despised the thing that he had done and crept back into his quarters to avoid seeing. Whole families huddled in their dingy living places, ashamed of the blood upon their hands, terrified of the punishment which might be wreaked upon them. But while these ordinary folk were hiding away, trained guerrilla squads of men and women pushed southwestward through the city, fighting from block to block, from house to house, driving Ronquista lines before them.

Later that morning when the frightened ones began to venture forth, they saw the market place and central plaza pocked with machine gun nests. Wide-eyed, they dallied in near-by alleys to gape at guerrilla gunners in peasant blouses and blood stained pantalones, at peasant guards with carbines slung and clusters of hand grenades dangling like hard, green pineapples from every belt.

Strange rumors passed from lip to lip among the watchers, and even while these simple folk were whispering, they heard a clatter of hoofs along the Avenida as Xlalak horsemen swept toward the center of San Marcos. They swept in from Chacala, these horsemen, jaunty and fierce on wiry mountain ponies, and they rode into the market place and plaza with carbines glittering. Great, lanky horsemen, they were, with heads held high. Great, lanky, magnificent horsemen with sombreros at a tilt! Great, lanky, fearless horsemen with lariats around the pommels! Great, lanky, terrifying horsemen with teeth filed, with cruel spurs upon their boots.

The people gathered in alleys in suspicious groups, passing rumors

from lip to lip. E-e-e-yah! Those Xlalaks . . . they swept into the
valley, those Xlalaks . . . down from the Fire Mountain, those Xlalaks
. . . with teeth filed, those Xlalaks . . . screaming, yelling, a thousand
riding . . . two thousand riding . . . a thousand thousand riding . . . and
the devil leading . . . Chichayan leading . . . El Casco leading . . . the
devil . . . Chichayan . . . El Casco . . .

E-e-e-e-yah! The Xlalaks rode into the plaza before the very eyes
of all and spread out across the city in groups according to the villages
from which they came. There they were — great, lanky, fearful men
just as the rumors said. They slid to the ground, unsaddled their
horses, watered them and fed them grain. They kindled fires in streets
and courts and alleys. They unlashed pouches of jerked mutton from
their pommels and roasted the meat over open flames, singing strange
songs while they worked.

Rumors travelled faster, now. E-e-e-e-yah! Those Xlalaks . . . they
swept into the valley, those Xlalaks . . . they killed a thousand Ronquistas, those Xlalaks . . . they raped a thousand nuns, those Xlalaks
. . . they filled fat gourds with babies' blood, those Xlalaks . . . they —

Two of the lankier, more fearful-looking Xlalaks were talking to the
Chief of Kalshayu who had built a fire near the bandstand in the
plaza. They spoke rapidly, excitedly, in their native language, both
at once, illustrating with many gestures. Gradually the old chief grew
visibly interested, leaning forward with sparkling eyes. "E-e-e-e-yah!"
he exclaimed. "Can that be so!"

Something in the Chief's tone caught the attention of El Casco,
who was sharing a near-by fire with Carlos. "What goes on?" he asked.

The Chief of Kalshayu explained in a flood of Xlalak. The other two
horsemen nodded continual agreement, pointing again and again at an
unguarded building that lay across the plaza from the Prettyman
structure. It was a new block of steel and concrete, eight or ten
stories in height, an office building, Carlos judged, or perhaps a bank.

El Casco chuckled. "These two men went into that place with their
village chief," he explained to Carlos. "There was a great big bird
cage just inside. The doors were all shiny gold. They went in and
found a row of knobs like teats on a sow. They pushed one button
and the door went bang shut and whoosh! up they went toward the
sky!"

The two horsemen grinned and jabbered, and one of them poked a forefinger upward. Carlos barely paid attention. Bored with this inaction, he was thinking up a reason for visiting Don Ricardo's headquarters — with the hope of finding Sapho.

"They went up fast-fast," El Casco interpreted, "and the floor pressed hard against the feet. Zup! They pushed another knob, and the cage fell down, while the stomach kept going toward the sky."

The Chief of Kalshayu gave El Casco a hopeful look. "I have heard such tales before," he admitted, "but I have never seen." It was clear enough that the old man was aching to ride an elevator. The horsemen were talking more rapidly than ever, gesticulating toward the building which housed this monstrous thing. The expression on the old man's face grew almost beseeching.

El Casco winked at Carlos. "Go see about this cage," he told the Chief of Kalshayu. "Look carefully so that you may tell me whether these men speak the truth."

The old chief jumped to his feet with boyish excitement and set off as fast as his knotty, bowed old legs would carry him. El Casco nudged Carlos. "In two-three hours I'll send a messenger to bring the old one back!"

Impatiently Carlos switched his gaze about the plaza. One noticed many changes after five years of absence. There was a new department store with wide show windows and a low arcade; there was a fireproof garage advertising the quick repair of "los flats"; there was a drugstore with chromium fountain fixtures and an enormous "hayscrim" sign; the Gran Hotel San Marcos had its name inscribed in neon tubes across its medieval front. There was the new Cine Jolliwood. These were strange sights made stranger by the fact that the buildings were all deserted, the windows smashed, the signs spotted with bullet holes. Only the Prettyman structure remained untouched, safe within its militia cordon.

Squatting near his fire, El Casco was watching Carlos. "That Felipe Cuerno!" he mused. "What a precious fox!"

Carlos glanced at the Xlalak curiously. "Why?"

El Casco shrugged indifferently, but Carlos guessed his thoughts. It was clear enough why Felipe Cuerno had been quite willing to keep his La Cumbre troops on the northern side of the river. Even

now guerrilla squads were setting up new machine-gun nests and
sandbag barricades about the plaza, and Carlos was certain that they
were not untrained. He suspected that Communist leaders, fore-
seeing a spontaneous uprising within the city, had taken pains to
organize and arm a small, tough army of laborers and peasants among
the alleys and slum courts of San Marcos.

The Xlalak chieftain took a chicken wing from his saddle bags,
skewered it on a stick, and held it low over a patch of coals. "Felipe
Cuerno understands how the poor man thinks," he said. "He also
knows how an empty belly feels. I like that."

Carlos was forced to admit that the Communist leader had snatched
a very real political advantage from the lap of the Liberales. For
Don Ricardo had been counting upon the influence which his militia
would wield as sole military force within the city. What would he
think when he saw these lean, ragged, well-trained assault squads
of alley and market place?

El Casco chuckled. "Don Ricardo thought he could win the revolution for his kind of people only," he said gleefully, "but you can't stop
a hungry gopher by stuffing up his hole. He just comes out somewhere
else."

Carlos ignored this comment. He knew by now that the Xlalak
chieftain had not missed a single move during that night of maneuver-
ing in the farm house near Santa Margarita. Sitting there on his bench
like a brown clay image, El Casco had seen each shift of eye, each
fleeting mouth expression, and from these observations and from the
talk he had heard, the Xlalak had formed his own opinions of Don
Ricardo and Felipe Cuerno and what each stood for. For these very
reasons Carlos was not anxious to discuss the Comunista or the judge
with the Xlalak leader.

El Casco pulled a burning twig out of the fire and applied the hot
end to the back of a spider that was crossing his knee. "Don Ricardo
has never had an empty belly," he observed as the hairy legs of the
spider quivered and shrivelled tight against the body sac. "Felipe
Cuerno has."

Carlos was watching the approach of a militia officer who had
crossed the plaza from the Prettyman building. Sunlight gleamed
sharply on the insignia that marked each shoulder. "Don Ricardo has
suffered much," Carlos said.

El Casco tossed the twig away. He was still holding the chicken close against a bed of coals, and the flesh was brown and sizzling.

The militiaman paused a few steps off; obviously he was searching for someone. He examined Carlos casually. "Tell me, hombre, where does one find General Chichayan?"

When Carlos made himself known, the officer hesitated. Carlos showed his commission papers signed by Don Ricardo. The militiaman saluted awkwardly, handed over a folded dispatch. "A message for General Chichayan," he said. "It came by phone from General Cervantes."

Carlos dismissed the officer as soon as he had read the note. "I go to see Don Ricardo now," he told El Casco. He approached his pony and began tightening up the saddle girths. Over the animal's back he could see the militiaman picking his way among lounging Xlalaks, and machine gun squads still busily digging up the face of the plaza.

With a wave in the direction of El Casco, Carlos mounted and set off toward the Street of the Holy Saints of the Cross. As soon as he had left the plaza he became aware of a morbid silence which seemed to have settled down over the greater part of the city. Except for guerrillas, there were few persons upon the streets. Now and then a band of ragged urchins might venture out of an alley, half terrified at prospects of the dangers which they had set out to find. But the crowds which Carlos remembered were not in sight today.

He missed the songs and shouts of vendors, the hoof-tramp of burros, the shuffle of heavily laden peasants on their way to market. It was as though a half of the population had taken sick and died of plague while the other half lay hidden away in fright.

Shops up and down the street had been looted during the night, but most were deserted now except for an occasional guerrilla pawing through the wreckage. Carlos was amused by the trophies which appealed to these peasant soldiers. This one straggled toward the plaza with strips of red ribbon streaming from his sombrero; that one toted a chamberpot and four brass knobs torn from a bedstead; a third was dragging a display dummy out of a half-wrecked tailor shop.

The skeleton of a burned-out sedan lay smoking in a gutter. As Carlos rode near, he heard a scrape of metal from within the framework. A ragged urchin had climbed inside and was tearing out whatever shiny contraption happened to meet his fancy. It occurred to Carlos that this gamin was not much different from the Pepillo that he had known so many years ago.

He urged his horse along, impatient to reach the station where Don Ricardo was and where he hoped to find the hospital train with Sapho on it. Within a few moments the hoof beats of his pony were sounding hollow on the river bridge. Standing in his stirrups, he saw that a company or more of militia had set up a perimeter around the railroad station, while freight yards beyond were swarming with guerrilla guards.

At the northern end of the bridge a militia sentry halted horse and rider. As Carlos reached for his papers, a guerrilla guard approached and challenged the militiaman's authority. This brought about a violent argument in Spanish mixed with San Marcos Nacheetl. Three more militiamen appeared, crowding around the guerrilla, their bayonets fixed.

Finding himself surrounded, the guerrilla hailed a comrade from near the station. The newcomer was a grimy-faced railwayman; Carlos noticed that he carried an automatic barely peeping from a shoulder holster. "Qué pasa?" demanded the grimy-faced one. He was examining Carlos with quick black eyes.

Once more Carlos showed his papers.

The guerrilla jerked his head in the direction of the station. "Pase!"

But the militia guard blocked his passage, calling, meanwhile, for his sergeant, who immediately appeared with a lieutenant to reinforce him. There were more explanations and another show of papers. A purplish tinge showed on the officer's face when he saw the name on Carlos' commission papers. "Do you know who this is?" he stormed at the guerrilla guard. "This is General Chichayan. He is on Don Ricardo's staff."

The guerrilla with the automatic interrupted sharply. "My guard did as he was told, Lieutenant, just as yours did."

The militia officer turned contemptuously. His eyes noted the railwayman's cap, the grimy face, the automatic peeping from under the left shoulder. "And who are you?"

"I am Colonel Duro," the guerrilla stated. He touched an insignia pinned carelessly to his railwayman's cap. "Come along," he said to Carlos. "I'll take you to Don Ricardo."

As they left the bridge, Carlos inquired about the hospital train.

"Felipe Cuerno took it down the Cocamba tracks," Duro told him. "Six trains of guerrillas started before dawn for La Trinidad. They seek to stop the retreat of Ronca."

A throaty beep-beep sounded close behind, and the pony shied. Carlos turned to see a tawny limousine with its nose pointed toward the station. The vehicle slid smoothly by as soon as the road was clear. Carlos watched it approach the depot and stop near a baggage platform. "Who is that?" he asked Colonel Duro.

The guerrilla's eyes remained fastened upon the limousine. "Every man in San Marcos knows that car," he said. "Surely you have heard of Frank Nash, amigo!"

2

CARLOS, DON RICARDO, General Ramírez, Frank Nash — they were hunched over a table in the ticket office of the railroad station, a map spread before them. There was a second table in a far corner where Don Ricardo's telegrapher crouched over a key. The clickety-click of his instrument sounded loud above the low, worried voices of those who studied the map. It was growing clear to Carlos that the revolution had leaped into a new stage. For the struggle was no longer a purely local matter, but a development of deep concern to Frank Nash and Mr. Prettyman and to diplomats and statesmen in important capitals throughout the world. Don Ricardo already had a pocketful of telegrams attesting to this wide concern, and Frank Nash had made no effort to conceal the fact that he was deeply disturbed.

General Ramírez was describing his militia's drive across San Marcos. "We ran into more Comunistas than we did Ronquistas," he concluded.

Don Ricardo frowned. "How many of Cuerno's troops are in the city now?"

Ramírez screwed his lips. "Who knows? One cannot begin to count."

Carlos watched Frank Nash closely. The Yanqui had not aged as much as Don Ricardo; the greyness in his sandy blond mustache and hair made him appear more distinguished but not much older. Carlos had scarcely been aware, at first, of the tiny wrinkles which creased the Yanqui's face, but Frank Nash was troubled now, and his muscles were tense. "We cannot confine ourselves to San Marcos," he reminded Don Ricardo. "Puerto Colón, Río Macho, refineries, oilfields, every mile of track — all Comunista."

The telegrapher left his table and handed a dispatch to Don Ricardo. A deep frown furrowed the judge's forehead as he glanced

421

through the message. "Santa Cruz!" he exclaimed. He picked at his teeth with a thumbnail. "Santa Cruz, too!"

Carlos got up and moved toward an open window that overlooked the switchyards. Guerrilla men and women had built tiny fires between the tracks and were heating tortillas and cans of coffee. They were laughing and shouting and singing songs in mellow, throaty voices. They were singing of mountains and skies and crops and rains. They were singing songs that mule drivers sing on the way to market. They were singing of Mamacita María and Jesusito in the manger and Sun breaking red over the hills at dawn.

Carlos turned back to the table. Don Ricardo laid both palms flat upon the map and faced Mr. Nash. "What does Prettyman want?"

"You've got to drive those guerrillas out of his refineries and oil-fields," Frank Nash said.

"They are his workers," Don Ricardo reminded the Yanqui.

Mr. Nash tapped one of Don Ricardo's wrists impatiently. "Why has Prettyman kept Ronca in power these twenty-five or thirty years? Why have we extended loans and paid up his rotten debts? Because José Ronca knew how to enforce law and order and protect property. And as long as Prettyman backed the Government, neither you nor anyone else could overthrow it. But Ronca guessed wrong during the war, and a lot of important people got peeved, and that's why Prettyman wants a change. This is the best opportunity you ever had, Ricardo. Don't lose it."

Carlos leaned forward. "What's the price?"

The Yanqui ignored this. "I know you want to clean things up," he told Don Ricardo, "but you've got to have a sound government first."

Don Ricardo removed his spectacles and levelled them at Mr. Nash. "The problem is ours, Frank. Prettyman has dictated long enough."

Mr. Nash seized the judge's arm. "You're an old hand at this game, Ricardo, and you know as well as any man around that Prettyman can't be bucked. Not yet, anyhow. But if you'll work along with him, you can slip in a reform now and then, and he'll never be the wiser. Then, when you're strong enough — "

General Ramírez nodded triumphantly. "That is what I told Ricardo when he came back from exile."

Carlos watched the judge anxiously. A great weariness spread across the old man's face as he drummed a tattoo upon the table top with restless, nervous fingers. The only other sounds were the clickety-click of telegraph and short wisps of guerrilla melodies that floated through the open window. Don Ricardo turned wistful, bloodshot eyes upon his Yanqui friend. "What else does Prettyman want?"

Frank Nash cleared his throat. "Have you thought about your cabinet? If you chose wisely — "

Don Ricardo breathed deeply. "I have made commitments, Frank."

"Break them!"

The judge spread his palms in a hopeless gesture. "I doubt if we are strong enough."

Carlos found himself gazing through the window again. The sun had climbed half way to its zenith, and heat waves were rising from the switchyard rails. He could hear the tinkle of a guitar along with the peasant singing.

Frank Nash studied his fingernails. "Perhaps you could pay this Cuerno off."

The Yanqui's words brought Carlos away from the window with a jerk. "Prettyman himself couldn't buy Felipe Cuerno off."

Mr. Nash raised his brows. "Oh?"

It dawned on Carlos that neither Don Ricardo nor Frank Nash understood what was taking place in Ronca's country. Neither one had come to realize that this was more than a surface revolution, more than a mere shift in government. But Carlos knew now, if he had not known before, that every city and town and village was seething with discontent. Whatever the Liberales had planned, this was no coup d'état. This was social upheaval. "What you see is an aggression of desperate people against a medieval state," he told Frank Nash. "If we do not lead them to something else, Felipe Cuerno will. He and his Comunistas have dedicated their lives. There is no buying off."

Don Ricardo sat bolt upright in his chair. "What is there to do, Carlos?"

"We might begin by disregarding Mr. Prettyman."

An expression of shock crossed Mr. Nash's face. "Don't you do it!"

"Why not?" demanded Carlos.

The Yanqui rose and paced the floor, hands thrust deep into the pockets of his suit. "That's the quickest way to put Ronca back in power." He spoke about credit and loans and concessions and the national debt. "Prettyman could ruin you in thirty days."

Don Ricardo faced his friend soberly. "Suppose we were to follow your advice, Frank. Where could we get the strength to oppose Cuerno?"

Mr. Nash peered at the map. The telegraph across the room rattled. Carlos saw the operator scribble down a message and hand it to Don Ricardo. After a quick glance, the judge stuffed it into the pocket of his black sack coat. Mr. Nash looked up through narrowed eyes. "How strong is Cuerno?"

General Ramírez slammed the table. "Hormigas! They are like hormigas! Believe me, I saw them crawling out of their ant hills at night. I saw the dust come alive with shooting Comunistas!"

Carlos flushed. "That is not true," he snapped. Pointing through the window, he indicated the guerrilla groups gathered about their open fires. "Those are not Comunistas, gentlemen, those are your own neglected peasants — men, women, and children whom no one but the Comunistas ever had time to notice."

Don Ricardo passed a hand across his eyes, rubbed his lids as though the orbs behind them ached. "Yet they follow Cuerno."

Carlos felt a potent anger flooding through his body. "Of course they follow Cuerno. So would you and I if we were in their places. Let me tell you, we must change our course while there is time." He turned on Frank Nash. "We have no further need for Mr. Prettyman. His day is past."

The Yanqui's eyes twinkled sympathetically. "I wish — "

Carlos cut him short. "This country is sick with many evils. If we cure those evils, we shall have the majority of our people with us. That kind of strength is real."

Mr. Nash came close to Carlos and laid a kindly hand upon his shoulder. "I like that kind of talk," he said. "I like your faith, I like your courage. But Mr. Prettyman is very powerful. He has influential friends. He can stop anything you try to do."

"I don't believe that," Carlos shot back. It was inconceivable to him that one man or even a small group of men could erect effective barriers to fundamental and necessary change. Ronca had blocked human progress with violence. That had succeeded only until the people had found strength enough to rise with another force. Well, Mr. Prettyman could set Ronca up again, or he could use any other kind of violence that money or power would buy, but the people in time would find their own force.

Now it was Mr. Nash who stared through the window, his back to the others. "You probably think that Mr. Prettyman is a kind of tyrant," he said softly. "But you are wrong. Mr. Prettyman believes that what he does is right. He sees only that he builds railroads across jungle country and gives jobs to native peoples. In his mind everything he does is for the good of other men. That is his reason for using power the way he does."

The Yanqui's words were a shock to Carlos. Mr. Prettyman a bene-factor! The idea was incredible. Someone would try to prove next that José Ronca was motivated through love of fellow men. Then the thought struck Carlos that perhaps the old Nacheetl *had* justified himself that way.

"I think every man is certain that his own way is just," Carlos de-clared. "Felipe Cuerno merely seeks a better world."

"He uses violence to do it!" Frank Nash shot back.

Carlos smiled wryly. "It appears that all men use violence in the name of what they think is right." He wondered suddenly whether violence were divisible into right and wrong; after all, these new Yanqui bombs could murder human beings for good cause as well as bad. "I think the time has come for us to take a greater, more courageous stand." He looked to Don Ricardo for support, but the judge did not seem to see him.

Eyes half closed, the old man had allowed his chin to drop upon his chest, and Carlos noticed how rapidly the arteries of his neck were pulsing. "Felipe Cuerno is very strong," Don Ricardo mur-mured. "I don't see how we can possibly oppose him."

"We might be able to arrange something," Frank Nash said softly.

The room was silent, even the telegraph having ceased its rattling. The judge's voice sounded low and far away and husky. "I don't know, Frank, I don't know."

3

AT NOON the new provisional coalition government proclaimed itself in power with Don Ricardo as its president, but the names of cabinet ministers were not revealed. By nightfall of the same day revolutionary forces had forged a line along eastern edges of San Marcos from the river down the Avenue of Bees to the Calle Bolívar, across Ronca's center at the Castillo barracks, to the suburb of El Limón which lay south of the Viceregal Palace. The sector from the river to the Calle Bolívar was held by General Ramírez and his San Marcos militiamen, while Carlos and El Casco had brought up their horsemen to tie into the militia's right flank, to face the Castillo barracks, and to hold Limón. Throughout the afternoon Felipe Cuerno had been leading guerrilla forces in attacks against La Trinidad on the Cocamba line, but San Marcos streets still swarmed with peasant soldiers, and the plaza was still pock-marked by their machine gun nests.

The Xlalak lines were a series of strong points tied together by intersecting lines of fire. The men were all dismounted, having concealed their ponies in clumps of trees and courtyards and even dwelling houses. Near the center, in a tiny, hidden patio, Carlos and El Casco maintained a headquarters. From the street outside one could see beyond a row of eucalyptus trees the wide open parade ground of Castillo barracks and the stone parapets just behind. Within those walls and southward along the Cocamba road lay Ronca's crippled forces.

Early in the evening a long, black sedan brought Don Ricardo to the rear of Xlalak headquarters. Carlos showed him through the hidden patio to a whitewashed, windowless room where a gasoline lantern hung. From a dispatch case, the new president took maps and papers which he spread across a wooden table. El Casco drew up a bench and sat upon it, his hoof-like feet dangling just short of the red tile floor. Carlos leaned against the table on the other side of Don Ricardo and listened while the provisional president described his plans.

"There is one escape for Ronca," Don Ricardo said. "He can fall back along the Cocamba road, and if he reaches the mountains, it will take much fighting to get him out. In addition, he will control Cocamba harbor and thus be in a position to receive supplies. But railway guerrillas control the tracks from San Marcos almost to La Trinidad. If Cuerno takes that town, he will control the Río Puma valley and be in a position to oppose any retreat of Ronca's forces."

Carefully Carlos examined the map. Southwest of San Marcos only the Río Puma separated the railway line from Ronquista territory. For the enemy to extend themselves across the tracks would be an easy matter, and if that were done, Cuerno would be cut off. Carlos realized that the guerrilla leader was prepared to operate without a base, to live by forage, but if Ronca could be struck off balance, if his troops could be annihilated quickly, the tracks would remain undamaged and contact could be maintained with Cuerno. "Why don't we strike tonight?" Carlos suggested. He found himself impatient to end the fight and move on to more constructive duties.

El Casco nodded agreement. "Now is the best time only."

"No, no!" Don Ricardo shook his head emphatically. "We cannot afford to leave San Marcos."

Carlos studied the new president critically. There were pinhead beads of sweat upon his forehead. The lantern, hanging by a cord from the ceiling, swayed gently back and forth; thus it played weird tricks with Don Ricardo's shadow, lengthening and shortening the shade of his beard upon the maps, distorting the cast of his face into the shape of a stubborn mask. "An attack tonight might be an early end of battle," Carlos said, "and the saving of many lives."

Don Ricardo turned upon him. "You know how delicate the balance is. It would be disastrous to extend ourselves beyond San Marcos."

Carlos noticed in El Casco's eyes the faintest kind of flicker. "If we do not strike," he warned, "Felipe Cuerno may be — "

A pounding on the door cut him short. From just outside came gruff words in Xlalak. El Casco answered. A horseman with glittering eyes and sweeping mustache burst in and stood before his chieftain, gesturing, grimacing, talking rapidly.

El Casco interpreted. "He says an officer has come across the field from El Castillo under a flag of white."

Don Ricardo spun about. "Send him in!"

The Xlalak leaned through the door and sang out an order in his native language. Instantly there appeared on the threshold a young lieutenant in the blue uniform of Ronca's National Army. He was ushered into the room at the point of a Xlalak carbine. Momentarily he hesitated, eyes dazed by the sputtering lantern, but when he spotted Don Ricardo, he clicked his boot heels and saluted smartly.

At a signal from Don Ricardo, Carlos and El Casco withdrew with the Xlalak guards and closed the door. The patio was dark except for the soft, pink glow of a charcoal brazier where three horsemen were brewing sarsaparilla tea. Carlos and El Casco squatted beside them, and the silence was heavy. One of the horsemen hummed softly a plaintive, mountain tune. El Casco stirred the coals, added water to one of the terra cotta pots. When the tea had brewed, he divided it between himself and Carlos.

After a time the door opened, flooding the patio with amber light. Don Ricardo called out for Carlos and El Casco. They entered to find the young lieutenant sitting contentedly on the wooden bench, a cigarette drooping from the corner of his mouth. "This officer will remain until I return," Don Ricardo told El Casco. He took Carlos by the arm. "I want you to come with me."

Carlos went with Don Ricardo to the long, black limousine that was waiting behind the headquarters. "We go to the church at Zamora," he told the militiaman who drove.

"Señor, that is a distance beyond El Limón," the driver protested. "It is almost Ronquista!"

"That is where we go," Don Ricardo insisted somewhat gruffly. He climbed into the back and drew shades across the windows. As soon as Carlos had seated himself beside the judge, the driver started his motor and eased away into the night. "Our passage is guaranteed," Don Ricardo said. "We shall have no trouble unless it is with Cuerno's men." He leaned forward to close the sliding window which separated them from the driver's seat.

The car slid into a smooth surfaced street and headed southward in the direction of El Limón. Don Ricardo shifted his position in order to face Carlos. "There is a wish for mediation." He spoke slowly with an anxious eye upon the younger man.

Carlos felt a sudden release from a tension of which he had scarcely been aware. The battle, then, was over! He settled back against the soft upholstery of the limousine. The driver swung into a narrow, cobbled street that led toward El Limón. The city was dark and still and seemingly deserted, as though the population had moved away en masse.

There was vast relief in the realization that the fight was finished, that there would be no further bloodshed. In a day or two he would be free to rejoin Sapho, to occupy himself with matters pertaining to the future of their newly formed government. Momentarily a vision of Felipe Cuerno flashed across his mind, and he wondered vaguely how Don Ricardo could possibly maneuver a middle course between the demands of the Comunistas on the one hand and Mr. Prettyman on the other.

As they neared the city's outskirts, a guerrilla stepped into the headlight beams ahead and flagged the driver to a stop. As the peasant soldier peered through a front window, Don Ricardo moved the sliding glass a trifle, passed a paper to the militiaman. "Show him this."

There was a mumble of Nacheetl conversation. The guard examined the paper curiously, handed it back to the driver. "He does not read," the militiaman told Don Ricardo.

Carlos opened the glass wider and spoke to the guard in Nacheetl. "This is the car of President Cervantes," he explained. "It moves across the city at night for the revolution only."

The guerrilla shrugged beneath his tattered serape. "What man is this Presidente?" he demanded. "I have never heard." He leaned deeper into the car, staring at Don Ricardo with narrow, suspicious eyes. Then he turned to Carlos. "What man are you?"

"I am Carlos Chichayan."

The guard hesitated, the pupils of his eyes widening slightly. "Not the leader of the Xlalaks?"

"That one."

The walnut colored face of the guerrilla split into an appreciative grin. "This is another matter!" He spoke to the driver. "Pass, amigo!" Backing off, he raised a hand as the car moved away. " 'diós, Carlos!"

The headlights bored southward through the darkness. Carlos settled back. "So Ronca gives up the fight?"

Don Ricardo breathed deeply. "We do not deal with Ronca," he said. "Ronca is out, altogether finished."

A disagreeable foreboding replaced the relief that Carlos had felt before. Uneasily he sought to discern the expression on the judge's face, but the interior of the car was dark. "With what man do we deal?" he asked.

There was the sound of tires humming over a stretch of brick roadway. Don Ricardo shifted in his seat. "Frank Nash is right," he sighed, evading Carlos' question. "We must get along the best we can till our government is strong enough to stand alone." The car jolted over an ancient stone bridge built by conquistadores and guarded, now, by a guerrilla squad. The driver slowed for the village of El Limón where horsemen patrolled the only street. Carlos waited for Don Ricardo to elaborate, but the president seemed to have lost himself in sober meditation.

A kilometer from the edge of town the driver halted at a Xlalak strong point. A troop leader touched his sombrero when he recognized Carlos. Beyond El Limón, he said, there was only darkness. He moved a forefinger back and forth just in front of his nose. "No Ronquistas! Since sunset, no Ronquistas."

Two horsemen removed a road block, and the car slipped through. Carlos noticed how the driver's fingers tightened about the wheel as they moved out into the eerie loneliness beyond rebel lines. Tall eucalyptus trees grew on either side of the road, and their trunks went whish-tah, whish-tah as the car picked up speed. The meter needle on the dashboard crept around its illuminated dial. The driver felt safer moving fast. As he bore down on his gas pedal, the car sped past adobe houses that carried a dark and deserted look, whisked through a village with empty streets.

Don Ricardo closed the sliding window which Carlos had opened at the road block. "I see no other way," he said in a voice husky with fatigue and resignation. "The Comunistas have gone too far. One way or another we must drive them out, or they will take the country over."

Carlos swung about.

The president stared intently at the younger man. "There is a rightist faction that is ready to consider some agreement." He spoke rapidly as though despising the words which he found himself compelled to say. "Let me repeat that Ronca is not in it. No, no, they push him out and come to us, turning their forces over to my command."

It was hot inside the car, and Carlos felt a stickiness where the serape fitted about his neck. He turned away to avoid the warmness of Don Ricardo's breath. The car was speeding between rows of cypress trees from which heavy moss hung in sombre festoons. When Carlos did not speak, Don Ricardo gripped him by the knee. "I have considered all the risks," the presidente said. "It is a dangerous thing I do, a backward step, but there is no other way."

Carlos disagreed. An alliance of force with any part of Ronca's following would breed catastrophe for the simple reason that Ronquistas stood opposed to necessary change. The only hope for peace, Carlos thought, lay in the fostering of sensitive governments capable of adjusting themselves to new conditions, to new human needs. "I think your way is wrong," he told Don Ricardo. "Our war has failed. We have defeated one enemy only to raise another. I think we must meet the challenge on a higher level."

The car slowed down at the edge of a deserted village. As it jounced over cobblestone streets, the headlights caught a church spire straight ahead. Don Ricardo leaned forward, his fingers still clutching at Carlos' knee. "I know the dangers of even a temporary backward turn," he insisted gravely. "It is contrary to all my years of struggle. Yet I see no alternative. Don't you understand, Carlos, that this split is too big a thing for us? Already the whole world is taking sides. I had hoped to steer a middle course, to work peacefully with the Comunistas. I saw that as the only hope. Now that hope is smashed. There is only one way left."

The driver swung close to a churchyard gate and stopped the car. Time was short. Carlos sought desperately to collect his thoughts, to marshal them against the old man's decision. Throughout the rest of Latin America, throughout Europe and Asia, in the whole world Comunista and non-Comunista stood face to face, each convinced that he was right. If Carlos and Don Ricardo failed here, what hope remained elsewhere?

"If we dedicate ourselves to curing evils at home," he told Don Ricardo, "and to building a free, united world — if we do these things, most men and women will be behind us. That is our only hope."

The president shook his head. "It is too late," he said huskily. "We cannot stand alone. This way the rightists give us help, and we do our best to make our government free. Later when we are strong — "

The driver opened the door. Carlos stepped out, and Don Ricardo came behind him. There was not a sound in all the village, and their footsteps echoed in the silent emptiness.

As they followed a cobblestone pathway around one wing of the shadowy church, Carlos remembered how, resting beneath a myrtle bush above La Cumbre, he had thrust aside his objections to the revolution. This war against Ronca is no ordinary aggression, he had told himself. This is a justified revolt against a feudal despotism. This is force dictated by a righteous cause.

Carlos now questioned whether the world could afford any use of violence, however justified the purpose. The self-interest of men and nations demanded effort of a higher order. What kind? Carlos struggled for the answer.

Don Ricardo touched him on the shoulder. "We must combine what we wish to do with what is practical."

Without stopping, Carlos shot back a challenge. "To preserve the world is practical." He wondered whether human beings were mature enough to do it.

The great tragedy, it seemed to Carlos, was that all these different leaders and their followings had convinced themselves that only they were right. Ronca, Felipe Cuerno, Don Ricardo, Mr. Prettyman — they followed different roads, but held two things in common: each used some sort of violence to gain his ends, and each was certain that his way was the only true and righteous one.

Carlos was not prepared to judge which cause among many in the world was most nearly right, but he was sure of this — that force in any cause, good or bad, was now capable of destroying Man. Unless peace met violence with peace, the world was lost.

Don Ricardo paused before a narrow door of the church, his hand upon the knob. "You disapprove of what I do!" His voice sounded flat and tired. Grasping the younger man's arm, he spoke again in an anxious, almost hopeful tone. "You are young, while I am old and not so brave. I do not advise you what to do. If you can manage something better — " He pushed open the door. "Shall we see who waits inside?"

Carlos stepped across the threshold. The room was an ancient sacristy with an odor of dust and mold. Along one side was a rack from which hung a row of cassocks and other vestments, while close against the farther end stood a table with a lighted candle around which a moth fluttered blindly.

Nailed to the wall above the table was an oil painting of the Last Supper. An officer stood gazing at the picture, his back to Carlos and Don Ricardo. A pearl-butted automatic hung heavy at his hip. He turned slowly as they approached, and his face showed brown in the candle light.

"Ho! Carlos!" he exclaimed. "Oh, you precious billy goat! Come to think of it, Frank Nash mentioned — cabrón! Sit down, amigos!"

Carlos ignored the chair which Pepillo offered. He noticed that the moth had fluttered close about the candle, beating its wings against the flame, and for a moment it looked as though the light would be extinguished.